Rare Blood

Susan Old

*For Joey,
Enjoy the Read!
Susan*

ZAIRESUE BOOKS
Arlington, Washington

"You will want to write about me."
—Tristan

MIRANDA'S PEEPS

- **Miranda Ortega,** author

- **Lena Hauser,** Book Agent
- **Baron Tristan Mordecai,** Head of Roman Books
- **Lolly,** BFF of Miranda, model
- **Alan,** engaged to Lolly, psychiatrist
- **Sergio Venturelli,** assistant to Lena
- **James Donelley,** friend of Alan's, Dentist
- **Simone Brown,** Mordecai's girlfriend
- **Professor Bishop,** Miranda's favorite teacher
- **Clive,** the Baron's butler
- **Tillie,** the Baron's housekeeper
- **Jasper,** the Baron's chauffeur
- **Pete and Connie Ortega,** Miranda's parents

- **The Magus aka Desmon Dontidae,** the most powerful vampire

Haute Caste Heads of Vampire Houses and their knights:
- **House of Pentacles (Europe),** Conrad Sudovian assisted by Stephen *CC
- **House of Swords (Middle East),** Omar Sadeghi assisted by Momand *CC
- **House of Wands (Africa),** Mbuyi Kananga, assisted by Samuel *CC
- **House of Cups (Asia),** Dr. Komaki Kyoto, assisted by Lady Lily
- **House of Plows (North America),** Sarah Lockporte, assisted by Sir Ruben
- **House of Arrows (Central & South America),** Jorge Diego, assisted by Sir Franco

Haute Caste Vampires known for Assassin skills:
- **Steve, Anastasia, Pauline and Cesar**

Other Common Caste Vampires:
- **Johann,** Kabedi and Antoinella
- **Monks on a Mission,** Benedetto and Grigoryi
- **The Magus' attorney,** Mr. Beaudine

---

*CC denotes Common Caste

A MEETING IN PARIS ~ 1306

"I KNOW OF your skills, Assassin." A cloaked older man stood under a bridge on the Seine, peering into the shadows. The pale moonlight outlined his gaunt features despite his beard. The stench of the river was hard to bear. He hoped to keep this meeting short. "The Lord has given your kind dark gifts. I have come to add to them," he stated boldly. He heard a footstep, and placed his hand on the hilt of his sword. A white tunic with a red cross showed beneath his dark garb. "I knew I would find you in this place where many disappear." He noticed a dark mass floating by and hoped it was the remains of a cow or horse.

"I should be honored," a man replied softly while remaining concealed, "but your kind has never sought my company before without bearing torches, weapons, and ill will." A tall hooded figure in black circled the knight, fading in and out of the darkness. His pale face could barely be seen. "You came alone, except for a sorry fellow who tried to follow you." The Assassin wiped his lips with his sleeve. "Why are you here?"

"Thank you for disposing of him. He was a spy for the king. There is little time left for my order. Treachery fueled by greed will cause the demise of my brethren. The king will not pay his debts; instead he conspires with the church against us. Since we are seen as a threat, it will take little to persuade the Holy Father to call us heretics. We will not bend, so we must be broken. I am one of the Templars." He paused and looked away to keep his composure. "They will arrest and torture me soon. I cannot stop this foul turn of events, but I can seek justice from beyond my cell or grave."

"Do you wish to become—" the Assassin began.

"No!" The old knight spit on the ground. "Never. I accept my fate." He reached into the folds of his cloak and pulled out an ornate wooden box. "I will give you the names of those who desire to betray my brethren, and the hiding places of a vast fortune. Our monarch and dignitaries of the church seek salvation with gold. They will never have the treasure they would steal. Unfortunately, my vows will not allow my sword to taste their blood, but you shall."

The Assassin pushed his hood back, revealing a pale, handsome, sinewy face framed by fair hair. His cool blue eyes were fixated on the warrior, yet he feigned a yawn. "Boredom caused me to follow you and kept me as an audience for your trying performance. The self-righteous succeed at betrayal on a daily basis. Your tiresome petty squabbles are of little interest to us. One immoral act condones another, all in the struggle for justice." He paused to consider the look of sorrow in the old knight's face. "This hardly concerns me." He started to walk away.

"I can think of no one else who exists beyond the reach of these tyrants," the Templar stated simply. The comment made the dark figure stop. The Assassin liked getting recognition from the holy warrior.

"I could easily take your life and that box. You know that, yet you stand here demanding help. Amazing." He turned back toward the old man. "Even if I were to agree to your request, what makes you think I would be compelled to keep a promise to a dead knight?"

"Because you were a man once." The knight stared at the dark figure. He spoke with urgency in his voice. "I have no one else to turn to. I assume you have no affection for the clergy. Your actions will serve a purpose, other than wanton slaughter. I desire what is right and fair. An eye for an eye. Perhaps making the royals and priests pay will relieve your boredom and appetite."

There was a long pause, then the Assassin responded, "I seem to remember a passage in a book, 'Vengeance is mine.' You give my kind your blessing to do what you are not willing to do. Am I to be your dark angel of justice?"

"Will you give me your word?" the knight asked in earnest.

"Very well. I give my word to the only mortal ever to require it." He held out his hand. The knight handed him a jewel encrusted box filled with papers, maps and keys. The name of the knight's family was engraved into the top: de Molay. The assassin was surprised. "The Grand Master seeks my help? Strange, how your foe can become your ally."

"I only want justice for my men." He took a step back from the blond killer.

"Sir de Molay, I know that holy men are often complicated souls. You're giving me a list of sinners to punish, and maps with keys to vaults of riches, but I imagine there is more that you require."

The old knight smiled briefly. "Ah, yes, your kind is very clever. You had to be to survive. There is someone I wish you to protect. I have a son. I ask that my lineage be protected. He is in Toulouse. I wrote it all down. His mother and I have kept his birth a secret."

"You have been a busy saint." The Assassin looked at him intently. "I understand the difficulty of being born a bastard. I shall protect your lineage." He bowed slightly and disappeared into the night.

Jacques de Molay whispered, "Thank you," and hoped God would forgive him for making a deal with the devil. The Grand Master would spend the rest of the night praying for his brethren. He pulled his cloak over his tunic and headed for the cathedral.

CHAPTER 1

THE FIRST TIME I met Tristan I thought he was a conceited, arrogant, womanizing bastard. Too late I realized those were his best qualities. It was a warm May evening in Los Angeles. A book party was being held at the Bel Air Hotel to promote my thriller *Obsession with Death*. Three years of disciplined writing and the luck of signing with a well-connected agent had put me on the brink of success. I stood in the middle of an oak-paneled conference room surrounded by literary notables who discussed restaurants in Paris and the latest opera in Rome. Chandeliers lit up the well-dressed gathering. I was thrilled, though their gems, couture clothing and sculpted hair made me think I had been invited by mistake. I had never felt farther away from the cornfields of Illinois.

"Why would Roman Books spend all this money on a nobody?" I overheard someone in the crowd ask.

The heels I wore kept sinking into the plush wine carpet, making me a little off-balance. *What a rube!* I thought, tugging at my simple black dress. It was short and tight. I had put aside my usual contempt for Barbie doll fashion to try and make a good impression. My long dark curls were pulled back with an ornate clip to make me look more mature. I was afraid I appeared more like a 13-year-old than the ripe old age of 23. Only the eerie posters of my book cover showing a menacing apparition assured me that I belonged.

When a man in a glistening suit asked about my inspiration for the novel's psychopathic ghosts, all I could think to say was "high school." An older woman, in an orange dress open to her navel and perfume that made me sneeze, wanted to know what writer most influenced my style. "St. Thomas Aquinas," I managed, without looking down or laughing. A young man with thick glasses wondered why I had chosen ghosts as the love object for neurotic women. "I grew up next to a mortuary," I responded. He thought I was joking but it was true.

I was just starting to feel a little less anxious when someone asked about my next novel. I did not have a clue about the future. I had poured all my time and energy into this book. Luckily, a waiter came by with a tray of shrimp and I excused myself.

I saw Lena Hauser, my agent, moving through the crowd like an empress bestowing favors. She wore a gray Chanel suit with long strands of pearls. She had short, straight brown hair slicked back in a boyish fashion. Her long red nails emphasized every gesture. "Elegant and tough" summed her up. Lena's assistant and lover, Sergio, followed close behind. Heavy eyebrows framed his intense hazel eyes. He had been a tennis pro in Italy and moved with the agile strength of an athlete. I liked Sergio. He had a warm smile and easy manner. I felt sorry for him because he adored Lena.

I whispered to my agent, "I need to find the ladies' room."

"Go through the French doors." Lena briefly put her hand on my arm. "Miranda, don't be long. It's almost time for introductions."

Happily, the powder room was empty. Three large mirrors, each outlined with small lights, made me even more self-conscious. I dug in my bag for lip gloss. I hoped it would help me look more something, anything but the innocent I was. My large brown eyes gave me the appearance of a deer in headlights when I was stressed.

Struggling with a touch of social phobia, I decided to get a breath of fresh air before going back to the conference room. I wondered how long before anyone noticed I was gone. The hotel grounds were lovely. Fragrant gardenias, roses and ferns lined the walkway. The tiled roofs of pastel bungalows lent an old-world grace. Show tunes drifted across the grounds from a patio bar. Sadly, the sight of couples communing in the romantic atmosphere tugged at my heart. The world of writing had left little time or energy for dating. I certainly could not be accused of misspent youth. At least the sacrifice was starting to pay off. I had received a $25,000 advance from my publisher. I imagined my mother at the village beauty salon, bragging about my book being published. My parents had sacrificed to send me to college. Now I could start paying them back, not to mention paying back my creditors.

The garden path led to a pond where swans floated among water lilies. It was like a scene from a fairy tale. Maybe I did belong here. A frog princess transformed by a book.

"I'll never wait on tables again!" I declared.

"Perhaps not," a man responded.

"What?" I turned, startled.

A tall figure was standing in the shadow of a sycamore several feet away. The sunlight had faded into twilight.

"Miranda Ortega?" he asked with a slight accent.

"Yes?" I responded uneasily. "Did we meet inside?"

"No, you would have remembered if we had." The most strikingly handsome man I had ever seen stepped before me. A thick mane of blond hair fell to his shoulders. He had a slightly jutting jaw and patrician nose. His complexion was pale, without a blemish. His eyes were river blue. His mouth wore a satisfied smile. A black silk suit draped his lean, muscular form. A starkly white shirt was left open at the chest. He wore a small gold medallion. Damn straight I would have remembered meeting him. At that moment, my brain was clearly registering attraction, anticipation and fear.

"And you are...?"

"Someone you will want to know better." He stepped closer, blocking the path.

The rape prevention course I had taken flashed before my eyes. I wondered if I could out-run him. It was getting darker by the minute. I regretted wearing high heels. I took a deep breath and tried to calm myself down. Maybe I was over-reacting.

"You're making me uncomfortable," I said, watching his response closely.

"I was hoping to have the opposite effect." He smiled.

I breathed a little easier.

"If you'll excuse me, I have to be getting back."

He moved but slightly, allowing me little space to pass by him. He smelled of musk and primal forest. I inhaled slightly. Heady stuff. His cologne seemed vaguely familiar. I am 5 foot 4 inches and he was about a foot taller than me. I guessed he was about 30. His eyes seemed old beyond their years. I started to move past him. He gently put a hand on my arm, just enough to make me pause.

"When I read *Obsession with Death*," he said softly, "I was surprised that such a young woman could write about violent creatures with such fervor and compassion."

"I take it you never read *Frankenstein*?" I moved his hand and took a step. "How did you get hold of an advance copy?"

"A friend," he smiled, "who thought I might enjoy reading you."

"I'm glad you enjoyed the book, 'cause you're not doing so well with the author. Excuse me!"

"You're not excused, Miranda," he laughed. "Not till you satisfy my curiosity." In an instant he moved so that I was between him and the pond.

"About what?" I asked nervously.

"What will you write about next?"

"I don't know, maybe I'll write a sequel. Look, I have to get back. I'll sign a book for you."

"Perhaps I can help you," he said with a self-satisfied smile.

"Yeah, right." *Like the spider to the fly,* I thought. "No thanks, I'm not interested."

"That's not what I sense," he said softly.

"Get out of my way." I tried to brush by him but my foot caught on something. I tumbled into his arms, just missing landing in the pond.

"You tripped me!" I gasped.

"I kept you from falling," he replied. "I followed you here because I thought it wasn't safe for you to be alone."

"You followed me? Who will protect me from you? Put me down!" I was about to knee him and scream when I heard someone call my name. "I'm over here!" I cried out.

"I was told you could be difficult." He smiled. "Talented but rather undisciplined."

"Who said—" I started.

"Miranda," Lena called out. "There you are. Well, I see you've met Baron Mordecai."

I swallowed my next protest. This was the head of Roman Books? I had signed a contract to write for this egotistical freak. My body and career were literally in his hands.

I was stunned. I could not believe my bad fortune. I stared at Mordecai's satisfied countenance.

Sergio was with her. He appeared mildly amused by my predicament. "Good evening, Baron. Perhaps she could sign books better if you allowed her feet to touch the ground."

He gently released me, then bowed slightly. "Tristan Mordecai, your esteemed publisher, at your service."

"You're not 'esteemed' to me. I thought royalty was supposed to have manners." I straightened my dress and tried to muster some dignity. I put my hand up to fix my hair clip but it was gone. My curls were now down past my shoulders. I looked at Mordecai as he slipped something into his jacket pocket.

"Come along," Lena urged. "Baron Mordecai, I'm so glad you could make it. Now the evening will be perfect."

Lena took his arm and left me staring after them, fuming. Sergio nudged me and we followed several feet behind. The way my agent was sucking up to the publisher made me want to puke. She was no longer the powerful woman I had imagined. I gave Sergio a sympathetic glance.

"They're old friends," he whispered. "Lena can handle the Baron but you should be, uh, more polite."

"Me be polite?" I started to raise my voice.

Sergio put his fingers up to his lips and shook his head. "Not now."

The crowd in the conference room had become less glamorous as celebrities left and more of the booksellers arrived. I was seated at a long oak table piled high with copies of my book. I had dreamed of such a moment, so why did I feel like my head was on the block?

"Ladies and gentleman, Ms. Ortega would be happy to sign books for you now," Lena announced. "We also have the pleasure of Baron Mordecai's company as we launch the publication of *Obsession with Death*."

A murmur went through the crowd as the reclusive publisher stood beside me. I knew his presence would be seen as a vote of confidence in my work, but he was the last person I wanted to feel grateful to. He placed a hand upon my shoulder, a very subtle caress.

"Miranda Ortega," he began, "has captured the depths of horror in her chilling story of lonely people lured into the seductive machinations of cruel spirits. It is a tribute to her talent that a first-time author could produce such an engrossing tale. I find her work reminiscent of Mary Shelley." I started coughing. He ignored me. "I know you will be pleased to tell your customers that her current success will be followed by a thrilling vampire novel."

I wanted to faint and kill at the same time. I must have suddenly looked pale because Sergio asked, "Are you okay?" My only response was a deep breath. I was expected to say thank you but I was speechless, though I could have managed a good scream. What gave him the right to decide what my next novel would be? I glared at my publisher.

Lena smoothed over the awkward moment by coaxing me to begin signing books. I forced myself to focus on the task at hand. I was pleasant with the booksellers but I was dying to express my indignation to Mordecai.

"Tristan," a petite blonde said as she took his arm, "we'll be late for the symphony." She wore a short gold mesh dress that hugged the small amount of flesh it covered. High heels showed off her shapely legs. Diamond bracelets glistened on her wrists. The woman's breasts were pushed up high against a scoop neckline. An architect must have designed her bra. Male booksellers were salivating, but Mordecai barely responded to her.

"Simone, you can go on without me," he told the whining blonde.

Through lashes thick with mascara, Simone scrutinized me with a cold, calculating look. A chill ran down my spine. Though she was a few feet away, I could smell the gardenia perfume she wore. Her interest in me was surprising. I was not in her league, nor would I want to be. She looked mean, and all the makeup in the world could not change that.

"I doubt you'll have any better luck with this author, Tristan. I'll be in the limo." She turned and walked away.

"I'll autograph a book for you, Simone," I called out.

The room became quiet. The blonde stiffened. She turned and gave me a stinging look, then she quickly walked out.

"Ouch!" I said with a little smile. A few of the booksellers smiled.

Mordecai leaned over me and whispered, "Perhaps I should take you to the symphony."

"Fuck you!" I whispered back. Mordecai laughed. I was not trying to be amusing.

A delivery boy brought a large vase of flowers to my table. There were lilies and bird of paradise flowers in a rather dramatic presentation. I read the card. They were from my best friend and her fiancé. She was a model shooting a commercial in New York, so she could not make the party. "Congratulations Randie! Now you can buy me lunch! Love, Lolly and Alan." Lolly had helped me through some hard times. I owed her more than lunch. Their thoughtfulness boosted my spirits. I placed the card face-down on the table. To my surprise, Mordecai picked it up.

"Hey, that's private!" I tried to take it from him.

"How nice." He smiled and returned the card.

"Miranda," Lena began in a condescending tone, "you might sign a few more books. Try to be professional, dear. Baron, I have a matter to discuss with you."

She went off to a far corner with Mordecai. Sergio neatly stacked the books. I was thrilled to have so many people interested in my book. Unfortunately, every time I looked up, I saw my publisher. He stood very close to Lena as they talked. My gut said he was bad news. My head said he was important to my career. My heart was silent.

"Aren't they a stunning couple," Sergio commented.

"Does it bother you?" I whispered and signed another book.

"What's more important is your reaction," he laughed. "You've only known him for 30 minutes."

"I don't give a rat's ass about him, Sergio. You saw how he treated me," I protested. Sergio walked away smiling.

"Miranda, congratulations." Dr. Bishop, my old English professor, stood before me. White wisps of hair lay across his balding head. He leaned on an ornamental cane and peered at me over thick glasses sitting precariously on the edge of his nose.

"Dr. Bishop, thank you for coming." I stood and gently took his wrinkled hand.

"I'm sorry to be so late." He spoke with a faint Irish accent. "You've done very well. Are you happy? Is this what you wanted?"

"Yes. It's always been my dream to be published. I wouldn't be here if you hadn't given my book to Ms. Hauser. I can never thank you enough." He looked a little sad. I thought perhaps he didn't feel well. He was considering retiring from teaching due to ill health. "Are you okay?"

"Yes, my dear, as well as someone my age could be. Thank you. Lena tells me you're ready to begin your next book, something about vampires?"

"It wasn't even my idea. The head of Roman Books made the decision without even consulting me," I replied indignantly.

"Yes, I've heard Baron Mordecai can spot talent." He glanced at Lena and the Baron. "I've also heard he can make or break writers. I'm not surprised he's partial to you. I've always thought you were exceptional. Vampires will be a challenge. Harder to capture in print than ghosts."

Presenting me with a challenge after stoking my ego by calling me exceptional would have seemed like a conspiracy from anyone but Dr. Bishop. I believed he had my best interest at heart.

"Your opinion means a lot to me, but this was not my idea. Anyway, I can't help but think that vampires have been done to death. Pardon the pun." I was hoping for some moral support.

"Miranda, don't let your pride get in the way of your future as a writer," he said sternly. Then a slight smile came to his lips. "None of this turning-into-bats nonsense. Make Dracula real. Imagine him walking among us at night."

Sergio interrupted our talk by handing me more books. Dr. Bishop said goodbye and slipped away in the crowd.

I felt the grounds for my artistic anger weakening. If Dr. Bishop thought it was a good idea to write about sea sponges, I would seriously consider it. I tried to ignore my gut feeling about Mordecai. Maybe it was a sound business decision, mandating writing about the undead. Maybe he just had poor social skills. It was useless. The scene at the pond kept coming to me, eating away at my attempts to be reasonable. Despite my mentor's words, I still wanted to express my moral outrage. I looked up, hoping to get Mordecai's attention, but he was gone! I would not even get the satisfaction of confronting him. I did not feel relieved by his absence. I felt more like I had been the victim of a hit and run.

It was about ten o'clock when the last bookseller scurried off with some autographed copies. Sergio began packing up the remaining books. He had been rather quiet all evening.

"Thanks for your help, Sergio."

"Sure, sure, remember me in your next book." He smiled.

"An Italian tennis-pro vampire?" I joked.

Sergio did not respond. He picked up a box and walked away. That was just great. The evening felt like a successful disaster.

"Miranda!" Lena called to me.

I approached her warily, like a puppy about to be scolded.

"You're lucky the Baron liked you. Why on earth did you give him those dirty looks? He holds the keys to your success." Her expression softened. "Still, you did not alienate him. He remains enthusiastic about your next book. I can only remember one other writer that he showed this much interest in, and that was some time ago."

"Lena, don't think I'm ungrateful. I'll try to write this book, but he's a total womanizing ass and he deserves his bitchy girlfriend."

"Keep your opinions about Baron Mordecai to yourself and stop complaining. I think the Baron was the only person you haven't offended tonight. Keeping the booksellers waiting, really! Start on your next novel soon so it won't be your last. I'll be in touch."

Lena and Sergio left without another word. I searched in my purse for an antacid. I looked at one of my book posters and felt disillusioned. "Damn Baron Mordecai!"

CHAPTER 2

SHORTLY AFTER MIDNIGHT Senator Thomas Bickwell's overweight form fell across his bed in a drunken stupor. From a corner of the bedroom his wife, Florence, began crawling to the door. Tears rolled down the petite socialite's cheeks but she kept silent. Blood dripped from her nose onto the emerald gown she had worn hoping to please him. She stopped for a moment as a wave of pain assailed her. Their evening at the symphony had started out well but Tom's vow not to drink had been forgotten by intermission.

"I saw the look you gave that guy!" he had whispered too loudly. "You think I'm blind! Stupid whore!"

She had said nothing until they had gotten into the parking lot. "That man asked what I thought of the concert, that's all. I answered to be polite. I've never seen him before."

His fingers had dug so deeply into her arm that she cried out but no one came to her aid. Tom Bickwell was a prominent politician. In the limousine, she was further assaulted with a barrage of accusations.

Once in their bedroom his fury knew no restraint. He struck her until the vodka rendered him unconscious. "Oh God!" she hissed in pain, cradling her bruised ribs. Florence bitterly regretted that she had once again believed his promise to abstain. Her head was pounding. Nausea welled up inside her as she reached the top of the stairs. No one witnessed her awkward descent to the garage. The servants had discretely vanished at Tom's first bellow.

Florence's Jaguar sped through quiet Beverly Hills' streets towards a very private hotel that would not spread rumors. For months, she had kept an overnight bag in the trunk. Suddenly, she pulled the car over to the side of the road; a torrent of tears made it impossible to drive. It was most difficult when Florence remembered the decent man Tom once had been, the brilliant student who had romanced her in law school. She thought of the promise she had made to stay with him until after the election. Florence focused on her immediate predicament. She found moistened hand wipes and began to clean the blood from her face. Carefully, she applied powder and lipstick. She would hide the blood on her dress with a cashmere wrap before entering the hotel lobby.

A tall figure, cloaked in darkness, approached the Bickwell mansion. Silently, he passed through the French doors from the balcony. The bedroom light revealed his well-sculpted features. Ignoring the jewelry and wallet on the dresser he walked to the bed, contempt shown in his eyes.

"This will be a pleasure," he announced.

Tom was groggy and confused by the presence of this strange man. "Who the hell...wait, wait you! You were at the concert! Son of a bitch. Florence!" He awkwardly pulled himself up on the bed.

"Baron Mordecai," he replied. "The lady left. I expect she found your affection a tad overwhelming." Malevolent hunger seized him. He could feel small, viper-like fangs start to protrude. Mordecai smiled just enough to display his unique dentition. "You don't deserve her."

"Get away from me!" Panic seized Tom as he realized he was not hallucinating. He fought off his drunken state and reached for a gun hidden under his pillow. Almost inhumanly fast, long pale fingers closed about Tom's throat before he could grab his weapon.

"Like a fat beetle on his back..." Tristan mused as he easily pinned his victim. Tom's stocky limbs wiggled frantically to no avail. The more he struggled, the faster his heart beat, the stronger the scent of his blood became. Mordecai found the macabre foreplay tantalizing. "No one will come. They think you are still enjoying marital abuse." The Baron looked at the terrified face of a man meeting his judge and executioner. "You beat a woman instead of making love to her. I find such behavior intolerable."

Mordecai skillfully applied enough pressure to cause the Senator to pass out, but would leave no telltale marks. He thought it was a pity that the blood would be slightly tainted with vodka, but the volume would be more than sufficient. Bringing Tom's fleshy wrists up to his mouth, Mordecai made razor like slits with a small knife the he had taken out of his pocket, then consumed the warm, salty, vital fluid. Tom gasped then made no other sound. Mordecai's body temperature rose as human sensations combined with his heightened abilities. Mordecai steadied himself as the initial rush subsided. For a few days, he would feel perfect. He dropped the dead man's wrists, allowing a small amount of blood to stain the bedding.

"I've spared your wife further beatings and the unpleasant experience of watching you die from cirrhosis," Mordecai said softly. He wiped the handle of the small knife to remove any traces of him, pressed it into the Senator's hand, then left it on the bed. He carefully added the final touches to the scene of the senator's demise and quietly disappeared.

In the morning, the butler was surprised to find that Senator Bickwell was not in his bed. He was about to knock on the bathroom door when he heard a scream from outside. The butler ran to the balcony. Senator Bickwell was laying on the wrought iron balcony. One arm was hanging over the edge. The cuts on his wrist had left a small pool of blood on the patio below and one on the balcony floor. The gardener who had spotted the body was on his knees, crossing himself and mumbling a prayer. Other servants rushed outside, their cries and gasps making it more difficult for the butler to decide what to do next. There was no sign of Mrs. Bickwell. Finally, he decided to call the senator's personal secretary.

The news of her husband's suicide was a shocking relief to Florence. Tears washed away much of her anger. When she emerged to face the press, Florence displayed grief with an amazing composure. Her ability to win public sympathy was not lost on her late husband's campaign manager.

When she returned home, the only trace of death was a stain on the patio. Florence ordered a potted plant placed on the spot. It wasn't until she went to her medicine cabinet that evening that she noticed an envelope with her name written in burgundy ink. She did not recognize the writing. Florence anxiously opened it.

"Lovely Lady, perhaps now you will be able to enjoy the symphony. It should not be difficult for you to find a more agreeable companion. T. M."

"I knew it," she whispered.

Her husband had been capable of driving others to taking their lives but not of killing himself. Florence had not misjudged Tom; he had been murdered. The emotional numbness that had held her together dissolved. Eyes brimming with tears, she thought of the violence he had suffered. It was not an end she would wish on anyone. The police had found no evidence of foul play, and surprisingly little blood loss after he had supposedly cut his wrists.

She stared at the note. The initials meant nothing to her. Then she recalled the handsome man who had been sitting beside her at the symphony. He had regarded the senator's drunken behavior with disgust. "Was he the assassin? But why?" Though her husband had many political enemies, she did not imagine that rivalry had led to murder. Florence had a gut feeling that the danger had passed, that the killer meant no harm to her. The idea of finding "a more agreeable companion" made her laugh; the last thing she wanted was another man to control her life. Florence winced from the pain in her bruised ribs.

"Well Tom, I was always good at keeping secrets," she whispered, "especially close to an election." Using the senator's sterling silver lighter, she burned the evidence.

Two months after Tristan "recalled" Senator Bickwell, Miranda was at an outdoor cafe waiting for her best friend, Lolly. It was perfect T-shirt and shorts weather. Eighty degrees and not a cloud in the sky. Miranda checked her watch, it was 5:00 pm. Lolly would be fashionably late. Miranda waved at the waiter to get his attention, then ordered a mocha shake and pulled the *L.A. Times* out of her backpack. Skimming the front page, she noticed that Bickwell's widow had won her late husband's seat in a special election.

She had a vague recollection of the suicide. Miranda considered the story for a moment but could not think of a way to use it in her new work in progress. She took a slurp of the shake and managed to get a glob on her Johnny Cash T-shirt. "Damn," she grumbled as it dripped onto her cargo shorts.

"Can't take you anywhere," Lolly remarked as she slipped into the chair across from her. They laughed as Miranda tried to repair the damage with a napkin.

The waiter came over immediately to take Lolly's order. It was always that way when they went out together. Lolly was a chic, perfectly groomed model. Glistening, ebony curls enhanced her expressive hazel eyes. She had pouting, full lips and high cheek bones and large gold hoop earrings that accentuated her graceful neck. She wore a sleeveless taupe dress with an animal print silk scarf.

"Iced tea. That's all, thanks." The waiter lingered for a moment. You could tell he was trying to figure out where he had seen her before.

"Victoria's Secret commercial," I said with a smirk.

"Oh yeah," he replied sheepishly and took off for her beverage.

"You know, I don't think that was my best work," Lolly said completely serious.

"Yeah, my favorite was when you captured the essence of being a home-maker by getting that tough stain out of Bobby's football jersey," I laughed. She had looked so wrong for that part.

"It was Billy and he was a brat! Since then I've refused to work with children," Lolly said a bit indignantly.

"Except Al," I responded with a grin.

"He gave me a diamond, he's allowed to be a brat now and then," she smiled and played with her 3-carat diamond engagement ring. "Anyway, I'm usually the one that misbehaves," she laughed.

"Yeah, Dr. Obsessive-compulsive. I think he should have been an engineer instead of a shrink." I chuckled.

"Randie! Don't say that." She tried to look indignant but could not pull it off. "Yeah, he's pretty up-tight white but I'm helping him learn to relax." She smiled.

"Poor Al, next you'll have him shaking his booty."

"Tried that...it was so funny...there's no way...you know I hate stereotypes but Al is just classic. Don't you tell him I said that." She started laughing. Her face was animated with love for the slightly nerdy psychiatrist who had won her heart. "He is so interesting, Randie. I love to hear him talk about his work. I sell underwear, he keeps people from killing themselves."

"And, he doesn't care if you have 75 pairs of shoes." I had to laugh.

"He likes my sense of style, and it's 77, there was a sale at Nordstrom."

"Lolly, doesn't he ever get irritated with you?" I asked with mock wonder.

"Yes, but only when I keep him waiting."

"You're never on time."

"I just tell him, I'm his moment of zen, a chance to learn to go with the flow." She smiled.

"Moment of zen? Lolly, really!" I had to laugh. "You should have tried that with Dr. Bishop when you were late for English. I'm going to see him tonight. He wants me to stop by his composition class."

"That old fossil? I thought he was dead." She sounded disappointed.

"You're still holding a grudge?" I asked.

"He almost failed me."

"You did your nails in class," I reminded her.

"I had an audition that day," Lolly replied indignantly. "Anyway, he always gave me the creeps."

"So, I can't invite him to your engagement party?"

"No! But there is someone..."

"Lolly, not again. C'mon, remember Fred? The pharmacist buddy of Al's...he had a better lingerie collection than most women. I don't think you know any normal people." I had to laugh.

My protests would be to no avail. Lolly knew I was tired of being alone. Sometimes you wish friends had less insight. She was on a mission and would not accept my refusal.

"There's a dentist in Alan's building, he's only been in L.A. about a year, he's like you..."

"A hick?" I laughed.

"Well, since you put it that way, sort of...he's from Montana or Wyoming. Al says he's a nice guy. His name is James Donnelley and he wants to meet you."

"I'm so far behind with my book. I'm under a lot of pressure to write a book I haven't even agreed to. If I don't, my agent can make my life pretty miserable."

"Randie, there's a gallery exhibit tomorrow night, just off Wilshire. We can grab a bite then meet them there when they get off work. Only stay a few minutes if you want, then go write...but I think you'll like him. Trust me," she said with an evil grin.

Lolly and I always joked that "Trust me" in Los Angeles was like saying, "You're about to get screwed" anywhere else.

"Yeah, I'll trust you!" I said laughing "But if he turns out to be bad news you'll never hear the end of it and you'll have to promise to stop setting me up with blind dates."

CHAPTER 3

I WALKED HOME glad for the slight breeze. The heat lingered despite the setting sun. It was good to see Lolly but I could feel my mood eroding. My apartment rent had almost doubled. My landlord, Mr. Olive, was of slight build, late twenties and looked sort of Greek or Eastern European. He was handsome but stern. He rarely made eye contact but when I walked away I felt his eyes on me. I caught a glimpse of him staring at me once when I got on the elevator. I thought he was probably just shy around women, or maybe a pervert. Still, he was patient when the rent was late, though I could not count on his kindness when my book advance ran out. I liked my quiet, old retro building. I was lucky the rent was so low when I first moved in. My debts had been paid. I could stay solvent a few more months if my rent did not go up again. I had to produce something that would satisfy my publisher. Perhaps after meeting the Baron I should have considered changing careers, but at that moment I wanted to be on good terms with him so I could negotiate an advance. I needed the vampire novel to be a big money book. I was hoping that seeing my old professor might help break my writer's block.

My apartment was a mess; not dirty, just chaotic, like my life. Books, CDs, papers, clean laundry I had meant to fold littered the living room. I had long ago decided it was impossible to be creative and tidy. I fished around my pile of laundry and found a neon pink T-shirt with Che Guevara's image and my favorite comfy blue jeans. Then I located my high-top lime green sneakers under the couch. Lolly once said I had all the fashion sense of a circus clown. I quickly brushed my hair and was almost out the door when my phone rang.

"Hello?"

"Miranda, I'm afraid you haven't grasped how important it is that you send me an outline of the new novel." Lena skipped pleasantries. "Mordecai demands more than promises from you. He has decided to be your editor. That is a rare honor. Give him something interesting to promote. He wants to build on the momentum of your first book."

"Yes, I know, but…" Mordecai my editor? That was good and bad.

"No excuses. Are you still interested in writing?"

"Of course I am," I responded though I really wanted to tell her to go to hell. "It's just that my brain is so full of bloodsucking fun facts I don't know where to begin."

"Start with a murder," Lena suggested. "That will get the reader's attention. Now tell me about the main characters."

"OK. Polly is a depressed photographer who goes to the Alps to get over breaking off her engagement to Sidney, a workaholic lawyer. In the picturesque village, the local vampire is more than willing to help her try to forget Sid. In the end, the Vamp will have to come to the U.S. to pursue Polly. Sidney will have to decide if his law practice is more important than the woman he loves. Polly will have to choose between human warmth and the fantastic nightlife of the undead. The vampire will not give up easily. I am also playing with the idea of a second love triangle involving the undead."

"Describe the vampire," Lena replied in a calmer tone.

"I wish I could. He's the problem. An undead enigma. I can't seem to capture him and, believe me, I've been trying."

"Apply yourself, or move back to Iowa."

"Illinois!" I dared correct her. "Why did Mordecai decide to be my editor? I was happy with Marcia. She did a good job with *Obsession*."

"You should ask him yourself. He's back in town. He'll contact you."

"Is that really necessary? He must have more important people to annoy." I had hoped His Highness had lost interest in me.

"Miranda, write! I want an outline and at least three chapters by the end of the month. You don't want to disappoint the Baron. Get on it or find a different agent." Lena hung up before I could respond.

I promised myself I would fire her ass after I sold my vampire book. I still needed her at this point in my career but with more success I would be able to start calling the shots. I hated to be talked down to, ordered around. Was she trying to motivate me with tough love? In any case, I knew she was not making an idle threat. Other struggling writers would gladly follow her dictates if she chose to represent them. What this businesswoman did not understand was that I loved writing. I wanted to be successful. I did not need to be coerced. I was thirsting for a magic elixir to get my creative juices flowing again.

I quietly tiptoed into the classroom while Dr. Bishop was still making some introductory remarks and took a seat in the back. A couple of years ago I was one of these students who listened attentively to his love affair with the creative process.

"Writing is a calling not meant for the faint of heart," Dr. Bishop exclaimed. "Even if you have been rejected a hundred times you press on. Every loss, every delight, every failure or tragedy becomes treasured material to weave into your tales." He coughed, then continued. "Ah, and here is our guest for this evening. One of my favorite young writers, Miranda Ortega." He gestured for me to step up to the podium. "It is my pleasure to present the remarkable author of *Obsession with Death*."

Although the applause startled me, I did not feel nervous. Looking about the room, I saw in the students' faces the hopes and self-doubts I struggled with. I felt an instant affinity with them. The literary true believers, out to make their mark on the world one book at a time.

"Thank you, Dr. Bishop. This room holds many pleasant memories. Dr. Bishop was the first person to encourage me to write *Obsession with Death*. My best friend thought I had lost it when I told her the plot of my novel. She said that with all the real people you could have sex with, why would anyone screw a ghost?" There was an awkward pause, then laughter erupted.

"The moral of this story is stick with the stories that flow out of you, regardless of the opinions of non-writers. The worst thing that can happen early in a writing career is to allow criticism to discourage you. My high school journalism teacher suggested I drop out of her class and take home economics since she assumed my goal in life was to continue to work at my after-school job at the local coffee shop. I surprised her by getting an A in that class. I also sent the high school autographed copies of my book." I could see that my comments were resonating with most of the students. One young man with curly blond hair and a pierced eyebrow raised his hand.

"Yes, you have a question?"

"Yeah, how do you find a way to support you writing habit? I want to continue writing but I have to eat too." There were a few chuckles from other students.

"Good question. You have to sacrifice for your art but don't starve. Some jobs like teaching work well for writers if you take summers off. I would be substitute teaching or waiting on tables if I had not sold my book. Maybe you should find an understanding girlfriend with a good job."

A young woman elbowed him and a few students laughed. There were several more questions about plot development, researching characters and getting attention for your endeavors. Then a young dark haired woman asked, "How do you stay with it, rewrite the same chapter over and over again and not get burned out?"

"Love the story you are telling, wake up worrying about the characters, then think of your bills, what a bitch your agent can be if she is disappointed and drink lots of coffee."

They thought I was joking. The students laughed but Dr. Bishop looked pensive. "One last bit of advice. Look over contracts very carefully before you sign away your talent. I wish you all good luck."

I was relieved when I was able to politely turn down the last request to read a manuscript. I did not like saying no to the students but I had a book to write at the moment. Dr. Bishop escorted me out. He seemed to walk slower than I remembered and leaned more heavily on his cane.

"Thank you for speaking to my class but I fear none of them have your talent or drive."

He stopped for a moment to catch his breath, then we continued on through the halls.

"I appreciate the compliment but I'm not sure it's deserved." It felt like the old days when I had sought his advice about writing as a career. "At this rate, I'm not sure I'll ever finish another book. My agent is not happy with me."

The professor looked concerned. "Is there some distraction keeping you from writing?"

"No, I've sworn off distractions. It's visualizing a vampire in this time. I don't see the undead using computers, going to the movies and getting stuck in traffic jams."

"Consider how the wealthiest people live, how servants take care of their every whim. Vampires would not have to soil their hands with the everyday concerns of modern man," he said in a serious tone. "I think that you must get inside the brain of a vampire. See the world as your domain, a place to prey upon the living as you see fit. It's a chilling thought." He coughed.

"Are you all right?" I inquired.

"At my age? Never," he replied with a flicker of a smile. "Tell me, is succeeding as a writer still so important to you?"

I nodded. "For a lot of reasons."

He smiled and seemed pleased with my answer. "Try some of the old writing exercises. Miranda, I'm going on leave soon, to get more rest...the years are catching up to me. Take care my dear." I held open the heavy oak door of the building. As he walked by me I thought I heard him utter "Forgive me" but decided I must have been mistaken. Then he slowly walked down some steps to a silver Cadillac that was waiting. He waved to me briefly, then disappeared inside.

I had a feeling that I would never see him lecture again. He was an odd man who never mentioned his personal life. The only picture in his office was a Victorian miniature of a beautiful young, blonde woman. I wondered if he was lonely. I decided to ask him out to lunch once my novel was underway and he was back from his leave. I appreciated the faith he had in my talent. I was still wondering if I had more than one book in me. I drove a Civic that was several years old with over 200,000 miles on it. It was comfortable to drive, like putting on an old pair of sneakers, but it tended to stall. Some nights when writer's block had the best of me I would drive to the beach, cruise along the coast highway with the windows down and blast rock n' roll till a new twist in the plot surfaced. I decided to drive straight home hoping that my conversation with Dr. Bishop would be enough of a catalyst for character and plot development.

Back in my apartment I checked my email before diving in. There was a reminder from Lolly about the art gallery tomorrow night. She was on a mission. Despite my protests, I hoped that the dentist would be more than an awkward incident to joke about later. I was tired of being a lonely writer. Maybe not having a sex life was part of my writer's block. It sounded stupid but maybe some intimacy would open another level to my work. At least that is how I was rationalizing going on another blind date.

Sometime around midnight I stretched and yawned. Then I deleted an hour's work because it was bullshit. If I didn't feel something for the vampire I was creating how could the reader? "More coffee," I mumbled. I put my favorite French roast blend in the coffee maker. Good coffee was a necessity of life. While it was brewing I looked out my window onto the boulevard. Not much of interest to inspire me, except a shiny black limousine parked down below. I wondered who in the building had a rich friend, or if some old couple had hired it for a wedding anniversary. I poured myself a cup of coffee, strong enough to wake the dead, and sat back down in front of my computer. Bela Lugosi loomed above my cluttered desk in a large black and white poster of *Dracula* with little bats in his eyes. "If you could only talk," I sighed. There had to be more to the undead than psychopathic horror, even Stoker's villain showed real depth of feeling.

I quickly wrote and printed out a list of undead qualities, then taped it under the poster:

Vamp:
1. Sadistic
2. Controlling
3. Without conscience
4. Secretive
5. Violent
6. Seductive
7. Powerful

I wrote a similar list for my heroine although it could have had my name on it, and stuck it above the desk:

Polly:
1. Hates pain
2. Can't even control checkbook
3. Feels guilty if doesn't floss
4. Open book and extremely curious
5. Won't even step on a cockroach
6. Vestal Virgin
7. Untested strength

Number six was one of the reasons I had not dated a lot. I had this unnatural desire to have the first time mean something. No one that significant had come into my life. There were times when it had been close. There was this Cuban poet I met at UCLA who had the sexiest voice, intense dark eyes and a profound appreciation of women. Luckily, in the nick of time, I found out he had a wife and seven kids back on the island. Feelings of sexual frustration and the sticky summer night started to prey on me, so while the coffee was brewing I decided to take a cool shower.

I cast off clothing as I walked down the hall to the bathroom with every intention of picking up my apartment tomorrow. I stepped into the shower and surrendered to the cool sensation of the cascading drops of water. I was a water baby; nothing soothed me more than a bath or shower. My thoughts returned to my work. Writer's block was a blow to my self-esteem and undoubtedly related to my publisher's insistence he choose the subject matter. My first novel had flowed easily. I had never imagined that creativity would become a chore. I stepped out of the shower and grabbed a soft pink, cotton robe. I was feeling refreshed and ready to get back to work. As I entered the living room of my apartment I picked up a familiar scent.

"Mordecai!"

"Good evening, Miranda." He smiled as though I would be glad to see him. "You really should lock your door."

The sinewy lines of his chest and shoulders were evident under the fine material of his partially buttoned pale blue shirt. It was neatly tucked into black jeans. A large ruby ring glistened on one hand. Despite the heat he showed no sign of perspiration.

"I could have sworn I did."

"You look beautiful," he remarked, staring at me.

I grabbed my robe and pulled it tighter "I better change, I wasn't expecting..." It dawned on me just how inappropriate his intrusion was. He had a way of throwing me off, making me feel like I had committed a faux pas. "I think you should leave."

"I think we should discuss your writing, or lack thereof. I presume Lena told you I wanted to talk with you." He walked over to my small dinette set. "May I sit down?"

I realized that my agent would have my head if I didn't hear him out. He sat down before I said anything. "Okay," I responded as though my opinion mattered, "but it's late."

"Isn't that when you write?" he asked with a satisfied smile. "I'd like some coffee, black." He swept a pile of papers and books out of his way. "Women are usually neater."

"Yeah, when they're medicated." I got two mugs, slammed the cupboard and poured the coffee. He appeared amused by my temper. I plopped his coffee mug down, spilling a little on the table. "Sorry. Now if you'll excuse me for a minute."

I went back to my bedroom and quickly put on an old Rossville Bobcat's T-shirt and jeans. When I returned he was standing by my desk drinking from his mug.

"Too bad, I prefer the more casual attire," he remarked. "Miranda, I've decided to avail you of my expertise."

"Save it for your blonde, Simone." I retorted.

"Simone? Interesting that you remembered her name. There's nothing more I care to teach her. You, on the other hand, are quite ignorant and perhaps more deserving. Let's start with the undead."

Indignation put me at a loss for words. It was the second time he had that effect on me in the last few minutes. "I think you need a hobby besides harassing writers."

"I have a cat but she is fairly self-sufficient."

Mordecai walked over to my desk, read the lists and smiled. Suddenly, he reached over and ripped the Lugosi poster off the wall.

"What are you doing? You have no right! That was expensive..." I protested.

He dropped two $100 bills on the desk and said, "That should cover it."

"Keep your money and get out!" I picked up the remnants of my poster. "You are the most arrogant, rude and entitled person I have ever met."

"Now you can begin to write about a vampire," he responded in a soft tone of voice. "That insulting caricature of Dracula could only inspire failure. I've come to salvage your career." His eyes held mine.

He was serious. I placed the poster on my desk. "What can you tell me about the undead? You act as if you knew Vlad the Impaler."

I walked to the table to get my coffee. I wanted to put a little more distance between us. His scent, there was something about his scent, like an old memory, and his eyes seemed to look inside me. I felt very vulnerable, like I needed a HazMat suit.

"He was a crude barbaric mortal." The Baron moved closer to me. "Vampires would never showcase their victims to frighten others. They practice a much more personally satisfying form of terror."

I had to brush past him to get back into the living room. I was trying not to react but there was a release of some kind of endorphins by my brain with even minimal contact. I had to wonder why I was reacting to someone I disliked so strongly.

"You talk as if they're real instead of mythological monsters." I sat in an overstuffed chair.

"They are not monsters, they are gifted," he responded and sat on the coffee table directly in front of me. His feet were on either side of mine. "I don't believe I have wrongly assumed you capable of grasping the vampire's significance."

"I'm not stupid..." my voice trailed off.

"Try to think beyond your limited existence," he demanded.

For a moment, there was nothing in the world but the Baron and me. His searching gaze captivated me. I wanted to know everything about him. He took the coffee mug from my hands and set it on the coffee table next to him.

"What if you had every right?" he asked softly. He stood and gently pulled me into his arms. I willingly complied. I felt like the rug was being pulled out from under me as I watched helplessly.

"The right?" I asked.

"To whatever you wanted."

His gaze was intense but his expression was softened by a slight smile as he tenderly cradled my face. Then Tristan's hands began to slide down my shoulders. I felt the slight pressure of his hips against me. He started to lower his head to kiss me. A weak voice in my brain began to protest the intimacy. For some reason, I remembered my Catholic mother's advice when I was 13 years old, "If it feels good, don't do it!"

"Let me go," I managed to say to his surprise. I pushed his hands away and stepped over to the window. I took a deep breath as though it might help clear my head. What was wrong with me? I was not sure if I was crazy for saying no or for considering saying yes.

"I'm sorry. I thought the attraction was mutual," he responded with a bemused expression.

"Apology accepted" was all that came out. I wanted to tell him he was wrong but I was not sure that was true.

"To write about the rulers of the night, you must shed your plebian reality," he simply stated. He did not move closer but kept his eyes on me.

"But I'm looking at this vampire through Polly's eyes. The American tourist who happens upon an intelligent, handsome, aristocratic, charming but arrogant…" I stopped because I saw Mordecai's smile.

"I think you have found your vampire," he laughed. "Just don't use my name." He bowed slightly and left. I stood at the window and watched his limousine drive away. I continued to stare at the dark street trying to understand what had just happened.

Baron Mordecai returned to his mansion in an unusually upbeat mood, only to find a disgruntled Sergio in his dining room with a bottle of wine.

"She's impossible!" the Italian proclaimed as Tristan entered the large room lit by two chandeliers.

"I could say the same thing," Tristan smiled, thinking about Miranda, and sat across from his friend. A servant brought him a silver goblet and placed it on the white linen table cloth. Tristan sipped the contents, leaving a slightly red tinge to his lips, then nodded approval to the butler, who quietly withdrew.

"You must talk to her, tell her I'm ready," Sergio pleaded loudly.

"I would not dare tell Lena what to do. There is only one who could. Why don't you talk to him?" Tristan was playing with Sergio.

He seemed to sober up. "Really, you think I could get an audience?"

"You are drunk," Tristan laughed, "and in love. Not a good combination. If Lena sees you this way she will never agree that you are worthy."

"Why were you chosen?" Sergio asked in earnest.

"For good and bad reasons, I suspect." Tristan drained his goblet.

"I didn't ask about your evening. How did it go with Miranda?" Sergio sounded concerned.

"She has great potential which is matched only by her difficult nature. An interesting combination," Tristan responded.

"You're in over your head, too. I never thought it would happen to you," Sergio mumbled and took another drink. "I wish Lena was as concerned about me."

"Miranda concerns us all," Tristan responded, then changed the subject.

"You must be patient and try to work things out with Lena. I have known her to become reasonable once or twice in the last 1,000 years."

CHAPTER 4

IT WAS A commonly beautiful, sunny day in Los Angeles and uncommonly good air quality was reported throughout the basin. James Donnelley seriously considered leaving work early to go fishing. He was intimidated by the reaction he might get if he asked his receptionist to cancel an appointment. His office manager, Mabel, made the mountain lions of Montana seem tame. She never had a problem collecting payments on bills. Sometimes he wondered if the old woman had connections to organized crime.

"Mabel, if possible I'll see the last patient early. See what you can do," he requested with a charming, boyish grin. He was 35 but looked like he might be in his late 20s. He had short, thick brown hair, green eyes and a slight tan.

"Don't forget your meeting Dr. Gottleib at the gallery tonight. It's at the corner of Melrose and Robertson at 8 o'clock." She checked off something in her appointment book like she was keeping score — Mabel, 300; Dr. Donnelley, 0.

He had wanted to forget the blind date. Nothing good had ever come from mystery dates. "Wasn't that for next week?" He knew it wasn't but enjoyed ruffling her feathers.

"I'm certain it is for tonight...if you would like I'll call his office." She tugged nervously at her blonde, bouffant wig.

"No, I'm sure you're right," he smiled "Just kidding, Mabel."

The receptionist blushed slightly, thinking about how handsome her young boss was and how she wished she were about 40 years younger. She hoped the young woman he would meet tonight would be good enough for him.

Several blocks away I was just rolling out of bed. It was 4:30 p.m. Sleeping most of the day had left me slightly disoriented. Mordecai had not stayed long but his visit had energized me. It was a relief to find I had not merely dreamed completing 12 pages. Gathering the precious sheets I had printed out before retiring, I started to tear up. Though I had no desire to get to know Mordecai better, his visit had undoubtedly kindled my creativity. Drawing from his haughty, self-indulgent and seductive behavior, it was easy to come up with the undead antagonist that had eluded me for months. My writer's block had vanished. I was happily pouring over my night's work when the doorbell rang.

"Lolly!" The blind date had completely slipped my mind. I just wanted to get back to my book. Lolly entered my apartment looking like she had stepped off the pages of *Vogue*. She wore an ivory silk tank top with an Aztec print mini skirt. Several gold bangles adorned her wrists and matched the long, dangling earrings that swayed as she moved. Tan leather sandals accentuated her long, shapely legs.

"You're just getting up?" She was surprised to see me still in a nightgown.

"I was working late, then overslept." I decided not to mention Mordecai's visit as Lolly's imagination almost equaled my own. She was already looking around the apartment like a detective.

"Let me grab a cup of coffee then I'll take a quick shower. You want some?" I headed for the kitchen to avoid her skeptical gaze.

"Miranda, you couldn't lie if your life depended on it," Lolly chuckled. "C'mon, 'fess up."

"OK, there is someone." I handed her the beginning of my new book. "The vampire I've longed for. Read it over while I shower."

Lolly did not look convinced but sat down to peruse the pages. A few minutes later the doorbell rang.

"I'll get it," Lolly called out.

To her amazement, a dignified white man in a dark suit and chauffeur's cap announced in a British accent that he had a few packages for Ms. Ortega.

"She's busy, do you want me to sign for them?"

"That won't be necessary," he smiled. "May we?"

Lolly stood aside and two men entered. The second man was a bit taller with a thin moustache, dark suit, perfectly combed short brown hair and an equally stoic manner. They headed straight for the coffee table in the living room as though familiar with the apartment. Without speaking, they cleared away books, papers and coffee mugs, then working in tandem neatly stacked several packages. The second man removed four dozen red roses from a box as the first man held out a crystal vase. He quickly arranged the roses and then placed the vase in front of the boxes. The chauffeur carefully placed a small white envelope beside the roses. The second man ran a finger nervously across his thin moustache as he surveyed the display. He then nodded to the chauffeur. The driver thanked Lolly and they left without another word.

I was vigorously drying my hair with a towel as I entered the living room. "Lolly, was someone at the...what is this?!" I stared at the beautiful roses, then the boxes.

"OK Randie, now tell me about last night," Lolly laughed. "A British chauffeur and another guy, maybe a butler, delivered these. Definitely not FedEx. More like Prince of Wales."

"Or Prince of Darkness," I muttered.

"Who?" She handed me the card.

"I have a bad feeling about this."

My name was beautifully written in burgundy ink on the envelope. It resembled the color of dried blood. The initials T.M. were embossed in gold on the outside of the card. Lolly peered over my shoulder full of curiosity.

Sweet Miranda,

I trust you had a satisfying night after our encounter stirred your creative juices. I look forward to helping you further. Your passionate temperament is quite compelling.

Please accept these tokens of my regard for your intelligence and beauty. I look forward to the scintillating pleasure of your company tonight.

—Tristan

"Randie, why didn't you tell me you were busy? Who is this guy? Scintillating?" Lolly started to laugh. "Creative juices?"

"English is his second language. Anyway, I didn't know... He didn't even ask...just assumed..." I stared at the card. "I'm going to the freaking gallery tonight...I'm not staying home."

"Okay! Okay! But who is he?" Lolly asked still grinning. "Where is he from?"

"Eastern Europe somewhere. He's my publisher. My career is in his hands and he is an entitled egomaniac. He is pressuring me for more than a book. Pisses me off, but he did help me last night." I knew I was not presenting my case well.

"So, is he married or ugly or is it his age?" Lolly inquired.

"He is hot! But that's not the point." I looked at Lolly trying to hold back her laughter and we both started chuckling. "Unbelievable. Let's see what he sent me. Maybe I can pawn some of it."

"Always the romantic," Lolly laughed.

I picked up one of the smallest boxes. Inside was a bottle of Magie Noire perfume. "Black Magic, how appropriate." I smelled the heady fragrance and it reminded a little of the Baron.

"You know they don't make that anymore. Here open this one." Lolly handed me a box from a Rodeo Drive jewelry store.

"It's a Rolex! A gold Rolex with diamonds!" I could not help but be stunned by this extravagant gift.

"Okay, so he's hot, wealthy, generous and interested in your career. I can see why you want to avoid him." Lolly rolled her eyes.

"I know this makes me look...oh no..." I opened a large box from an exclusive boutique also on Rodeo Drive. Out spilled the most gorgeous red silk kimono with delicate chrysanthemums embroidered in gold thread on the sleeves. The soft, delicate material shimmered in my hands. I knew it would feel heavenly against my skin. I quickly placed it back in the box.

"Ungrateful," Lolly joked.

In another small box, I found a silver and gold Mont Blanc pen with my name engraved in an intricate script. "Damn, the engraving will make this hard to sell."

"One more to go. He knows what you like!" Lolly remarked. She handed me a large box with Godiva printed on the side. It contained 2 pounds of chocolate truffles and 2 pounds of French roast coffee.

"Not fair," I mumbled as I popped a truffle in my mouth. "All these presents were to remind me to get to work. Something to write with, something to keep track of time, food and drink to keep me going, Magie Noire to remind me of..."

"Sex?" Lolly chuckled

"Probably! But we haven't...I mean...it's business. My publisher thinks silk robes are work clothes! Lolly, he's not right," I protested.

"Business? Yeah, right. Whatever you say. But he does have exquisite taste or his personal shopper does. Randie, maybe he's not as bad as you think," she smiled as I slipped on the Rolex.

"I'm keeping this. I think I earned it for putting up with him." I looked at the magnificent watch and thought no one in Rossville would believe it was real. It was weighty yet comfortable on my wrist. Then I grabbed another chocolate truffle. It melted in my mouth, bittersweet heaven. I had to draw the line somewhere. "Lolly, you want the kimono?"

"No, I don't think you should give it away."

"Then I'll put it in the back of my closet. I mean it. He can pressure me about writing but that's all. This is nuts. I am not sticking around my apartment tonight. So, you think pants are okay for the gallery, or maybe a skirt?"

"I think the dentist would prefer the kimono," Lolly quipped.

"You're not helping." I tried to be serious but had to laugh. "C'mon, I'm actually asking for your fashion advice."

We began rummaging in my bedroom closet. Lolly found a simple black skirt and a red, sleeveless blouse.

"Randie, I haven't seen you this upset about a man since that Cuban poet fiasco."

Lolly grinned and shook her head as she handed me the clothes.

"You want me to bring up some of your Dating Hall of Famers, like Sven, the Swedish rocker and part-time professional wrestler?" I started changing and grabbed some black flats.

"I was young," Lolly protested.

"That was only two years ago," I laughed. "Hair up or hair down?"

"Up. I'll do a French braid for you," Lolly said, amazed that I was being so cooperative. As she started working on my hair she added, "You should pick up a little before you have any more company. If you need a cleaning lady I know...."

"Clutter helps me write."

"Whatever," she sighed and put the finishing touches on my sophisticated look.

"You should go see Rigoberto, his new salon is amazing and you could use a trim."

"Lolly, one more *should* and I won't need to call my Mom this month," I laughed. I grabbed a black tote bag and discretely placed a few overnight necessities inside along with a notebook and my wallet. I was not sure what I was going to do other than find a way to avoid the Baron. We took my car as Lolly had come by taxi. She would go home with Al. We darted in and out of rush hour traffic to the Hard Rock Cafe. We parked at the Beverly Center garage and walked to the restaurant. Lolly had a VIP card so we never had to wait for a table. It had been a gift from a record producer she had dated just before meeting Al. We declined menus and soon I was eating a black bean burger and fries while sipping iced tea with a sprig of mint, Lolly had her usual turkey burger. Tourists stared at the rock memorabilia. Steven Tyler's black and yellow striped suit. Some woman in her 60s stared at Jimi Hendrix's suede, fringed jacket like she was having a religious experience. I loved the music and all the hype. I thought it was a shame that there were no groupies for writers. Then I thought of the Baron and changed my mind.

"So how did Al pop the question?" I asked, hoping to avoid more inquiries about last night.

"It was so funny. He was so nervous he dropped the ring in the wonton soup. The soup was hot so he had a hard time fishing it out. The waiter came over to see what the problem was. He thought something was wrong with the soup and tried to take the bowl away from Al. It was like a scene from a Marx Bros movie," she laughed.

"I wish I could've seen that. I bet he was nervous. He's 40, right? And this is the first time he's made the big commitment. Maybe he should start seeing a shrink."

Lolly threw a French fry at me. "Knock it off or I'll name one of the dogs after you."

"Dogs?" I asked.

"Al wants to get a couple of springer spaniels. Sweet dogs. We looked at some puppies last week. He thinks it will help us prepare for having kids. You'll be an aunt," Lolly laughed.

"You two deserve each other. You're spoiled, the dogs will be spoiled and I don't even want to think about the kids!"

It was getting late so we decided against desert and took off for the West Hollywood gallery. Alan Gottlieb, a tall, sandy-haired man in a dark suit, was standing outside checking his watch as we pulled up. A slightly shorter, nicely built man in cowboy boots, jeans and a striped shirt stood beside him.

As we approached them, Lolly whispered, "He's the shy guy from Montana."

With a firm handshake, James Donnelley introduced himself and made me feel instantly at ease. I noticed his boots were comfortably worn, not just for show. He had a Cheshire grin like he might let me in on a joke. There were blond streaks in his thick, brown mane from hours in the great outdoors. It was easier to imagine him building a house than filling a cavity.

Lolly started to introduce him. " Miranda, this is Dr…"

He cut her off, "Hi! Please, call me James. Nice to meet you, Miranda."

"Thanks. Have you been waiting long?"

"No, but I think Al was."

We glanced at the couple just in time to see Al's look of impatience vanish with a kiss from Lolly.

"But I guess he doesn't mind," James remarked with an amused expression.

"It will probably get worse before the night is over," I added which caused him to laugh.

I noticed he was wearing a Timex watch, the kind my Dad wore. Nothing pretentious about him. It made me wish that I had left the Rolex in my apartment. I was starting to have a good gut reaction to this man.

"So pardner," I teased. "What brings you to these parts?"

"You don't like my boots?" he said looking down. "Hey, Lolly said you were nice and I should try and draw you out."

"De-fang me is more like it," I laughed, "and you're doing a pretty good job. So how long have you been in our fair city?"

"About a year. I've been building up my practice. I heard you're a foreigner, too," he remarked

"I'm from the land of acres of corn and soy, da Bears, the Cubs, Blackhawks and Al Capone. Illinois. I like your boots, they remind me of home downstate." I smiled.

Alan ushered us into the gallery. An uncomfortable silence fell over us. The art exhibit turned out to be an international photo display of women's breasts. There were no faces, arms or even necks. Just extreme close-ups of mammary glands from around the world. After wandering about for a few minutes in disbelief, James confessed his embarrassment at such a backdrop for our first meeting.

"I'm sorry, I don't get this, but I've got a six-month-old nephew who would love it," he chuckled.

"This is so wrong in so many ways." I began chuckling as well.

Our laughter began to attract attention. The owner of the gallery, a burly man dressed all in black, approached us.

"Does there seem to be a problem? May I help you?" he asked with a slight scowl.

"We were just wondering how much this photo might go for?" James managed to ask in a serious tone of voice. He pointed to a picture of a woman who must have been about 90 years old.

"Three thousand dollars," the owner responded.

"I'll tell a friend of mine, a plastic surgeon about it, might be good in his office," James added.

I grabbed his hand and pulled James away as I started laughing. The owner walked away in a huff.

"You are too funny." I released his hand but wished I had not.

"I don't think Alan is going to invite us to a gallery again," he said with mock disappointment. We stepped outside to avoid being asked to leave.

"Well, now I know what to get Alan for a wedding present," I laughed.

Alan and Lolly followed us out. Just as Al was about to comment on the gallery Lolly suggested going somewhere for dessert. It was such a beautiful, clear night we decided to walk to a coffee shop on Beverly Boulevard. En route, Alan began his lecture on the importance of viewing the human body impartially without emotional discomfort. As we were seated in the '50s diner, I challenged his intellectualizing. "But wouldn't you have been upset if Lolly had participated in that exhibit?"

After a pause Al responded, "It would have been anonymous."

"Al, you wouldn't care if my naked breasts were displayed in public?" Lolly asked with raised brows. The waitress dropped her order book. "You know I don't do nude modeling."

"Honey, I wasn't suggesting you should..." Al patted her hand.

There was a brief respite from the debate as the waitress took our orders. We all ordered freshly made doughnuts, a specialty of the coffee shop, except for Al who asked for dry, whole wheat toast. He was a serious vegan.

"You see, I'm right," I remarked smugly. "People will never be dispassionate about being naked in public."

"Yeah, I can tell you never spent the winter in Montana," James chuckled.

"Or Illinois. In any case I had an ethical problem with that exhibit. I think it lacked integrity."

"And faces," James quipped.

We gave each other a high five.

"Al, I understand about seeing beauty in the human body but that was rather sexist. I mean, don't you think they could have included men's chests as well?" Lolly asked.

"The impact is greater when it is women. The meaning is so clear..." Al began.

"Yeah, people are getting ripped off for thousands of dollars by a guy who had a thing for his mother. I'm sorry, Alan, but that was trash," James commented.

I was growing fonder of the dentist by the minute. The waitress brought our orders.

"Eating a doughnut," Al felt compelled to warn us, "is like putting a lard plug in an artery." For a psychiatrist, or maybe because he was one, he sorely lacked social skills.

"I just don't have your self-discipline," Lolly commented. It was a moot point as she had a metabolism that would burn up a side of beef in an hour. Lolly bit into a large raspberry-filled pastry, sending a dollop of the sticky red jelly on to Al's perfectly white, pressed shirt. Despite his displeasure, her repentant expression made him laugh. I watched them and thought of how well they balanced each other. She brought spontaneity and fun to his rather serious and regulated life. He provided stability and unconditional positive regard. She would always be lovely in his sight.

James suggested we take the long way back to where the cars were parked. There were lots of interesting shops on Melrose. We stopped in front of a clothing store that had a man's T-shirt with Mona Lisa painted on it for $700.

"Maybe I should give up my practice and start painting Fruit of the Loom," he quipped.

We noticed the reflection of a street person who walked up close to us. He was a young man in dirty clothes with a scruffy beard. His expression was flat and distant.

"Spare change? I'm starving."

I began to dig around in my purse but James stopped me gently.

"There's a soup kitchen at the Catholic Church by the park."

The man looked directly at James for a moment then disappeared down a side street.

"Why didn't you let me give him a dollar?" I asked.

"Because it wouldn't have gone for food, believe me. Someone like you, so trusting, you're a drunkard's dream," he said with a slight smile.

Alan and Lolly caught up with us at that moment.

"We're about ready to call it a night," Alan told us eager to be alone with his fiancé.

James and I were disappointed our first encounter was over but politely agreed and walked to the parking lot. It was about 10:30 p.m. when we reached the cars.

James turned to me and said, "I've really enjoyed meeting you. Lolly was right, you're not an airhead." He saw my puzzled expression. "That was my criteria for going out on a blind date."

"Thanks, I think," I laughed.

Out of nowhere, a black Mercedes limousine pulled up beside us. The chauffeur got out and approached us.

"He was one of the guys who delivered the presents," Lolly whispered to me, though I'm afraid it was loud enough for everyone to hear.

He greeted us with a classy British accent. "Good evening, Ms. Ortega, it is time for your meeting with Baron Mordecai."

My friends looked on in amazement. I felt angry and embarrassed.

"You must be mistaken. I'm not working tonight."

The driver looked uncomfortable with my response. "Is that the message you wish to be conveyed to the Baron?"

"Absolutely, and please add that I'll contact him to arrange a meeting when I'm ready to discuss the progress on my book," I replied indignantly. I was hoping to emphasize that this was a work-related matter.

"Very well," he replied curtly, clearly displeased, and returned to the limo. The sleek transport sped rapidly out of sight.

"That's the first time I've ever seen a limo burn rubber," James commented, hoping to ease the tension. "He's a Baron?"

"That's what he's called. He's my publisher."

"He is kind of pushy," Lolly commented. "Maybe you should stay at our place tonight." She spoke before thinking about how it might sound to my date.

"It's okay, really, Lolly. He's just obsessed with publishing deadlines and I'm a little behind." Alan started to say something but Lolly elbowed him. I noticed that James was staring down at his boots. "Are you going to the engagement party tomorrow night?" I boldly asked.

A smile lit up his face "Now I am." Then his expression became more serious. "Look, I know this is none of my business, but I don't think that guy is going be too happy you turned him down. I know I wouldn't be. Maybe you should…"

"I wouldn't turn you down," I replied. "I'll be fine. I'm glad Lolly and Al arranged for us to meet. I'm looking forward to tomorrow night."

We said our goodnights and headed off with a slight sense of discomfort. I knew they were worried about me but not as worried as I was. Who could know what crazy shit the Baron might pull. I just did not want it to be in front of James. I started my car and considered where I might go to avoid Mordecai.

CHAPTER 5

I DROVE AROUND the gallery neighborhood for several minutes until certain I was not followed. I knew my apartment was not safe from my bizarre benefactor. I got on the 405 freeway and headed towards the airport. LAX had a lot of hotels that would be open and well-lit anytime of night. Also, it was not an area where I would normally hang out. I hated feeling so vulnerable. The evening with my friends and James had been more enjoyable than I expected. The Baron's intrusion was making me wonder if should get some legal advice about getting out of my writing contract or even contact the police to report stalking. I took the exit and dodged in and out of traffic. L.A. never slept. I kept glancing in my rear view mirror but no cars seemed to be following me. The hotel parking structure gave me the creeps. I walked quickly to the lobby. While checking into a room at the Hilton, I felt a small bit of satisfaction when I paid for the room using Mordecai's money. I had to admit it was kind of exciting hiding out from a handsome, crazy millionaire. I just was not sure how crazy.

I got on the elevator with an older couple. The only place I would feel safe alone would be in my room with the door locked. It took forever to get to the 12th floor. I thought of how the Baron might react to being snubbed again. I imagined a royal temper tantrum with the servants scurrying. I was glad I would not be experiencing it tonight.

Finally inside the room, I double locked the door. The room was tastefully decorated in shades of pale peach and mint green, soothing colors. I dropped my large purse on an overstuffed chair and looked around. Finally satisfied that no one, that is, that the Baron was not hiding in the shower, I breathed a sigh of relief. Maybe I was a little too paranoid. It was beyond me why he was so concerned with my life, or even with my writing. He had the means to hire any writer. Maybe he was just a nocturnal control freak when it came to publishing.

The last thing I wanted to do was run back to Illinois. I had to figure out how to deal with someone like him.

I pulled a comfy T-shirt out of my bag and ran some water in the tub. The hotel soap smelled of lemongrass, which was relaxing. I only soaked in the tub for a few minutes as I wanted to tell Lena I had a productive night if she questioned my behavior. Lena was still scarier than my publisher. I put on my Bear's T-shirt and started the coffee maker. I promised myself that my second cup would be decaf, anything to help calm me down. I probably did not need coffee but caffeine abuse was the least of my problems at that moment. I started to put some lotion on my hands when I suddenly picked up a scent that was not calming. "No! I don't believe it." I turned around to see the Baron sitting in the overstuffed chair. "Damn it! How did you?"

"GPS," he smiled. "You like this room? Rather drab. I prefer boutique hotels." He stared at me with a bemused expression. Tristan wore a navy blue silk shirt and blue jeans. The dark hue made his fair skin appear even paler. For a second I wished our relationship was not so hostile, then sanity returned. "Your bourgeois tastes are to be expected."

"You're hard on locks," I replied, ignoring his condescending comments. "Don't you ever knock?"

"I can't decide if you're acting out of ignorance, stupidity, or ingratitude," he stated, as though not wanting to waste time explaining his burglar abilities.

"None of the above. I simply don't like you," I quipped and reached for the phone but it was missing.

Tristan held up the room phone then placed it on the floor along with my cell phone. He shook his head as though reprimanding a child then let loose an audible sigh.

"If you don't leave this minute I'll scream bloody murder!" I threatened.

"You are wasting what is left of a beautiful night your with histrionics. The hotel staff have been paid well to ignore the sounds caused by a sadomasochistic romp with my spouse. Besides, you picked a hotel that is fairly well insulated for sound because of the airport," he yawned. "Enough adolescent rebellion for one night, don't you think? You know I mean you no harm."

"Imposing your company on me makes you a sadist, but I'm not deriving pleasure from it. I don't intend to be pleasant no matter what Lena says, and I don't believe your intentions are saintly. Why waste your time with me? That trashy blonde must be on speed dial." Even I was surprised by how bitchy I sounded.

"Jealousy becomes you," he smiled, "but she was merely a distraction." Tristan stood up and started to unbutton his shirt, while staring at me.

"Keep your clothes on! I mean it!" I demanded.

"Ah, wishful thinking, but I'm only removing my shirt. It's for educational purposes," he said calmly. "Though you did choose a hotel for our meeting tonight."

"I'm dropping out of your class," I responded nervously and took a step back.

"My class?"

"Abnormal psychology," I said, taking another step back.

"Too late." He carefully laid his shirt across the chair. He was muscular and lean. His body reminded me of the pictures I had seen of white marble Greek statues. He exuded strength and grace.

"I don't think seeing you shirtless will help me write my book," I lied. He made a great, seductive villain. "Okay! This has gone far enough, leave me alone now and I promise, in the morning, I'll send you the chapter I write tonight." I was trying to get my mind back on our business relationship, which was not easy at that moment.

"I am growing impatient. It's time for show and tell." He stepped closer. "Bishop thinks you are intellectually capable of grasping the truth."

"Dr. Bishop?" I looked puzzled.

"I've known him a long time. We discussed you but I requested he not mention it. How much I reveal and when is my prerogative. Tonight, I've decided to lecture you on vampire basics. Think of your time with me as a field study course. Stand over there." He pointed to the floor in front of the dresser.

"Your manners suck. I don't like how you try to boss me and I don't think you're a friend of Dr. Bishop. I think you could benefit from a different kind of doctor like my friend Al." I bolted for the bathroom and tried to lock the door. He pushed the door open with such force that it sent me flying backwards into the tub.

He stood over me smiling. "Are you finished?"

"Bastard!" I cursed and tried to get up with some dignity. I would be sore in the morning.

"Yes, I am, but I've gotten over that," he quipped and returned to the sleeping area.

I glared at him but decided to take a different tact. "I will stand over there so that you will finish harassing me and leave," I replied indignantly, which was not easy considering I was only wearing a T-shirt. I walked across the room and stood with my back to the dresser.

The Baron moved beside me facing the dresser. His scent evoked a response like a pleasant memory. I scooted over a little. He smiled at my reaction. He had the most beautiful eyes, cool and mysterious. Fighting my attraction to him was hurting my brain.

"I never said I was his friend. Turn around," he demanded.

I saw my reflection and was horrified by what a mess my hair was. Then it dawned on me the Baron was gone. I turned and looked at him standing beside me, then back at the mirror.

"What the fuck! How did you do that?" Then I noticed his blue jeans were visible but that was all. His gold medallion was floating in the air.

"It's because of cellular differences. I'm only visible to the naked eye," he replied. "For such a sweet young woman, your language is rather raw."

"It's not possible." I stared at him and then looked back at the mirror hoping for some plausible explanation of how he did the trick. I touched his arm and it looked like I was touching nothing. "You're invisible." My stomach began to flutter and my pulse throbbed. "I've got to sit…." Then everything went black.

I felt a cool, damp cloth on my forehead. I was not sure how much time had passed. I opened my eyes slowly. I was laid out on the bed. It took a minute to remember I was in the hotel. A pale lock of hair fell along Tristan's jaw as he stared down at me. He was fully dressed again. His eyes showed intense concern, like I was the only person in the world that mattered. I will never forget that look. I can't explain it but at that moment I started to trust him. He covered me with a sheet and put another pillow under my head so I could sit up a little.

"Room service is bringing up espresso. That stuff you brewed was not worth drinking." He gently stroked my hand. "I think you'll be fine now. I know my reality is a bit of a shock. Not seeing is believing in my case. I can have a doctor attend to you if you'd like."

"So, what happened…it was your way of telling me…"

There was a knock on the door. "Room service!" The interruption gave me a chance to breathe. I struggled to make sense of the last few minutes. The young man who delivered the coffee and croissants barely glanced at me. He had probably heard about the "romp." Tristan handed him a $50 tip. Then to add to my amazement, the Baron brought me a cup of coffee. I think serving someone else was a novel experience. I stared at him while I took a few sips of the bitter brew. Such a hauntingly handsome face. He was waiting for me to say I accepted his bizarre reality.

"So now you expect me to believe you are a vampire. Maybe it was just an optical illusion." I stopped. His look silenced me.

He took the cup from my hand and sat on the edge of the bed. He gently raised my hand to his chest. He ran my fingers over the only imperfection visible on his flesh, a tiny scar. "That is the point of transformation. The neck is for feeding. The heart is for passing on the gift. It happened when I was a young man."

I liked touching him. The feeling of being embraced by his eyes, his surprisingly gentle touch. I wanted to kiss him. Self-preservation kicked in at that moment as the battle in my brain continued. How could I believe him? How could I let myself be seduced by him?

"This is all wrong. A gift? It's a curse. You can't be a vampire, it's not possible." Tears welled up in my eyes. "No!" I started to push him away but he just held me tightly. I thought I was going insane. That had to be the explanation. His hold felt like a strait jacket, keeping me immobilized until I calmed down. Instead of fear, a sense of being protected came over me. I could not explain why I felt safe. His scent seemed comforting.

He whispered, "I am Tristan Mordecai, one of the vampires of the Haute Caste. You are important to me." Tristan stroked my head while holding me against his chest. "I have waited patiently to share my world with you. It is a hidden reality that you are being granted access to. This is just the beginning, Miranda." He then released me and looked upon my face. Eyes that had seen the passage of centuries gazed at me longingly. Carefully he unloosed my curls from the remnants of the French braid. "Always wear your hair down for me." His tender actions were incredibly powerful.

"I can't think clearly when you're so close to me," I managed to whisper.

"As you wish," he responded and moved to the overstuffed chair. I didn't know what was weirder, his confession or the fact that he obeyed me.

I sat up straight and took a sip of coffee. Suddenly I was hungry. My dad was a volunteer EMT, he told me trauma tends to screw up your blood sugar. So what effect would talking with the undead have? I needed to calm down. I started to eat a croissant. "Do you want one?"

He shook his head. "I follow a special diet."

I put down the croissant. "What do you want from me? Why me?"

"For now, what Bram promised but did not deliver." There was a hint of irritation in his voice.

"Bram? You don't mean..."

"Stoker!" He stood and walked to the window. The Baron looked out at the street far below lost in thought for a moment. I stared at his striking profile, so pale against the night sky. "He agreed to write an accurate account of my existence. Much was revealed to that wretch. He expressed his gratitude by portraying me as a hideous, loathsome monster."

"That's why you hated my poster, you think you're Dracula." I stared at him. How could this be true? My mind was trying to piece together all the things he had said and done.

"That was Stoker's invention. I know who I am. Baron Tristan Mordecai, born in the year 1090 in Eastern Europe."

"Next you'll be telling me werewolves exist."

"Only in Hollywood. Come on, Miranda," he said impatiently.

"Right, but vampires run around L.A. Excuse me if I'm struggling here." I took another sip of coffee. "That would make you over 900 years old."

"Your IQ was 157 in the fifth grade. It is my goal to rescue you from the common beliefs of the unenlightened masses." He returned to the overstuffed chair—which now seemed more like a throne—and stared at me.

"How did you know that?"

"I know everything about you, everything. You're not ready for more revelations tonight. my dear."

"What the fuck does that mean? You have no right to invade my privacy, I don't care if you are the Prince of the Undead." My indignation was taking the place of fear and wonder. My mom always tried to warn me about my temper.

"Don't be so provincial. I have any right I choose. No one can restrict me. Your rules don't apply to my kind," he smiled. "Tell me, do you think Stoker was very productive after writing about me?" He rose and walked over to the bed.

I felt like I was being tested. "Besides something about a mummy, I can't remember anything else he wrote." I swiveled around and sat on the opposite side of the bed. Then I stood and faced him, keeping the bed between us. He merely smiled.

"Precisely. His disagreeable nature cost him dearly. It is important to keep one's word."

"Are you insinuating that could happen to me? That you could ruin my career if I didn't appease you?" I stared back at him, unflinching.

"It's more like please me and you do, except for your vocabulary when angered," he laughed. "In fact, your behavior continues to peak my interest." He glanced at the Rolex on my wrist. "I'm glad you like it."

"Take it back! Leave me the hell alone!" I fumbled with the watch.

"Keep it. The watch will be the least of the presents I give you."

"Gifts? Really? More like bribes."

He walked around the bed and stood in front of me. My anxiety level was rising. I was on an emotional roller coaster. I felt trapped.

"I'm hoping to wake up any minute from this nightmare."

"Shall I pinch you?" he smiled.

"No!" I blurted out.

"Admit who I am and I will regretfully leave you alone for the rest of the evening."

"What if I just admit you make me crazy?"

He stepped closer and lightly placed a finger on the side of my neck. "You have such lovely, throbbing arteries." His eyes showed a longing which made me push his hand away.

"You're a freakin' vampire. I believe you. Go away!" I started to tear up.

"Very well." He walked over to the dresser and placed a credit card on top. "It is in your name but I will pay the bill. Buy whatever suits you. Your apartment rent is paid. I don't want financial concerns to be a distraction. When you write tonight consider my supernatural state. Try to imagine what it is like to never be ill, to never grow old and to never die," he added with a slight smile. "I assume you will be discrete about our encounter."

"Don't worry. I don't want to get locked up. Does Lena know?"

"She is a trusted friend." Tristan replied as he walked back over to me. He gently took my right hand and, in courtly fashion, raised it to his lips. He lightly kissed the tips of my fingers. I felt warmth envelop my body. "I will share my secrets and more with you. I do not believe you will ever betray me."

"What happened to Bram?"

"There are worse fates than dying." he replied. "Until tomorrow night, Miranda." He left without another word.

Simone had followed the Baron to the hotel but did not have the patience to wait till his business with the writer was complete to try and find out more about his current pet project. She grew bored after a few minutes and decided to engage in her favorite activity, prowling the airport. Airport bars, where the servers would quickly forget their customers, were a perfect place to pick up a late-night snack.

She walked into a sports bar where a plumbing supply salesman from Ohio was drinking beer, clearly not his first, and staring at a waitress instead of the game. "Perfect," she thought. Simone sat down beside the overweight, middle-aged man and ordered red wine. "My flight was canceled. I've got three hours to kill," she said.

"My name's Bill. I've got about 90 minutes before take-off. I have to say you smell great," he said, "kind of like geraniums."

This was going to be easier than expected. "Gardenias," she smiled. Simone smelled his AB blood type. "I like your cologne."

"I only wear Brut." When Simone's wine came he said, "Here, that's on me."

"Business must be good," Simone remarked.

"Yep, everybody needs to have their plumbing working. They are installing our toilets in city hall. That was a big contract."

"You don't say," Simone tried to sound impressed. "Why don't we celebrate some place a little less public."

Bill started to choke on his beer. This was going to be the best business trip ever. Wait till he told the boys in the front office about this woman. He did not care if she had a boob job, she was stacked. He wanted to take her picture but was afraid his wife might see it.

"Sure," he replied and finished his beer.

Simone led him to a remote corner of the air terminal all the while asking questions about his trip to flatter him. Then she pointed to a family bathroom.

"There's a couch inside," she smiled, "and you can still make your flight." She took his hand and blew softly in is ear. "I'll go in first, then in a minute join me."

Bill suddenly felt apprehensive. He started doubting the wisdom of having sex in an airport bathroom with a stranger. Then he thought about how his wife had not touched him since menopause started six months ago. "You only live once," he told himself and followed her in.

She grabbed him as he entered and slammed the door. She began to kiss his neck. As Bill felt her breasts crush against his chest, he said, "Whoa! Slow down!" Those were the last words Bill ever spoke. His bloody body was found by a janitor a few hours later. His throat had been slashed. The security footage showed him walking through the airport alone, though there was a bit of a blurred shadow beside him that the airport personnel decided was a bug in the system. He was not robbed but his wedding ring was found in his pants pocket. The police had suspicions that his wife might have hired a hit-man but the case would remain unsolved. Simone left the airport just before sunrise. She saw the gray sky appearing behind the old palm trees that lined the boulevard. She burped a little of Bill's beer-enriched AB blood. The evening had worked out fine after all. There would be time tomorrow night to pursue her revenge on the Baron.

CHAPTER 6

JAMES RETURNED TO his West Hollywood bungalow feeling confused about the way the evening ended. His Dalmatian, Gracie, gave him an enthusiastic greeting. The sparsely furnished home smelled faintly of Pine-Sol. Though neat and orderly, it was comfortable. There was a small leather couch with a throw his mother had knitted and an old rocking chair. His most prized possession, his grandfather's banjo, leaned up against his desk. He let the dog out the back door and gazed up at the few stars that managed to shine through the glare of the city lights. When the old dog returned he sat down at the kitchen table and scratched behind her ears.

"Gracie," he mumbled. "I'm not sure what I'm getting into here but she is very pretty and bright. I think you'll like her, but I'm warning you, she's complicated."

The dentist tried to keep his life simple. He was a minimalist. He had one frying pan for breakfast and a stock pot for everything else. In his cupboard there were four mugs, four plates and four bowls, just in case he had company. In his closet, he had a functional amount of clothing and one suit for weddings or funerals. James joked that if he never got married, at least he could get his money out of the suit when he passed away. He prided himself on being rational and reasonable when he was sober, which had been his choice now for five years. It seemed like Miranda was trying to cover up something with her publisher. That was causing his gut to be a bit uneasy. Still, a smile came to his lips when he thought of her debating nudity with Al. She could hold her own. He liked that. Despite any misgivings, he wanted to see her again.

He ran a hand through his hair and sighed. In the past, he would have silenced his thoughts with alcohol. He went into the living room and picked up his banjo and began playing an old Southern dancing tune. After about 20 minutes of strumming he felt more relaxed.

"Well Gracie, I just hope she likes dogs." His canine companion wagged her tail and followed him down the hall to the bedroom. It would be hard to stay focused on molars tomorrow.

At the crack of dawn, I returned home. After the Baron's alarming revelation, I could not sleep. I had paced, switched to decaf and finally completed two chapters. My mind seemed quickened by our interaction. Exhausted, I collapsed on the bed without taking off my street clothes. My writing focused on the naive Polly's reaction to the charming and overwhelmingly seductive count. Polly's lingering affection for her ex-fiancé helped her fend off the vampire's advances for the moment. I left Polly feeling confused and gazing out of a hotel window at the Alps. While the aristocrat plots to make Polly his undead bride, her ex, Sidney, is flying into Geneva hoping for a chance to salvage their relationship. The scenes with the count flowed easily, but Sidney was a little more difficult. His character was a combination of Al and James. Something told me not to make him look too much like James. Also, to appease my publisher and Lena, I described the vampire as exceedingly attractive. That was not a lie.

I fell into a deep sleep. Six hours later the heat of the day disturbed my rest. A thin layer of perspiration made me feel sticky. It was impossible to go back to sleep. I opened a window and let a cool breeze into the room. I tried to take stock of the last 24 hours. The shock of what I had experienced at the hotel had worn off. There had to be a rational explanation for his vanishing act. Tristan had been in the room for a few minutes before I came out of the bathroom. He had time enough to adjust the lighting, do something to the mirror, or maybe it was sleight of hand like a magician. With his money, he could have hired the best special effects techs in Hollywood. It seemed far-fetched but not as bizarre as believing his claim to be a vampire. The Baron was probably chuckling about my reaction. Perhaps he just thought his theatrics would help me write. It did. The trick would be to find a way to set limits with him. What I did not see in the mirror had compelled me to believe that Tristan Mordecai was a creature of the night. The rational part of my brain now countered that it was a clever trick, a practical joke. There was only one person who might be willing to tell me the truth and it was not Lena. I called Dr. Bishop's office but he was still out on sick leave. So much for a reality check. I looked at my calendar. The engagement party! James would be there. A promise of normalcy, at least for a few hours. I remembered the slow, easy cadence of his speech and how relaxed I felt with him. I wanted to know what motivated him to come to the West Coast. Perhaps we were kindred, restless souls. Hopefully the scene with the Baron's chauffeur would not scare James off. For the moment I would try to focus on the party and worry about his Royal Bizarreness later.

I found a dress in my closet that Lolly had pressured me to buy against my better judgment. It was a purple satin cocktail dress with spaghetti straps. She said I would need it for the next book party. She would be delighted if I wore it to her celebration. I held the beautiful garment up to the mirror and freaked. "My hair!" This occasion called for the professional help I often scorned. I would wear my hair up. Take that, Baron Mordecai. At this point being passive-aggressive was my only weapon. My gut told me the Baron would keep his word and visit me later. I decided that since he was throwing his money at me I would use the royal credit card to make the salon visit even sweeter.

I dialed Rigoberto's Salon and begged him to fit me into his busy schedule. I used to hang out there while he was styling Lolly's hair but had never gone under his scissors. He always said I was a walking hair disaster.

"Rigoberto, please, please, style my hair today. I surrender my unruly, unworthy, wild mane to you." I waited for a response.

"Miranda, sweetheart, I have been waiting for this day. Is it for Lolly's party? She was already here this morning."

"Yes, it is. Whenever you can fit me in will be fine."

"For this historic event, I will work over lunch but you must pick up an order at that Thai place around the corner."

I set out to primp, So. Cal style. I was considering a manicure/pedicure as well. Then maybe I would have time to shop for a new pair of high-heel sandals. Lolly would be proud of me.

My old Civic looked out of place in the Bel Air parking lot full of Mercedes, Cadillacs and Lexus. Gleaming brass handles adorned the dark glass doors of the chic salon. I entered the intimidating world of pampered, wealthy women carrying two bags of Thai take-out. The young woman with perfectly straight hair behind the counter thought I was making a delivery.

"Just put it in the back."

"I have an appointment with Rigoberto," I told her, a bit annoyed.

Before my claim could be verified, a high-pitched, somewhat nasal voice welcomed me. "Miranda, at last!" He was a wiry little man, with a neatly trimmed beard and short, curly hair. He always wore beige and black, even away from the salon. Though he went by Rigoberto, he was actually Bob from Moline, Illinois. That was our secret. Ethnic and exotic was better for business. He said I was one of the few "real" people he knew. I wondered what he would think of the Baron. We grabbed a bite while catching up on life.

"I have never seen her so content. Alan is eccentric, but he is exactly what she needed, and you, there must be someone you wish to impress."

"Maybe," I replied with a grin. "He's a friend of Alan."

"Then let's get to work. Let's make you more interesting. A few steaks of magenta."

"I don't want to be that interesting," I replied. He made a sad face. "Okay, one streak, a small one, on one side." He clapped his hands. "Very good. Let us get to work."

The color consultant did my streak. Then my hair was shampooed by a woman who tackled my scalp like it was a wrestling opponent. My neck hurt. Finally, Rigoberto's assistant combed out my wet hair.

"You want to wear your hair up, have a casual, chic look, right?"

I nodded. His sheers started flying. Clumps of hair fell to the floor. I felt tightness in my stomach. After 20 minutes of blow dryers, curling irons and assorted chemicals, he turned my chair around so I could see his creation.

"Wow!" I exclaimed.

"I always told Lucy there was a beautiful woman under all that hair."

Lightly feathered bangs emphasized my eyes. A small rhinestone clip pulled the streaked hair up behind one ear, emphasizing the oval shape of my face. Glossy ringlets cascaded down just to my shoulders. He had cut off about 3 inches of split ends. My hair looked healthy and glossy. I started to pull on one of the ringlets. He grabbed my hand.

"Let someone else do that tonight," he smiled

"Will you be at the party?"

"Of course. I want to thank the man who motivated you to come here."

I gave him a kiss on the cheek and left the salon feeling like a different person. I cannot explain how a hairstyle could make such a difference. I felt more sophisticated, worldly and daring. It did not feel like a disguise, more like a hidden side of me was revealed. My next stop was a chic shoe store. I spent $450 on a pair of black sandals that had 2-inch heels adorned with tiny crystals. I could walk in these heels. Well, actually, the baron spent $450, which I enjoyed to no end. I even stopped for a manicure/pedicure in two shades of plum. Back at my apartment, I blasted rhythm and blues while I primped for the party. I wasn't big on cosmetics so I didn't have a lot, but I used them all. Lipstick, blush, mascara and pale, violet eye shadow. A little Magie Noire perfume by my ear lobes added to my *femme fatale* feeling. After I got dressed I used a trick I'd seen Lolly employ; I added a little blush to my cleavage. It helped if you were barely a B cup like me. In my mind, I was doing it all for James, but the thought of appearing more sophisticated to the Baron when he dropped by later was not unpleasant.

The sprawling, hillside home of Dr. Gottlieb was full of light, soft music and laughter. An odd mix of Al's professional buddies and Lolly's Hollywood crowd filled the spacious, modern living room that looked out over a canyon. A couple of friends said they almost did not recognized me. Lolly said I looked amazing. Even Al said my hairstyle was becoming. I found James out on the balcony alone. He was looking down into the canyon. He was wearing a tailored, short-sleeved shirt and jeans. I wondered if he felt a bit out of place.

"It's a beautiful view," I commented.

"Randie?" He looked surprised.

"I clean up good," I replied.

"You certainly do. I think that purple dress might get you arrested in Rooster, Montana."

"I'll take that as a compliment."

"Oh, it is." James appeared to have a bad case of infatuation. A slow song could be heard from the living room. "May I have this dance?"

"Absolutely. It's why I wore this dress."

I stepped into him. He held me gently, lightly putting his arm about my waist. When I rested my head on his shoulder I felt him relax. It was a beautifully normal moment. An attractive, bright, funny man was dancing with me at my friend's party. He smelled of soap and water. He was unpretentious and comfortable, like his Timex watch. When the music stopped we reluctantly moved apart.

"I've seen coyotes in the canyon," I remarked.

"I miss the open spaces of home. Drive a little way out of my town and you won't see anything but wild critters and cattle for miles."

"Yeah, but can you buy a teriyaki pizza or a kosher burrito there?" I was trying to keep the conversation light.

"Nope, and you won't find a Miranda Ortega there either," he smiled.

"I know it's hard to adjust to this place but at least it's never boring. Think of the millions of lives all around us."

"I'd rather not. I'll just think about you."

"Nice!" I laughed.

"You're alright. You haven't asked for free dental work yet."

"Not me, I hate dentists," I quipped and he pretended to be hurt. "Present company excluded, of course."

Hunger drove us to face the multitudes inside. Lucy seemed quite content to be the center of attention but not Alan. As they stood at the buffet table the psychiatrist whispered to James, "I'm trying to convince Lolly to elope."

"Fat chance," James responded as he watched Lolly show off her engagement ring for the hundredth time.

We both declined wine and set off for the kitchen in search of root beer. The old-fashioned soda was one of the few likes I had in common with Alan. I told James, "Al usually has a case of the good stuff in glass bottles, it's his weakness. I've even seen the fitness fanatic down a root beer float. Pretty shocking, eh?"

James' expression became pensive as I handed him a glass and started to pour. "I'm glad you don't drink," he told me and looked at me squarely, "because I can't, or maybe it's better to say I won't. I'm in recovery." He looked like he expected me to run away.

"My mom raised me to abstain. It stuck with me. Thanks for being so honest. How long have you been sober?"

"I'm really glad I met you." James smiled and relaxed a bit. "It's been five years, three months and six days. I could calculate the hours and minutes."

"That's okay. You're sober now. I had an uncle who used to get wasted at family gatherings but then he got a DUI. That helped him quit. It's just hard to imagine you like that."

"It was a nightmare towards the end but now I really like my life. Enough about my misspent youth."

"It's ironic. You're looking at the designated driver of my high school senior class. I was the only one who didn't drink or smoke pot."

"You're mama raised you right. You're lucky, very lucky."

"Are you sure you don't know her?" I laughed. "She would love you."

"I think I'll just focus on her daughter," he smiled. "Still want to dance the night away?"

"Yeah. Maybe we can get Al to play something from this century."

He followed me into the living room. I was not bothered by his Achilles' heel; we all have something we struggle with. He had faced his problem. I respected that. There was a spot by the grand piano with enough room to dance. We were headed there when Rigoberto caught my attention and communicated a questioning glance towards James. I was about to respond when Lolly called out to me loudly.

"Miranda, why didn't you tell me the Baron was coming?"

Conversation in the room lessened noticeably as heads turned towards the elegantly attired new arrival. A gray Italian suit draped his athletic form. A barely buttoned red silk shirt partially displayed his muscular chest. Lolly wrapped her hands around the guest's arm and smiled flirtatiously as she guided him towards me. I was mortified.

"Baron?" James wondered out loud.

"Baron Shithead," I responded. "I'm so sorry he showed up. It's about my next book. He's financing it. Believe me, I didn't invite him but there's no getting rid of him."

"Business, huh?" he questioned.

"Unfortunately, yes." I looked at him with disappointment. "I had looked forward to spending the evening with you but he can't be dismissed easily."

"I want to stay but I'd hate to make a scene at Al and Lolly's party."

"Thanks for being so understanding. Al's got my number, call me, okay? I mean it."

"Miranda, you can count on it." He squeezed my hand before leaving.

"Of all the piss-poor timing." I turned to face the Baron. Repeated contact with him was having a deleterious effect on my vocabulary.

CHAPTER 7

A LARGE RED ruby glistened on Tristan's right hand, the same ring he had worn to the hotel, as he dislodged Lolly and stared at the polished version of me. "Miranda, why didn't you inform our lovely hostess that I would be joining you?"

Matching his steady gaze, I replied, "Because I hoped you wouldn't."

After being charmed by the mysterious aristocrat, Lolly appeared astonished and embarrassed by my rudeness. "You know, she did say something about bringing a guest. Please, join us for a toast." She glanced at me with an evil eye.

"Delighted," his voice and demeanor were sweet as honey. "You're gorgeous!" Then he whispered, "Except for your hair." He pulled lightly on one of the cascading curls just as my hairdresser approached.

Rigoberto looked at my new escort approvingly, as though appearance was a valid measure of a man.

Tristan put his arm about my waist. All I could think of was how much I wished the simply clad dentist was by my side. Unwilling to disrupt the celebration, I resigned myself to my unwelcome date for the time being. We followed Lolly thru the guests to where Alan was waiting by a small table with dozens of glasses of champagne. I noticed several women giving Tristan indiscreet visual appraisals. He acknowledged them with a slight smile.

"Go for the redhead, I won't mind," I whispered.

"Not tonight." His hand began to play with the delicate strap that held my dress up on one side. "Very nice."

"Stop that!" I said loud enough to evoke snickers from those standing nearby.

"If you move away from me," he whispered, "the fragile material that covers your heart will not be able to withstand our separation."

I started to blush. I fumed but I did not move. Alan asked the caterers to start passing out the champagne and sparkling apple juice. Tristan chose the intoxicating beverage. When I asked for the juice drink he gave me a questioning glance.

"I don't drink because it makes people stupid."

"Then what is your excuse for this evening?"

I managed to spill some of my drink on his Italian loafers. My hostile act was witnessed by several people nearby, straining his façade of gentility. With subtle anger in his eyes he whispered, "Perhaps Lolly would be better company tonight."

I looked at my dear friend. Though she was ready for the engagement toast she kept looking at the Baron. "What do you want?" I whispered.

"Appear to enjoy my company," he said in a serious tone.

I managed a weak smile, raised my glass "To Lolly and Alan, my dearest friends." The couple embraced to the cheers of well-wishers. Even at that tender moment I noticed my best friend glance at Tristan. What was it about him that made women so vapid? Is having a royal title that hot? I knew it was something else that emanated from him. Lolly was always very focused on Alan; this was so out of character for her. I was not immune but I was also not as blindly effected by his charms. I had to get him away from her.

"The show is over. I want to leave, now!" I said quietly.

"Your wish is my command, Miranda," he replied in courtly fashion, causing a few envious stares. I was slightly nauseous. The Baron kept one arm about my waist as we said goodnight to the officially engaged couple. Lolly asked us to stay longer but Tristan politely refused. "We need a little time alone, I'm sure you understand."

Once we got outside, I tried to break free of him. "We need to be alone? I need to be alone! Fascist creep!"

"Temper, temper," Tristan said, laughing as he threw me over one shoulder and carried me to a black Bentley like I was a backpack.

"Put me down!"

The chauffeur opened the door as he deposited me in the back seat. It was plush and dark inside, creating fleeting images of a coffin's interior. I sat up and scrambled into a corner. He sat beside me and looked quite content.

"Party crasher," I snarled. "I'm driving myself home."

"Party crasher? I've never been called that before." He chuckled. It seemed so out of character. "This is what I love. You make me laugh. When you've lived as long as I have, it becomes difficult to find anything or anyone amusing, but you are full of surprises and so indignant. Amazing. You are a de Molay, after all."

"de Molay? I don't know who you're talking about. Amuse you? I amuse you? Go to hell!"

"That's not possible." Laughing harder he added, "Think about it."

"Tell me what you want, then I'm out of here." It was taking all my self-control not to hit him. I did not like being thought of as entertainment. He was acting like such an arrogant son of a bitch. Yet, I saw desire in his eyes. He was not lying about having strong feelings for me.

"A book about my unique reality to start."

"Should I search for articles in psychiatric journals? I don't know how you did that trick at the hotel but I'm over it." I looked down at my dress and started smoothing it to avoid his gaze. "I want you to leave my friends alone. They aren't part of our agreement."

"Like James Donelley?"

I looked up and anger flashed in my eyes. "All my friends."

"I have little interest in other people. I hope you never call me a friend. How boring."

"I don't think you ever have to worry about that," I said with a flat expression.

"I've rescued you from a mundane existence," he said with satisfaction. "Nice shoes."

"Go fuck yourself!"

"I don't have to," he replied with a smile.

"Neither do I!" I responded angrily, not sure I'd said the right thing.

"Agreed!" Tristan looked at me like he was about to dig into a hot fudge sundae. He acted like my attempts at self-preservation were flirtatious banter. I had to get out of there.

"Sorry, but my boss is extremely demanding. My 15 minutes of allotted fun was up a half hour ago. I have to go home and write, alone." Despite my words I could feel myself starting to react to his scent, to his masculine charm. "Don't force yourself on me. C'mon, is your ego so fragile that rejection by any woman is intolerable?"

"You're not any woman." There was a longing in his voice that caught me off guard.

He touched me only with his eyes. "Though my presence may at times seem overwhelming, I would never take advantage of a woman. I sincerely care for you, which is why I abide your insults."

Arrogance was easy to combat but his compliment, his admission of high regard and ethics, left me almost speechless. "Let me go."

"As you wish."

The limo door opened suddenly. I almost fell, scrambling out onto the driveway.

"Until tomorrow night," the Baron called out. Then the black limousine sped away down the canyon.

Benedetto was tired of being in Los Angeles. After 20 years of tracking vampires all over the great cities of the world, he disliked having to survive in this gross capital of material consumption. He was constantly averting his gaze from the scantily clad women in a place that knew only summer. The Brethren had a contact who might give them information that would permit a crippling blow to the conspirators of evil. The monk desired to give back to the church the riches that were given away by the Templars. He could forgive the misguided warriors but not the undead. He had vowed to spend his life hunting them down. Unfortunately, he had never been successful. His one encounter with a tall, blonde vampire had been quite humiliating. The demon mocked him by reciting a sacred verse, "Judge not lest ye be judged," then disappeared. He tried to squash that memory as he got ready for the evening encounter. Benedetto adjusted the small bronze cross he wore on a leather cord. It was his only adornment. The monks had shaved heads they disguised with assorted ball caps. He chose the Dodgers for tonight. The rest of their uniform was comprised of a plain, dark colored T-shirt, jeans and leather sandals. The clothes were meant to blend in with the locals. He was gaunt, due to the small amount of food he allowed himself. His deep-set brown eyes made his slightly hooked nose appear more prominent.

He shared a white van with another monk, Grigoryi. His holy partner was about 10 years younger and much more fascinated by the thought of one day encountering the undead. Benedetto admonished him at times to remember their goal was to destroy the blasphemers. While Benedetto was about 6 feet tall, Grigoryi was only about 5 feet, five inches. His diminutive stature made it easier for him to do surveillance. Grigoryi returned to the van with day old bagels and cream cheese from a Jewish deli. Benedetto was not sure it was appropriate to shop there. Sometimes he wondered how committed his holy brother was to their mission, though Grigoryi had come up with the idea of painting the wooden stakes with crosses, hopefully making the stakes more potent. Benedetto began putting their saintly weapons in his backpack, along with several small bottles of holy water and more stakes. Benedetto had to assert his authority over Grigoryi when he suggested they use squirt guns instead. That would just be wrong. He threw in a garland of garlic because of tradition. Since neither of them had ever laid a hand on a vampire they were merely following the teachings of their predecessors. They had practiced throwing fake holy water into each other's eyes, then thrusting the stakes at their chests. They stopped practicing when Grigoryi bruised Benedetto.

"What did you do with that note from the woman?" Ben asked. Someone had left a note on their van window last night while it was parked near the home of a suspected vampire. She asked the Brethren to meet her by the carousel at the Santa Monica pier at 10 p.m. She told them they shared a common enemy. She promised to help them. The note was signed "Cindy."

"It's stuck on the driver's side visor," Grigoryi responded. "When we meet her, promise you'll use my American name. We don't want to seem too foreign. It might scare her." Grigoryi was looking forward to talking with an American.

"Right Greg, we're just two ordinary guys who shave their heads, go to mass every day, live in a van and hunt vampires." Benedetto gave him a what-is-wrong-with-you look. Grigoryi made himself busy packing his gear. "We must have faith. Divine providence has sent us aid."

"What bothers me is how she knew about us. It's possible this is a trap. The undead tend to ignore us. All these years and only once did they acknowledge you," Grigoryi continued to question, "Why would they bother with us now? We never do anything but follow them around."

The last remark hurt Benedetto's pride. He squared his shoulders, and faced Grigoryi. "That is about to change. I had a vision last night. The Virgin Guadalupe appeared to me and blessed my hands. I did not tell you as visions are private affairs, but you seem to lack faith in my leadership. Apparently, the Virgin Guadalupe feels otherwise. It is why I know we must meet with this Cindy tonight and see where it leads."

Grigoryi merely looked down at his feet and muttered something about convenient hallucinations. He dared not say what he was thinking too loudly. He found it odd that whenever Grigoryi questioned Benedetto about his decisions, or the way they were carrying out their mission, the elder brother would talk about some holy vision. If Grigoryi could just meet a vampire once, he might become more dedicated, that is if he survived.

They drove down to Santa Monica with Benedetto humming *Ode to Joy*. It was Benedetto's habit when he was nervous, which further irritated Grigoryi, who proceeded to hang his head out of the window. It was moments like this that made Grigoryi consider joining the order he had heard about that baked fruitcakes in Texas.

The Brethren slowly walked towards the carousel on the pier. They noticed teenagers with skateboards and several couples. No one seemed to pay much attention to them. Benedetto kept his hands on his backpack in case he would need to pull out a holy weapon. Grigoryi dropped his pack and pulled a granola bar out of his pocket.

"You can't wait, really?" Benedetto whispered.

Grudgingly he returned the snack to his pocket. Just then a young, white woman with brown shoulder length hair approached them. She was wearing a white shirt, which showed a bit of cleavage, and tight blue jeans. She stopped a foot away. The scent of Gardenia wafted over them.

"I'm Cindy. We are after the same demons. I've been tracking that blond one since he killed my brother three years ago."

"What are you talking about?" Benedetto had an uncomfortable feeling.

Grigoryi just stared at the attractive woman, hoping to think of something intelligent to say.

"I need help. I've watched you tracking him. You must know he is after this woman, Miranda Ortega. She lives in that apartment building he's been visiting."

"Wow, someone else is hunting vampires, too," Grigoryi blurted out.

Benedetto and the woman both glanced at Grigoryi, making him hang his head a little. "You two should try to be less obvious. I'm surprised the Baron doesn't get you arrested for stalking him," she added.

"You know about Baron Mordecai? How is it you have not been harmed?" Benedetto questioned. It was difficult for him to fathom a woman capable of vampire hunting.

"I'm very careful. That's why you did not see me following you."

Grigoryi smiled at her response. Benedetto was trying to keep his gaze at eye level. Sensing she could win the monks over she stepped closer.

"This woman is in danger. I followed her once to a hotel but before I could speak to her the Baron showed up. I know I can't deal with him if I don't have help," she admitted. "He is very powerful." That was the cue for the Brethren to come to the rescue. She waited for a response.

"We are obliged by holy oaths to assist you in any way we can," the older monk responded. "I'm Brother Ben and this is Brother Greg. We have waited for many years to fight the undead but lacked opportunity. They are cunning and fast. Physically we are no match. Our weapons are weapons of faith." Benedetto touched his backpack.

"We have wooden stakes and holy water," Grigoryi said with enthusiasm, as though hoping to win a Boy Scout badge for preparedness.

"Great. I've been planning this vampire intervention for months. I've followed him enough to come up with a way to grab her to protect her from becoming his victim," she said with a tone of disgust. "Meet me at the parking area by the Bel Air Gates tomorrow at 10 pm and I'll fill you in on the details. I'll be in a silver Lexus."

"If we can save one soul it will all be worth it," Benedetto responded.

"Amen!" Grigoryi responded.

CHAPTER 8

I HAD STAYED up writing till about three in the morning. The character and plot development flowed easily. The innocent and smitten American discounts the villagers' warnings about the count as folklore. When her old flame, Sidney, shows up he investigates the count and is fearful for Polly. She decides he is just jealous and that his criticism of the aristocrat is self-serving. By the time I went to bed Sid was getting an earful from an old woman in the village who hates the count. Polly was feeling pressured to choose between the two rivals. The count was planning to make her choice easy by getting rid of Sidney. I was left with trying to figure out the weaknesses of the undead. I decided to ply my vampire expert for answers at our next encounter, which I predicted would occur much too soon. I needed rest, interactions with my bizarre publisher were exhausting me. For four hours, the arms of Morpheus cradled me in a deep sleep. I woke from a dream about Tristan feeling a bit shaken. He was sitting on a throne, barking orders and I was brought into the room with a single gold chain about my waist. When I sat up I could not recall what he had been saying. He was evidently troubling me at a profound level where rational thinking could not protect me. *I can't turn back now,* I thought. The profane barter of my writing was now more to protect my friends than to ensure success. I hoped that the sooner I finished the book, the sooner I could distance myself from him. I tried to go back to sleep but the phone rang.

"Miranda, tell me, is he there?" Lolly inquired. I looked at the clock in disbelief. She never called this early.

"Let me check," I responded. "No, I don't see anyone."

Lolly was oblivious to my sarcasm. "You won't believe all the people who asked about him and I had nothing to tell them."

"James wouldn't mind if you talked about him." I was hoping she would get a hint.

"Stop it, Randie. Come on. How could you have kept the Baron a secret? Even Al was a bit jealous, can you imagine?"

"Yes," was all I said.

"You've got to fill me in. Is he really a Baron? How long have you been seeing him?"

"I haven't eaten yet. I'll call you tomorrow," I replied flatly and hung up.

Before my friend could call me back, I switched off my phone. The thought of her being taken in by that arrogant prick had made it impossible to get any more rest. I doubted that revealing what an eccentric freak he was would make any difference to those affected by his extraordinary charisma. I also knew it would take Lolly about 45 minutes to drive over after she realized what I had done. I fixed a cup of coffee and rummaged in the fridge. Stale bread, moldy cheese, a limp carrot, a bottle of hot sauce and half a burrito from a week ago. I pulled out the Godiva chocolates and let a truffle melt in my mouth. It was bittersweet heaven. I stepped in the shower and washed away all the glamour from the night before. It felt good to put on my comfy blue jeans and an old Save the Polar Bears T-shirt. When I brushed out my hair it fell in neat layers. I slipped on some flip-flops and sat on the couch. The thought of going to the store to avoid Lolly was appealing but I feared she might contact Mr. Olive to break into my apartment when I did not respond. So I read over the pages from last night while I waited for the inquisition. In the book, the vampire was much more polite and restrained than the Baron. He used longing looks and the attraction of being a sophisticated aristocrat to lure Polly to his side. Polly was an avid photographer and a little miffed the count had not let her take a photo of him. Sidney will use the photo issue to start to shake Polly's confidence. The count looked exactly like my publisher. I made a mental note to get a better look at his medallion when the doorbell rang.

That was record time, I thought, and opened the door. "What are...."

The chauffeur handed me a garment bag from a Rodeo Drive boutique. "Good morning, Miss Ortega. The Baron sends his regards."

"Ms., not Miss," I replied. "What is this about?"

"You'll have to ask Baron Mordecai yourself." The chauffeur glanced at my attire and smirked. "Good day, Miss Ortega." He got back on the elevator with a satisfied grin.

I wondered if being an annoying snob was a prerequisite for his job. Curiosity won over my resentment as I zipped open the bag. It was a beautiful blue silk gown. Against my better judgment I decided I had to try it on. Though ankle length, it was split up past the knee on one side. The plunging neckline descended into a delicate flower outlined with caviar beads. It was an exact fit as though tailor made for me. This gorgeous gown made my purple dress look like a blue light special. I quickly changed back into my jeans and banished the gown to my closet. I was not about to show it to Lolly.

A very fashionable Lolly arrived a few minutes later. She took one look at my outfit and said, "I guess you are alone."

"He only comes out at night," I quipped.

"Funny. So who is this guy?" She continued the interrogation.

"Dracula. Hey! I was about to go to Trader Joe's. Want to come with me?"

"I guess so," she sighed. Her irritation with me was showing.

Once in the car she continued. "So where is he from? I couldn't place his accent."

I tightly gripped the steering wheel and replied, "I'm not sure."

"Why all the mystery? He must have told you something."

"Lolly, this guy is a high-class shithead. He is conceited, controlling and treats women like door mats. Our relationship is strictly business, at least on my end," I replied, hoping to end her line of questioning.

She became quiet for a couple of minutes. I regretted getting so upset with her. She was my best friend. Lolly had always been there for me.

"Al said he was narcissistic," Lolly responded in a contemplative tone.

"Thank God!" I muttered and parked the car. As we walked into the grocery store I added, "I'm sorry. I'm just stressed about writing deadlines." It wasn't easy to apologize when I knew I was right.

"Randie, we never keep secrets from each other. Then you're with this handsome, rich, sexy guy who sends you fabulous presents and I'm supposed to think it's business? Maybe I should start writing," she whined.

That was it. My apology had only encouraged her. I grabbed some cartons of yogurt, a bag of salad, a bottle of dressing and a few frozen dinners. Then walked quickly to the checkout. Lolly noticed the credit card. "Since when did you have a platinum American Express card?"

"Don't you realize what a fool you made of yourself last night?" I lashed out. The cashier's eyes got big. "Grabbing Mordecai's arm, hanging on him? Then even during your engagement toast you were staring at him. Remember Al?

You're supposed to be in love with him!" I grabbed my bag and headed out to the car.

Lolly followed me out. She appeared astonished and hurt by my outburst. After we got in the car she said softly, "I hope you're not jealous."

Those words made me realize that she was under the Baron's influence. She would not be able to see the truth in my portrayal of her behavior. She protected herself by finding fault in me. We drove back to the apartment in silence. When we arrived at the parking garage, I said, "Lolly, I wish someone was a threat to my relationship with the Baron. Just give this a rest. I'll call you in a few days." Her sad expression caused me to add, "I'll see if he has time in his schedule for us to stop by and see you and Al sometime." She brightened a little. We hugged and went our separate ways. "Damn Mordecai! This had better be a bestseller," I muttered in the elevator to my apartment.

I saw messages on my phone but decided to eat first. I was really hungry, so I heated up veggie lasagna in the microwave for breakfast. Filling up with pasta helped calm me down. Then I let a couple of chocolate truffles melt in my mouth. It gave me a moment to come up with a game plan to deal with the Baron, at least for tonight. Finally, I listened to the phone messages. I quickly deleted two from Lolly, then to my delight there was an invitation from James to go to Sunday brunch in Malibu. I hoped Mordecai's fixed delusion would prevent him from making a daylight appearance. It would be a chance to make up for the abrupt end of our date last night. Perfect. The dentist's receptionist took a little persuading to let me talk with him.

"Howdy, some person from Rossville that I wanted to hear from," James laughed.

"Hi James, I just wanted to apologize and accept your invitation."

"No apology needed. It wasn't your fault, but don't invite Baron Albino on Sunday."

"No problem," I stated, hoping to sound confident.

"Good. Now, you'll have to excuse me, I have to do battle with a couple of cavities."

"Thanks for being so understanding," I replied in earnest.

"I'm not. I almost waited for you to call first but I like you too much. Bye." He hung up quickly to avoid making a bigger fool of himself.

Trying to stay in the moment I thought about where the budding relationship might go. It was easy for me to imagine my parents liking him — a successful dentist who came from a rural area. A thought of the Baron meeting my folks shattered my happy moment. His royal status and wealth would trump a dentist in their eyes, no matter how bizarre he might be. I sipped another cup of coffee and considered how I would deal with a visit from my intimidating benefactor. This time I would be ready. I set off to visit a Mexican market, a Catholic church and a hardware store.

As the afternoon, waned, Sergio paced in a hotel room off Sunset Boulevard. He dialed Lena's number knowing she had been awake for about an hour. She did not pick up. She had refused to speak with, or see him, since he had pressured her to transform him. There would be no going back. Sergio glanced at his reflection and noticed the slight signs of aging. This would be his last glimpse of himself. His vanity strengthened his resolve. He would never need plastic surgery.

The door opened suddenly. Simone arrived dressed to kill. She wore 4-inch heels, a skin tight red dress with a wide, black patent belt and a Tahitian pearl necklace that adorned her cleavage. The scent of Gardenias was a bit much even for Sergio. Simone had a black alligator overnight bag. She closed the door quickly.

"You told no one?"

"Not a soul. I mean no one," he was not sure if that applied to the undead.

"Not even Tristan?" she pressed.

"No one. I even checked to be sure I was not followed," he insisted. "Lena is ignoring me. Why are you willing to help me?"

"Help you? I couldn't care less about you. I want to send a message to the ruling caste. I'm tired of being under their control, having to seek their approval for my meals and not being allowed to pass on the gift to whom I chose," she announced coldly.

"I appreciate your honesty," he responded, though her words struck a nerve. "Can we get it over with?"

"Take off your shirt and lay on the bed. I will muzzle you and turn on the TV to cover any unpleasant sounds that might alarm others."

He did as he was told but before he was muzzled said, "I thought the bite would numb any pain." His eyes became large as she put the cloth across his mouth.

"Normally that's true, but the transforming bite is above the heart. You shall feel your heart fail, then suddenly my blood will revive you." Simone traced his veins with her finger then let her hand rest on his beating heart, "Lovely."

Sergio began to perspire, his pulse increased. Simone sat on the bed and savored the moment. She had waited many years to get revenge on the elder vampiress who had snubbed her. She had not imagined that an intimate companion of Lena would present such an opportunity. Simone opened her bag and pulled out an IV bag, tubes and needles. She hooked the bag up to the lamp with a technique a medic would envy, quickly found a pulsating vein and inserted the IV needle. Sergio grimaced but said nothing. She took out a large syringe and withdrew blood from her arm, then emptied it into the IV bag. She filled a second syringe and emptied it again into the IV bag. Sergio began to feel the effect of her blood, like an amphetamine rush.

"I won't be here when you wake. Just take it easy for a couple of hours. I'll leave a bottle of O positive in the fridge. It will hold you over for a few days until you have the balls to confess to the Haute Caste." Simone lowered her head. She bit into his chest and drank deeply. Now she felt the exhilaration as the warm, salty fluid entered her body. The excruciating pain made Sergio pass out. The trauma of blood loss was weakening him. His heart failed for a minute. Then Simone withdrew one more large syringe and emptied it into the IV bag. His heart started again but he remained unconscious.

"Normally it is better to receive than to give but tonight it was worth it. Tonight I gave Lena a gift she won't forget," she said with a smile. Simone bandaged her arm and steadied herself. She pulled a pint of blood from her bag and gulped it down. Then she placed another pint in the room fridge. She looked down on him and removed the muzzle. Simone pulled a Tarot card from her bag and placed "The Fool" on his chest.

"Welcome to the family!"

CHAPTER 9

THE ODOR OF burning wax and garlic was noticeable as the Baron silently entered Miranda's apartment. All about, holy faces illumined by candles in jars stared at the intruder. Two garlic wreaths hung from the light fixture over the dining table. The Baron fought back the urge to laugh. He saw Miranda curled up on the couch asleep with a copy of Stoker's *Dracula* on her lap. For a few minutes he just observed her. She was wearing the same casual clothes from that morning. Bathed in flickering light he noted the rhythmic rise and fall of her chest. He later told Miranda that the sight of her so innocent, tender and appealing stirred the depths of his neglected human nature. His desire for her was increasing with each contact. She had no idea how well he had studied her and, though he tried to predict Miranda's behavior, she was still able to surprise him. Like this night.

I woke suddenly with the Baron leaning over me, his strong, cool fingers about my throat.

"Stop it! What are you trying to do, strangle me?" He let me push him away and I sat up. The book fell to the floor.

"Merely adorning your ungrateful neck," he replied with a satisfied smile.

My hands went up to my neck and touched a large pendant hanging from a heavy gold chain. I ran to the bathroom where my reflection revealed a magnificent square cut ruby. A smoldering fire glistened from within the jewel. "This belongs in the Tower of London!" was all I could think of to say.

"Yes, it once did, but then I did a favor for a queen and so it goes. I had my favorite ring turned into a pendant for you." He stood in the hallway quite pleased with my appropriate awe.

Instead of thanks I pulled a tiny bottle of water out of my jean's pocket and poured it on his shirt. Nothing happened. I realized he had not even pretended to be affected by my horror movie props.

He blotted his shirt with a towel. "Holy water, I presume."

"From St. Michael's. It wasn't easy to steal." I was sure there was a special spot in purgatory for someone like me. "Now you have to admit you're not a vampire."

"I was a bit put off by the smell of garlic but not because of my identity." He was obviously amused by my theatrics.

"But the holy water should have made you burst into flames," I insisted.

"Where's the wooden stake?"

"In here." I went into the bedroom with him on my heels. A small stack of wood was on the floor. "They wouldn't let me buy just one."

"You're pathetic." The Baron tried to contain his laughter.

"Here!" I held up the two stakes I had glued together like a cross.

"Really?" He sighed. "Think about it, Miranda. If religious symbols were unbearable to vampires how could we ever rise from the grave?" Then to my horror he grabbed the stake, rolled up one sleeve and pierced his forearm. He never even grimaced. I felt sick and handed him a hand towel. He wiped the wound and said, "A warm-blooded being cannot harm my kind."

I was stunned. "You want a bandage?"

There was very little bleeding. "We heal quickly."

It was getting more difficult to explain his extraordinary abilities. I tried to unfasten the heavy pendant. "I can't accept this."

"I bent the connecting link together when I put it on you. It is now an endless chain." He buttoned his cuff. There was no blood on his shirt.

"You should put some antibiotic ointment on that wound," I admonished him.

"It's nothing. You should put on the gown I sent you." He clearly expected me to change.

"When hell freezes over," I replied, looking at him squarely. "I want a cup of coffee. Excuse me." I slipped past him. I swear I heard him laugh but I did not turn around.

The Baron followed behind me and sat at the dining table. "I'd like a very hot cup of black coffee, thank you."

"No problem." I brewed a cup of Sumatran, put it in the microwave for 30 seconds and, with my back to him, added a tablespoon of Tabasco sauce. I carried it over to him. As I placed it on the table he put his hand on mine. It was very cold. "You're freezing."

"60 degrees, give or take a few. But that will change when I drink this." He put the cup to his lips and stopped. "Hot sauce? Arsenic I would expect, but this? Very well." He downed the tainted, boiling brew.

"Are you okay?" I was amazed. He waited a minute then put his hand on mine again. Now it was warm. "Who the fuck are you? How did you do that? Any of that?"

"I would prefer it if you called me Tristan." He appeared calm and satisfied with himself. "Do you still require more proof?" His eyes became serious. I wondered what he had in mind.

"You have a weird appetite and a strange metabolism. You heal quickly, I'll give you that. Also, you are good at hiding your reflection. Bizarre. Impressive. Even unique. But, it doesn't make you a scary creature that only exists in B movies," I responded, trying to sound matter of fact when in all honesty I was starting to wonder big time. "You're just some freak of nature."

"How can someone so bright cling to stubborn ignorance? Come along then. Time for field study." He walked out the door. Curiosity proved greater than fear. I was voluntarily going with him. I grabbed my purse, sneakers and a notepad. In the elevator, I dropped the notebook as I struggled to tie my shoes. He shook his head, "You won't need that. You won't forget tonight."

A sleek, customized black Corvette was parked in front of the building. "The Batmobile? Really?" I joked. Tristan did not smile.

"Get in!" he commanded and went around to the driver's side.

For a second I doubted the wisdom of complying but there was an adrenaline junkie hidden deep inside my brain longing for adventure. An itch I could not scratch. It was one of the reasons I left Rossville. I got in. The seats were soft leather. The interior had a bit of the Baron's scent. I had never been cool in my life but sitting in his sports car I felt like it. He turned the key and the powerful rumble of the engine echoed in the street.

"Where are we going?"

"The ballet, it's why I had the blue gown sent over. Apparently, you've chosen to wage a class war with ugly clothes."

"You're going to bite someone at the ballet?" I asked in disbelief.

"I like light entertainment prior to a meal."

"Which ballet?" I asked. I regretted wearing jeans, though in L.A. I would not be the only one in casual dress. I loved the ballet but he must have known that. In undergrad Lolly and I used our student discounts to get tickets. The beautiful movements and music were captivating. Although my first ballet was a local production of *The Nutcracker Suite* back home, I had been to dozens since coming to L.A.

"*The Rite of Spring*. Hopefully there won't be a riot today," he remarked.

"You want me to think you were there, in Paris, at the first performance?" I had to ask.

"It's when I lost all respect for mortal men," he responded.

The Baron had a special parking spot by an elevator which opened to the lobby of the Center for Performing Arts. The usher merely nodded at Tristan; apparently no tickets were required. The Baron did not go unnoticed by women as we made our way to the elite seating section. At every opportunity, he touched my arm to guide me. A petite brunette looked apprehensive as we passed in front of her. The Baron nodded to her and she responded in kind.

"Do you know her?" I asked as we sat down.

"The Senator?" he smiled. "I know a lot of people."

As the lights started to fade the powerful woman left and did not return.

"Do you really like the ballet, or is this just for me?"

"Motion pictures, plays, they just regurgitate man's banal existence. Opera I find pompous and lifeless. The ballet brings vital desire to the stage. It creates a love affair with the audience," he whispered. "It is one of the few distractions that gives me pleasure besides chess and women."

"I'll leave so you can have your pick," I started to get up. He placed his hand on my arm.

"Explore the pleasure of my existence," he implored. "It will be invaluable research."

I looked into his impenetrable blue eyes as the music began. I felt like I was drowning. I turned back to the stage. The sounds of primal rhythms and the desire which would fuel the sacrifice of a virgin began to be artfully played out. I wondered why he had chosen this particular ballet.

My writer's instinct surfaced to distract me. I imagined Polly at a performance with the Count. She is wearing my blue gown and is surrounded by his old-world wealth and knowledge. They are in a special balcony box. Looking down at the dancers' ritualistic movements, she suddenly starts to feel anxious and sad for the victim in the ballet. The Count notices her discomfort and touches her hand. Polly is feeling overwhelmed by the vampire's presence. She tries to tell herself it is just because of suspicions that Sidney has been raising, but she starts to feel faint. "I need some air," she states and hurriedly exits the box. I would write that scene tonight.

Running sounded like a good idea to me as well but I did not want to seem afraid of the Baron. I tried to stay focused on the ballet but his scent, his profile, kept diverting my attention. I felt relieved when the ballet was over.

Tristan noticed that my applause was hardly enthusiastic. "You found the performance lacking? It wasn't Nijinsky but still..."

"No. It was fine. I'm just concerned about what happens next," I asked bluntly. I was becoming more concerned about what lengths he might go to prove his delusion.

"Then let me take you for a bite," he replied and led me out of the theater.

"I'm not very hungry," I said as the evening appeared to be taking an ominous turn.

"I have quite an appetite," he replied.

We drove to Marina Del Rey in silence. It was a beautiful night to be by the water but it was difficult to appreciate the scenery. I wondered if he was taking me to a night club. We pulled into a parking lot by an upscale bar. There was a white BMW with its lights on. Tristan parked nearby.

"Here is your proof. I hope you won't be squeamish. Stay in the car. I must meet with Phillip, he's a drug dealer and a pedophile. Watch closely." He looked at me for a moment, then got out of the car. "Dinner time" he said coldly.

"This has gone...." I started to say but a glance from him stopped me.

As the Baron approached the BMW, the window lowered slightly in anticipation of a lucrative deal. Tristan tore the door open as a gun went off. The few people in the parking lot disappeared into the bar. He pulled the short, bald man, who was hitting him, into the street. Tristan glanced back at me for a second to display his fangs. Fear gripped me but I did not look away. I had to know. Tristan pierced the soft fleshy neck and the man instantly stopped struggling. After he had consumed enough blood, he took a small knife from his pocket and slashed at the man's throat to erase the bite marks. Then he threw the body back in the BMW like a bag of trash. He steadied himself by placing one hand on the car roof, then wiped his mouth with a handkerchief. As I watched the horrible murder take place, my writer's fantasies about the undead vanished. The harsh reality of their cruel existence flooded me. He was a monster! I started to feel sick. I had to get away. I jumped out and ran towards the marina. I don't think I ever ran faster in my life. I fell by a dumpster and ripped a hole in my jeans, cutting my knee. I gasped for breath. Tears started to pour down my cheeks. I was not sure who they were for.

"Grab her," a woman yelled. "Use the rope. The ruby! He gave you the ruby!"

I looked up to see Simone standing over me wearing a wig. She started to reach for my pendant, then vanished. Suddenly two white men in baseball caps grabbed my arms.

"Let me go!" I cried. They tied my hands together.

"It's for you own good," the taller man said as they hauled me kicking and screaming towards a van. "We're saving you."

"He'll kill you. Let me go!" I yelled.

Simone had disappeared. The smaller man was shaking. He apparently was new at abducting someone. The taller man opened the van door. "Quickly!" he ordered. I heard the sound of screeching tires, followed by the sound of his body being smashed against the van, then I saw him collapse. The smaller man took one look at the enraged vampire and fainted. I was left lying on the ground. Tristan untied my hands and gently helped me to my feet.

"Don't hurt them," I pleaded. "I believe you now." There were tears in my eyes.

"You are safe." He touched my cheek. Then he scooped me up in his arms and carried me to the car.

"I'm sorry I did not protect you," he added.

"I just saw you execute someone," I replied.

"I will never harm you," he stated as though it was a sacred oath.

"How can I ever feel safe with you after tonight? That was horrible! They probably tried to abduct me because of you!"

At that moment police sirens could be heard heading towards the murder scene. "We must go now!" The Baron quickly deposited me in the Corvette and sped away towards downtown. He took side streets where there were no traffic cameras.

"I witnessed you killing someone. This is a moral dilemma for me." I rubbed my sore wrists.

"Should I drop you off at the police station?" he smiled.

"You fucker!" I spat out.

"He molested three children but got off on a technicality. He also sold opiates. My meals are carefully chosen."

"What if you decide I'm not worthy to live?"

"That will never happen. You matter to me, you will always be under my protection, though it wouldn't hurt if you were more respectful." The Baron glanced at my bloody knee. "That needs attention."

"Not from you. If you don't mind." I replied curtly.

"My appetite has been appeased," he smiled briefly at my discomfort. "Those two are buffoons, someone put them up to this," he muttered.

"It was Simone. She was with them."

"You are sure?" he asked in earnest. "This is very important."

"She was there, barking orders, then she left them to do the dirty work. She wore a wig but I could smell that awful perfume. You know them?"

"Benedetto and company. They are devout zealots on a mission to rob Vampires, give our riches to the church and thus secure their places in heaven. The inside of their van looks a bit like your apartment at the moment. They don't have a clue about us. They obviously didn't realize Simone was one of their holy foes. What she did was unthinkable."

"What *she* did? Unbelievable!"

I was too tired and upset to argue about his absurd, warped point of view. I just wanted to go home, to be left alone. I stared at the man sitting next to me. Damn it! He should not exist. He was handsome as ever. His scent was appealing as always. I had never met anyone more interesting or frightening. My brain was trying to separate the sin from the sinner.

"I wish you were not undead," I told him in all honesty

He gave me a touching glance then rested his hand on mine. "I'll take that as a compliment. I have no regrets." Tristan lightly caressed my hand. For the first time that night I truly felt in danger. "You are very strong. You have witnessed the violent side of my nature and kept your wits. It seems you have the *sangfroid*, like one of your ancestors."

I pulled my hand away. "Don't talk about my family. Leave them out of this. Just take me home, I'm done for this evening."

"Very well." Tristan used a hands-free phone to talk with someone in a language I did not recognize. I noticed that we were near Westwood, close to Bel Air. Not exactly my neighborhood. "Where are you going?"

"We are going home," he replied. "My home, as your apartment is no longer safe."

"Yeah that sounds like a great idea. Let me out! I'll call a taxi." I tried to sound commanding.

"Simone would give you a ride, she has been following us since we left the marina," he replied.

I looked in the side mirror. There was a gray Lexus with a blond that resembled Simone keeping a safe distance behind us.

"She noticed the pendant. I thought she was going to tear it off my neck."

"She always wanted that ruby. I would never give it to her," he glanced at me. "It suits you somehow."

I did not mind upsetting Simone one bit. "I can't believe she set those monks up knowing you might kill them. Then she just left them suffering in the parking lot. Aren't you worried that they will tell the police you're the killer or they will identify you with finger prints or license plates?"

"Miranda, my kind has perfected the art of not being seen. I will appear a mere blur on video. There will not be any fingerprints. Two men living in a van making accusations about vampires are hardly credible witnesses. The police will suspect the monks of attacking the drug dealer when they find his wallet in their van. Also, my license plates are covered by a film that keeps them from being photographed."

"So how do I fit into this mess?" I inquired.

"Nicely," he replied and turned onto Stone Canyon Road.

There were glimpses of mansions as we drove along past security walls disguised by lush foliage. The car turned down a side street and passed through an ornate electric gate. They drove around a large fountain that could have been in a park and stopped in front of a sprawling, gray stone, country manor. It was set on about a half-acre of the most expensive land in L.A. County. The opulent gardens were surrounded by a very high stone wall. I wondered if it was to keep people in or out. In this neighborhood, no one would ever stop by to chat.

The chauffeur appeared and opened the Baron's door. I did not wait. I should have been afraid but the unique opportunity of exploring a vampire's lair beckoned. I could not imagine that my night could get worse. When my dad took foolish risks, my mom would say he was feeling bulletproof. I was feeling that stupid.

"Thank you, Jasper. Tell Clive we'll have coffee in the library."

I followed the Baron through heavy wooden doors into a marble tiled entryway that led to a foyer that was the size of a small ballroom. Exquisite, huge tapestries hung from the walls depicting scenes from the Middle Ages. A magnificent crystal chandelier cast sparkling light on the ornate Persian rug in the center of the room. By every door there was a gold-leaf table with a vase full of fresh-cut roses. At the far end, a dramatic stair case rose to the next level.

The butler smiled politely as we entered the library. It was the stuff writer's dreams are made of. Thousands of books lined the shelves from floor to ceiling. There were four ornately carved ladders, one leaning against each wall. But that was not what stopped me in my tracks. It was a painting.

"Incredible!" I gasped staring at the self-portrait of Van Gogh with one ear bandaged. It was hanging above a huge mahogany desk. "It's the original, isn't it?" Tristan merely nodded with a slight smile. Then I looked around and noticed a Renoir hanging on the opposite wall. "This place is a museum. What, no Gauguin?"

"It is in the dining room, Miss. Would you like coffee now?" The butler asked.

"Yes, please, I like it...."

"Black. Yes Miss Ortega." He had a tiny self-satisfied grin.

Tristan sat in an overstuffed dark green velvet chair and gestured for me to sit on the brown leather couch. There was a large ebony and malachite chess set nearby. It appeared a game was being played.

"You really play chess?" I asked. It seemed too normal a past time.

"With an old friend," he responded.

It was weird to be in such an opulent setting after witnessing a murder. It seemed as though we had just returned from a B movie, which was not worth discussing further. The butler handed me a fine bone china cup and saucer. My hand was shaking slightly. I placed it on the lacquer coffee table and took a breath to calm myself before sipping from the delicate cup. The scent of dark roast coffee was soothing. It was a delicious blend. Then Jasper placed a silver tray with several petit fours in front of me. I was starving. I ate three, to the butler and Tristan's surprise.

"Shall I bring more?" he asked.

"No. I'm good, thanks."

Jasper appeared at the door looking distressed "Excuse me sir, but there is a visitor."

"Show them to the sitting room, I'll be there shortly," Tristan replied, sounding annoyed.

"I will be seen now!" Simone responded in a loud, shrill voice. She pushed past the chauffeur, almost knocking him over. "How dare you give a Short the ruby! Have you lost your mind? What can you possibly see in her? Choosing her over your own kind!"

"You have never been of my caste," Tristan began in a low, threatening tone. He rose to his feet and stood in front of me facing her. "Miranda is under my protection. The ruby has always been mine to give as I choose. Leave. You'll be hearing from the Parliament about your offensive behavior."

"You will regret treating me so badly!"

"You are only making your situation more critical," he warned. "Leave now!"

Simone leaned to the side where she could clearly see me and sniffed the air. "Ah, delicious, it is true!" She looked at me coldly. "Save the Polar Bears? You should save yourself!"

"I may not have your abilities but I can recognize trash, and all the expensive perfume in the world can't hide your stench," I fired back.

"Stupid bitch!" she muttered as Jasper showed her out.

"You were impressive," he stated looking at me with surprise.

I started to take another sip of coffee and noticed my heart beating quickly. I put down the cup. "What did she mean by Short? And why did she say I was delicious? Why exactly did you bring me here? I want out of here."

"I have business to attend to this evening though I will answer your questions before Clive shows you to your room. Short does not refer to height, rather it denotes lifespan."

"Short life? Really?" I responded.

"When she said delicious she was responding to your quite rare blood type. We can smell blood types like you might smell something cooking on a stove. And," Tristan held up his hand to stop me from interrupting him, "you are here for many reasons besides protection that I can't possibly begin to explain tonight since you don't want to discuss your family."

"You ass... "I started but was interrupted by Clive.

"Miss, I'll show you to your suite now."

"Hole!" I blurted out and followed the servant. He led me through the foyer and up the magnificent staircase. "I could use a tooth brush and if I could borrow a T-shirt."

"This way, Miss Ortega."

We took the grand staircase to the second floor then walked down a hallway with Asian lilies in Chinese vases sitting on small, lacquer tables by the closed doors to several rooms. He stopped at a room near the end of the hall. He pointed towards the last door. "That is Baron Mordecai's suite."

"Thanks for the warning. How many other guests are here?" I inquired.

"Just one other." Clive opened the door to a beautifully decorated suite in shades of lavender with large bay windows that overlooked the garden. The bed was king size, covered in a plush comforter and several satin pillows. "I think you'll find everything you need but if you still want..."

"My computer!" It was sitting on a small desk by the window, "and my notebooks."

"You'll find a complete wardrobe in the closet and dresser, though if you still want a T-shirt just let me know the size, color and style," he added with a smirk.

I opened the closet. It had silk blouses, high-end jeans, skirts, pants and several pairs of shoes in my size. There was even a stack of cashmere sweaters. Then I noticed the gown I had refused to wear.

"I want my sneakers, my jeans and my T-shirts. The clothes in my dresser." I turned to see Clive's reaction.

"Sorry Miss, but that is contrary to the Baron's wishes. There is a first-aid kit in the bathroom. Here is the intercom if you wish anything to eat or drink. Imagine that you are staying in a fine hotel. The staff will try to make you feel as comfortable as possible."

"More like a fine prison. Who is the other guest?" I pressed him.

"An old acquaintance of the Baron. Good night, Miss Ortega," he answered and closed the door behind him. I tried the door, it was not locked. He must have thought that I would not chance running into Simone, or that the grounds security was so tight I could never sneak out. I still had my cell phone but was afraid to get my friends involved. I opened a dresser drawer and found a delicate lace nightgown in ivory with a matching robe. Another drawer had several pairs of silk underwear. There were even a couple of 32B bras. I wondered how he could know so much about me. My knee was hurting. I peeled off my well-worn clothes and decided to take a bath. It was a very large, marble whirlpool tub. The fixtures were gold plated koi fish. I soaked in the bubbling, rose scented water for 10 minutes. It was difficult to feel relaxed considering the Baron was probably monitoring my every movement. I reluctantly put on the luxurious nightgown. I hand washed my clothes and laid them out on towels to dry in the tub. I bet that did not happen every day in Bel Air. The first-aid kit had everything. I wrapped my knee and it felt a little better.

Out of curiosity, I found the credit card the Baron gave me and called the customer service representative. After being grilled about who I was and my mother's maiden name, I asked a question, "What is the credit limit?"

There was a pause, then the woman replied, "It's $250,000."

"Thank you," I replied and hung up the phone. *Maybe I can use it to escape,* I thought.

There was a knock on the door. Then a small, thin Asian man about 30 years old entered wearing a tan suit and tie. He smiled and bowed slightly. "I'm Dr. Kyoto, the Baron asked that I look after your injury."

"I'm okay. What kind of doctor are you?" I stared at him trying to figure out if he was warm-blooded.

"I'm board certified in several specialties. I started out in Ob/GYN but pediatrics and hematology are my main interests." He paused and smiled politely. "Yes, I'm like the Baron. He insists I attend to your injury."

I assumed this was not a service I could refuse. He motioned me to sit in a chair and I complied. The doctor bent over as I pulled the gown up to my amateur bandage job. He removed it with little discomfort. Then he took a tube of salve from his pocket and applied it to the scrapes and bruises, then covered them with a dressing. There was instant relief from the soreness.

"Thanks!" I responded.

"It looks like the bath cleaned the wound nicely. I will tell the Baron you will be fine. It is a pleasure to meet you." He stood and gently patted my hands. "Is there anything else I can do for you?"

"Not considering your specialties," I responded but he did not laugh. "Isn't being a doctor a conflict of interests with being a vampire?"

"Not at all," he smiled. "We specialize in matters of life and death." He started to leave.

"Would you tell Tristan that I want to speak with him?"

"I'm afraid he is occupied at the moment. He has pressing matters to attend to," he said in a somewhat condescending tone. "Good night." He bowed slightly and left quickly.

I was hungry, irritated and I did not like being dismissed by the Baron or his minions when I had so many questions left unanswered. I was hoping that

Simone would be dealt with soon so I could go home. I decided to make the best of my situation. I pushed the intercom button.

"Yes, Miss Ortega, may we assist you?" Clive answered.

"I'd like caviar with lemon and crackers and a mango smoothie." I just wanted to see if the butler could deliver.

"Any preference with regard to the type of caviar?" Clive asked snidely.

"Nope" I responded, ignoring his tone.

"We will bring it up as soon as possible," the butler replied and hung up.

I had had caviar once at Lena's office to celebrate book sales. It looked weird but the tangy, salty taste was delicious when you squeezed a little lemon juice on it. I sat at the desk and tried to write. It was hard to focus with the events of the last 24 hours playing over in my mind. Polly's situation began to melt with mine. It was going to be a long night.

CHAPTER 10

TRISTAN WAS TROUBLED by Simone's behavior but knew that alone she posed no serious threat. It was a comment she made about Miranda that alarmed him. He sat alone in the library for a moment before calling one of the few vampires he trusted completely.

"Magus, I must talk to you about a situation that concerns me," Tristan spoke candidly.

"Tristan, is Ms. Ortega well?"

"Yes, she is fine but Simone attempted to abduct her and then made a remark about her that indicated knowledge she should not have been privy to."

"You are right to contact me. Where is our protected Short?"

"With me but she resents having to stay here. She is the most obstinate, disrespectful and ungrateful, woman I have..."

"So, you still adore her," the Magus quipped.

"Unfortunately, yes," Tristan replied with a soft sigh. "My fear is that one of the Haute Caste may be involved. No one else knew."

"This is not the first rumbling of treachery I have heard of. The Parliament must be convened. I shall order a meeting of the Houses in two nights. Speak to no one about your suspicions. Simone's misconduct will be enough to warrant a discussion and judgment," the leader of the vampire world spoke with authority that none questioned openly.

"I feel it is my duty to deal with her," Tristan told him.

"We will consider your request," the Magus responded.

"Of course. As always I am in your debt," Tristan replied, though he wondered why the Magus had not mentioned alerting Lena to the possible traitor. Vampires were a secretive lot. Unfortunately, it increased their tendency to not trust one another. There were alliances within the Houses but all appeared to give their loyalty to the Magus.

"This move by those who would stop us has only allowed us to progress more quickly. Be patient with Ms. Ortega, she will respond best to a gentle touch," he stated confidently.

"Her vocabulary is loathsome."

"She just needs a soft polishing cloth," the elder vampire assured him.

"She tries my patience like no other, but of course you're right. Thank you, dear Magus."

"Good night Tristan. You'll be notified of the meeting details."

I was restless, curious and irritated with my host. In my opinion, I deserved more than being brushed off and set aside after having witnessed a murder and almost being kidnapped. My mind was buzzing with questions. Sleep was out of the question. I put an ivory silk robe over my night gown and set off for some answers. I cracked open my door and looked down the hall towards the stairs. I saw the butler leave a room carrying a tray. I closed my door then waited a couple of minutes before leaving my room. I tiptoed down to the door where the butler had been. I knocked softly on the door. I heard someone cough.

"Get away from that door!" the Baron ordered from the top of the stairs.

"Who is in there?" I boldly asked.

"Someone who does not want to be disturbed by you." He walked past me then turned and asked, "Aren't you tired? If not, why don't you go write?"

"I've had a rough night. I saw someone get sucked dry, then Cruella and the Strange Rangers tried to abduct me and now I'm in protective custody in the Transylvanian Embassy," I replied.

Without a word he turned his back to me and walked to his suite. He knew I would follow behind. I must have seemed like a troublesome pup, barking at his heels.

"You may enter," he called out as I approached the open double doors.

The room was twice the size of my suite. It was entirely in black and white. The carpet was an intricate paisley pattern. There was a black leopard skin rug at the foot of a king bed covered in white satin sheets embroidered with black Fleur de Lys. The windows were covered by black drapes. Tristan sat on a loveseat by the bed and removed his shoes. I noticed an Escher print on the wall; it was the design where angels appear to be turning into bats. The room was softly lit by a few art deco sconces and two candles on the bedside tables. I walked to the far side of the room and a sudden movement made me freeze. The rug lifted its head and two gold eyes stared at me.

"What the fuck! It moved!"

"Delilah," Tristan called to his pet, "meet Miranda."

The black panther rose to its feet slowly, approached me at a languid gate, then sat perfectly still. It stared at me and I stared back, afraid to move.

"This is your cat? Damn, Tristan! What should I do?" I demanded.

"She won't harm you. If she didn't like you, you wouldn't have made it past the doorway. Hold out your hand to her, then scratch behind her ears," he suggested as though she was a common house cat.

I followed his direction and the powerful beast gently rubbed its chin against my arm. I was thrilled. Her fur was soft and thick. Delilah made a throaty noise that indicated she approved of me. I was learning to expect anything and everything where Tristan was concerned. The butler paused at the bedroom door then entered with a tray of caviar, crackers and a mango smoothie. Clive managed to step over the panther's tail. "Will there be anything else, sir?" He placed the snacks on a small table set for one.

"Just feed and walk Delilah. Then you may retire."

"Of course, sir. Come, Delilah." The butler had a leather leash which he attached to a golden chain about the panther's neck and they strolled out of the room.

"Your neighbors don't mind?" I asked.

"Clive takes her to a special enclosure where she can play. She does not leave the property. I have never spoken to my neighbors, though the servants have. They don't interest me," he responded flatly.

"I bet you would interest them," I replied. "So why do I deserve your attention?"

Tristan gestured for me to sit at the table. "Please, help yourself, you must be hungry."

"Thanks," I responded and started to eat, but the feeling of his eyes upon me made me stop. "Why me?"

"It's not because of your upbringing," he replied.

"At least it didn't turn me into a blood-sucking toad," I retorted. He moved closer and seemed to take a breath to calm himself, like a parent dealing with a difficult child. "Those anger management classes are paying off," I added.

"It is because of your potential. Your unique bloodline. That is all I will reveal tonight. It's why Delilah accepted you." Tristan moved behind my chair. He placed a hand lightly upon my shoulder. He was warm now. Then he placed a hand upon my other shoulder. He softly caressed my tense muscles. If I had been his panther I would have purred.

"So that's your bed? No coffin?" I had to ask.

He sighed audibly. "You believe everything you see in the movies? No vampire is so poor he could not afford a decent bed." He replied.

"I don't think decent is the right adjective," I moved to stop his contact with my tired muscles.

"Coffins are very uncomfortable, trust me," he remarked and ran his hand through my hair.

"Maybe I should eat in my room." I stood and started to pick up the tray.

Tristan swept me up into his arms. He kissed me softly at first, then the pressure began to part my lips. He started to carry me to the bed. I pushed against his chest.

"Vampires can't have sex!" I blurted out.

"Why not?" he asked while laying me on the satin coverlet.

"They just don't. They don't get past the neck," I protested

"In Hollywood," he replied and gently cupped one of my breasts.

My brain's circuits were fried all I could think of was, "I'm a virgin!"

"I know," he whispered and lay beside me with one arm across my waist. He started to kiss me again. I could feel fight or flight set in. I started to tremble. Just as our lips touched I bit him. He held his mouth against mine for a few seconds. Then slowly sat up. I experienced a sweet and savory aftertaste. His blood! I began spitting on the dark sheets. Tristan had a tiny cut on his lower lip. He appeared amused. "You will feel a bit of an adrenaline rush. Your mental abilities and stamina will be slightly heightened even with that small amount." He stood and helped me to my feet.

"It tasted familiar, like your scent," I said, wiping my mouth again.

"In time it will all make sense." He looked at me with an expression of mild wonder. "You are the only woman I have ever wanted who refused me. Miranda, despite my behavior, you must know that I will wait till you welcome my affection."

"You will have to wait until hell freezes over," I said indignantly. "You think you are better than other men but you are no different. All you care about is sex. Hundreds of years and you haven't evolved at all." I grabbed the tray and headed out of the room.

"Sex with me would hardly be like sex with other men," he replied.

I stopped in the doorway. "Your ego is the same size as other men so I imagine the rest of you would be too," I retorted.

"I've had hundreds of years to perfect my technique," he said confidently.

"Do me a favor, don't waste your expertise on me."

"You may keep your date with Donelley tomorrow"

"James! I almost forgot." I wondered what kind of spy equipment he used.

"Understandable," he smiled. "You're not a prisoner. You are in my safekeeping. Jasper will drive you. He is a student of the martial arts and an excellent marksman."

"A chaperone? What if I don't want Jasper to tag along?" I protested.

"Then, my brash guest, you will have to cancel your date. Suit yourself," he replied calmly.

"I want to go," I responded angrily. "Where will you be?"

"Sleeping, so I'll be ready for my next encounter with my troublesome, immature and oddly charming antagonist," Tristan told me and bowed slightly.

"Fuck you!" I replied.

"You changed your mind?" he asked with an amused expression.

If looks could kill, even the Baron would have succumbed. Then I turned and secluded myself for the rest of the night. I really had to watch what I said to him.

Across town Sergio awoke in a cold sweat. He felt shaky and nauseated, like he had the flu. He remembered what Simone had told him. In the fridge was a bottle of O positive blood. The thought was repulsive but he knew he could not turn back. Sergio took a sip and felt a little relief. Then he drank a few more mouthfuls. The liquid of life soothed his stomach and he started to feel more comfortable. He put the bottle back to give himself a chance to be accustomed to his new diet. He felt exhausted. He touched the small cut on his chest. For a moment he remembered the intense pain of Simone's bite. He looked in the mirror and could tell that his reflection was fading. To his surprise he started crying.

"What have I done? Lena will hate me!"

After a few minutes he gained his composure and called the front desk. He told them he would be staying another night and asked not to be disturbed. Sergio needed time to recover, adjust and decide how to approach his love. He hoped his vampire qualities would aid in his ability to understand her. He drank a little more blood and the taste was more acceptable this time. He left about a third of the bottle for later. "A nightcap," he mused. He knew that Lena could no longer view him as a Short, a limited being. Though he realized he would be of the lowest caste, he would have eternity to win her back if needed. He made sure the hotel curtains would block daylight and went to sleep as dawn approached.

CHAPTER 11

ABOUT 10 AM there was a knock on my door. It had been difficult to fall asleep in the vampire lair/five-star hotel. I opened my eyes and felt a little disoriented. A plump older woman wearing a maid's uniform with short brown hair and a sweet smile brought me a breakfast tray.

"Mornin' Miss. Thought you might want a bite to eat before you set off. I'm Tillie. I was asleep when you got here last night. We weren't expecting you quite so soon. Will you be needin' anything else?" She prattled on while I woke up. "The Baron chose the colors for this room, had it decorated just for you. Never seen him carry on so about a guest." She had an English accent like Clive and Jasper. She wore a wedding ring.

"Are you related to the other staff?" I asked while taking a sip of coffee.

"Yes, Miss. Clive is my better half," she said with a proud smile.

"Do you like working for the Baron?" I inquired.

"He's a good man Miss. Very kind to us," she replied.

"You know he's a ...."

"Vampire. Why yes, Miss. I suppose it seems odd to you but everyone has their quirks, don't they? You get used to it." She picked up my tray from last night. "Jasper will be ready to drive you at 10:30. Just come downstairs when you are ready."

"Thank you," I replied, a bit surprised by her casual acceptance of the undead.

"Nice to finally meet you," she added and quickly left.

So far, I was not finding any allies in the asylum. Why were these people so devoted to him? When had they expected to see me? Perhaps Simone's bungled abduction messed up the Baron's plans. I had this uneasy feeling in my gut when he mentioned my family. I was afraid he would tell me something that would turn my world upside down forever. I was still holding onto the hope that I would be able to sever my connection to Tristan and go on with my normal "Short" life at some point. I was thinking of him by his first name now, not his royal title, but that did not mean anything. Sometimes denial is all you've got. My torn jeans and T-shirt had vanished from the bathroom. I looked in the wardrobe and decided on a floral wrap dress and pink sandals. There was a matching pink clutch of the softest leather. I threw my wallet and phone in the purse. The ruby necklace was a bit much but I had no choice. On the dresser was a small jewelry box with gold hoop earrings and matching bangles. I thought of Lolly. I took a quick photo of my look, sent it to her and texted I was about to see James.

In minutes she responded, "What about the Baron?" I didn't reply.

I figured they must have had hidden cameras all over the mansion so I did not try the door to the other guest's room as I left. Sooner or later I was bound to find out who that poor soul was. When I stepped outside I took a deep breath of freedom, however fleeting. Jasper was waiting for me. He opened the door of a gray Rolls Royce. Unbelievable.

"Good morning, Miss. Paradise Cove?"

"Yes, thanks," I responded as I got in. I was not sure if you were supposed to thank chauffeurs. Servant etiquette was never covered at Rossville High. "How many cars does Tristan have?"

"In Los Angeles or worldwide?" he responded.

"Never mind," I sighed as he closed the door.

The ride to Malibu was quiet and comfortable. It gave me a little time to consider my options, which was more than enough time since they were fairly limited. Despite the Baron letting me go on a date, he was still human enough to get jealous. I had to protect James. This would take more tact than I usually displayed. We pulled into the seaside parking lot. James was waiting in front of the restaurant. I could see a mixed response to my arrival on his face.

"Hi Miranda, you look great!" He glanced back at Jasper and the Rolls. "Are you alone?"

"No, I'm with you," I replied and took his hand. I refrained from a kiss on the cheek, thinking it would be reported.

"Nice ride," he quipped.

"It's a loaner," I smiled.

We were seated at a table on the patio with a beautiful view of the coastline. He looked tan and healthy. Very appealing in a warm-blooded way.

"Thanks for inviting me, I really needed to get away for a few hours," I said sincerely.

"So, what's with the chauffeur?" he had to ask.

"It's the book. I'm trying to meet deadlines." I could not help but think that deadlines had new meaning for me. James did not look convinced. "It's the wacky world of writers. I'm sort of sequestered while I try to finish my book. My publisher is putting me up in his house so I can access his library of vampire books and not be disturbed. The chauffeur is part of the deal."

"That explains why Lolly has been blowing up my phone leaving messages about trying to get a hold of you." James seemed to be willing, or wanting, to make sense of my behavior.

"Sorry about that. We kind of had a fight. It'll be okay eventually, but right now I'm just limiting my contact with her." I was relieved he was accepting my story. It was partially true.

"I hope you and Lolly bury the hatchet soon 'cause Alan was complaining about her mood."

"I can imagine. I hadn't thought about him. Good thing he's a professional." I tried to lighten the conversation.

"I don't think that helps with Lolly," he laughed.

We ordered omelets with juice and rolls. It was delicious. It was the kind of date I had imagined when I moved to California. I was not sure it would ever happen again.

I sprinkled some hot sauce on my eggs. "Do you think it would be possible to drink Tabasco?"

James laughed. "Only if I were drunk out of my mind, why?"

"Nothing," I replied.

"There is one other thing. Lolly wants you to tell that royal freak her agent wants to talk with him. So, what do women see in him?" James inquired.

"I think you mean what do I see in him? An expert on vampire mythology. They are rare. I'll tell the Baron about her agent but the Royal Freak is not a people person. If it's okay with you, I don't want to talk biz anymore. So, tell me about Montana."

"Absolutely fine with me," he stated. "It offered some novel experiences for a dentist." He took a drink of coffee and got into story telling mode. "A rancher brought a horse halfway into my waiting room. My practice was in a one level building on Main Street. She demanded I pull out her mare's rotten tooth because the vet was out of town. Said she'd report me for animal cruelty if I didn't help."

"Did you do it?" I liked the way his face lit up as he talked.

"I was afraid of getting my hands bit off or being trampled to death. I was also worried about refusing services. This woman could scare a bear." He took a bite to add to the suspense.

"So what happened?" I inquired.

"I called a high school buddy, a vet in the next town and he was able to take care of the mare. The cranky woman expressed her thanks by dropping off a side of beef."

"Cranky and scary, don't you think you're being a little hard on her?" I replied.

"I had to leave Montana because of a woman. They're tough and sneaky on the plains," he responded.

"You're demonizing the women of your state," I laughed. "Besides, I grew up on the plains."

"You never met the mayor's daughter," he replied and proceeded to finish his omelet.

"The mayor's daughter? This has to be good."

James sipped his coffee, then said, "You want another roll?"

"When writers are unable to satisfy their curiosity, they can become violent." I picked up a cherry tomato and aimed for his head.

"Don't hurt me, I'll talk," he said loud enough to make a few heads turn.

I lowered my weapon. "You were saying..."

"His Honor's 17-year-old daughter grabbed me while I was examining her teeth. I had to yell for the technician to pull the cute, eager thing off me."

"Poor baby," I responded.

"Me or her? The mayor never did believe my side of it. That was the last straw. I moved six months later," he replied, feeling properly defended. "So, what brought you to the coast?"

"A Rolls Royce," I smiled.

James picked an ice cube out of his water. "I have really good aim," he said, looking at my cleavage.

"You wouldn't!"

He grinned.

"Tamales...I didn't want to end up running my parents' restaurant when they retired."

"I like tamales," he replied.

"Then go to the Rossville Diner. I'm not a good cook. Trust me," I laughed.

"Maybe I will someday, but for now would you like to go for a walk? I have a friend I want to introduce you to."

He reached for the bill but I grabbed it first. "I'm paying," I insisted. "I got a big bonus." After a couple of protests, he agreed and I put brunch on the Baron's card with a big tip.

We walked into the parking lot under the watchful gaze of Jasper. James had parked his truck in the shade of a couple of palm trees. In the back was his dog Gracie. She was tied up with a bowl of water and a chew toy. I was impressed by the loving care he took of her.

"Gracie, this is Miranda." He untied the energetic pup and she jumped out of the truck. I patted her on the head and she wagged her whole body. We were a few steps from the sand so I slipped off my heels and put them in the back of the truck.

A mild offshore breeze and clear skies made it a perfect day for a stroll. James threw a tennis ball for Gracie and she ran down the beach.

"Even though I like you," James began, "don't expect me to read your books. I love to read Tolstoy and Louis L'Amour but not the horror genre. It's not my thing. No offense." He was hoping that my ego could take his honesty.

"Well, as long as you like to read something," I punched him in the arm. "So, you must like soap operas, too."

"I do have a little TV in my office." He stopped talking when I started snickering.

"*Young and the Restless*?" I laughed.

"I can do some divining myself. I bet you're a democrat," he stated with confidence. Gracie ran up to us and dropped the ball at our feet. James threw the retrieved ball. It almost went in the water.

"You insult my writing and now you're picking on my political party!"

"Peace! Lucky guess. I don't even vote, it gets in the way of my fishing," he replied.

"Not registered? Why you...." I turned to face him.

"I belong to the Sierra Club, that must get me some points," he smiled.

"Subversive," I replied. "I like the World Wildlife Fund."

He high-fived me, which caused Gracie to jump up on me just as the high tide unexpectedly hit us. We fell laughing onto the wet sand. James stood, helped me up, then politely tried to brush some sand off my dress.

"Ms. Ortega!" Jasper came running down the beach, looking like an over-dressed penguin.

"Thanks James," I grabbed his hands for a moment. "I really enjoyed spending time with you and Gracie." I let go as the chauffeur got near. "I'm sorry but I've got to go."

"I can give you a ride," he offered.

"Another time maybe when I've finished more chapters, in a couple of weeks."

"Shall we go now?" Jasper asked, but it was more like a strong suggestion.

I nodded and we walked behind the chauffeur, snickering at his jerky movements as he tried to shake the sand out of his dress shoes.

When we got to the truck I retrieved my heels. James gave me his arm to steady me as I slipped them on. His smile was warm and endearing.

"I like you better barefoot," he quipped.

"Me too," I laughed and hugged him but avoided a kiss.

"Don't keep me waiting too long," he called out, "and give my regards to Edgar Winter."

"I will!" I loved his sense of humor and hated to leave him.

When we returned, Tillie made a fuss over my dress being ruined. Then she ran a bath for me. I was told the Baron would not be available until 9 pm and that he would see me then.

"I might be too busy writing tonight," I told Tillie, which seemed to fry a few brain cells.

"Oh, Miss Ortega, don't joke like that," she replied and excused herself.

The warm bath felt great. The rose scented water was very relaxing. I thought *So this is what it's like to be the prom queen*. I could not help wishing I was a little less popular, at least with the undead. Afterwards, I decided to take a nap. I had a feeling it would be a very long night.

Benedetto and Grigoryi had been put in the same cell with the usual collection of drunk drivers, druggies and petty thieves. The guards were worried about the monks getting killed trying to save souls as they had blessed the arresting officers. A psychiatric evaluation had been ordered.

"I can't believe we trusted that woman," Grigoryi said for the hundredth time.

"The Lord sent her to help us. We were unable to thwart that blond demon. For a moment we fought him," Benedetto responded and patted Grigoryi on the shoulder.

"He assaulted us!" Grigoryi responded, shaking his head. "Being in the county jail might make you feel closer to God. I much prefer a church with a bathroom, thank you very much," he replied and rested his head in his hands.

A guard approached and the door clicked open. "Hey saints, you're being released on bail, your lawyer is here."

Grigoryi jumped to his feet. "Thank God," he muttered.

"But we don't have a lawyer!" Benedetto blurted out. They had not made a call when they were arrested because they did not want their church contact in Rome to know about their screw up.

"You do now," he replied and showed them out.

A young man in a very nice suit with a leather brief case greeted them as they were released. He had short brown hair, a tan from sailing and looked pressed for time.

"I'm Victor Schnelling. I agreed to represent you on behalf of Ms. Simone Brown. The charges against you have been reduced to petty theft due to lack of evidence and some judges in my yacht club," he explained as they left the building. "I'll drop you off at your van."

"She did not abandon us," Benedetto whispered to Grigoryi.

They followed the lawyer into the parking lot. A black Jaguar was parked in a reserved spot. The monks got in without question; they did not want to look their gift horse in the mouth.

"Ms. Brown went to a lot of trouble on your behalf. I suggest, as your legal counsel, you avoid trying to save any more drug dealers. Your impound fees have been taken care of. The keys are in the van." As they got out of his car he added, "You might ask your benefactor to pay for a hotel room. Believe me, she can afford it."

CHAPTER 12

JAMES PARKED HIS truck in the driveway and let Gracie into the back-yard. He was mulling over his feelings for Miranda when he noticed a large package on his front porch. It was wrapped in silver paper with a matching bow.

"What in the world?" he looked around but did not see anyone he knew on the street. He opened the card.

"James, I'll come by later to party. Love, Miranda." He got this funny feeling in his gut. The card did not sound like something Miranda would write. He had known his fair share of women who liked to party, and Miranda was not one.

He picked up the heavy box and felt the contents shift and then a familiar clinking sound. "Damn it!" he growled and hurried around to the trash cans by the garage. Angrily, he threw the box down and heard bottles breaking. The smell of whiskey permeated the air. Liquid began to seep from the box. He went into the garage and got out some work gloves. He opened the package and saw six bottles of expensive Irish whiskey. For a moment he felt queasy. He steadied himself and took a deep breath. "That Bastard," he spat out. He had no doubt the Baron was behind this. He knew Miranda would never jeopardize his so-briety; she did not even drink. He poured out the bottles that had not broken. Then he put the box of broken glass in the trash. *What an asshole!* he thought. James took a couple of deep breaths. He was worried about Miranda. He was not sure how he could help her.

It had been a few weeks since he had been to a meeting. He let Gracie in the back door to the kitchen. He filled her bowl of kibble, then glanced at the meeting list on his fridge. He decided it was going to be a two-meeting night. "I've got to get my head right before I do anything," he thought. Impulsive behavior had always gotten him in trouble. He called a friend to see if they could meet for coffee. He was not ashamed to ask for advice; he was afraid not to.

At the hotel, Sergio woke in the late afternoon and finished off the O positive blood. He had gathered from years of being privy to the vampire world that it would take several months for his transformation to be complete. He felt better than he had expected. As a former athlete, he had always been in tune with his body. To test his strength, he lifted the dresser in the hotel room. It felt like he was picking up a chair. Sergio's reflection was faint. He felt regret that Simone had been the source of the blood that was enhancing his cells. He wondered if Lena would believe that he did it to be with her forever. The new vampire drank a glass of water. He was thirsty but not hungry. It was important to find protection and hopefully forgiveness within the undead community. *Surely they will understand my desire to be one of them*, he thought. He decided to return to his apartment, put on his best suit, order flowers for Lena and then beg the Baron to intervene on his behalf. He could not think of anyone else who might be sympathetic. There would be no turning back.

Across town the monks were not happy with the condition of their van when they got it out of impound. Their vampire hunting supplies were missing. Their cots had been turned upside down and their clothing was tossed on the floor. Benedetto pondered their financial difficulties. They had $65 to live off until their next payment from Rome in 10 days. What bothered him most was the inability to buy gas so they could follow-up on any leads.

"This is all the food we have left." Grigoryi sadly held up a box of granola bars. "Good thing it wasn't doughnuts."

"You think about your stomach too much. The Lord will provide," Benedetto proclaimed.

"At the soup kitchen," Grigoryi replied.

"That is for the poor and unfortunate," Benedetto said.

"Good. Then we qualify," Grigoryi quipped.

Benedetto drove the van back to the street where Simone had first contacted them. They had a quarter tank of gas. He decided to pray about their dire straits and requested that Grigoryi join him at the church that was nearby.

As they knelt in the pews, Grigoryi whispered, "That was exciting. I mean seeing a real vampire."

"Yes," Benedetto whispered back. "Let us pray for more excitement but no arrests."

"Gentlemen," a woman said softly. "May I see you outside?"

They both turned to see Simone wearing her brown wig with a scarf over her head looking quite modest. She wore a blue knee-length dress and flats. Only her heavy makeup hinted at her worldly ways. The monks nodded in unison and followed her out.

"Thanks for getting us out of jail," Benedetto said.

"That's the least I could do. I hope you are recovered," she feigned concern.

"We're kind of hungry," Grigoryi responded.

Simone eyed him and considered how resistant he might be. Grigoryi squirmed a little under her gaze.

"Not now," Benedetto told him sharply.

"That's fine," Simone said and pulled an envelope out of her purse. "This should help support your mission. It's the least I can do." She handed it to Grigoryi as she guessed that Benedetto would try to refuse it and she did not want to waste time.

Grigoryi's eyes got big as he counted ten $100 bills. "Thank you!"

"There is another way to hurt that undead demon and save another unsuspecting soul," Simone began. "I have a plan that will force his hand. Are you interested?"

"We did not do so good at saving..." Grigoryi said but was interrupted.

"Be quiet, let us hear the plan. Please continue," Benedetto asserted his rank as elder monk. He was embarrassed by Grigoryi's manners. "We will assist your work in any way we can."

"Excellent," she responded, "It will happen tomorrow night." She proceeded to talk in a very quiet voice for 15 minutes. The monks hung on every word. "Gentlemen, that is how we will make that vampire pay for his crimes."

They agreed on a rendezvous point and Simone drove away in her Lexus. She did not realize that a tracking bug had been attached to her vehicle by Jasper the last time she visited the Baron. Her every move was being reported to him. Benedetto walked back to their van feeling exhilarated by the convincing plan that he thought would lead to validating his life's work. Grigoryi was happy about the cash but still could not shake a feeling that Simone was not quite a saint. Sitting in the jail cell had changed his perception of their patron.

"Do you really think we can trust her? She deserted us last time," he protested.

"We are being given a great opportunity. Let us not squander it," Benedetto said then quickly added, "Let us celebrate. In-N-Out Burger?"

"Yes! I want a double cheese with chili! And a milkshake!" Grigoryi became distracted by the thought of such a glorious feast, which was Benedetto's hope.

I woke up from my nap and stretched. The normalcy of the walk on the beach had lifted my spirits if I could just untangle myself from the Baron. I was about to request coffee when I remembered the other pampered prisoner down the hall. I opened my door slightly and found the hallway empty. I walked to the door and knocked softly.

"My name is Miranda, maybe I can help you," I whispered. There was a fit of coughing followed by silence. "You can trust me, I'm not like them."

"That is very true," Clive's voice startled me.

"Don't sneak up on me like that!" I responded.

He had come from the Baron's suite. "Our other guest is resting. The Baron has decided to take you out for dinner."

"I don't like his diet," I interrupted. "I'll eat in my room." I started to walk back.

"The Baron has reservations at the Golden Duck restaurant at 9 p.m."

"I'm here to write, and that's exactly what I plan to do tonight. I'll have dinner in my cell." I replied.

"But the Baron..."

"Can do whatever he has done for hundreds of years before meeting me. May I please have some coffee sent up and some of those little cakes? Thanks." I quickly sequestered myself.

I put a couple of pillows against my headboard and sat up in bed with my laptop. The next chapter flowed easily. The Count gives Polly an extravagant ruby necklace. She tries to politely refuse but she is so impressed by his charm and wealth that she accepts it. The necklace is a symbol of the Baron's station and claim on her. Sydney becomes alarmed when he sees it. He goes to great lengths to investigate the Baron, using some of his legal skills to question the locals. Sydney even bribes some of them to talk about why they fear the Count. He secretly meets with the local priest who becomes his ally. I gave Sidney James' warm smile and kind heart with a touch of city sarcasm. Upon first seeing his handsome, muscular opponent, Sidney whispers to Polly, "Royal inbreeding." A knock on the door interrupted my efforts.

"Miss Ortega," Tillie entered with the coffee and a dozen petite fours. "How are you feeling?" She placed the tray on the bedside table. There was a red rose in a crystal vase.

"I'm fine. Thanks." I took a sip of the coffee, it was dark roast, probably Sumatran.

"The Baron wanted the rose on your tray," she almost sighed. "Will you be needing help getting ready for your date? It's a very nice restaurant."

"Maybe you could order a cheese pizza," I replied. "I'll be working tonight and I can still dress myself." I was annoyed that Tillie was trying to pressure me.

"Yes Miss, I'll let Clive know," she replied and left quickly.

I returned to my writing. Polly was basking in the attention of two romantic rivals and feeling torn between her fascination with the Count and her affection for her ex-fiancé. The Count was making plans to rid himself of the irritating and far too curious Sidney. I found myself touching the ruby pendant as I explored plot lines. I wanted to know more about how vampires acquired wealth, how their community could thrive in a high-tech world and not be exposed.

Content with the progress I made, I decided to catch up on emails. Lolly had sent three messages expressing her concern. I decided to send a short email assuring her that I was fine, just immersed in finishing my book. Within a few minutes she replied with an invitation to bring the Baron to dinner. I could not help but think that would be a fascinating meal and decided to keep that as an option. However, I did not respond to Lolly. There was a guilt-inducing email from my mom asking why I had not called. I sent off a busy writing excuse to her as well. I avoided calling her because she always knows when I lie. I was not up to a maternal interrogation.

I looked in the armoire for some casual clothing. To my surprise I found my old jeans and T-shirt laundered and folded. Putting on my own clothes empowered me a little. I hoped to set some limits with the Baron tonight. Suddenly I heard a loud crash. I ran out into the hallway. I heard men's voices yelling. One of them sounded like Tristan. It was coming from downstairs. I quickly descended the stairs and saw a stuffed chair fly out of the library. Clive was standing a safe distance from the room and began righting the thrown chair. He motioned to me to go back upstairs. I crept to the doorway and peeked inside. "Oh my God!"

A murderous expression distorted Tristan's features. The elegant room was in shambles. Tristan heaved the heavy roll-top desk at Sergio, knocking him to the ground. A vase full of roses exploded when it hit the floor. The young vampire pushed the desk aside and started to stand.

"Ungrateful bastard!" Tristan yelled. He grabbed Sergio by the neck. "You have disrespected the High Caste! You were not ready! How could you be so stupid?" Tristan bellowed. Sergio did not struggle. He tried to look respectfully at Tristan despite the blood dripping from his nose.

"Stop it! What is wrong with you? Put him down!" I yelled.

Tristan dropped Sergio and turned towards me. Sergio got to his feet and wiped his face with his sleeve. He apparently was not hurt that badly. I noticed that the Van Gogh painting was askew.

"You could have ruined this treasure, you idiots! You don't deserve nice things." I carefully centered it.

"Miranda, this is none of your business, please return to your room. I'll be with you shortly," the Baron told me as though I could be easily dismissed.

"Are you okay?" I asked Sergio.

"Not really but..." he stopped speaking and looked at the Baron for help.

For a moment I could not understand why he was unharmed, then I realized. "You heal quickly. I can't believe it, you're one of them."

"Only recently. I feel very lucky. Don't be upset with the Baron. He has a right to express his disappointment," he replied.

"Why? Didn't he think you deserved to be a bloodsucker? I'm surprised he doesn't high-five you." I snapped angrily, staring at them.

"High five?" Tristan looked at me like I spoke a foreign language.

"It's like this." I held up Tristan's hand then slapped it. "It means congratulations. Since he chose to be like you, shouldn't you be happy that you ruined someone's normal life?"

Sergio looked anxiously at Tristan, fearing his wrath might be unleashed once more.

"High five!" Tristan said and to our surprise walked over to Sergio and slapped the hand he had raised in self-defense. The vampires started laughing. "Let me be the first to congratulate you on your transformation. Good job, citizen."

"Asshole." I hated to be mocked. They started patting each other on the back. I noticed that despite the wrecked furniture and torn drapes, the chess board had not been touched. It stood like the Water Tower in Chicago after the Great Fire. I walked over to it.

"No!" Tristan cried.

"Oops!" I tipped the small table over. The pieces went flying.

"I've been playing that game with the Magus for a month!" he sounded truly upset.

"The Maggots?"

"Miranda," Sergio said with a look of concern. "You should go upstairs right now."

"Before I carry you upstairs," Tristan added as he righted the chess table. "Luckily for you I remember where every piece should be. Now go!"

I walked out of the room as I sensed it would be reckless to provoke the Baron further. Clive had been joined by Tillie and Jasper. It appeared they were waiting to pick up after the boys. As I went upstairs, a feeling of sadness over-whelmed me. Sergio would never welcome the sunrise. He would be a night dweller forever. I had to wonder about Tristan's game plan for me.

The Baron turned to Sergio with a look of concern. "You had better stay here while you are adjusting to your new state and trying to apologize to Lena." Then he smiled. "Perhaps Miranda is right that I should be more appreciative of your decision."

"I don't know if it was the beating or the new diet, but I could've sworn you just said Miranda was right," Sergio remarked.

"I said it in confidence," Tristan smiled. "She is amazing. She did not show any fear when she entered the room during the fight. She is not like any mortal I have ever encountered."

"Women are consistently confusing, frustrating, demanding and yet we crave them like our existence depends on their approval. We are doomed," Sergio responded, shaking his head.

"Sir, may we restore the room?" Clive requested. Jasper and Tillie stood behind him in the doorway.

"Yes, that will be fine," Tristan replied. "Tillie, please show Sergio to a guest room, he will be staying with us for a few weeks."

"I will never forget your kindness. I'll do anything to show my gratitude." Sergio bowed slightly to the Baron.

"Simone must be dealt with. You will have a chance to prove your worth."

"Jasper, please have the Spyder ready. Tillie, see to Bram. It is time," Tristan said and headed upstairs to change. He could not remember taking a normal woman on a date. The Magus had emphasized using a gentler approach. Lena encouraged him to take her out and utilize the tactics of Short men to woo Miranda. It seemed that watching him slay the drug dealer might have gotten their relationship off on the wrong foot. There was some unfinished business before going out. The Baron hoped it would open Miranda up to him more. It could also turn her more against him. In any case, he decided an evening with her would not be dull. He selected dark slacks and a pale gray silk shirt. He slipped something into his pocket.

I heard a knock on my door and expected to see Tillie. "Do you have my coffee?"

"No, but I'm sure you can request it at the restaurant, though most people drink tea with Chinese cuisine," The Baron replied.

"You knocked!" I was in disbelief. He looked so handsome. All the traces of anger were gone from his countenance. There was an unmistakable delight at being with me that I could not ignore or understand.

"I thought you might be changing," he responded. "No matter, please come with me, someone wishes to speak with you."

I followed him out into the hallway. Tristan stood by the guest room. He unlocked the door and allowed me to enter first. I saw Tillie fixing the pillows of a very old white man.

"I must honor a promise," Tristan said. "May I introduce Bram Stoker."

As I got close to the bed I recognized him. "Dr. Bishop!" He looked nearly dead. "You're Bram? I don't understand. What has he done to you?" I cried as I went to his side.

He coughed to clear his throat. "Miranda," his eyes welled up. "I was born Bram Stoker a very long time ago. Now, because of you, he is finally allowing me to die," he stopped to take a breath. "Long ago, I loved Simone but she just used me and then I became jealous of the Baron." He took a breath "I wanted revenge. I'm sorry. I hope you understand," he coughed. "I lied about them. Please tell the truth, be their historian."

"You were preparing me?" I questioned.

"I had no choice. The vampires found you, not me." He started coughing and Tillie gave him a drink of water. "Tristan has promised me that he will protect you." Bram glanced at the Baron, who nodded.

"I'm sorry that you have suffered," I said softly through silent tears.

"I'm sorry I will not be able to read your book," he said with a slight smile. Those were his last words, then he slipped into a coma.

Tillie said, "It won't be long." She placed his hands upon his chest. I walked out into the hall trying to compose myself. Tristan handed me a silk handkerchief.

"He was Stoker. You kept Bram Stoker alive all these years?"

"A tiny amount of our blood on a regular basis will provide longevity, slow down aging," he explained. "I promised to let him go after he mentored you. He'll be cremated. You may choose his final resting place if you like."

"Now I am supposed to take his place?" I asked.

"Suffice it to say your station is far beyond his understanding," Tristan said with a smile. "Why don't we discuss this further over dinner?"

"Will you excuse me for a few minutes," I said, handing back the handkerchief.

"Of course," he replied.

I sat on my bed and felt very alone. I expected to feel anger at my mentor's betrayal but instead I just felt sadness. Tristan had held a grudge for over 100 years. Stoker had become tangled up with Simone. I realized that she was the blond in the miniature painting in his office. He had been paying for years for his insult to vampire pride. Now, because of my entrance into this bizarre world, he was free. Was I supposed to view Tristan as a cruel tyrant or an honorable despot? Death seemed to follow him closely. In this case it was a mercy to end a torturous existence. What did this mean for me? I should have felt more upset but instead I just felt hungry. There is a reason people eat after funerals. I needed to feed my growing anxiety. At that moment, I could have eaten half a cow.

I splashed water on my face, then looked in the armoire. I wanted to take off the clothes that had witnessed Bram's passing. Black seemed appropriate. I put on a black satin tank top, a subdued floral skirt and black strappy sandals. My focus had to be on how I was going to survive. I told myself there would be time to process the loss later. I wanted more information about my predicament.

The Baron said nothing more as we walked downstairs. Clive looked up from the debris in the library with a solemn smile. Jasper opened the front door and then was dismissed by the Baron. A sleek, red sports car that looked like NASA might have designed it was waiting for us.

"Wow!" I said out loud despite myself.

Tristan was amused by my response. "This is one of my favorite cars and the fastest." We drove through the winding streets of Bel Air to Sunset Boulevard. I noticed other drivers taking a second look at our car. Tristan's scent added to the moment. I glanced at him and felt an undeniable attraction to this powerful, undead man. Conflicting emotions were doing battle in my brain. I felt like hitting him but instead sat quietly.

"Here we are," Tristan said as we pulled up in front of an exclusive Chinese restaurant almost hidden from the street with lush bamboo plants and flowering shrubs. The parking attendant was excited to get the keys to the Spyder.

"Welcome," an Asian man in a black suit greeted us. "Ms. Hauser's table is this way." He guided us past the patrons seated in the public dining area.

Red, black and gold dragon designs were beautifully painted on the walls. The tables were bathed in flickering candlelight. Small trees grew in ornamental pots by a large fish tank next to the bar. We were led to a small private room that was curtained off from the other diners.

"Was this Lena's idea?" I inquired as we were seated at a table set for two.

"She recommended it. If you don't like Chinese..."

"No, that's fine. I do. I just wondered if she was like you," not wanting to blurt out vampire in public.

"Yes," he replied, "though she is much better at interacting with Shorts. She likes being a literary agent. I don't normally associate with people from your world," he explained.

"Lucky for me and Bram," I declared. Tristan did not respond. "That explains a lot about Lena. I should've guessed it by the way she orders people around. Poor Sergio, he loves her."

The waiter politely interrupted and took my order from a menu with no prices. Tristan ordered in Chinese, which delighted the server.

"I think Dr. Bishop, I mean Bram, hated you and respected you."

"You look lovely tonight," he responded with a smile.

"So, you're not going to talk about him?"

"No. Not tonight. I would prefer to talk about you."

"But someone died," I protested.

"He died many years ago when he fell in love with Simone," he replied.

"Did you love Simone?" I had to ask.

"Never," he responded. "She was merely a distraction at times. She has never felt a genuine emotion except envy. She lacks depth and self-respect."

"Yeah, I must be much more fascinating than a shallow vampire," I replied and tasted the tangy, sweet and sour egg drop soup. "This is great." I noticed that Tristan was merely sipping the broth.

"You are far from uninteresting, though Rossville seemed unbearable at times!" he said. I almost dropped my spoon.

"When were you in Rossville?"

"My visits started the week after you were born when I learned of your blood type," he replied and continued to sip the broth.

"Visits? What are you talking about?" I put my spoon down.

"I have been waiting for a long time to have this conversation with you. Miranda, your life and mine are linked by an agreement I made with your ancestor, Jacques de Molay. He was your very great grandfather on your mother's side. He was one of the last Templar Knights, an honorable gentleman betrayed by greedy nobles and clergy. He requested I look after his line in return for great treasure. I have kept my word," Tristan said with a soft smile. "This coin came from the treasure." He touched the gold medallion he always wore. "It would have been preferable to watch over you in Chicago."

I had a million questions but at that moment three servers began removing the bowls and filling the table with savory dishes. I waited till they had been thanked and dismissed. A large brandy glass, filled with a dark red fluid, was placed in front of Tristan.

"I'm not sure where to begin, but first I have to know what you are drinking."

"Cranberry juice, would you like some?" he smiled. "This evening there will be a goblet of my preferred beverage when we return home. I buy it from a blood bank."

"That's nice that no one gets sucked to death on date night," I quipped. "I want to know more about de Molay but first I have to know how you could have been in Rossville without being noticed. Sheesh, we have neighbors that count the squirrels in town." I managed a forkful of broccoli with almonds and rice in a savory sauce.

"We have spent centuries perfecting how to be invisible in a warm-blooded world. Do you remember the accident when you fell off a tractor and your lung was pierced by a broken rib?"

My eyes got big and I stared in disbelief. "How could you know that?"

"They could not find any blood that was compatible with your blood type except your dad, who was being treated for hepatitis," Tristan explained. He reached across the table and touched my hand.

"I was 10 years old. My mom said I almost died. My recovery was..."

"Miraculous?" Tristan took a drink. "Not really. I visited the hospital that night while your parents were praying in the chapel. I gave you some of my blood."

A vague memory came into my mind. Someone leaning over me with white hair, the bright hospital lights were behind his head leaving his features hidden but there was this scent. "I remember you!"

"I will answer your questions but please eat."

I sat staring at him. "You saved my life?" I was taken aback.

"You have been looked after, without your knowledge, all your life. My visits to rural America were brief and discrete but other vampires and trusted Shorts, dozens of them, took jobs working nights at the gas station, bars and even washing dishes at your parent's café. Do you not like the meal?"

"I'm stunned. The food is fine," I picked up a spring roll. "I never knew."

"Once one of my kind stopped a mugger who was going to attack you when you were jogging at UCLA."

"Do my parents know about any of this?" I asked.

"Your maternal grandmother knew. She never wanted your mother to be told. She was afraid your mother would not handle it well."

"Grandma Genevieve? I think she was right." I could not imagine explaining having vampire buddies to either of my parents. "She died when I was about 5. I heard she was a bit wild in her day."

"She was beautiful, intelligent and stubborn, like you," he replied.

"You and my grandma?" I dropped my fork.

"She was devoted to your grandfather," Tristan replied tactfully.

I tried to eat a tofu and snow peas dish with a delicate sauce. It was hard to enjoy the meal when my brain was being bombarded with an alternate reality. "I can't help but feel I'm missing something here. I still don't understand why me. You could have left me in the dark like my mom," I responded. It was strange how I was coming to accept that everything he said was true.

"You have de Molay blood from your mother and HH blood from your father, the rarest blood type in the world. Your very great grandfather asked that we protect his lineage. We took revenge on those who betrayed and murdered the Templars. We have looked after your family for generations. When you were born, the Parliament of Houses held a meeting to consider what your remarkable heritage might mean for our kind." He took another sip of cranberry juice to give me a chance to take it all in.

"Parliament of Houses?" I felt my anxiety level rising higher.

"It is our international governing body," he replied.

"Vampires without Borders? Really? And you are all just fascinated with my lineage?" I pushed the plates away. "Bram encouraging my writing was just a way to ease me into your world."

"We were glad you chose English over psychology. Freud tried to understand us, it's why he was obsessed with sex and death."

"You knew Freud, that explains a lot. He had women all wrong, by the way."

Tristan reached into his pocket, pulled out a card and handed it to me. "We invented Tarot cards as a way to communicate more than 1,000 years ago. This card symbolizes you. Notice the plants," he pointed out.

I stared at a woman sitting on a throne with a cornfield at her feet. "The Empress" was written across the bottom. She had a crown of stars and a shield with a feminine symbol. "Your destiny was written long ago."

"I don't understand. Tarot cards are bullshit, like Ouija boards. What does this have to do with me? Why do you care about my bloodline?" I had a sinking feeling I already knew but wanted to hear it from Tristan.

"The vampire Haute Caste also has HH blood. The Magus is the first vampire, we are all descended from him. He shared his gift. You are the last of the de Molay line and you have HH blood. It seems that you are fated to be one of us."

"I'm not an Empress. I'm not some candidate for a genetic experiment. You may have made an agreement with one of my ancestors but I didn't! I want to leave now."

"Of course." He put the card back in his pocket and stood up. The servers appeared and thanked the Baron. The man in the suit guided them to the front door babbling on about how he hoped they had enjoyed the meal. The Baron merely nodded. We stepped outside and waited briefly for the car.

"You didn't pay the check!"

"Lena owns the restaurant," he said. "I'm sorry if I upset you. Perhaps I should have given you more time."

"Which card symbolizes you?" I asked.

"The Emperor."

I had to escape. I could not stand the thought of being alone in a car with him at that moment. The car arrived and I told Tristan, "You should at least tip the parking attendant."

The attendant helped me into the car, then Tristan stood behind the car to hand the attendant a $100 bill. At that second, I jumped into the driver's seat and hit the gas, burning rubber as I sped away. The car was going so fast I was afraid to take my eyes off the road to look behind me.

CHAPTER 13

I SPED INTO the night trying not to kill myself as I adjusted to the amazing machine. I stayed on side streets when possible and headed towards the one haven the Baron might not know about. Forty-five minutes later I was in the Hollywood Hills near the reservoir. Los Angeles has reservoirs in the middle of densely populated areas which serve as lakes with trails and bike paths. Though the Hollywood Lake would be closed, I knew a way into the park. Lolly and I used to go running up there when she was on a fitness kick. I pulled off the road and felt bumps as I drove over gravel and parked the car under some pine trees. I looked back in the direction of the road; no one followed me. I took a deep breath and exhaled slowly but it did little to calm me down. I knew there would be hell to pay. There were several hours till sunrise. If I could hide here till then, I would have a day to consider my bizarre situation without the Baron's interference.

I threw my sandals over the fence. The chain metal gate scraped my knees and tore my skirt as I made it over. Pine needles poked my back as I landed on the cool dirt. "Damn it!" I yelled. I made my way to some old oak trees on a small hill that looked out over the lake. I sat on the solid ground and leaned against one of the trees. We used to rest here after a run. The scent of the trees reminded me of the Baron. "Damn him!" I focused on the lake. A cool breeze played with my hair. The water shimmered in the moonlight like the lakes back home. I remembered fishing with my dad. I hated baiting a hook but it was worth it to have time with him. He was so easy to talk to. I had always been honest with him. Now I was afraid to be honest with anyone. Who would believe me anyway? I watched Bram Stoker's cruel death. Poor man. How could I expect my association with the undead to have a happy ending? I was trying to make sense of what Tristan had said over dinner. He told me he had saved my life but did not explain why. I did not like the direction it was going.

It seemed the vampire ruling class had decided I was pretty special. "Fuck them!" I swore out loud. They had no right to take over my life. It was weird how their machinations brought up the same feelings of resentment I felt when my high school guidance counselor told me to forget about college and focus on helping my parents with the café. I could not go back to Illinois even if I wanted to. I feared that wherever I went the undead would find me eventually. I remembered the image on the Tarot card. I did not doubt they had invented them. That made perfect sense. A way for a secret society to communicate before computers and encryption. Regardless of what Tristan said, cornstalks and all, that card did not resemble me in the least. Who the hell was de Molay? I did not, would not, fit into that world. I had to find a way out.

I heard leaves crunch nearby. I looked over my shoulder but not a soul could be seen in the dark landscape. It was probably a squirrel or coyote. Suddenly, a huge bearded man dressed in old, soiled clothing appeared from behind some bushes. He had a scruffy beard and reeked of urine. He looked from side to side, then approached me quickly.

"Leave me alone!" I cried and started to get to my feet but slipped.

"Princess," he hovered over me. His deep-set eyes scrutinized me. It looked like his nose had been broken and healed without medical attention.

"I'm not a princess and I don't know you. I'm leaving now." I tried to sound calm as I scrambled to my feet and slowly backed away.

"Princess, you returned. They could not hold you forever. I have been waiting to take you to safety. Quick, before the Riders find us!" He grabbed my arm and started to drag me towards the bushes.

"Tristan!" I screamed for some unknown reason. "Let me go!" I yelled and pounded him with my free arm.

"Quiet! I'm taking you to my fortress, not even the CIA will find us there," he hissed and jerked my arm almost out of the socket.

"Help!" I screamed in pain. Then I kicked his leg with all my might but he barely winced.

My attacker pulled a tarantula out of his pocket and dropped it on the ground. "Don't let the Riders follow us!" The delusional man started to pick me up. I struggled against his size and strength but he was winning.

"Let her go! Hands above your head!" a man's voice demanded.

He dropped me on the ground as two security officers shined flashlights in his face. One of them started patting down the bizarre man who was suddenly quite docile, while the other helped me to my feet.

"Are you okay miss?" the guard inquired.

"Yes, just a little bruised. Thank you." I answered, trying to straighten my clothing.

"You do not know your assailant?"

"No, I was just looking at the lake and he attacked me," I replied.

They escorted us back to my entry point.

"Is that red sports car by the gate your vehicle?"

"It belongs to a friend but yes, I drove it here," I replied.

"Did Fred here force you to enter the park?" He asked while the other officer took the park dweller to their SUV.

"He grabbed me while I was sitting by the pine trees." I could see that his expression was becoming less sympathetic. "I had a fight with my boyfriend and wanted to be alone," I added.

"Sorry, but you are being charged with trespassing. The LAPD will be here shortly to assume custody," he said in a monotone voice he probably practiced at home. "They will also assist you if you want to press charges against Fred."

"He attacked me and I'm getting arrested?" I shouted in disbelief.

"There's also the matter of this vehicle. It was reported stolen. You can explain your side of it to the LAPD."

"Shit!" I replied.

At least they put us in two different squad cars. I was trying to figure out who I could call. I did not want to drag Lolly and Alan into this. I was shown into a holding room that smelled of cigarettes and unwashed bodies. The cuffs were very uncomfortable. I sat at a heavy wooden table with chipped paint while a female officer questioned me. She was a hard-looking bottle redhead, about 45 and not in the best mood. The overhead lighting did not flatter her.

"I'm Sergeant Quinn. Do you want to tell me what happened?"

"I was attacked by that park dweller. I went to the park after I had an argument with my boyfriend. I drove his car but I didn't steal it."

"Do you want to press charges?"

"Not against him. I mean, he's delusional," I replied.

"Did you have permission to take your boyfriend's vehicle?" she asked flatly.

"Well, not exactly. I mean I didn't have time to ask." My handcuffs clinked against the table as I tried to use my hands when I responded.

"Can you give me your boyfriend's name and phone number so we can verify your story?"

"Sure, he's Baron Tristan Mordecai but I don't know his number, I mean I never call him." My anxiety was increasing, "But the car must be registered to him."

"What about an address?" she demanded, looking a bit skeptical.

"He lives in Bel Air, sort of near the hotel on Stone Canyon. I don't know the street address."

"Right, he's a Baron somewhere in Bel Air. Are you sure he's not a prince?" She picked up her clipboard and walked out. I heard her yell, "We need a psych eval."

"I'm screwed," I sighed and put my head down on the hard table. I was exhausted. At least I would not have to smell Crazy Fred or hang out with vampire royalty in jail. I resented having to tell people Tristan was my boyfriend but I was trying to keep my story understandable.

I had lost track of time. Suddenly, the door opened and a gray-haired policeman entered. "I'm Lieutenant Sparks. Sorry for the misunderstanding, Miss Ortega." He took off my handcuffs. "Your lawyer is here, you're free to go."

A thin man with glasses and a nice suit stood by the door. He gazed at me intently with a professional smile. "I'm Nathaniel Beaudine, the Baron's attorney."

"All charges have been dropped," the officer assured me.

"My lawyer? Damn it, Tristan!" The lieutenant looked surprised by my response. "Shouldn't you hold me for trespassing?"

Lieutenant Sparks smiled awkwardly. "It was all a misunderstanding. Apparently, your fiancé did not realize you had taken the car and mistakenly reported it stolen. It was obvious you did not know the park hours, so you're free with a warning to only visit the reservoir during the day."

They walked me out into the hall. Clive was there and in a rare show of compassion put a cardigan sweater from my armoire over my shoulders. I saw Sgt. Quinn watching the show and shaking her head in disbelief.

"I'm sorry to have met you under such trying circumstances," the lawyer said. "Here's my card. If there's anything else I can do for you don't hesitate to call."

"What about an order of protection?" I was serious.

"I'm sure that won't be necessary." Mr. Beaudine smiled and looking at the officer and added, "Young and in love, somehow we all survive it."

The officer nodded and handed over my belongings. Clive and the lawyer ushered me out of the building.

"Miss Ortega, you don't realize how many expensive favors it took to clean up the mess you made tonight." Mr. Beaudine had dropped the faux charm. "You just might express a little gratitude when you see Baron Mordecai," he added in a condescending tone. "Good night."

Gratitude was not at the top of my list. Instead of repentance I felt moral anger welling up. The book had just been a ruse to get to know me. Tristan and his nocturnal gangsters had plans for me because of a hyper-religious ancestor and a recessive gene. What the fuck. I was too tired to run for it again. A Bentley was parked in front of the station. Apparently, no one would dare ticket it. I slowly started to descend the stairs but Clive motioned to follow him around the corner. The Spyder was waiting and I could see Tristan in the driver's seat.

"I'll ride in the limo," I said. Clive merely shook his head and opened the passenger door. If it had been possible I would have climbed under the seat. Tristan looked at me briefly, then started to drive.

"Are you all right?" he asked rather coldly, keeping his eyes on the road.

"I think so."

"He did not harm you?"

"Everything kind of hurts," I replied.

"That's not what I mean," he stared ahead. "Did he rape you?"

A hollow laugh escaped my lips. I looked down at my soiled and torn skirt

"You want to know if I'm still a virgin?" Tears began to roll down my cheeks. I crossed my arms tightly and sobbed, "I'm an exhausted, battered, infuriated virgin who wants nothing to do with men, alive or undead, at the moment!" I took a breath. "That crazy bum thought he was trying to rescue me." I crossed my arms over my chest.

"Then I'll let him live," he said coldly.

"But what are your plans for me?" I implored. "I want my life back. I want to go back to my apartment. I didn't ask for any of this! I want to be blissfully ignorant again."

The Baron said nothing and just kept driving. The sky was becoming gray as we pulled into the drive of his mansion. Tillie was waiting to take care of me. Tristan parked the Spyder by the front steps and sighed softly.

"You are safe now, that is all that matters." He turned to me with eyes that had witnessed ages. "I will try to make you blissfully wise. But not tonight. It is almost sunrise. We will have much to discuss this evening." He lifted my hands to his lips and lightly kissed my fingertips. "I could not bear anyone harming you."

I pulled my hands away. "It would be better if you yelled at me."

A smile came to his lips. "I yelled until I found where you were. The servants were quite relieved when the police called about the car." His face became serious. "Never do that again."

Tristan disappeared into the house as the light of dawn began to appear in the east. I did not argue as Tillie fussed over me. The knowledge that would turn my world upside down was just beginning to be revealed. Emotionally and physically exhausted, I took a quick shower then she literally tucked me into bed.

CHAPTER 14

AUGUST BEGAN WITH unhealthy air quality warnings. A smoggy layer enveloped the city. Dr. Donelley looked out his fourth story office window at the discolored haze Angelenos called sky and thought of Montana. He was done for the week. The harsh voice of his secretary disturbed his reverie.

"Some people think money will get them whatever they want." Mabel looked at the inquisitive expression of her employer and continued. "Some foreign woman called and demanded an evening appointment, said she'd pay any fee to be seen at her convenience. The nerve, doesn't she realize you're a dentist!"

James fought back a laugh. "What did you tell her?"

"I told her the office hours would not be changed for anyone and then she said something I won't repeat," Mabel replied indignantly.

"Well, we can't have that. If she calls back just hang up." James replied, trying hard to sound serious. He decided not to tell her to notify the FBI.

"I certainly will, Dr. Donelley," she said with satisfaction. "Also, Miss Lolly Johnson is on hold, do you wish to take the call?"

"Sure, I'll take it in my office." He hoped to have a confidential conversation.

"Hi James, I'm sorry to bother you but have you heard from Miranda?"

"Hi. Nothing new. I think she's just trying to finish her book," James replied. "I'm sure she'll call when she isn't so busy."

"You're probably right. Al says I'm obsessing, that I should just trust Miranda's ability to take care of herself. All the same, let me know if you hear from her."

"I will Lolly. Goodbye." He ended the conversation quickly because it was fueling his anxiety about Miranda's situation. He had not told Al and Lolly about the box of bottles left on his porch because he did not have any proof about who sent it. He did not want to alarm Lolly further. He was planning on telling

Miranda the next time she contacted him. He sighed and hung up his white coat.

"Mabel, I'm going fishing. Have a good weekend." He was going home to grab his fishing gear and Gracie. Then he would go to the Santa Monica pier. It would not be hazy at the beach. He was hoping for a beautiful sunset and maybe some beautiful tourists to watch as he fished. Anything to get his mind off Miranda.

The monks followed James as he left his office. Their unmarked white van blended into the traffic. Benedetto was the designated stealth driver. He would position the van a car behind James. Grigoryi was fascinated with the GPS that Simone had provided. He pulled up James' address in case they lost him.

"He is 12 and a half miles from his house," Grigoryi said enthusiastically.

"Yes, we will keep an eye on his whereabouts until our benefactor joins us."

"He is now 12 miles from his house."

"Very good." Benedetto was starting to sound annoyed.

"Eleven and a half," Grigoryi said. "Look you have to turn right here!" He shoved the GPS in Benedetto's face.

"Stop it!" Benedetto yelled. He swerved and the van almost hit an Escalade. The older woman driving the SUV shouted a string of obscenities that left the monks speechless for a moment.

"We lost him!" Grigoryi exclaimed. He wanted to repeat some of the choice phrases he had just heard.

"Put that down!" The elder monk appeared to lose his cool. "I studied the map. I know where he lives."

"I'm sorry, Brother Benedetto." Grigoryi sounded sufficiently ashamed of his outburst.

"It is good that you are passionate about hunting vampires." Benedetto had regained his composure. "But let us not lose our civility." There was a pause and Benedetto heard some clicks. "Put down the GPS."

"Sorry," Grigoryi replied sheepishly.

There was unusual activity in the Baron's suite before sunset due to the emergency meeting. A time had been chosen that would be most conducive to the undead international community being able to participate. He put a royal blue robe on. It had two gold rams embroidered on the shoulder denoting his station as the Emperor. Delilah glanced at Tristan in a disapproving manner and went back to sleep. "Sorry old girl," he said as he opened the mahogany antique armoire that held a communication center. Vampires loved technology. Monitoring blood banks, hematology research, hiding assets, creating new birth records, blackmailing and spying had become so much easier. A few members of the highest caste were M.I.T. graduates. Tristan had to get through four different security screens to enter the meeting place online. Nine smaller screens appeared on his monitor. Each screen had an avatar which would interact with the others during the meeting as it was impossible to capture their images. Each avatar was crafted to "reflect" their real world appearances. The avatars of the six members of the Parliament of Houses acknowledged him.

The Lady Mbuyi Kananga of the House of Wands in Kinshasa smiled and nodded. Gold beads decorated her avatar's shoulder length braids and a 7-carat diamond glistened on a chain about her neck. On each hand she wore a gold lion's head ring. Sir Conrad Sudovian of the House of Pentacles avatar in London gazed at him momentarily. His three-piece gray suit made him look like an English banker. An intricately carved bull's head was on the wall behind him. He wore a large platinum ring with a jeweled pentacle design. His short brown hair was neatly combed straight back. He was very proud and only showed deference to the Magus. Dr. Komaki Kyoto of the House of Cups of Tokyo's avatar bowed slightly, from his second home in Los Angeles. His hair was put up in a knot on top of his head. He wore a light blue kimono layered over a silver kimono. A koi fish in white gold with sapphire eyes hung about his neck. A green jade goblet with carved dragons sat on his desk. Lady Sarah Lockporte's lovely avatar represented the House of Plows. She chose to govern from Toronto. She was the least formally dressed. She wore a black lace top and a black leather jacket. A large golden platter with an embossed wheat design was beside her. She wore several turquoise rings. Her curly red hair fell to her shoulders. A painting of a buffalo herd was on the wall behind her. The avatar of Sir Jorge Diego of the House of Arrows, which represented Central and South America, appeared from Caracas. He smiled warmly at his old friend. A small golden bow rested beside an arrow on his desk. He wore a tailored red shirt. A gold ring with a butterfly design could be seen on his hand. His thick mane of curly dark brown hair was pulled back. Sir Omar Sadeghi's avatar nodded to Tristan. He represented the House of Swords in Qatar. He wore a long, flowing black cloak and white headdress with black silk ties. Beside his stack of Tarot cards, a falcon sat on a perch. His dark countenance showed strength and intelligence.

Tristan's screen was above the others, on the right of the Magus, who was still unseen. Lady Hauser appeared in a screen on the left side of the Magus. Her avatar wore a simple white gown with a large platinum crescent moon on a chain about her neck. Behind her hung a black and a white curtain panel. Her station as High Priestess made her second to the Magus. She barely acknowledged the six Houses and made only brief eye contact with the Baron. She never revealed how close she was to the Baron, and the rumors of her past involvement with the Magus were legendary.

The Magus was the most ancient and most powerful of the undead. Lady Hauser was also ancient, extremely intelligent and arrogant. Baron Mordecai was younger but when his DNA was transformed by Haute Caste blood it produced an amazingly strong and brilliant vampire. He was considered the third most powerful vampire in the world. Though envy and jealousy were rampant within the caste system, the Magus was able to keep order through fear and respect. His powers and authority were very rarely tested, which made the current situation with Simone especially troublesome.

"All the Houses are represented, we may now proceed," Lena announced.

The image of the Tarot card, the Magician, appeared on the Magus' screen. All the vampires stood. Then his avatar appeared seated wearing a black robe with gold trim. He wore the symbol for eternity as a pendant. His straight black hair framed his angular features. A large jeweled goblet and a stack of Tarot cards were before him. He glanced at the others and they sat down.

"I am pleased to see you all but unfortunately we must discuss treachery against the Haute Caste," he said bluntly.

There were audible responses of disbelief. Lady Hauser and the Baron watched their reactions closely.

"Who is responsible? Which realm? What did they do?" Lady Lockporte blurted out. The youngest member was not aware that she had to wait for permission to speak. The other Houses looked at her with disdain.

"When the Magus has finished you may inquire further about this situation," Lady Hauser stated authoritatively. Lady Lockporte bowed her head.

"Simone Brown of the Common Caste of the House of Pentacles has gone rogue," the Magus informed them.

The representatives from the other Houses glanced at Sudovian, who briefly looked uncomfortable. He quickly regained his stoic composure. The Magus gestured to the Baron to continue. "Her lesser offense was to transform a member of Lady Hauser's retinue, Sergio, without permission. The more serious offense involved the traitor divulging information about my activities to the monks who hunt us and then utilizing them to try and abduct someone under my protection, Miranda Ortega," Tristan added. "Ms. Ortega was upset by their behavior but is unharmed."

"Unbelievable," Lady Lockporte said softly, shaking her head.

"I called this meeting of the Parliament to discuss the appropriate course of action to ensure just retribution," the Magus continued. "Our society adheres to a strict code of loyalty that is crucial to our existence. Any breach in trust must be dealt with swiftly and severely. I welcome consultation on this matter."

"I'm just glad Ms. Ortega is fine. Do we know what motivated the vampiress to go rogue? Was anyone else involved besides those idiotic monks?" Lady Lockporte inquired. She had watched Miranda over the years as she grew up in her domain. Lady Lockporte's concern for her was genuine. She also found it difficult to believe a member of the lowest caste would pull off such detestable acts alone.

"We are all grateful for Ms. Ortega's well-being but what about the new vampire?" Kyoto asked. "What of his condition?" Being a doctor, he was naturally concerned with the newly transformed.

"We have concluded that the vampiress acted alone. It seems she is jealous of Ms. Ortega and unhappy with her position in our society. She hopes to use her crimes as leverage to upgrade her status," the Magus explained. He could lie most effectively. "Sir Kyoto, your concern for the young vampire is appreciated. He is under the care of Lady Hauser and Baron Mordecai."

"Her behavior warrants the most severe punishment available. As the vampiress is of my House, it is my responsibility to see that she pays for her transgressions," Sudovian announced.

"That is not your decision," the Magus said sharply.

Sir Sudovian looked down at the stack of Tarot cards in front of him. The others took note of Sudovian's faux pas. "I have chosen Baron Mordecai to carry out our decision as he was one of the targets of her crimes with the assistance of any members of the Haute Caste that may be required."

Lady Hauser responded. "I might add that we all will keep close watch on Sergio till we are assured of his loyalty, though he appears remorseful." She always seemed to use the royal "we," which annoyed some of the others but they did not show it.

"I appreciate the importance of this task and I will act according to the wishes of the Magus and the Parliament," Baron Mordecai said. "Desire for personal vengeance will not cloud my judgment or behavior."

"As Simone's behavior is an insult to every vampiress, I gladly offer my skills," Lady Kananga added.

The Magus smiled. "Lady Kananga and Sir Sudovian, your offers are appreciated." It was a face-saving comment for Sudovian. "Sir Sadeghi, we may need your expertise if you could be available."

"Her treachery is quite disturbing. I am relieved to hear that she acted alone. My House would be honored to offer protection to Ms. Ortega or to be of any assistance in this matter," Sir Sadeghi responded.

"Perhaps we should discuss what sort of punishment the Magus has in mind," Sir Diego interjected. "Simone could be made quite uncomfortable or she could taste mortality. Or perhaps there is some more creative way to ensure she does not repeat her unfortunate behavior. Also, I would like the pleasure of punishing those annoying monks."

All eyes were upon the Magus. Though his word was the law he still enjoyed the appearance of having support for his decisions. "Your offer regarding the religious fanatics is accepted, Sir Diego, though they may be of some use." He paused for a moment to give the proper build-up to the next announcement. "As there are only two possible responses for Simone's crimes, please find the cards for Temperance and Death. Hold up the card that you believe suits her acts of treachery."

The members of Parliament quickly found the card that would seal Simone's fate.

One by one they held up a card. It was unanimous. Then the Magus raised his card. "So it is Death!" The members of Parliament were glad they had chosen correctly.

I woke up at about two in the afternoon, slightly sore and very hungry. I pushed the button for Tillie, then fell back into bed. In minutes brunch was served. I savored the dark roast coffee while my mind tried to focus. I had a goal when I got into this mess, to write a best-seller. I was not about to leave Polly hanging. I would finish my story, damn it! Though I realized that more pressing goals were presenting themselves, like not becoming a vampire or falling in love with one. My grip on denial had loosened considerably. Tristan had touched me deeply. I lay back in bed and felt the toll my nocturnal crisis had taken on me. Instead of getting up I fell back asleep.

I was walking down Wilshire Boulevard, wearing my comfy jeans and a Bear's T-shirt. It was sunny and warm. There were the typical afternoon business people and a couple of guys on bikes. I saw a taco truck parked on a side street and decided to buy dinner. As I approached it suddenly felt cooler and the sunlight faded. I hurried to the taco truck. It started snowing. It never snowed in L.A. I had to get some food and get home. When I reached up to pay, someone with long black nails grabbed my arm. Simone glared at me, her teeth were long and pointed. I got free and started running home. The wind began howling and the snow was piling up. Suddenly, someone grabbed my hair, causing me to fall. I looked up to see Simone holding a long, sharp blade. "Tristan!" I cried and tried to roll away. All I could see was snow. I could not see where she had gone. I struggled to stand. I felt an arm about me. "Stop it!"

"Miranda, you are safe," Tristan said softly. He tried to untangle me from the sheets.

"I had a nightmare," I mumbled as my brain tried to orient itself. His gaze showed tender concern. I pushed my hair back out of my face and sat up. "What time is it?"

"About six o'clock. I heard you cry out," he replied.

"I woke you up? I must have been loud."

"I got up earlier than usual but yes, you were loud," he smiled. "Quite understandable after last night."

"Is it cold in here? I was dreaming about a snowstorm and Simone was after me," I said still a bit shaky.

Tristan pulled the comforter up about my shoulders and drew me close to him. He was warm. I just wanted to be held at that moment, it did not matter that he was undead. I rested my head against his shoulder. His strength, his scent and his voice were comforting. He was sheltering me, protecting me. With sudden clarity, I knew that he was the home I was running to. As crazy as it seemed I felt somehow whole and safe with him. I did not want to lose him! Tears started to well up in my eyes.

"What are we going to do?" I asked, feeling helpless.

"About Simone? The Parliament has voted tonight to take action against her. The plans are being discussed now," he responded in a typically male fashion, ready to problem solve, not really hearing me.

"About us," I said. My feelings for Tristan were suddenly so obvious. I could not go back to blind childish hostility and deny my heart. I had no doubt he loved me. "I don't begin to understand my feelings for you but damn it, I recognize them. Maybe I do need a psychiatrist."

He gently put his hand under my chin so my face looked up at him. "I should get up early more often," the Baron softly chuckled with a bemused expression. "You said us. You are certain?"

"When I was in trouble at the reservoir I called your name. While I was dreaming I called for you. My conscious mind has finally admitted my desire for you. I don't understand this. I should be fighting against you but I just want to be in your arms."

He lowered his lips to mine and kissed me softly, then I found myself kissing back till he pulled away with a look of surprise and delight. "I want to show you something. Come to my room."

Without hesitation I gave him my hand. When we stepped out in the hallway I saw Tillie standing by. The Baron merely said "Tonight" and she scurried off smiling. In the suite Delilah came over to me and gently rubbed her great muzzle against my side, almost knocking me over. Instead of going over to the bed, he opened an armoire to reveal a computer system. Quickly, he pulled up a file. The Baron reminded me of a child excited about sharing a prized toy. "Look!"

Dozens of photos appeared on a large flat screen on the wall beside the armoire. It took a few seconds before I realized that they were all of me. Tristan put his arm about my shoulders as much to steady me as to express affection. The first row were pictures when I was a baby and as a toddler. There were images from elementary school.

"I can't believe this. I don't think I've ever seen these photos before. My high school prom! Look at my hair!" The last photos were while I was at UCLA. "Lolly and me at Starbucks. I don't understand how you could have done this without me noticing. Stalker!"

"I was keeping an eye on you but keeping my distance, so as not to interfere in your life. I have protected, cherished and adored you always. Your existence gave new meaning to my very long life. I was sent weekly updates when I could not discretely check on your status personally."

I turned to Tristan with tears in my eyes. "Why didn't you introduce yourself sooner? I have felt so alone for so long."

"I wanted to but your normal development was important. I'm grateful to your parents for the stable, loving home they provided for you. If they had ever mistreated you I would have taken you away from them. There were times when I wished they would have," he replied. He picked up a small framed picture off his desk. "This is my favorite when you were 8 years old."

"Oh no," I started laughing. "I'm so sorry." I was dressed as a vampire for Halloween. Huge fake teeth, a horrible black wig, cape and a purple bat necklace.

"You are forgiven," he replied. He stood before me with a longing that captured my heart. He took a small box out of a desk drawer. "I humble myself before no one except the Magus," he stated, then he got down on one knee, "and you. I will honor, protect and love you with all my heart. All that I am, all that I have, I pledge to you. Will you marry me?" He held up a blue sapphire ring circled by diamonds.

I cannot explain why but serenity took hold of me. I looked at my destiny on bended knee before me with love in his eyes and somehow the most insane marriage proposal seemed right.

"As a mortal?" I asked. "You accept me the way I am?" Tears welled up in my eyes.

"Yes. I ask only for the honor to have you as my wife," he replied.

Tears rolled down my cheeks. "Damn you, Tristan Mordecai, I accept!" I blurted out.

He tried not to laugh as he slipped the ring on my finger. Then he placed his lips on mine and I melted into him. It was a long, slow kiss that caused my knees to weaken. The most passionate, sensual, promising kiss I have ever experienced and I did not care if I had made the right decision. Too soon he stopped and said, "Wed before bed, to protect your virtuous honor my lady. The judge will be here in two hours. Tillie is waiting to help you get dressed."

"Seriously, in two hours? That must be the shortest engagement in history. My mother will kill me. How will I explain it to her?" I asked.

"We eloped. Honestly, you'll have much harder things to explain," he smiled. "Off with you!" He patted me on the ass.

CHAPTER 15

I HURRIED TO my room while glancing down at my ring. The ocean blue sapphire reminded me of the color of Tristan's eyes. I tried to stay in the moment, not think about how this would impact others. I was afraid I might talk myself out of marrying a nocturnal serial killer. Tillie was pulling the blue gown out of the armoire. Now I understood why he had sent me that gown, it was not just meant for a night on the town.

"It's a lovely evening for a wedding. You will be a beautiful bride," she smiled warmly. "I prepared the bath for you. I also brought up some coffee and pastries."

"Thanks. How long have you all been planning this?" I inquired as I got into the soothing bath. Rose petals floated in the sweetly scented water.

"Since you arrived in Los Angeles. The ring suits you."

"I'm marrying a vampire," I sighed. "I must be crazy. This makes no sense."

"He is the Baron Tristan Mordecai and you will be his Baroness. You are very lucky if you don't mind me saying so," she replied.

"Keep saying it, Tillie, and maybe I'll start believing it," I smiled. "Maybe you should tell my mother about the wedding."

She merely smiled and helped me out of the tub. She styled my hair in long ringlets down my back. I drank the coffee but was not at all hungry, which was a first. Then she handed me a small black box. Inside was a pair of dangling earrings that had sapphire and ruby flowers attached to diamond stems. They were exquisite.

"The Magus sent over the earrings," Tillie said with reverence.

"When did the ruler of the night send them over?" I inquired.

"About six months ago," Tillie said in a reverent tone. "You'll be honored by his presence tonight."

I was not certain I wanted the nocturnal kingpin's blessing but I loved the earrings. The dress was so feminine and alluring. The gems were so incredible. There was one problem — no matching shoes. Okay, that was not my only problem but it was the only one I was willing to focus on at that moment. I considered going barefoot as no one could see my feet, then I looked in the armoire for something to give me a little height.

"I almost forgot. Please forgive me. Your shoes." Tillie handed me a pair of golden silk heels with a royal crest. "It's the house of Mordecai." The shoes were a perfect fit.

"Tillie, how many times has the Baron been married?" I had to ask.

"As far as I know, Miss, never. He told Clive he never had a reason or inclination to get married until now." Tillie handed me the bottle of Magie Noire. "They don't make this perfume anymore but the Baron had me do a computer search to find it for you. When it comes to you he is very particular."

"So it seems," I smiled and placed a little behind my ears and on my wrists. "Thank you, Tillie, for everything. You have been very kind." It was hard to imagine Tillie using a computer.

"It has been my pleasure, Miss," she responded. "I believe the Baron is waiting for you in the grand room." She opened the door for me then followed a few steps behind. I felt like I had matured greatly since encountering Tristan at my book signing. I was accepting my place in a secret world that operated without the normal constraints of life. I would have to lie to my family to protect them from this bizarre reality. I suddenly felt sad that my parents could not be at my wedding. I had to let Lolly know. I took a selfie and sent a message stating I was eloping with Tristan. I added that he was much more than he seemed, that I would explain later, and not to worry, but she might want to read Dracula. I carefully went down the staircase taking slow, even breaths to steady myself. I thought of how I arrived in a T-shirt and jeans. I realized that these seemingly sudden changes had been years in the making.

Then I walked into the grand room. The Baron looked at me with eyes that reflected his love for me and my resolve strengthened. He was wearing a black suit with a white shirt and a black tie. For a moment I only saw him, then I noticed Lena in a beautiful gray satin dress with Sergio at her side. Lilies and yellow roses were arranged in several large ornate vases. A dark-haired man stood with his back to me talking with the Baron. Lena approached me and briefly held my hands. I think it was the first time she had ever touched me.

"Try to be worthy of this incredible honor," she said.

I wanted to respond with "Fuck you very much" but it was not the time or place. I managed to hold my tongue and respond with, "Thank you for coming."

I smiled at Sergio who looked happy but a little pale. He leaned in to kiss my cheek and whispered, "Tristan is a good vampire."

I whispered back, "You're not helping." Then hurried over to my groom. I just wanted to be alone with him. The man beside him turned towards me.

"Mr. Olive!" I exclaimed. His demeanor was self-assured. He wore a beige silk suit and an ivory shirt. I had always been in their world, I just never saw it.

"Miss Ortega, soon to be Baroness Mordecai, delighted to see you again," he bowed his head ever so slightly.

"He is the Magus," Tristan explained. "The most learned, respected and powerful of our kind. It is a rare privilege to have his presence at our wedding."

"You own my building?" I asked.

"Of course, it was the easiest way to protect you," the Magus replied with a slight smile.

"Judge Ryan has arrived," Clive announced at the door. A somewhat obese man in casual slacks and shirt entered the room and narrowed his gaze upon Tristan.

"Baron Mordecai? The senator sends her regards. May we begin?" It was obvious Judge Ryan was not delighted to be working overtime.

The Magus remained beside Tristan. Lena and Sergio moved to my side perhaps to keep me from bolting. Tillie, Clive and Jasper stood by the door. Tillie held a handkerchief to her nose and sniffled. Even Clive looked like he was tearing up a bit. They were truly fond of the Baron. I tried not to look at the bizarre, dysfunctional family that surrounded the judge. He had no idea that any slight to the rulers of the night could have ended his judicial career. Not long ago I was like him, a Short without a clue. I envied his ignorance.

Sergio handed a piece of paper to the Judge. It appeared the lowest ranking vampire was given the task of interacting with him. "Read this." For an instant, the Judge started to question the demand but Lena's glare caused him to stop.

"Very well. On this night, Baron Tristan Mordecai, do you pledge your heart, your hands, your blood," here the Judge paused for a second, "your honor and all your wealth to Miranda Ortega?"

"I do," Tristan responded without hesitation. Lena gave me a platinum diamond eternity band, which I placed on his left hand.

"Miranda Ortega," the judge glanced at me for a moment as though checking to see if I was agreeable to the ceremony. "Do you pledge your heart, your loyalty, your unwavering trust and your blood to the Baron Tristan Mordecai?"

I took a breath as all eyes fell upon me. "I do, except for the blood part." Then I looked at my groom. You could have heard a pin drop in the room.

"So be it," Tristan stated. Then Sergio handed Tristan a matching platinum band, which he slipped on my finger beside the sapphire ring.

"By the powers vested in me by the State of California, I pronounce you husband and wife."

My husband kissed me gently to murmurs of approval. Then for just a few minutes there was a quite normal display of affection and congratulations. Lena hugged me, though it felt a bit stiff. Sergio slapped Tristan on the back like he had made a touchdown. Clive and Jasper shook Tristan's hand. Tillie kissed my cheek, which made me miss my mom. Only the Magus stood apart and watched with a contented expression. Tristan did not shake the judge's hand when it was offered, he merely said, "Tell the senator her debt has been repaid. You may leave." He exited quickly.

As the Magus approached me the room became silent. The greatest vampire took one of my hands and raised it to his lips in a courtly fashion. His hand was cool but soft. The other's watched with looks of surprise. His scent reminded me of the ocean. He kissed the back of my hand so lightly it almost tickled. "Welcome to the family." He then released my hand and left the room with Jasper and Clive following behind.

"He rarely touches anyone, let alone kiss their hand. That was to grant you high status," Lena said. She and Sergio made their goodbyes brief to my relief. I was feeling a bit overwhelmed at the moment.

Tristan took my hand. "Baroness, would you like a picture for your parents?"

"You read my mind. I didn't ask because I thought it was impossible." I started tearing up.

Clive entered with a camera. Tillie handed the Baron some thin pieces of latex that looked like a mask and gloves. He tried to smile as the mask was fitted on his head. Then Tillie took a wig out of a box and helped style his hair. Before putting on the gloves he put blue contacts lenses in his eyes. From across the room he looked normal.

"This is a bit uncomfortable, my love. Please stand beside me," he requested.

I grabbed a few roses from a vase. Clive took a dozen pictures, staying about 15 feet away. It was important to have something to send to my family. It was also important to me to have a wedding photo, a shred of proof. He was glad to remove the latex and contacts.

"Shall we go upstairs?" he asked.

"I would love to be alone with you right now," I responded with anticipation. "The judge, he was the real deal?"

"Yes."

"Some senator owed you?" I had to ask.

"I helped unburden her," he replied and took my hand. "Baroness suits you," he said as we walked upstairs.

I had so many questions but I knew they could wait. The master suite was bathed in candlelight. Some of the wedding flowers were in smaller vases scattered about the room. The silk bedding was pulled back. A silver coffee service was set on the small table. I noticed a small tray with caviar, lemon quarters and water biscuits. Beside the bed a dish of chocolate covered strawberries beckoned.

"Where's Delilah?"

My husband smiled. "She'll stay with Clive tonight." He walked over to the coffee service and found a lone cupcake. It had white frosting and T and M written on top with dark chocolate. "Tillie said I am supposed to feed this to you."

I was amused as he awkwardly tried to unwrap the cupcake then hold it up to my mouth without getting frosting on either of us. Cake, as with most solid foods, did not agree with my husband's physiology, but he did not want me to miss out. I loved his attempts to accommodate me. I bit into the cake, getting the sticky, sweet butter cream on my mouth, then kissed him. The Baron sputtered, wiping the frosting off his face and started laughing. "You twit!"

We fell onto the bed and all laughter stopped. The gown mysteriously slipped off my body. Tristan's suit and shirt were soon on the floor. His kisses gently wakened all my senses. I felt my nipples become almost painfully hard. I responded to his passion measure for measure. The scent and taste of his skin was an aphrodisiac. My body arched against his. He explored my clitoris to be sure I was sufficiently aroused to receive him. It was achingly beautiful pleasure. I felt a slight tear as he entered me. Then rhythmic movements which seemed to match the *Rites of Spring* drumbeat. It was like small, electric pulses began to run through me, building with intensity. We were lost in a carnal moment.

Just when I felt like screaming he covered my mouth in hot, hard kisses. I felt like my heart was about to explode. I cried out just as Tristan climaxed and collapsed on top of me. I felt very warm, juicy, content and suddenly hungry. It was the most excruciating pleasure I have ever experienced.

I remembered reading about how men would fall asleep after sex but I was wide awake. I reached for a strawberry and felt a slight twinge between my legs. It was to be expected. My husband slid off me but kept one hand on my thigh. The strawberry was delicious but not sufficient. "Caviar," I declared and slipped out of bed.

I squeezed lemon on the luscious fish eggs and in minutes had emptied the silver bowl. My naked state dawned on me and I started to grab Tristan's shirt.

"Don't you dare," came from the bed.

"Go back to sleep," I laughed.

"Make me," he taunted.

"In time," I smiled. "Coffee!"

"Whatever brings you back to my bed."

"Are you satisfied with me?" I asked. I could not help but think of the thousands of women he might have had sex with.

"Satisfied? Not yet," he smiled.

I gulped down my coffee and climbed back into bed. His arms, his body, engulfed me.

"I feel like the happy truck just ran me over."

"You are insane," he laughed and started kissing my neck.

"I had to be to marry you. It's the only explanation."

There was a knock on the door. I tried to ignore it. I saw his expression change from lover to protector.

"Clive would not disturb us unless it was urgent." The Baron got up and grabbed a robe. "Come in." I held the comforter up to my chin.

"Sir, the psychiatrist has been taken to the ER at Cedars-Sinai. I'm afraid it was Simone. Lolly is unharmed. She is at the hospital with him."

"She attacked Alan?" I blurted out.

Clive nodded. "I'm so sorry. We were tracking Simone but she got away."

"Meet us downstairs with the Bentley!" Tristan turned to me "Get dressed quickly.

I wrapped a sheet about me and ran to my room. I threw on jeans and a T-shirt. I had flip-flops in my hands as I ran down the staircase and out to the car. Clive burned rubber as he spun out of the driveway. When I started to talk Tristan stopped me.

"There is a chance he can be saved but you must do everything I say. Lolly has to cooperate. You must convince her," he said in earnest. He briefly explained what needed to be done and handed me his phone. "Call Lolly, let her know we will help him."

"Lolly, we are almost at the hospital. Tristan is with me."

Through tears she went on about how weak Al was and about the attack, "We were at the park and this bizarre woman attacked Al, she had fangs, and ran off when the police got there."

"I know this is crazy but you are right about the fangs, she's a vampire. So is Tristan, he is like Al's attacker, but he would never harm either of you. He can save Al but you'll have to trust Tristan and do what he says."

Lolly was silent for a second then she blurted out, "I don't care what he is just help Al!"

Clive dropped us off at the ER where Jasper was waiting. "They started a transfusion but it is not sufficient," Jasper said. He led us to the curtained cubicle where Alan lay unconscious. The ER staff were busy with trauma patients from a multi-car collision so they did not notice us as Tristan and I entered the cubicle with Jasper. Alan's neck was bandaged and he was very pale. There was a bag of blood slowly dripping into an IV line running into his arm. There were monitors keeping track of his vital signs. You didn't need to be a doctor to see that he was slipping away.

Lolly, standing at his bedside and holding his hand, was fighting back tears. She turned to us. "Please! Don't let him die!"

"You must follow my directions!" Tristan demanded.

Lolly took a deep breath, wiped her eyes, and gave him her full attention. Tristan told her that his blood could save Alan, but it had to be given now. Tristan whispered something to Jasper who glanced at the nurses' station and quietly walked the other way. Tristan turned back to Lolly.

"What do you need me to do?" she asked.

"You have to make sure that we aren't interrupted. No one can see what we are doing."

Lolly nodded then stepped out and pulled the curtains closed behind her giving us a chance to act without detection. Jasper returned and handed Tristan the largest syringe I had ever seen and a length of rubber tubing that he obviously had lifted from a supply cart. My husband told me to hold the IV line in place. He removed his jacket, rolled up his sleeve and tied the tubing around his upper arm like a junkie, then he put the needle into a vein and slowly filled the syringe. He then inserted the needle into a port in the IV line, depressed the plunger and emptied the syringe into the IV line. Within a few minutes Alan started to mumble. The Baron repeated the procedure a second time. This time Alan's vital signs started improving. He opened his eyes and seemed to recognize me. Tristan injected Alan's IV bag with one final full syringe of his blood. I was so focused on Alan's recovery I did not notice my husband grab the bed rail to steady himself until I saw Jasper take his arm. At that moment we heard Lolly began talking loudly. "Nurse, please, I feel faint." She stood in the way of the RN who was about to check on Al. A male nurse with a Filipino accent could be heard asking her to move out of the way. Lolly collapsed at the nurses' feet. After a moment Tristan straightened up, pulled the rubber tubing off his arm and handed it and the syringe to Jasper. He rolled his sleeve down, put his jacket back on and all appeared as if nothing had happened. I let out a breath that I hadn't even realized I had been holding in. As the poor nurse helped Lolly into a chair and started to take her blood pressure, I opened the curtain and gave Lolly a thumbs up. She pushed the confused nurse away, saying she was fine and ran to Alan's side. He was smiling and the color had returned to his cheeks. An older doctor entered, prepared to see a fellow physician on his death bed. To his amazement the psychiatrist was alert and engaged in conversation with an elegantly dressed man while his patient's wife was admiring the wedding rings on a casually dressed young woman's hand.

Lolly went over to Dr. Bernstein and grabbed his hand. "Dr. Bernstein, thank you so much for taking care of my Al. I don't know what I would have done." She even managed to shed a couple of tears of gratitude and succeeded in distracting the physician while Tristan apologized for his kind's attack and finished explaining the effects of the transfusion to Alan. Lolly introduced Miranda to the doctor who was trying to get to his patient.

In a hushed tone Tristan continued to warn Alan. "As the sweet taste in your mouth diminishes, you will start to feel withdrawal symptoms, similar to opiate withdrawal. Drink this tea." He handed Alan a small packet that Jasper had passed to him. "It will greatly reduce your discomfort. Your wound will heal quickly."

"It's not permanent? Uh, you know..." Alan whispered trying to grapple with the thought of being infused with vampire blood.

"No," Tristan smiled, "but I've been told mortals feel younger. I am truly sorry I put you in danger."

Alan placed his hand on Tristan's sleeve. "I don't blame you for what happened. Thank you, my friend, your secret is safe with me." It was an odd sensation for Tristan to be forgiven by someone who had just been attacked by a vampire.

Finally, Dr. Bernstein managed to break away from Lolly to check on his patient. He told Alan that his recovery was nothing short of miraculous and he was at a loss to explain it. While Alan was talking to the doctor Tristan quietly cautioned Lolly. "You must both leave at daybreak. We will feel much better knowing you are safe. Do not go home first. In a few days Miranda will call you when you can return. I promise you I shall punish those responsible."

"Will he be okay?" Lolly asked.

Tristan gave her a reassuring smile. "It will take a few days for him to fully recover but don't worry, he won't become like me."

I thought for an instant that Lolly almost looked disappointed, "Thank you for everything you have done. I know you will protect me, I mean us." She looked at me, "When this is over we have to talk."

I interjected, "You have to get out of L.A. Find some nice hotel where Al can rest."

They promised they would do as we asked. As we left I was afraid of what might happen next. Jasper walked by the Baron's side still holding his arm as we came out of the ER. Clive was waiting with the car door open. I got in and then Jasper assisted Tristan into the car. His hands were trembling slightly as he sat back against the leather seat.

I had never seen Tristan look so weak before. "Are you alright?" I asked, trying to keep my voice steady.

"Not really. It is dangerous to give away so much vital fluid. At this moment, I could hardly fend off Simone, let alone restrain someone to quench my thirst." He closed his eyes. "Generosity can be a character defect at times."

Tears welled in my eyes. I could not stand to see him like this. I took his cold hand and placed it on my neck. He felt my pulse and his eyes opened.

A look of great appreciation came to his face. "Remember you said no blood." A faint smile came to his lips, "I will always cherish this moment."

I rested my head on his shoulder, hoping he would not see the tears in my eyes. How could love make me so reckless? I was relieved he had not accepted my offer.

The car stopped at the back of a medical center building. Jasper disappeared into the building, then a few minutes later opened the door and handed Tristan three bags of blood. "O positive, sir," he said and quickly closed the door. The car sped away home.

I watched my husband finish off the bags of blood and was surprised that I did not feel repulsed. It only mattered that he recovered. His body quickly began utilizing the blood to replenish his energy. Vampires had a right to exist. I could accept and try to understand his reality or go crazy fighting it. He put his hand tenderly on my cheek, then gently kissed me. He was warm again.

"I will be fine," he said. "Alan will feel quite rejuvenated after his transfusion. Let us hope Lolly will keep our secrets."

"Simone is a monster!"

"Worse. A jealous, ambitious vampiress." The Baron looked at me with a slight smile. "Be grateful Lena likes you."

"I'm not sure she does. What will happen to Simone?"

"I will discuss those details with the Magus shortly," he replied.

"What a wedding night!" I grumbled.

"I can promise your life will never be boring, my Baroness."

CHAPTER 16

JUST AS WE arrived at the mansion the Baron received a text message to meet with the Magus. He held me in his arms for a moment then sighed, "I'll return to you as soon as possible." I got out of the Bentley and watched them drive off. Tillie was waiting at the door to smother me with concern. I headed for the kitchen to her dismay.

"Please Baroness, I'll serve you upstairs, whatever you would like," she pleaded.

"The Baroness wants to scrounge for a snack," I said to her disappointment. "But I would like a cup of coffee in a mug. Coffee in tea cups is just not right." I opened the huge refrigerator and reached past some bags of blood to a carton of yogurt.

"Of course," she replied, content to be given a task. "Is your friend okay?"

"Yes, thanks to Tristan he is recovering, and no thanks to Simone for almost killing him," I replied. "I can't help but feel somehow responsible."

"Couldn't be helped. I never liked that Miss Brown," Tillie said in a rare moment of unprofessionalism. "But it was a lovely wedding," she said, trying to get back in form. "Shame that your special evening was interrupted." Terrible events in this household were just a common nuisance to her. She handed me a porcelain Queen Elizabeth mug trimmed in gold.

Tillie made up a plate of Camembert cheese, red grapes and a sliced baguette. She kept hovering around wanting to be helpful till I told her I needed some time to myself and excused her. Then I sat at the large white kitchen table and pondered my current state of affairs while I stared at the image of the queen. She certainly was a survivor. She weathered storms well. I only hoped I would be able to. "Long live the Queen." I raised my cup to the empty room and took a swig of coffee. I felt emotionally hung over from the wedding and the hospital. Now all I could think of was, "What the fuck have I done?" It all seems right when I am with him but when we are apart the weird reality is sobering. The fated-to-be-together fairy tale was not so easy to accept with the coming light of day. Though I chose to marry him, I was still a Short. My poor friends! They were in jeopardy because of us. They did not deserve this. I could not allow myself to put anyone else in danger. With each passing night I seemed to be pulled further into this fine mess. I wondered what the Magus and my husband were planning. I must have been sitting there staring out of the dark kitchen windows about 10 minutes before footsteps startled me out of my ruminations.

There you are, Baroness," Sergio entered the kitchen and sat beside me. I realized that I would have to get used to my royal title.

"You heard about Alan?" I asked.

He nodded. "I'm to be your body guard." His countenance became serious. "I just got a message from the Baron. You are to call James and tell him to leave L.A. and not return till he hears from you."

"I just met him, why would Simone...." I started to protest but was stopped by Sergio's serious expression, realizing that she would stop at nothing to get what she wanted.

"We are wasting time," Sergio insisted.

I knew he was right, I pulled my phone out of my pocket and searched recent calls. His number was there. I put it on speaker phone. It rang a dozen times then, "Hi Miranda, I'm glad you called. Lolly has been driving me crazy."

"James! Where are you?"

"At the pier but fishing is lousy tonight," he complained. I felt very relieved.

"Listen to me. You have to trust me. I'm fine but Alan is in the ER at Cedars-Sinai. Someone attacked him and they may be after other people I know."

"Is Alan okay?"

"Yes, but you have to get out of L.A. for a few days. Lolly and Al are leaving in the morning. I'll call you when it's safe to return."

"What are you talking about?"

"I can't explain it now. Just leave as soon as possible," I replied.

"Is it your freakin' publisher?"

Sergio's eyes got big. I was sure he would report every word to my husband.

"No, he is helping. It's this psycho woman. His old girlfriend." That was all I wanted to tell him at the moment.

"I'll come get you, we can go away together," James insisted. Sergio looked down at the table. He felt sorry for the clueless man.

"There is no time. I'm very safe. She is going after others because she can't get to me. You must leave now. Just take your dog and go!"

"I can't leave you here," he responded.

"I'm not in danger. Call Lolly, she'll verify what I'm saying. Please, just go!" I demanded. "I need to know you are safe. Please do this! I'll call you in a few days."

"Alright, I'll call Lolly," he assured me and hung up clearly unhappy.

True to his word, he talked to Lolly who told him in no uncertain terms to believe me and get his ass out of town immediately. She and Alan were headed for the Biltmore near Santa Barbara soon. Sergio and I sat in an uncomfortable silence. It was broken by a text from Lolly saying that James was going to meet them north of L.A. "So, is this going to be my life?" I finally blurted out.

"Honestly, Miranda, life got much more interesting since you moved to Los Angeles. We all hated those trips to Rossville," Sergio replied. "I was sent out your senior year. I had to watch your basketball games. You should've worked on your free throws. Go Bobcats!" he chuckled. "Too bad I wasn't on a liquid diet then; the food was terrible." He was trying to distract me. "But I did get quite a collection of John Deere baseball caps."

"You know why vampires fit in so well in L.A.? It's a culture that worships youth. When you don't age, people just think you have a great plastic surgeon."

"Perhaps that is why there are more vampires in L.A. than New York," Sergio mused.

"Maybe I should move back home so my friends will get a chance to age," I responded.

"Tell me you're joking," he said and poured himself some coffee. "You couldn't wait to leave the cornfields."

"And soybean fields. No one ever mentions them," I added.

"That's because they are even more boring than the corn," he retorted.

"Shouldn't you be assisting blood donors?" I quipped.

"C'mon Miranda. You just married a fucking billionaire Baron! A jealous vampiress is stalking your friends. You are now the darling of a powerful secret society. You have servants who think it is an honor to serve you. The Haute Caste of the undead will hope to win your approval. With all your imagination, you could never have made this up. Your life has become exciting."

"Stoker did not seem excited," I replied.

"I heard he was, back in the day with Simone," Sergio smiled.

"How will it happen. How will Simone be..."

"Punished?" Sergio noted my emotional state and replied more seriously. "She will be taken care of quickly. The Lower Caste, young bloods, like myself are not as hardy as the more experienced, ancient vampires. All vampires can be damaged but we always heal. The catch is that we must be whole to repair any injuries."

"That's your Achilles' heel," I sighed. I had mixed feelings knowing they had a weakness. "No one is immortal," I flatly stated.

"We usually are. It's extremely rare for a vampire to be disposed of. The Haute Caste have strengths beyond the rest of us. The Magus, Lena and the Baron will see to it that justice will prevail. Vampires are very keen on that," Sergio said. "I thought you should be prepared."

Though his words depicted a brutal end for Simone, his words calmed me. There was a sense of order, rules and consequences in the vampire world. It seemed that my love and my friends would be safe. I excused myself to get some sleep.

"You may not be aging but being with vampires is making me feel 100." I went to Tristan's room. I wanted to sleep with my husband on my wedding night.

James' head pounded as he opened his eyes to darkness. Cold steel cut into his wrists when he tried to move. A cloth gag kept him from crying out. His ankles were bound. He was handcuffed to a heavy wrought iron chair in the middle of a room. The room felt damp and the scent of the ocean filled his nostrils. As he became more alert his eyes adjusted to the relative obscurity. He appeared to be in a garage with no windows. The gray light of dawn outlined the door. The last thing he remembered was stopping at a rest stop on his way up the coast to walk Gracie. He took her over by some trees, then everything went black. He hoped his dog was unharmed. "Dumb shit! I should have just gone back to Montana," he thought to himself. "Well, at least I'm alive."

Bright light blinded him for a second as a door to the house opened. A tall, thin, bald man approached him followed by a smaller man. They studied James for a moment as though not sure about how to treat a prisoner. James realized that they could not be the brains behind the kidnapping. He noticed they were wearing crosses.

"We mean no harm. We hope to trade you, in order to harm a very bad fellow," Benedetto explained.

"Maybe we shouldn't tell him anymore." Grigoryi was afraid to displease Simone.

"We will give you food but you must promise not to scream," Benedetto continued. "If you scream, you will only get nourishment through a straw. We are trying to be merciful."

James nodded, hoping to try and reason with his bizarre kidnappers. They removed his gag slowly. "I'm not feeling the mercy. Where is my dog?"

"Your dog is being cared for. Quite a sweet animal," Benedetto replied. He motioned to Grigoryi, who held a peanut butter sandwich close to James' mouth. "You'll be with your dog again soon."

James took a bite considering he would need every ounce of energy to get out of this mess. "You've made a mistake. I don't know any very bad people. Let me go and I promise that I won't go to the police."

"We will let you go tonight. Until then you must make the best of this situation," Grigoryi said and gave him another bite. "You are serving a great cause."

"Right now, I have a great headache," James responded. "Will one of you lunatics get me some aspirin?"

The monks talked quietly in a corner of the garage then returned to James. The tall one spoke, "The medication we have will knock you out again. Do you wish to sleep?"

"No more drugs, thank you. What about coffee? It helps a hangover."

Benedetto nodded to Grigoryi, who went back into the house.

"Who is in charge?" James demanded. "Who are you working for? I want to talk to them."

"Our benefactor is asleep right now. She is resting up for tonight," Benedetto replied in a hushed voice.

Grigoryi returned with half a cup of barely warm coffee. "Here." He held up the cup, allowing James to take small sips. "We don't want you to drink too much as we are not to let you out of the chair."

"Idiots. Then you better stop feeding me peanut butter," James responded. "So, am I your first kidnapping?"

"Second attempt," Grigoryi blurted out before Benedetto silenced him with a disapproving look.

"I had a feeling," James said. "My wrists are pretty sore. Can you put some bandages on them where the metal is cutting into the skin?"

Benedetto decided it was only right to attend to the prisoner's wounds. He instructed Grigoryi to get the first-aid kit from their van and wrap James' wrists with bandages by unlocking one at a time. James let them wrap the first wrist then place it back in the cuff. When they had finished wrapping the second wrist he hit Grigoryi squarely in the jaw, sending him flying.

"Help! Help! Help me!" James screamed as he struck at Benedetto. "Call the police! Call the police! Help me!"

Grigoryi got to his feet holding his jaw. The door to the house opened. An angry blond woman began yelling at the kidnappers. Her face showed nothing but malice.

"Silence him!" she shrieked. Simone leaped upon James, knocking over the chair and shoved the gag almost down his throat. "Medicate him!"

James continued to struggle with his free arm trying to push her off. Benedetto handed her a small bottle. She poured something on the gag and soon James was rendered unconscious again.

"Your hair," Grigoryi blurted out. They had not seen her without the brown wig.

"I like wigs," she said, realizing her mistake. "Sit him back up. He'll be out of it for a few hours at least. If he wakes, please dose him again." She was trying to regain her softer demeanor.

"And you are very athletic," Grigoryi added.

Benedetto intervened, "You have to stay in shape to hunt vampires. I'm sorry we let him trick us. It won't happen again."

Simone was hungry and angry enough to make a nice snack out of Grigoryi but she still needed her minions. She was also longing for a taste of James but not in front of the monks, not yet. At least she would not have to wear that stupid wig anymore.

"We can't afford to get the police involved." Simone glared at Grigoryi for a second. He felt a chill go down his spine. Then she turned and smiled at Benedetto. "I trust you will be more careful now. I will try to get a bit more rest. Please have Grigoryi deliver the messenger in a few hours while you watch our valuable guest."

Tristan quietly entered his bedroom with Delilah by his side. The great cat sniffed the air by my head, then silently laid down by the door. Tristan disrobed and slipped under the covers slowly. He tried to move beside me without waking me. It had been ages since he had allowed anyone to share his bed. He wondered about how a husband should behave. Being a bastard child, he had no role models. The Haute Caste were never obliged to take or make romantic vows, until now. He noticed my scent had a subtle difference, which made him smile. The Baron had everything he wanted at this moment. I stirred and placed a hand on his thigh. He gently cupped my breast. I turned to kiss him. One kiss turned into 50. He found every pleasure cell in my body. I still wonder if everything we did that night was legal. At one point I heard Delilah grumble as our passion was disturbing her sleep. There was no pain when he entered me this time, just an explosion of pleasure, then exhaustion. Neither of us spoke. We fell asleep tangled in each other's arms.

CHAPTER 17

THOUGH THE ROOM was dark, my internal clock woke me about noon. To my surprise my husband was snoring softly. Vampires snore! One of his legs was across mine, properly pinning me to the bed. His body temperature had cooled. I seemed to be getting used to that. I wondered if a heated blanket would work for both of us. He was my emotional and physical shelter against the storm brewing outside. I remained in bed about half an hour, absorbing his presence. I wanted to have sex but thought he would need more rest to deal with Simone. All my self-discipline pulled me away from his amazing body. I very slowly, carefully, untangled myself from my love. I pulled on my clothes and stepped around Delilah, who raised her head, blinked at me, then went back to sleep. I quickly went out through the door.

Sunlight through windows greeted me as I stepped into my room. I would have to find a balance between the worlds of light and darkness. Perhaps I would write in the early afternoon before he woke, then have the night with Tristan. Though I realized I did not have to write to support myself, I would still pursue my calling. I checked the messages on my phone. Lolly and Alan were safe but James had not yet arrived. I hoped he had decided to go back home. I felt sorry for him. In another life we might have had a chance but that was not in the Tarot cards. With any luck, Lolly would tell him I got married, but my luck had not been great lately, though Sergio seemed to think I hit the jackpot. How would I explain all this to my parents? Would the wealth be enough to make them happy for me? At least I could offer financial security to them. I got on the intercom and asked for lunch. In a few minutes Tillie entered with a cheese omelet, fruit, yogurt and a small green salad. I bypassed everything for the coffee. It had a little different taste than the Sumatran she usually served me. "What kind of coffee?"

"Congolese, Baroness. The Baron ordered it for you. Did you sleep well?"

"Yes, thanks. What about Bram, is he...."

"Cremated? Yes. We will get the ashes back tomorrow. Anything else Baroness?" Tillie asked.

"I guess there is no hurry to make the funeral arrangements." I wondered about which name to put on the tombstone. "Thanks, that will be all."

I was glad to be left alone. I decided to soak in the tub. Water rituals were soothing. My mental compass needed to be reset. I was struggling to get my mind around being married to a vampire, being called Baroness, not to mention the violence and intrigue that was apparently acceptable in this new culture. I turned to an old friend to help calm my brain, Polly. I had left her in the middle of a struggle between the Count and Sidney. Her situation had seemed rather black and white when I began writing but now was shades of gray. Sidney at first glance seemed the hero but his lack of attentiveness to Polly had been the catalyst for her trip to Europe. If she went back with him, would he get caught up in his career and neglect their relationship again? Was his motivation his love for her, or a desire to have his woman back? The Count knows that eventually his true nature will come out if he stays involved with Polly, yet he is willing to risk exposure for a chance to be with the woman he appears to love. He could have easily disposed of Sidney but his ethics would not allow for taking the life of a romantic rival. Even before Polly knows the truth about the Count, she has started to gain an understanding of a world, an existence, she could not have seen herself a part of until now. An old-world order trying to adapt to technology that prizes efficiency over graciousness. All the players find themselves changing. Sidney is becoming much less self-absorbed. The Count is gaining respect for Shorts, as he sees Sidney willing to take him on. Polly is becoming more aware of her power to choose her fate, though I could not help but wonder how much of an illusion choice really was. In my case, fate seemed to withhold the options I could give Polly. I got out of the tub and picked out clothing that might be appropriate for a vampire conflict. Tristan would want to spare me but I wanted to be there. I was hoping it would happen tonight so I would be able to stop worrying about what Simone might do next. I put on black pants and a black top with tiny silver flowers embroidered along the V neckline. It showcased the ruby necklace. I would have begged Tristan to give it to her if it would have satisfied her, but I knew she wanted more. She wanted to be as powerful as Lena. Seriously, wanting to be like Lena? That assured me she was a crazy bitch. I devoured the eggs and the rest of the meal. I preferred to not eat in front of my husband, as it made me a little self-conscious. I sat at my desk and opened the last chapter on Polly. Would she make the same choices that I did?

Grigoryi liked dogs. He petted the Dalmatian, Gracie, as she rode beside him in the van. He briefly considered running off with the dog but feared Simone would track him down. He worried about Benedetto as the elder monk was trying so hard to please her. Grigoryi trusted his gut. He knew she was a vampiress. Grigoryi also realized the monks were in over their heads when it came to the undead. As soon as he had the chance, he would find a way to get himself and Benedetto to safety. For now, he had to obey orders and hope for a way out. The younger monk parked close to the gates of the Baron's residence. He got out with Gracie and quickly tied her to the gates, patted her on the head and slipped a rolled-up note into her collar before running back to the van. He silently prayed for protection for himself, Benedetto, their hostage and the dog as he drove away. Grigoryi drove slowly back to the beach house. He was not looking forward to spending more time under Simone's thumb.

About 5 p.m., I heard someone yell in the hallway. I opened my door to find Gracie, who promptly jumped up and almost knocked me over. Jasper and Clive were not far behind. I knew this could not be good news.

"Where is James?" I asked.

"Simone has him, Baroness. We found the dog tied to the front gate," Jasper replied, holding up a small, curling sheet of paper. Clive handed me the note.

Tristan,

Congratulations on your pathetic choice of a mortal wife. As a wedding present, I offer to exchange the life of your romantic rival for the ruby, forgiveness of my alleged transgressions and entrance into the Haute Caste. Surely my ability to successfully attack your household and transform Lady Hauser's lover should garner respect for my intelligence and abilities. I only demand what I truly deserve.

Our rendezvous shall be at Point Mugu at 1 a.m. You will stay by the limo while your bride brings me the ruby. Do not make the mistake of crossing me. I shall have what is due me.

Lady Simone

"She is mad," Clive added.

"I have to tell Tristan," I started down the hall but Clive stepped in front of me.

"Baroness, he will need a good rest to be sufficiently restored for tonight, especially after assisting your friend, Alan."

"Is there nothing we can do now?" I asked, feeling useless.

"Help us get this dog to a room off the kitchen so Delilah doesn't turn her into a snack," Jasper replied.

I looked down at the sweet, confused dog and realized the danger she was in. "Yes, of course, I didn't think about Delilah. C'mon girl."

"And we can help you prepare," Clive added. "You will need different attire, Baroness."

We took Gracie downstairs. I patted her head in the kitchen while Tillie cooked some chopped steak. I became a little tearful, imagining what James must have been suffering at the hands of Simone. I put Gracie in a guest room with the meat and a bowl of water. I returned to my room to wait for sunset. I paced until Tillie entered with a small duffel bag.

"These are the clothes the Baron has ordered for your protection," she said as she placed the bag down.

"When did he order these?" I inquired.

"Must have been about a year ago. He has always been quite concerned about your safety." Tillie began pulling out dark items of clothing.

"Apparently," I responded. The top looked like a turtleneck with matching leggings. The material had a silver, metallic sheen.

"The material is very strong," Tillie informed me.

It fit perfectly. Despite the material's protective properties, it was quite easy to move in.

"I can't imagine needing this kind of suit."

"Here are the boots, Baroness." Tillie handed me knee-high leather boots with thick rubber soles. "And this, it goes in the boot on your right side." She gave me a gold dagger with a small dragon design on the hilt.

"Really?" Then I considered Simone. Tillie just nodded.

I looked like a ninja. My hair hung loose. I decided to put it in a braid. The ruby necklace weighed heavily against my chest. I excused Tillie, saying that I wanted to be alone. Then I did something that I had not done in a very long time — I prayed. I asked for my husband and friends to be safe. Vampires were part of creation, which is how I justified praying for them. I offered nothing in return, as I thought that might insult God, especially after all this time. Perhaps I was just acknowledging the tiny amount of control I had at that moment.

After a few minutes, I asked Tillie to bring up more coffee. I requested Sumatran. The African coffee did not have the same kick. When she brought it up, I could tell by the first sip it was the Congolese blend.

"Tillie, I know you have a lot to be worried about, so I understand that you might have not heard me, but I asked for Sumatran," I stated a bit strongly.

"The Baron was very specific about the coffee he wanted me to serve you. It's organic. He is concerned about your diet. Will there be anything else Baroness?"

I shook my head and she left. My husband was going a little overboard about my well-being. The discussion about personal boundaries would have to wait till the Simone crisis was settled. I pulled the dagger out of my boot and practiced throwing it at the bed post. My dad had shown me how to throw a knife when we went camping when I was 10. For years when I got pissed at home, I would go out back by the garage and throw my knife. If I needed a weapon, I hoped it would involve throwing, not hand to hand. I had not been in a fight since the seventh grade. Surely my husband would be able to protect me from Simone if it came to that. I picked up a small spray bottle of perfume and stuck it in my pocket, just in case. Then I stood in front of the mirror and practiced giving Simone an evil stare down.

"Horrifying," Tristan exclaimed. I jumped.

"You startled me," I responded. Then I ran to his arms. "How are you feeling?"

"I'm rested. The Magus gave me some of his blood which helped restore my energy and abilities," Tristan responded. "So, you know about James. I'm sorry. We will rescue him tonight."

"I'm afraid of what Simone might do. She has no moral compass," I said.

"You must trust me and follow my instructions to the letter, do you understand?" he asked, though it was more of a command.

"I will. Whatever it takes to stop her and rescue my friend."

"The Magus and I expected she might try something desperate. Several of
the Haute Caste and their knights have arrived. They shall be witnesses to a
swift but just response." He gently cupped my face and kissed me tenderly. Then
he rested his hands on my shoulders. "Listen carefully. In several hours, Clive
will take you to the Bentley. You will sit in the back with Dr. Kyoto and Clive. I
will be in the front with Jasper. Do not try to talk with me. Do you understand?
I must focus on what I have to do."

"Okay. Whatever you say," I responded softly. I was starting to understand
the seriousness of the situation.

He breathed a sigh of relief when I did not question him. "When we arrive
at Point Mugu, you will get out of the vehicle with Dr. Kyoto and Clive by your
side. I will stay in the limo with Jasper waiting for Simone to make her move.
You will follow Dr. Kyoto's directions. Is that clear?"

"Will Lena and Sergio be there?" It was my only question.

"I can't tell you anymore. Secrecy is protection, my dear Miranda. I must go
and prepare." He moved towards the door then stopped. "Just know I will do
everything possible to protect you, James and bring down Simone."

"I love you!" I called out as he went into the hall.

He called back. "I know!"

In a private room of the Golden Duck Restaurant, a rare gathering of the vampire elite waited for the Baron. As much to be present at an historic event as to
find favor with the Magus, they had traveled in private, darkened jets. It had
been centuries since a vampire had been judged unworthy. In that case it had
also been a member of the lower caste. There were rumors that the Magus and
possibly Lady Hauser knew a way to be rid of someone from the Haute Caste
but none could remember it ever happening.

Six golden goblets filled with O positive were served to the heads of the
houses by their personal assistants. Lady Kananga was waited on by her knight,
Samuel, who she had transformed a few centuries ago when she saved him
from the slave trade. He was short, with delicate features and a warm smile. Sir
Sudovian barked at his knight, Harold, stating the blood needed to be warmed.
Harold, a tall, strong blond Englishman jumped up and immediately took care

of his lord's displeasure. Dr. Kyoto's knight asked if the beverage was satisfactory; he merely smiled. Lady Lily sat down in a chair behind him. She wore a silk dress he had bought for her in Hong Kong. Their relationship had been more than official for two centuries. Lady Lockporte unconsciously drummed on the table with her fingernails until a glance of annoyance from Lady Kananga stopped her. Behind her sat her knight with short red hair and light brown eyes. Sir Ruben wore a black leather jacket and black leather pants. He was Lady Lockporte's brother, the only known vampire siblings. They both had HH blood. Their relationship was much less traditional than the others. Sir Diego wore an amused expression. His knight, Sir Franco, appeared bored, though secretly the tall, muscular vampire was excited to be back in Los Angeles. He and Sir Diego enjoyed the nightlife of the West Coast. Sir Sadeghi straightened his white robe. He bore a stoic expression while contemplating the destruction of one of their kind. His knight Momand was attentive to the vampire who had taken him from a nomadic existence and saved him from death 150 years ago. He was slight and graceful, like a dancer. He wore jeans and a tailored shirt in contrast with the traditional attire of Sir Sadeghi. He was also attracted to Lady Kananga, who seemed oblivious to his discrete glances.

The Baron arrived followed by Sergio, Clive and Jasper. The Parliament members were astounded to see the young vampire who had been involved in a treacherous act with Simone. They also did not expect non-vampires like Clive and Jasper to be present.

"The Magus and Lady Hauser send their greetings and their regret at not being able to attend this meeting, but Simone's actions since we had our online gathering have made it imperative that they make preparations for tonight. Before I go further I must give you the news that Ms. Ortega and I were wed last night. It was witnessed by Lady Hauser and the Magus."

"Splendid," Sir Diego exclaimed. The others nodded approval.

"The Magus attended," Sir Sudovian remarked. "Well, well."

"This is a night full of surprises," Lady Kananga remarked.

"When may we become acquainted with the bride?" Sir Sadeghi asked.

"After we deal with Simone," the Baron responded. "The rogue vampiress has attacked one of my wife's dear friends and is holding another hostage. She demands that we meet her to exchange his life for the ruby I gave to Miranda. She also demands to be allowed back into our good graces and to be made a member of the Haute Caste."

"She could never be worthy of such an honor," Sir Sadeghi stated solemnly.

"She is deranged," Lady Lockporte responded. "Is your wife's family safe?"

"Yes, Lady Lockporte, Simone has only gone after her friends here but precautions have been taken."

"How may we be of assistance?" Sir Kyoto inquired.

"The Magus has asked for your medical expertise tonight, along with the assistance of Sir Diego and Lady Lockporte."

Tristan looked at the other members closely, watching for some telltale sign of treachery. "The Magus has requested that our other esteemed members of the Haute Caste would be kind enough to stay at an observation point to witness for the vampire world how justice will be meted out." They all nodded in agreement. "Very good. My trusted servant, Clive, will give the details to you." Tristan turned to Dr. Kyoto, Sir Diego and Lady Lockporte. "If you will please join me with your knights." Then he paused and looked at the head of the House of Wands. "One more thing, Lady Kananga, if I could trouble you to see that my wife gets home safely after this sad event, as I may be occupied with the aftermath."

"Of course," Lady Kananga replied, bowing her head slightly.

The room was filled with murmurs as Tristan and his most trusted allies left. Clive gave the details about the midnight rendezvous as politely as possible, ignoring the cold stares from Sudovian. There was an uneasiness in the room as those left behind considered why they were being excluded.

"I should not have to sit in the spectator gallery," Sudovian complained.

"The Magus insisted that there be witnesses of the highest integrity for this momentous event." Clive was hoping to sooth royal egos. Sir Sadeghi and Lady Kananga sat quietly taking in Clive's instructions.

"I should be hearing this from the Magus himself," Sudovian told him, clearly unhappy. "Sir Sadeghi, Lady Kananga, I will see you later tonight." He turned and walked briskly out the door. His assistant, Harold, followed. Clive knew better than to argue and merely bowed his head.

After Sir Sudovian stormed out, Lady Kananga exclaimed, "What a pompous asshole!"

"Indeed" Sir Sadeghi remarked.

CHAPTER 18

AT MIDNIGHT, I was taken to the limo by a very somber Clive. He wore a black dress shirt and black slacks. Dr. Kyoto was seated in the back. He wore a light gray linen suit. He nodded slightly and smiled grimly when I got in with Clive. I could see my husband seated beside Jasper in the front. He did not turn to acknowledge me. I noticed Tillie wave to Clive as we drove off. She looked scared. I truly hated Simone at that moment. We rode along in silence for several minutes.

"Could Simone hurt Tristan?" I asked Dr. Kyoto. "Is there some kind of undead Kryptonite that no one has told me about?"

"I have only seen vampires fight once before, centuries ago," he paused to consider how much information to reveal. "The Magus was offended by the actions of a young vampire who challenged his authority. The first strikes are key and can do a lot of damage," Dr. Kyoto said and then became quiet. I did not feel reassured.

"Baroness," Clive began, "here are your instructions from the Baron. We will go to Sycamore Canyon Beach. It is our understanding that the vampiress has leased the entire campground and paid off the park guards to disappear. We will be in a very secluded area. She has planned this well, for months, maybe years. The Magus believes she is working with another vampire of higher standing." He paused to fish something out of his pocket. "I must remove the ruby." He clipped the gold chain around my neck and placed the pendant in a velvet pouch, then put it in his pocket. I felt relieved of a heavy weight.

"Who would help her?" I questioned.

"Someone extremely ambitious," Clive remarked.

"I think it will become apparent tonight," Dr. Kyoto responded. "When we arrive at the meeting point, the Baron and Jasper will remain in the limo. Clive and I will stand with you until Simone tells you to bring her the ruby. You must seem to comply with her demands and trust that the Haute Caste will protect you."

"As long as they aren't conspiring with Simone. Will they protect James?" I asked.

"Of course," Dr. Kyoto responded and patted my hands. I think that because he was a physician, he had more practice at feigning compassion than the other vampires.

"Baroness, I will keep the pendant. When you have no choice but to give it to her, call to me and I will bring it to you, allowing me to get closer," Clive instructed.

"No offense, Clive, but I would feel safer if it was Dr. Kyoto," I replied.

Clive started to respond but Dr. Kyoto raised his hand, which silenced him.

"Baroness, just follow the plan and you and your friend will be safe."

"Why do some high-class wannabe vampires want to bother with me and my friends? Surely they realize we are just Shorts!" I said, irritated by his dismissal.

"Baroness, that question will be answered soon," Dr. Kyoto said in a slightly condescending tone. "We have more pressing concerns at the moment."

The doctor was looking out the window as a red convertible Jaguar pulled up beside us. An unconscious James could be seen propped up in the back seat with Grigoryi. Benedetto was behind them in the white van. Simone flashed a satisfied smile then hit the gas and raced ahead. A terrible feeling of guilt overcame me, causing tears to roll down my cheeks. Clive pulled a handkerchief from a coat pocket.

"Thank you."

"Now is not the time for sadness, it is the time for focused anger," Dr. Kyoto remarked.

"I've got plenty of focused anger." I blew my nose into the handkerchief, looked at Clive and held out the handkerchief.

"You may keep it, Baroness," he said with a polite smile.

We rode in silence towards the rendezvous. When we got to Point Mugu Park, the gates were open and no guard was in sight. After several minutes, the limo stopped at the far end of the beach parking lot near a few oak trees. The lighting was minimal but the moon was full, casting eerie shadows. It was a stark landscape with rocky points.

Simone's car and the van were parked a hundred feet away by some shrubs. James was still motionless in the backseat with Grigoryi. I wondered how stupid the monks had to be to work for Simone, or how afraid. I heard the ocean waves crashing on the sand as we waited for instructions. Clive got a text message from Tristan, then looked over at Dr. Kyoto, nodded and said it was time to begin.

We got out and stood on the gravel parking lot. I took a deep breath of cool ocean air to calm myself down. Clive and Dr. Kyoto were standing on either side of me. Tristan and Jasper remained in the limo. I imagined that having to follow Simone's orders was killing my husband. Simone began yelling at the monks.

"Get him out of the car! Lay him on the ground, over there!" Simone pointed to the ground several feet in front of her car. I heard James groan as the monks awkwardly tried to get him out of the backseat. I started to go towards him but Clive and Kyoto held me back.

"Wait, Baroness," Clive whispered. "Go slowly, stall as long as possible and keep about 10 feet away from her. Follow the plan." I watched helplessly as the monks carried James over by the vampiress and placed him on the sandy gravel. She stared at me with a self-satisfied grin.

"Bring me the ruby, bitch!"

Did I mention how much I hated her? Double that. I slowly walked towards Simone, meeting her stare. The scent of her perfume made me slightly nauseated. I stopped halfway. Simone snarled, "Hand me the ruby." I turned my head and called to Clive to bring the ruby to me. Dr. Kyoto would probably not have been allowed to get closer but she did not fear the butler, a Short. I began to understand the plan now. Clive slowly walked over and handed me the pouch. It felt heavy in my hands. The monks stood nervously by watching the scene unfold with questioning glances. I could tell they were no longer sure about their patron saint. "Hold up the ruby! Do it!"

My hands trembled as I opened the pouch and it fell to the ground. When I bent down to pick it up I glanced at James. He opened his eyes groggily.

"How could anyone think your blood is better than mine? I deserve the royal jewel, not you! I should be the Baroness! Give me the ruby and I'll let him live." Simone spat at me.

"You never said you were going to kill anyone," Grigoryi blurted out, now clearly feeling distress at having aided her with her murderous plan.

"Shut up!" Simone shrieked, which caused both monks to take a step back. She pulled James up, exposing his throat. For a second, she flashed her frightful bite. "The ruby, now!"

I looked back at the limo. Tristan was still inside with Jasper. "If you won't do anything, I will!" I yelled.

With all my might I threw the necklace into the bushes. Simone screamed, "No!" She yelled at the monks, "Find it!" Grigoryi and Benedetto ran to the shrubs.

"I'm suddenly very hungry," Simone pulled James up to her mouth.

A shot rang out, hitting Simone in the shoulder. I looked back. It came from Clive. She dropped James and yelled at Clive, "I always hated your arrogant ass!"

Simone ran toward Clive. I made it to James and cradled him protectively. His eyes opened again for a moment and registered recognition. Suddenly a figure in black jumped out from behind her car and grabbed Simone as she reached for Clive. "Tristan!" Simone and I yelled at the same time. She turned and slashed at his throat. I saw a small amount of blood. Then Tristan put her in a choke hold. She screamed and bit down on his arm. Tristan pulled her head back and bit her neck. The coppery scent of blood filled the air.

"Help!" Simone yelled but her speech suddenly ended.

The van door swung open and Harold, Sir Sudovian's aide jumped out screaming, "I will destroy you!"

Harold brandished a large knife and stabbed Tristan in the back of the neck. Dark red glistening blood flowed down Tristan's back. He dropped Simone and tried to shake Harold off but blood loss was making him weak.

"Tristan!" I screamed and threw my dagger deep into Harold's side. He looked surprised by my attack. Harold pulled the dagger from his side and threw it in my direction, I ducked and it sailed over my head. He then pushed Tristan to the ground and started to come after me.

"How dare you! This is all because of you!" he yelled.

Grigoryi got between us and held up his cross. Harold hit him so hard he landed on his knees and began spitting teeth. Benedetto cowered. Clive threw his body over me and James. Harold grabbed Clive and tossed him against some rocks. I sprayed Magi Noire in Harold's eyes; he screamed. Then I grabbed the dagger that had fallen on the ground. I plunged it deep into his thigh, hoping to hit an artery. Then I tried to drag James away.

"You don't have a chance," Harold bellowed. "I will kill you and destroy the Baron's plans to dishonor our kind." He stepped closer. "I will be a hero!"

"The others will stop you!" I yelled, hoping someone would save us.

He leaped over James and grabbed my arm. I felt his cold hand start to circle my neck. He lowered his head close to mine as I struggled against him. "So, it is true," he sniffed me. "Delicious." Then I screamed as I felt his cold breath on my neck.

Suddenly someone took hold of him and threw him so hard he flew into the side of the van, making a large dent. I looked up at my husband. "You're not hurt!" I exclaimed with great relief. Sir Diego took off Tristan's wig and mask. It was the Cuban poet I had dated at UCLA. "Is everyone a fucking vampire?" I exclaimed.

"I'll explain later," he said and walked towards Harold.

I was confused and stunned by everything that had happened since we got to the beach. I saw Dr. Kyoto bandaging the knife wounds on my husband's motionless body. The sound of a helicopter overhead brought me back to reality. It landed at the other end of the parking lot. I looked around and noticed that Jasper had handcuffed Harold and Simone before they became conscious and started tying them up with heavy rope. Clive was on his feet, cradling his side, and heading over to help Dr. Kyoto. The Magus, Lady Lena and Sergio alighted from the helicopter. James was still on the ground at my feet, apparently more confused than I was and more than a little groggy. "James, you will be safe now," I told my dazed, bruised friend.

"Thanks," he mumbled. "Gracie?"

"She is fine, you'll see her soon," I assured him.

I left him to rush to my husband's side. "Tristan," I uttered and took his hand. His hand was ice cold, he barely acknowledged me. I turned to Dr. Kyoto. "Help him," I pleaded with tears running down my cheeks. I tried to clean the blood from Tristan's face with my sleeve. I could not stand seeing him so helpless. "You can't die! You told me you can't die," I uttered. He made eye contact for a moment then he slipped into unconsciousness. "Tristan!" I wailed.

Lady Hauser, the Magus and Sergio arrived with a vaguely familiar red haired woman wearing a pilot's uniform just as two men and a woman came down from a nearby rocky hill. The woman wore African dress, one man was in Arabian robes and the other wore a suit. I realized the pilot, used to work the night shift in my parent's café. She stopped and leaned over me.

"I'm Lady Lockporte but you can call me Sarah. We'll take good care of the Baron," she whispered.

"Lady Hauser and I will take the Baron in the helicopter with Dr. Kyoto," the Magus said.

"I must be with him!" I blurted out. I was having a hard time making sense of anything.

"Not now, Baroness," the Magus replied sternly. "Lady Kananga, Sir Diego and Sergio will take you and your friend back to Stone Canyon. Lady Lily, Dr. Kyoto's assistant, will be there to look after your medical needs."

To my amazement, Lady Hauser picked up Tristan like he was a child and carried him back to the helicopter with Dr. Kyoto and Lady Lockporte following close behind. All attention fell to the rogue vampires.

"You disgust me!" Sir Sudovian exclaimed and kicked Harold's head. "How could you dishonor my house? Traitor!"

"Simone and I are true vampires," he uttered with blood trickling down his chin. "We are trying to protect our purity! We should be Haute Caste!" He spit on Sir Sudovian's shoes.

The Magus spoke with authority, "You have failed to understand that our great calling is perfecting life in this world. You used your gifts to betray our kind." He dropped a Death card on the ground. "You will suffer the fate of the people you would have killed."

"May I have the honor?" Sir Sadeghi asked. The Magus nodded and walked back to the helicopter.

"No!" screamed Harold, which caused Simone to open her eyes. Jasper and Clive propped up the vampires against a pile of rocks. Sir Sadeghi pulled a sword from beneath the folds of his robe.

"It was Harold's idea. He put me up to it!" Simone pleaded.

"Why you ungrateful …." Harold's response was literally cut off as his head went flying across the beach. Simone's head quickly followed, landing a few feet from him. They seemed to stare at each other with angry expressions.

"Well done," Sir Sudovian said with satisfaction.

"Jasper and Clive," Sir Diego spoke. "Here is the slip number and keys to my yacht in the Channel Islands Marina. Please dispose of this trash. Thank you."

"With pleasure," Clive responded.

SUSAN OLD

"I am Lady Kananga," the African woman introduced herself. "I suggest we get back to Stone Canyon now. You and your friend could benefit from some medical attention."

"Yes. You're right. Poor James." I saw Sergio helping James to his feet. Then I noticed Sir Diego approaching the frightened monks. I ran to them. "He tried to help me!" I pointed to Grigoryi.

"It was my fault," Benedetto stood and faced Sir Diego. "I stupidly believed Simone and made my brother do her evil bidding."

There were tears in Grigoryi's eyes. "Please! We promise never to hunt vampires ever, ever again!"

"I'm sure you won't!" Sir Diego responded with disgust. "Idiots! You're not even worth killing. Go back to Rome!"

"Yes sir! Thank you sir!" Benedetto responded.

"But I thought I might get a job at a Bagel Shop here," Grigoryi whined, looking at the ground.

I held my breath, expecting to see Grigoryi's body thrown into the sea. "Please! He really did help me." I put my hand on Sir Diego's arm looking up at him, pleading for Grigoryi.

"Alright, he can stay. But only that one," he said, pointing at Grigoryi." Sir Diego started walking towards the limo, then he paused and turned to me. "Miranda, we must leave!"

It was strange to hear and see my old boyfriend and know he was not at all who I thought he was, and that the redheaded waitress was, in fact, a vampiress of the Haute Caste and a helicopter pilot. My poor brain was reeling. I watched the helicopter take off and fly south back towards L.A. I was responsible for James but I wanted to be on that helicopter. Sergio helped James into the limo with Lady Kananga. As I approached, Sir Sadeghi was waiting for me.

"Baroness," he said in a soothing voice. "I'm sorry to meet under these circumstances. I am Sir Omar Sadeghi of the House of Swords. You have proven yourself today. You must know that the Baron could not be in better hands at this moment. He will heal fully but it will take time. I must return home. Please know that my sword and my house will always be at your disposal."

Tears started trickling down my cheeks again. There was something about this proud warrior's approval and concern for me that melted my heart. "Thank you," was all I could say.

"My personal assistant, Momand, will stay with you for a couple of days."

A white Rolls Royce drove into the parking lot. A man in jeans and a white shirt helped Sir Sadeghi into the Rolls then he approached me carrying a small satchel as the car sped away to the airport. The vampire's one eternal foe, daylight, would appear soon. There was no time to spare. I saw Clive and Jasper put the dishonored parts of the undead in plastic garbage bags, then load them into the back of the Jaguar as Sergio drove us out of the park. Sir Sudovian was standing on the beach looking at the sea, probably considering the effect this night would have on the House of Pentacles. A Mercedes with darkened windows was parked nearby with a chauffeur. There were dark blood stains on the ground. I did not envy the park ranger who was supposed to be on duty trying to explain this, but maybe he would be lucky enough to find the ruby. I didn't think I would ever want any part of it again.

CHAPTER 19

SIR DIEGO OPTED to ride in front with Sergio, probably to avoid the millions of questions I wanted to ask. Lady Kananga removed a long panel of ornate cloth from around her waist and wrapped it gently around James' shoulders. Momand gave him sips of water when he was conscious. The assistant smiled warmly at Lady Kananga.

"He is slowly coming out of shock and sedation," she said. "How are you, my dear?" It was a simple, common question meant to convey concern. I had the feeling she already knew more about my situation than I did.

"Just great. My friends have been attacked, my husband has been whisked away in a helicopter in a coma, I just saw two people get their heads chopped off and I'm supposed to trust my life and the life of my friend to strangers," I looked out the window as the tears began to trickle down again. "What is wrong with all of you vampires? For such supposedly advanced creatures, you all seem pretty fucked up to me."

With a patient grin, Lady Kananga replied, "I appreciate your unbridled honesty. You don't hear that amongst vampires. Don't be too hard on us, we were all human once after all." She pushed back her ornate braids and added, "This was a difficult night for everyone." It was the perfect response to politely kick my self-centered ass.

"I'm sorry for being so unfiltered," I responded. "Where did they take Tristan?"

"To the home of the Magus. He will be well cared for, have no fear. Just know his recovery will take time," she warned.

"I guess the honeymoon is over," I quipped.

She glanced at James who appeared to be sleeping off the drugs, then whispered, "Since this is the first instance of a vampire ever getting married, there is no expectation of what should happen next. Your relationship has been kept a secret from all but the highest caste and their personal assistants, their knights. The Haute Caste's presence this night sends a message of support and acceptance to the Houses, so when they hear the news, they will respect your unique station. You showed bravery tonight and self-pity, a strange combination."

"Not when you consider what my life has been like the last few weeks," I responded.

"You'll do," she smiled.

"Do what?" I asked. I was still a little pissed.

"May I respond?" Momand directed his question to Lady Kananga, who nodded approval. His voice had an Arabian/British accent. There was a look of familiarity between them. In a hushed tone, he said, "Baroness, we were told to wait and observe before responding tonight. The Magus wants the vampire world to know you are worthy of being the Baroness. When you stood up to Simone to protect James and when you attacked Harold with a mere dagger to save one of our kind, that showed incredible valor," Momand said in earnest.

"A Templar Knight's blood runs in your veins," Lady Kananga added.

"Glad I passed the test," was my only response. James was conscious by the time we arrived at Stone Canyon. Sir Diego approached me on the mansion steps and placed a cool hand lightly on my arm. I remembered those handsome brown eyes gazing intently at me. He promised to talk with me tomorrow night, then he and Lady Kananga excused themselves to retire. Sergio and Momand helped James walk to a servant's bedroom off the kitchen that appeared to have been turned into a doctor's office. Lady Lily was waiting there to take care of him.

"I could use a cup of coffee" James sighed. Hearing that, I knew he would be okay. Lady Lily also appeared quite concerned about me. Tillie began cleaning up James, and Lilly insisted on taking my vital signs and doing some blood work.

"I'm not hurt. Really!" I protested. "It's James who got drugged and beaten." Lady Lily insisted so I finally cooperated.

"Are you a knight?" I had to ask.

"I am the Knight of the House of Cups," she said proudly. "It is an honor to care for you." She gave me a small bow, causing James to look at me for some explanation.

"How is my friend?" I asked. She turned her attention to James. "He is lucky, just some bad bruises and cuts, but no broken bones." She held a light up to his eyes. "No signs of a concussion."

I heard commotion in the hall and suddenly Gracie came running in. She stood on her hind legs and covered James' face in dog slobber. I helped restrain Gracie while Tillie handed James a wash cloth. "I was so worried about Gracie, I was afraid they had left her at the rest stop." He scratched her head, fighting back tears.

"Have you heard from Clive?" I asked Tillie.

"Yes, he is a little sore but fine. He and Jasper went fishing," she glanced at James, "and should be home about noon."

"Baroness," Sergio appeared in the doorway, "some of us must retire now. I can tell you that the Baron is responding to treatment and that more information will be given to you tonight."

Lady Lily and Momand left with him. Tillie brought James some clean clothes. "These are Clive's, I think they will fit Dr. Donelley. Would you like breakfast now, Baroness?"

"Yes, thank you," I replied. James looked at Tillie then back at me, clearly confused.

"Would the Baroness like to freshen up first?" Tillie looked down at my blood-stained ninja suit.

"Yeah, I would." I looked at James. "Be back in a few and then I can try and explain all this."

"Sure, Baroness," he replied in tone that was equal parts confusion and sarcasm. I was relieved to take off my bloody clothes and shower. I must have used twice as much soap and shampoo as usual, hoping to wash away that horrible night.

I put on my old comfy jeans and a T-shirt, wanting to restore some sense of normalcy. Before going downstairs, I checked in Tristan's Suite for Delilah but she was gone. I had a feeling she was taken to Tristan's side. I stood alone, breathing in the faint scent he had left behind and looking at the bed we had briefly shared. My ability to experience pleasure and pain seemed to have increased since I met him.

I slowly walked down the staircase rehearsing what I would say to James. When I entered the kitchen, he was on his cell phone. "Yeah, I think the good vampires got rid of the bad vampires, I'm not sure how. My truck is parked by the vending machines at the rest stop before Goleta. There's a spare key stuck behind the front license plate. If Al can just leave my truck at my house, that would be fine. Thanks Lolly." He handed me the phone and added, "I think I've lost my mind."

"Hi Lolly. How is Al?" I asked.

"Better, I mean he says he feels better than he has in years. What happened? How is Tristan? James said he was hurt, is that possible?"

I explained what happened with a few more details than James' account but glossed over the blood and gore. "Lolly, I've been told Tristan will be fine but I'm not sure how long it will take for his recovery. There are a lot more vampires than any of us imagined and I mean the nice, protective kind. Well, you know, civil. Anyways, it is safe to come home. I'll catch up with you in a few days. Give my love to Al. See you soon."

"Nice vampires!" James said and shook his head.

"Let's eat and I'll try and explain." I was really hungry. Tillie had left a plate of Danish pastries, a bowl of fresh berries and a platter with scrambled eggs and sirloin tips on the counter. I poured us both coffee, then we loaded our plates and ate without speaking for several minutes. It had been over 24 hours since he had a meal. James gave Gracie a few pieces of steak.

"So Baroness," he said in a slightly surly tone, "tell me what the hell is going on."

"I will try," I said and paused for a moment. "When I met you at that gallery, I didn't believe in the undead any more than you did. I just thought my publisher was eccentric and pushy. Now we know there is this whole vampire society operating in our midst. I really like you but as I came to know Tristan I felt this deep, strong connection. He has been looking out for me for years. In a nutshell, apparently, he and I are fated to be together."

"Nuts is right. Were you forced into this?" James demanded.

"Not at all. He proposed and I accepted. We were legally married by a judge two nights ago. Now, I don't know when I'll see him again he was hurt so badly, he lost so much blood." I started to cry.

"Miranda, I'm sorry," he started to hug me but stopped, clearly not sure what to do.

"I'm sorry I got you into this mess." I was trying to regain my composure.

"What do you remember about last night?" I asked, hoping not very much.

"I came to laying on the ground then Simone kicked me and was yelling. I kept losing consciousness. I heard a gun. Then I remember you next to me looking scared. The only other thing I remember was a scream and Simone's head flying through the air. I'm not sure about that, maybe it was wishful thinking or the drugs, but I don't think I really want to know." He looked at his dog. "As long as Gracie is fine."

"They didn't harm her. And we kept her away from Tristan's panther," I added with a smile.

"Panther? Really?" he responded. "It's not your fault but all the same, I think I'll leave California. I don't care if they are 'nice,' there are just too many fucking vampires in L.A.!"

"You're telling me," I responded. James called a taxi. I offered to drive him home but he seemed to want to get away from me. I could not blame him. James promised that he would never discuss the undead with anyone besides me, Lolly and Alan. After he left I went upstairs and collapsed on my bed. I was starting to keep vampire hours.

At the Magus' mansion on the coast near Paradise Cove, a team of the most trusted Shorts were treating the Baron's wounded body. A world-renowned hematologist had been flown in from the Mayo Clinic. Also, a neck surgeon from Harvard Medical school. The Magus' generous support of research had given him access to brilliant medical experts who promised to ask few questions and tell no one about their special patient. All they were told was that a member of some royal family had been hurt in a fight with his wife's lover. Public knowledge was to be avoided at all costs.

Tristan's rare HH blood type could be explained by Eastern European royal inbreeding. The baron remained unconscious due to sedation during the neck surgery. Little did the medical staff know that he was being given a transfusion of blood that was enhanced by the undead elite. Lena, the Magus and Dr. Kyoto had each donated blood to him. No one had ever received the vital fluids of all these three ancient vampires at the same time. The medical staff were amazed at the improvement in his vital signs and blood work in just a few hours, and would be flown home that evening as Tristan would be out of crisis. They were carefully searched as they departed to be sure no samples of the Baron's unique blood type were being taken for research. He would be faithfully cared for by Dr. Kyoto, Lady Lily and the Magus' staff. I would not be allowed to see him until his neck had healed. Lena sent word that it would not be right for me to see the Baron in a weakened state. The time apart would be used by the visiting Haute Caste to educate me.

I had passed Vampires 101, now it was time for some graduate classes.

CHAPTER 20

IT WAS ABOUT 6 p.m. when I woke up. The mansion was eerily quiet. I splashed cool water on my face to shock my brain into functioning. I checked my phone; there was a message from Lolly that they were home safe and that James had decided to close his practice so he could leave town ASAP. I felt like I had so much to explain and so much to ask at the same time. I now knew vampires could be destroyed if they were permanently decapitated. Apparently, the Haute Caste had tough necks. It was also apparent that Harold resented me, a lot, enough to literally stick his neck out to preserve vampire purity. This logical sequence was taking my mind to a place it did not want to go. I needed to talk with Dr. Kyoto or Lady Lily about the lab tests. I put on a white tailored shirt with my jeans, hoping to look a little more stylish when I faced my old boyfriend. Somehow that still mattered. I was famished. When I got to the kitchen, Tillie was waiting for me.

"I've made some waffles with fresh blueberries, Baroness," she said, handing me the queen's mug. "Would you like an omelet as well and maybe some orange juice?"

"Sure, thanks. It all sounds good," I replied. "Did Clive and Jasper get back okay?"

"Yes, Baroness. They are still sleeping. Thank you for asking," she said while putting the food on the table.

"They were something else last night. I am grateful to them."

Tillie smiled. "I heard you were too, Baroness, if you don't mind me saying."

"Could you ask Lady Lily to meet with me when she gets up?" I asked.

"I believe she stayed at the Magus' mansion last night. Are you all right?" she looked concerned.

"Yes, thanks. I just want to know about Tristan's condition," I responded, which was true but I did have other questions for her.

"Clive told me it might be a week or two," Tillie said and excused herself as though worried she might say too much.

The coffee was the new blend Tristan ordered for me. It did not have the punch of Sumatran but I would drink it until he got back. Maybe keeping us apart right now made sense as our conversations could get pretty intense. I didn't want answers from anyone but my husband, but I would not wait a week to find out more about my position in the grand vampire scheme of things. Once you go down the rabbit hole, there is no turning back. This rabbit hole was quickly becoming a mine shaft.

I was surrounded by brilliant, lethal, somewhat sociopathic egomaniacs with unlimited resources who considered me a novelty. They also seemed concerned about the approval of their peers, especially the Magus and Lady Hauser. As Baroness, it seemed they might even want to curry favor with me. That was my leverage within this, dare I say it, cutthroat community. I also wanted an apology, or at least an explanation from Jorge. Apparently, he was a sir or something grandiose but I was not sure I would ever be so formal with him.

I was antsy and decided to explore the grounds of my new home while I waited for the undead to rise. I needed to distract my brain from the gore of last night. I wandered down a hallway past the library. I saw some double doors where Clive would go out with Delilah. I went through the doors and noticed a garden path to a large building and wondered if there might be an indoor pool. I could never have imagined what I found there. It was a half court ice hockey rink! The ice was beautifully maintained as though ready for a game. There was even a Zamboni parked to the side. Banners of the Blackhawks, Chicago Wolves and Maple Leafs hung on the walls. Ice hockey gear was neatly placed in lockers with the players' names. The first of course said Mordecai, then Diego, Venturelli and Lockporte.

"Want to play?" Sir Diego asked from the door, startling me.

"Ice hockey?" I asked with disbelief.

"I suppose the Baron didn't have time to show this to you yet," Sir Diego responded. "He plays well. It's all part of his plans for you. It's because he knows your parents like hockey. You have no idea the lengths he has gone through to accommodate you."

"Like having you pretend to like me?" I had to ask.

"Dear Miranda, I do like you," he smiled, "and especially impressed after seeing you in action last night. But, Tristan chose me to look after you at UCLA for two very good reasons, because he trusts me and because I'm gay."

I sat down on a bench and started to laugh. "I guess vampires are just like Shorts, the good ones are either crazy, taken or gay."

He smiled and said, "Two out of three," and sat beside me. I still liked being around him, whoever or whatever he was.

"I've missed you, Jorge," I smiled. "Why ice hockey?" I asked.

"He knows Americans bond over sports. Your parents are Cub's fans but baseball is too slow a sport for him to even pretend to be interested by it."

"You got your intel wrong. My mom is a White Sox fan," I smiled and added, "Besides, most baseball games are played in the sun, so I guess that would be a problem."

"Tristan likes football too but he needs a sport that had only indoor night games. Basketball was just not physical enough to keep his attention. Ice hockey has just enough skill and violence. He has been worried about your family's re-action to him. He wants to win them over to make you happy."

"All this is to impress my parents?" I asked. "I think being a billionaire baron is enough."

"It also helped us get by during those long winter vigils in the frozen tundra of Illinois. I will never forgive your parents for living in Rossville," he sighed.

"You were there too?" I asked, still surprised by the Haute Caste's unde-tected surveillance for so many years. I stood and picked up a hockey stick and puck. I hit it as hard as I could. It bounced off a side of the rink.

"As little as possible. I wore a fake beard and pretended to shop for antiques at the one shop that had evening hours near your parent's café. It was painful. If it's not 500 years old, it's hardly an antique," he complained. "But I was able to keep up on the gossip."

"I should be pissed off that you pretended to be attracted to me," I pouted.

"But you're the only Short that I adore," he smiled. "Forgive me?"

"Never." I responded, trying to sound stern, and sent another puck flying into a trash can. "I think that should count."

"You and the Baron deserve each other," he smiled.

"I agree," Sergio said from the doorway, yawning. "You're making enough noise to wake the undead. Shall we play?"

"Not without Sarah," Sir Diego replied.

"Sarah?" I asked.

"Lady Lockeporte," Sergio responded "She suggested ice hockey to the Baron. She's from Toronto. She's better than the rest of us, so we made her the goalie."

"You're afraid of a girl," I laughed.

"A Canadian vampiress with a hockey stick? Absolutely," Sergio responded as he entered the rink. Sir Diego threw a hockey puck at his head but Sergio caught it easily. His powers were increasing by the night. "Clive asked me to announce that dinner will be served at 8."

"Thanks, but I just ate," I responded. "Any news about the Baron?"

"He is responding well to treatment as expected, Baroness," Sergio answered.

"Even if you just have soup, it's important you attend. We dress for dinner," Sir Diego stated looking down at my blue jeans.

"All right. I'll change, fuckers," I laughed.

"That's Sir Fucker," Sir Diego responded, "and only you can call me that."

"Thanks, but I'll save that title for my husband." I headed for my room. "Ice hockey, unbelievable," I muttered. Tristan probably knew that my family had gone to Wolves' games every year. We could not afford the Blackhawks' tickets. I imagined that he already planned to take my parents to a Blackhawks' game. That would win my dad over. It would take more to win over my mother. He might have to at least attend a midnight mass. That would be amusing. I stood in the middle of my room trying to absorb everything that was happening. I was still having a hard time getting my head around my new life. I picked out a lavender lace blouse with delicate shell buttons and a gray skirt. When I entered the dining room I was surprised to find most of the elite vampires present. The grand chandelier added flattering light to the room. Sir Sudovian in his banker's suit chatted with Lady Kananga in her ornate African robes. Momand wore a tan suit and sat quietly beside her. I started to sit at the head of the table but Jasper showed me to a seat by Sir Diego, who was impeccably dressed in a gray Italian suit. Even Sergio wore a brown sport coat and tie. He appeared to be having an animated discussion about ice hockey with Lady Lockporte. She wore a black cocktail dress with tiny caviar beads sewn about the low-cut neckline. Clive entered with a large tray of silver goblets and placed them at everyone's place but mine. Tillie followed behind him with a large bowl of French onion soup for me.

"The Magus," Clive announced from the doorway. Everyone stood but me. I decided to test the strength of my position. They ignored my rebellious, rude act. Sometimes rude is all you've got. The Magus wore a dark blue suit and matching tailored shirt with a small red geometric pattern. His hair was slicked back almost like a Mafia godfather. He glanced over at me and I thought I saw a little amused smile, then he took his seat and gestured for all to be seated.

"Good evening to you all," he said looking around the table. "We were successful last night in ridding our civilization of unworthy members. Unfortunately, as you know, Baron Mordecai was injured protecting us. He is responding well to treatment and would like his beloved wife to know he will see her in several days."

"Good news," Sir Sudovian and Momand said almost in unison.

"Lady Hauser, Dr. Kyoto and Lady Lily wanted to be with us this evening," he continued, "but felt it more important to stay at the Baron's side."

"I should be at the Baron's side!" Everyone tried to ignore my comment.

The Magus smiled. "He knew you would say that. He asked me to tell you that he will heal more quickly without being distracted by your charms."

"He would say that," I responded a little tearful "Damn it." The Magus looked amused, which caused similar responses from the others.

"I would like to have a toast to the loyal warm-blooded servants who so bravely assisted us last night," the Magus held up his goblet. The others joined in and I held up a crystal glass of water. "To Clive and Jasper, you have our deepest respect and thanks."

Clive and Jasper looked very uncomfortable with the high praise they were receiving. The Magus pulled a small box out of his pocket. Inside were two gold rings adorned with large sapphires. He gave the rings to Sir Sudovian, who handed them to Clive and Jasper with a slight bow. It looked like Jasper was tearing up a little.

"We desire to properly welcome the Baroness Miranda Mordecai into our family. Also, we wish to commend her for her courage, use of a dagger and a certain *sang froid*. The Baron has wisely chosen you to be his wife," the Magus stated.

Murmurs of approval could be heard from the vampire elite. Sir Diego whispered, "His words will cause your actions to become legend by the time the news is spread."

"Yeah, but you saved my ass last night," I whispered back.

The Magus began to drink his supper and the others joined in. I ate my onion soup. It was delicious. I somehow was starting to feel at home with this bizarre group. Maybe being around Sir Diego again helped.

After several minutes, Lady Kananga spoke up. "To properly welcome you, each of the Houses would like to present you with a wedding gift." She removed a golden cuff from her wrist and handed it to me. It was a regal lion's head with green tsavorite eyes and a diamond encrusted mane. I placed it on my wrist immediately. "It's exquisite!"

"From the Amazon," Sir Diego gestured towards the door. Clive wheeled in a very large ornate cage with two Toucans with brightly colored feathers.

"They're beautiful, but what about Delilah?" I asked

"They've already met," he smiled. "She has learned to leave them alone."

"From Sir Sadeghi and the House of Swords," Momand passed a gift wrapped in red silk and tied with a silver cord. I removed the cloth to reveal a rather large dagger with a gold handle. There was an eye decorated with emeralds, rubies and sapphires at the base of the handle. "Wow!" I gasped. Momand looked pleased.

"From the House of Plows," Lady Lockporte said. Tillie entered carrying two silver goblets trimmed in gold with bird's-eye blue turquoise stones and opals. The letters 'T' and 'M' were engraved on them.

"Dr. Kyoto and the House of Cups sent this over for you," Lady Kananga said. Clive presented me with a delicately carved, 12-inch red jade dragon on a gold stand.

"From the House of Pentacles." Sir Sudovian handed me a small silver box with golden hinges and a blue sapphire moon on the lid. Inside I found my ruby pendant which now had an ornate diamond studded clasp.

"I can't believe it! My pendant!" I exclaimed.

Sir Diego whispered, "He stayed behind to find it for you himself. It has a new clasp."

I asked Sergio to fasten it for me. "I thank you all for these amazing gifts. I just wish that Tristan could have been here."

"In a way he was," Sir Diego said and pointed to a camera in a corner of the ceiling "Live feed."

"Tristan! I miss you!" I called out and then saw the blinking camera light stop.

"I think that is about all the excitement he could handle at the moment" Sergio said.

Lady Kananga and Momand excused themselves, stating they had to begin the first leg of their night flights home, which would take them to New York. I imagined they were looking forward to a little time together in the Big Apple before returning to their respective realms. Sir Sudovian also said he must begin his travels home. I overheard him talking to Sergio.

"I must choose a new knight. If you are interested in the position let me know soon."

"I appreciate the honor, Sir Sudovian. I must discuss this matter with Lady Hauser," Sergio responded.

The Magus rose, nodded to the assembly and left the room without a further word or waiting for anyone to respond. Most of the members of the Haute Caste respectfully said their goodbyes to me and took their leave. Sir Diego and Lady Lockporte stayed behind. I asked Clive and Jasper to take the gifts to my room except for the Toucans, which were moved to the informal dining area off the kitchen. I started to follow them when Sir Diego stopped me.

"The Magus wishes to speak with you in the library," he said in a serious tone. Sir Diego and Lady Lockporte walked with me toward the library in silence. When we entered I was directed to sit on the couch. I was afraid it would be about my husband, something that the others should not know. I was afraid it might be bad news.

The Magus sat across from me in a stuffed chair. The others then seated themselves. "My dear Baroness," the Magus began, "I have great news for you. The Baron's rate of recovery is amazing. Though I am more excited to tell you that against all odds, to our delight, you are with child." He looked like someone had just given him the best birthday present ever.

"That's not possible," I uttered and my hands went to my tummy. "You're saying I'm pregnant?"

"May I?" Lady Lockporte asked the Magus. He nodded. "Until now we would have agreed. A vampiress is unable to conceive and no male has ever fathered a child. Dr. Kyoto theorized that a warm-blooded female with HH blood who had been exposed to a vampire's blood might be compatible enough for a pregnancy to take place."

"My life is just some damn experiment to you! What is wrong with you?" When I raised my voice to the Magus the others seemed quite uneasy and glanced at the Magus, who showed no reaction. Sir Diego lightly touched my arm but I jerked it away from him.

"Fate has led you to this moment" The Magus replied calmly. "The blood the Baron provided to save your life when you were a child was the event that made this possible."

"But my baby, it might be..." I became tearful. Lady Lockporte moved closer and handed me a black lace handkerchief.

"A vampire?" Sir Diego finished my question "No, dear Miranda, that gift requires a transformation."

"My baby will be normal?" I asked the Magus.

"Hopefully much more intelligent and gifted than that," the Magus said with a smile. The others relaxed a little.

"But this is the first. I mean, you don't have a clue about how the child will be effected." There was an uncomfortable silence. "Tristan knows about me being pregnant?" I asked.

"Yes," Lady Lockporte responded, "and he is very happy about it."

"The medical office set up by the kitchen was originally set up for your pregnancy," the Magus explained.

"The coffee, it's decaf!" I exclaimed.

"The Baron has been concerned about how caffeine might effect the baby," Lady Lockporte responded somewhat amused. "He didn't consider how lack of it might have effected you."

"I never thought to use birth control. He's ancient, how could his semen be fertile? One night together and I got pregnant! Unbelievable! That's why Lady Lily did the blood test last night!"

"The Baron thought he detected a difference in your scent," Lady Lockporte said. "If we can do anything for you, just ask."

"Indeed," the Magus added. "Dr. Kyoto and Lady Lily will attend to your medical needs as soon as the Baron returns home. If you have any questions or problems now, Lady Lockporte will be glad to assist you. Good night Baroness Mordecai." He stood and walked out of the room without another word. He knew I had a million questions that he was not ready to answer. I watched him walk out somewhat dumbfounded.

"What an arrogant prick," I said and no one corrected me. "I'd like to be alone."

"Of course," Sir Diego responded and they quietly left. Despite their powers, no one wanted to argue with a Baroness, much less a pregnant one.

CHAPTER 21

I SAT IN the library alone, staring at Van Gogh's self-portrait. He was the poster child for inner turmoil. His painting reflected his great difficulty coping with the insanity of being. I had to cope. I was bringing a baby into this world. The painting also reminded me of the beauty that can come from painful difficulties. A new life was coming into my unpredictable existence. I could only hope the child would bring out the more human side of the undead. Though I had disrespected the Magus at dinner, honestly, I was in awe of his knowledge and power. I feared bringing my baby into this hidden, violent culture of intrigue ruled by an archaic caste system. What if I was considered a disloyal Short? Would I lose my head after my child was born? I believed my husband truly loved me. It would not be wise to put him in a position to choose between me and the Magus. I could try to be polite to the head of the nocturnal world as long as my child was safe. How would I introduce my undead family to my Rossville family? When my husband returned, we would discuss how to let my parents know about the wedding and the baby. Perhaps I could explain that we eloped because of an unplanned pregnancy. My mother would accept that explanation. My father would want assurance that I was happy and well-treated. My brain needed a break from stress. I was almost as worried about my parent's reaction to my wedding and pregnancy than I was about living in a house full of vampires. I took a few long, slow, deep breaths.

The Magus returned to his mansion on a cliff above Paradise Cove. He went straight to the room where the Baron was recuperating. Lady Hauser sat beside the Louis the XIV bed where the Baron was hooked up to vital sign monitors. His head was propped up on goose down pillows. The bedding was light blue silk with tiny silver birds embroidered on the edges. His neck was still heavily bandaged. His skin was paler than usual and more translucent. The veins in his arms were more visible. A bag of red IV fluid hung on a pole beside the bed. The medical equipment looked out of place in the opulent setting. Lady Lily sat in a corner of the room in case she might be needed. She knew better than to try and engage Lady Hauser in conversation. When the Magus arrived, Lady Hauser excused her.

"How is Tristan?" the Magus inquired, resting his hand on her shoulder.

"He can tell you himself," she replied with a smile. "Dr. Kyoto has decreased the sedation."

"Better," Tristan replied in a soft voice. "Much less pain. I watched my wife receive the presents."

"Splendid. You are healing well," the Magus stated.

"Dr. Kyoto believes that the serum he produced when our bloods were combined is rapidly improving Tristan's cellular health. He believes his stamina, strength, speed and self-healing ability will be better than before," Lady Hauser explained.

"Thank you," the Baron responded weakly. "How did Miranda take the news?"

"She is amazing. She has let me know that she will be an overprotective mother," he said with a look of amusement. "I don't know if you saw it on camera but she did not stand when I entered the room. Also, her temper flared when she found out about the pregnancy."

"She is rude," Lady Hauser responded indignantly. "She should be honored and have shown the Magus proper respect."

"She is American. They have no sense of their place in society," the Magus corrected her. "I don't want to encourage her behavior but it was amusing."

"She is Miranda," the Baron said. "She will surprise us at every turn," he managed a smile.

"Perhaps you are right," the Magus responded. "Her closest friends are aware now. Perhaps it will be good for her to have someone to confide in. Hopefully her friends will be discrete."

"You believe that we can trust them?" Lady Hauser asked the Baron.

"The doctor, without doubt. His fiancé? I'm not sure but then who would believe her?" the Baron answered.

"Yes, indeed," the Magus replied. "I will let you rest now. You will need all your new-found strength to heal your wounds."

The Magus walked down the hall and entered a large room that looked like a hospital laboratory. Dr. Kyoto was looking at a computer screen that was set up at the end of a long stainless-steel table covered in medical research equipment. Lady Lily was assisting him.

"Good evening, Dr. Kyoto," the Magus said.

"Magus," the doctor bowed respectfully "The blood results are fascinating."

"Yes. Lady Hauser told us the Baron's powers have increased."

"Not the Baron, the Baroness," he said with a smile. It was a rare moment for the doctor. He actually thought he possessed knowledge of Miranda of which the Magus was unaware. "Her blood work is not normal either for the warm-blooded or our kind. Apparently, the blood transfusion she received as a child was very compatible with her HH blood. I noticed how comfortable she was around us when I first met her. I was surprised by the accuracy of her use of a dagger against Harold but now I know why. It also explains how healthy she was growing up. She is a sort of hybrid. It is why she became pregnant so easily. We thought that the baby she carries would be the first to have a dual nature but the Baroness seems like she already does."

"That explains her strength on many levels," the Magus responded. "Yet she walks in sunlight and prefers vegetarian meals. What does this mean for the baby?"

"May I?" Lady Lily asked.

"Please," Dr. Kyoto replied.

"The Baroness," Lady Lily began, "I believe is quite fertile. The Baron is also quite healthy in this regard. What I can gather from the medical tests and my research is that there is a great likelihood of multiple births."

"Twins?" the Magus asked.

"Probably," Lady Lily responded. "We also hypothesize the children will be, in a manner of speaking, greater than the sum of their parts in ways we can't yet calculate."

"This is wonderful news. I will inform Lady Hauser and the Baron. I do not want anyone else to know of your findings yet. I shall let the Baron explain this to the Baroness. You are free to answer any questions the Baron may have," the Magus instructed. "Splendid work." He bowed ever so slightly to Dr. Kyoto and hurried off.

I had fallen asleep about three in the morning and slept until 11 a.m. When I woke up there was a text message from Lolly saying that I was invited for lunch. I replied that I would be there. I needed to see my old friends and get away from my golden cage for a while. I put on a UCLA T-shirt, jeans and my high-top sneakers. A small bit of my former self. When I went downstairs I found Tillie, Clive and Jasper having lunch.

"I'd like to run over to Lolly and Alan's for a few hours. Don't get up, I can drive myself."

"Beg your pardon, Baroness," Jasper responded, "but if you went out alone I would lose my job."

"OK, you drive." I did not want to cause any problems for the staff.

We took the Bentley. I was starting to get used to luxury. I remembered the first time I had ridden in this car with Tristan. He smelled so good and looked so much at home leaning against the leather seats. I wished he was with me now. I felt his absence like a wound that would not heal. I rested my hands on my belly. He would return soon.

When Lolly opened her door we both yelled, hugged and started crying. James and Al were just standing back looking at us awkwardly. Al disappeared for a moment and returned with a box of Kleenex. Good thing we had a psychiatrist present. Somehow our tears turned into laughter.

"Damn it, Miranda, I should have put on waterproof mascara," Lolly laughed grabbing some tissue. "You're sure you're okay?"

"I don't think okay exactly covers it," I smiled.

"We've all been through a lot," James said. "Hello Miranda." To my surprise he gave me a hug.

Al ushered us into the dining room. They had several trays of assorted sushi, bowls of rice and cucumber salad. I loaded my plate with futomaki rolls and started in. Al served as host, pouring cups of green tea. At last my brain was getting a little caffeine.

"You look okay, James." I turned to Lolly. "He was really beat up."

"Just a few scrapes and bruises. I'll be fine," he replied.

"I can't imagine what it was like being abducted by her," Al responded. There was a shadow on his face for a moment as though recalling Simone's attack. "But we are all safe now."

"But changed. Knowing about them, believing in them, it alters us," I said.

"It's why I'm leaving," James stated in earnest. "I'll stay in touch but I'm leaving. I want to go back home where I hope I'll never run into one again."

"It's funny, it's like we are afraid to say 'vampire' out loud," Lolly commented, "even when it's just us."

"I guess we're a little paranoid now," James responded.

"How is the Baron?" Al asked.

"Recovering. He's in a private intensive care set-up. I'm not allowed to see him until he gets his strength back. Vampires are very proud and hate to show any weakness. He should be home in a few days," I replied.

"I'm so sorry," Lolly responded. "James said he was injured. I didn't realize how serious it was."

"I'd like to speak with him when he has recovered," Al added. "I just have some questions about the lingering effects from the transfusion."

"Sure, we'll have you over for dinner," I replied.

"Or maybe a Bloody Mary," James quipped.

"Nice," I responded with a laugh. The others chuckled and we all started to relax. "It's certainly an alternative lifestyle that takes…"

"Lifestyle?" James questioned.

"Fuck you!" We started laughing. "If it had been possible, I would have kept all of you out of their world. Without my knowledge, vampires have been looking after me since I was born because of my family blood lines. I'm HH."

"I've never heard of that blood type," James said.

"It is extremely rare," Al responded.

"It's a funny thing about having a similar blood type to vampires, it makes you compatible. I'm pregnant," I said calmly and emptied my cup of tea.

"Tristan?" Lolly asked and looked at James.

"It wasn't me," James sighed.

"Mazel tov!" Al started filling our cups.

"Because it wasn't me?" James asked.

We all started laughing at the bizarre moment we were sharing.

"Thank you. You are the best friends a woman in my freakin' weird situation could hope for." Then I added, "Also, though you were kind enough not to ask, I can tell you the baby will be like us. It will have our appetite."

"Thank God!" Lolly exclaimed. Her honest response incited even more laughter.

"Crazy as this might sound," James began, "I would like to be the child's godfather."

Tears came to my eyes. "That is so sweet of you. Thanks."

We talked for another hour about our experiences with the undead. It felt good to have normal people I could open up to. I had no doubt James would stay in touch with the three of us.

"We should call ourselves the F.O.V., Friends of Vampires," Al announced.

His comment was met with total silence. The rest of us looked at him like he was crazy.

"Okay, maybe not."

"It's time I get going. I still have some packing to do and arrangements to make," James said.

I walked him to the door. "I treasure your friendship. I'm really glad you want to stay in touch. I'll talk to Tristan about the godfather offer."

Before he walked away he said, "I think you and the baby might need some regular people who understand in your lives. It's funny but because of my drinking problem, I know about how difficult keeping secrets and fearing people's reactions can be. Maybe that's why I came over today." I watched him walk out the door and felt a little sad.

Lolly put her arm about my shoulder, "I can't believe you told me to read Dracula."

Sir Sudovian was in a foul mood on the flight back to London. He lay in the bed in the rear section of his private jet. The House of Pentacles would be under close scrutiny by the Magus. "Damn Harold! Damn Simone!" he exclaimed. He hoped Sergio would agree to be his knight. Though he was inexperienced, he was favored by Lady Lena. Sir Sudovian wanted to please her at all costs. He considered giving another vampire, Johann, the job on a temporary basis. He was a bit of a dimwit but it would never do for the Head of the House of Pentacles to have to wait on himself. If he never traveled to L.A. again it would be too soon. He was not favorably impressed with the Baron's choice in a wife, though she did have courage. She did not rise for the Magus. That was inexcusable. He had difficulty seeing a Short lauded by the Haute Caste but dared not draw anymore suspicion upon himself. He settled into his black satin sheets and drifted off thinking about the night when the House of Pentacles would once more be the envy of the vampire world.

CHAPTER 22

WHEN I ARRIVED home, Clive informed me that I could make the funeral arrangements for Bram. I supposed that my husband would not want to be involved, even if he were well. Vampires may cause funerals but avoid attending them. I was able to arrange for a burial on short notice in the Westwood Village Cemetery, close to UCLA. It seems if you throw enough money around just about anything can be arranged quickly. I requested the best casket, which probably helped. His box of ashes would be placed inside. I decided to put Dr. Bram Bishop on the gravestone and make up some birth/death dates. He would always be my old professor. The funeral would take place tomorrow morning. I considered inviting Lolly but then I might have to explain who he really was. She had been through enough lately. I decided to attend his burial by myself. There was noise in the house as the guests began rising. I went down to the kitchen for coffee and hoping for some of Tillie's scones and jam.

"Good evening, Baroness," Tillie said. "I've got some baby mozzarella with fresh basil and tomato slices for you as an appetizer." She also put out some fresh berries, a bowl of roasted almonds and a baguette. "You must eat well now," she smiled. "I'm making vegetable lasagna for dinner if there is anything else you would like?"

"Beats canned chili, thanks Tillie," I replied.

"As I remember, you were never very particular when it came to food as long as it didn't have eyes," Sir Diego stated from the doorway of the kitchen and yawned.

"My funds were limited," I replied.

"Korean tofu tacos? The smell was an abomination," Sir Franco said as he walked into the kitchen past Sir Diego. He wore a gray silk shirt and skinny black jeans.

"Franco! You're one too?" I exclaimed.

"Happily, no longer disguised as a UCLA Bruin. That was painful," he smiled and gave me a hug. "I'm with Sir Diego. I'm the knight of the House of Arrows."

"Very close knight," Sir Diego responded. "We've been together a couple of centuries."

"Who else at UCLA was in the coffin?" I laughed. At least I was fairly certain Lolly was not undead. I started to wonder about some of my night class professors.

"Really?" Sir Franco tried to look offended. "There is one other — Ruben, class reunion time!"

Sir Ruben walked in and ran his hand through his curly hair. His jeans and T-shirt were a bit wrinkled. He also looked like he could use a shave.

"Hi Miranda, I mean Baroness," he smiled. "You seemed interested in the crap they were teaching in Western Civilization."

"You always sat behind me when I took night classes! I thought it was weird that you never talked to me."

"That was Sir Diego's job. The Baron was very strict about who would be allowed contact. I was just keeping an eye on you," he smiled. "I'm Lady Lockporte's knight. She's my sister. We are of the House of Plows."

"Plows? No wonder your sister hung out in Rossville. I guess you didn't get the undead dress code."

"My sister would agree but I prefer more casual contemporary attire." He sat on a stool next to me. "Welcome to our world."

"Are you on the hockey team too?" I asked.

"No hockey puck is coming near this face," he smiled and sat on the kitchen counter.

"Might improve it," Lady Lockporte said as she entered the kitchen and leaned on the counter. She wore a navy blue silk, short-sleeve blouse and very tight indigo leggings with black boots.

"How is Tristan?" I asked.

"Remarkably well. The Magus, Lady Lena, and Sir Kyoto all donated blood to him. His response to their serum has been amazing. He may be coming home tomorrow night. They were able to remove the bandages," she replied. "He would be home now but Lady Hauser and Dr. Kyoto insist he rest one more night."

"I hate not being allowed to be with him," I responded.

She patted my hand and replied, "He will be home tomorrow."

"Thank you," I uttered, tearing up.

"I believe we should celebrate!" Sir Ruben exclaimed.

"Perhaps it would be good for the Baroness to be seen!" Sir Franco was looking at Sir Diego.

"Seen?" I asked.

"By the people who matter. At the Narcissus club in Venice Beach," Lady Lockporte responded.

"Do we have the Baron's permission?" Sergio asked. He had been standing in the doorway. Tension seemed to be building in the room. It felt like I was surrounded by caged animals.

"It's my executive decision," Sir Diego responded. "Lady Lockporte and Sergio, would you protect the honor of the Baroness this evening?"

"Of course," Lady Lockporte responded and Sergio nodded.

"What's the Narcissus Club?" I asked. "And do I want to go?"

"It's the reason vamps love L.A.," Sir Franco stated. "It's a nightclub where Shorts are not normally allowed. Lady Hauser made an exception with Sergio and now we will make an exception with you. The Magus owns the place."

"We must change," Lady Lockporte said. She glanced at her brother. "Even you."

"The Houses," Sir Diego began, "try to impress each other. Be sure and wear the ruby necklace. It will announce your status."

"Why is it called Narcissus?" I inquired.

Sir Ruben replied, "You'll see when we get there and I mean that literally."

Tillie set out cut crystal shot glasses filled with blood. They were quickly consumed. Then the guests dispersed to get ready for the evening.

"We'll leave about 10," Sir Franco said.

I sat quietly eating the dinner that Tillie had prepared for me. I never had a lot of friends and suddenly I was hanging with the cool kids, no pun intended. Lolly would love going to a new nightclub, but I would rather read a book. I decided to go to further my understanding of this other world and get my mind off my husband's recovery. I considered how Tristan had surrounded me with his undead cohorts without my knowledge. It was interesting how few he trusted. After the unfortunate encounters with Simone and Harold I could understand why. Yet, it now seemed like the threat had passed. I would be presented to the larger undead community tonight. How many vampires could there be in L.A...? I filled up on veggie lasagna and tried to focus on what I would wear instead of how much I missed my weird husband, and the pregnancy.

In my suite, I rummaged thru the armoire. I picked the outfit least likely to embarrass my entourage. It was a little black dress, black heels with cut-out toes and the pendant. Then I soaked in the tub. It was major primp time. I got on the com and asked Tillie to help me with my hair. She used a curling iron to give me long tendrils. I used all my makeup to try to look a little more sophisticated. As I was about to leave, I put on the bangle from Lady Kananga. Now I felt ready. I wished that Tristan would be there.

They were all waiting for me in the library. They looked amazing. Lady Lockporte wore a black satin halter dress and black diamond jewelry. Sir Diego wore a glistening dark gray suit and black shirt. Sir Franco's black suit was of a similar material and cut, with a gray shirt. Sir Ruben had on tight black leather jeans, a red silk shirt, and a bolo tie. Sergio wore a white tailored shirt, a black vest and tuxedo slacks.

"Lady Lockporte and Sergio will be at your side the whole night," Sir Diego told me. "The rest of us will take turns watching over you."

"Fine, whatever, I could use some fun," I responded. "I just planned a funeral."

"I'm sure the dead appreciated your efforts," Sir Franco quipped.

"Cooking shows and funerals just don't hold our interest," Sir Ruben added.

"I appreciate your concern for me but won't the others treat me like you all do?" I asked.

"Your scent is like the smell of a very rare and coveted wine," Sir Diego responded.

"They will crave a taste," Lady Lockporte added. "Here, it's coffee, Sumatran," she smiled. "They won't serve anything that you'll want." She handed me a small silver travel mug.

"Sumatran? Thanks!" I followed them out to the vehicles.

Lady Lockporte and I rode in the Spyder with Jasper driving the others in the limo. For some unknown reason, I trusted my vampires. Maybe because they had watched over me for years. The evening felt like the bachelorette party I never had.

"Are you okay? You've been through a lot in the last few days?"

"As long as Tristan will be fine, I can deal with it. Though I have to say I was not prepared to witness a beheading," I replied.

"Yes, that was crude. Normally, it would have been a guillotine," she said in a matter of fact tone.

"Guillotine?" I asked.

"I guess the Baron didn't tell you about our invention," she responded with a bit of pride. "The Magus gave the plans to Dr. Guillotine, who was allowed to take credit. It has been centuries since it was used. It was not possible to set one up on the beach that night."

"Wow," I replied. "I thought the guillotine was supposed to be a merciful way to execute people."

Lady Lockporte had a slight smile when she responded, "It was more for show. It made the lower cast quite nervous about crossing the Magus."

We pulled into a small, dimly lit parking lot by a two-story art deco building. There were no signs to indicate that it was a club. I will never forget the gathering inside. A man about 5 feet tall stood at the door. He had very short brown hair and a handle bar moustache. He was very muscular and wore a sleeveless T-shirt, jeans and a huge sapphire ring.

"Steve!" Sir Ruben called out as we approached the door.

"Long time no see Ruben!" They hugged.

As we came to the door, Sir Steve's demeanor changed. He bowed to Lady Lockporte and myself as we passed, then he bowed to Sir Diego. I looked back to see him high-five Sergio and Sir Franco.

"He is of our House, very accurate with knives," Lady Lockporte said.

The building had been gutted and turned into a ballroom. The walls were trimmed with elaborate art deco designs in gold. On the far wall was a large mural of the handsome Narcissus gazing into a pond to the dismay of his lover. A hundred small crystal balls hung like stars, lighting up the lapis blue ceiling. There were about 50 round tables on the sides of the dance floor. Each table had a small reflecting pool in the middle. In the center of the dance floor was a larger pool of water. I think there may have been 200 vampires dressed for a ball. The sound of jazz drifted through the room. The music stopped and the voices hushed as we were seated at two tables.

"I never imagined that there would be so many..." I uttered.

"They all know who you are," Lady Lockporte said. "Nod to them."

I did my best to give them a royal nod and smile of approval. The noise of whispered conversations and music returned. The table seemed to be bolted to the floor. "What is it with the tables and water?" I asked.

"Look into the water," Sergio said, "but don't breathe on the surface of the water."

I leaned forward and noticed my reflection. Lady Lockporte leaned forward and I saw her image as well!

"It is the only way we can see ourselves," Lady Lockporte explained.

The music changed to a waltz, not at all what I expected. There would be no dancing for me tonight. I took a sip of coffee, it was delicious. "Thanks for the Sumatran, I won't tell Tristan," I promised.

Graceful couples began gliding across the floor and they all took turns pausing by the large pool to admire themselves. A fair number discretely glided close to our table to get a better look at me. One tall blonde man dancing with a voluptuous redhead stared at me coldly.

"Who is that?" I asked Sergio.

"A Pentacle, his name is Johann. He is interested in Harold's position," he replied, "but it has been offered to me. I think that look was for my benefit."

"You're a Pentacle?" I asked Sergio.

"Yes. Simone transformed me, so there is an expected allegiance," he sighed.

"The proud House of Pentacles has been shamed by Harold and Simone. I'm surprised any of them showed up tonight," Lady Lockporte said, "present company excluded."

As the couples maneuvered close to our table, I had this sense that many of them sniffed in my direction. They were 20-something, beautiful people without tans. The dresses, heels and expensive suits were amazing. Each had a bit of drama and mystique to their look. All the Houses were represented. The music became international. A woman from the House of Cups appeared in a gorgeous glistening silver kimono and did a graceful dance with fans. Sir Diego and Sir Franco performed a tango. How could I have ever thought he held passion for me? What a great actor. Sir Ruben was sitting at the bar talking to a member of Lady Kananga's House. He brought Lady Kabedi over to the table for an introduction. She had graceful long limbs and her hair was braided with golden threads.

"It is an honor to meet you," she stated. "Lady Kananga will be pleased to know you are wearing the bracelet. She wanted me to tell you to push on the lion's head if you are threatened." Before I could ask what she meant, Sir Ruben pulled her onto the dance floor.

"They are a sweet couple," I said to Lady Lockporte. I looked at the bracelet, but did not press the head as I was not sure what would happen.

"She is the only member from another House my brother has been allowed to date," she noted my surprised look. "The Houses are very competitive. The Magus likes to keep it that way but, between you and me, that is changing. Lady Kananga and I are encouraging alliances between Houses. Though why an exquisite, brilliant vampiress like Lady Kabedi is interested in my brother I will never know." I laughed.

The Narcissus staff placed small plates with cubes of raw steak on each of the tables. Small three-prong silver forks were used to eat their only meal. "Angus, my favorite," Lady Lockporte said.

I watched Sergio devour a few pieces. It left a slightly red stain on his lips. He self-consciously dabbed them with a napkin.

"It's just very rare," he said.

"You won't believe this," Sir Ruben sat down with Lady Kabedi. "They are calling you Dorothy, you know like the drop-a-house-on-a-witch girl" he laughed.

"They are a bit afraid of you. Amazing!" Sir Franco added.

"Because," Sir Diego added, "they can't just dismiss you as a 'Short,' lines are being blurred. That is quite unsettling for vampires. To put it frankly, it's the thought of our prey fighting back."

"So, you're saying I freak-out the undead. Unbelievable."

We sat silently after that watching the dancers as I started to comprehend my unique status. Suddenly there was commotion at the entrance to the club. Sir Steve moved the dancers off the floor and signaled for the music to stop.

"This is a first," Sir Ruben said. "The Wizard of Oz has arrived."

The Magus walked out on the dance floor wearing a black suit with shimmering lapels and a black shirt. All the vampires stood and bowed slightly. I stood and bowed but only after Sir Diego gave me a nasty look. The Magus had two attendants following a few feet behind. He stood in the center of the room and held up his arms as though giving his blessing to the gathering. Then he walked over to our table. A red velvet stuffed chair appeared out of nowhere. After his highness was seated, the rest of us followed suit. The music resumed and the dancers returned to the floor.

"Lovely to see you, Baroness. The Baron will be joining you tomorrow evening. Ah, Lady Lockporte and Sir Diego, thank you for letting the Baroness experience our larger community. Splendid idea."

"They have been very kind and protective of me," I replied. Lady Lockporte gave me a look of appreciation.

"I would expect no less," the Magus replied. "Will you join me for a waltz?"

"I don't know how to waltz. I'm sure Lady…" I stopped as I felt Lady Lockporte elbow me. "Uh…I can try to follow your lead," I quickly added.

The Magus stood and once again the music fell silent. He took my hand and we walked onto the dance floor. We stopped by the gazing pool. The reflection showed an attractive, dark haired, young couple. It was strange because he felt so much older than me but looked so young. The vamps in the club stared in silence. The Magus raised his hand and *Greensleeves* started playing.

"Follow my lead," he said "We will step to the four corners of a box. Breathe, you will be fine."

I let his body guide my movement and, after a few missteps, I found myself able to glide back and forth in an invisible, moving box. The waltz was a beautiful, graceful response to the music.

"You learn quickly!"

I knew I was supposed to say something about what a good teacher he was but no compliment was forthcoming. I still had a lot of mixed feelings towards this ruler of the night. "Do your friends call you Gus?"

The Magus stared at me in disbelief and then started laughing. The vamps in the room seemed to lean forward to get a better look at this strange phenomenon. The Magus signaled with his hand and others began to join us on the dance floor.

"Even my intimate companions call me the Magus. No one has ever given me such a nickname." He appeared amused.

"But don't you have another name, like Abraham or Moses?" I was just pulling up old names I could think of at that moment.

"My name is not in religious writings," he almost laughed again. "Tristan said you were quite entertaining, he did not exaggerate. Perhaps one day I will tell you my birth name."

"So why are you here tonight?" I asked frankly.

"He also said you lacked tact. It was important to communicate to the Houses that you are under my protection," his tone was quite serious now. "After word gets out about our dance this evening, there will be no doubt that you are favored by me. They will not dare disrespect you in any manner. Tristan asked this favor of me, which I was delighted to fulfill."

"You are way too happy about my pregnancy," I replied. "But I thank you for your protection."

"You are welcome," he smiled. "I know you don't like me but I hope you will trust me."

"I don't think I have a choice, Gus," I said. He seemed amused by my response. We continued to dance until the music ended, then he walked me to the table.

"Good night Baroness, Lady Lockporte, Sir Diego," the Magus said with a nod as he took his leave. Everyone in the room stood and watched as he walked out followed by his entourage. Once Elvis had left the building the sounds of conversations again filled the room. The music started again and couples spilled out on the dance floor.

"Can we go soon?" I asked Sir Diego.

"Of course," he replied. "You must be exhausted after spending so much time with the Magus. He has that effect on all of us." As we all walked out the vampires watched us intently.

When we got in the car Lady Lockporte asked, "What did he say to you?"

"He told me his nickname was Gus," I replied.

"Unbelievable," she uttered.

CHAPTER 23

I WAS A little late getting to the small cemetery. The all-nighters were taking their toll. A dense marine layer made the world appropriately overcast and gray. Jasper and Clive accompanied me, though they stayed by the Bentley when I approached the burial site. My shoes sank into the damp grass. A couple of cemetery workers stood at a distance. I slowly approached this strange goodbye. I stood alone with the casket that held my old professor's ashes. I held a single red rose that I had taken from the mansion's garden. I felt sorrow for the man who had become caught up in the world of the undead. It was hard to accept how cruel my husband had been towards the writer who had betrayed him. Bram had deceived me too but he was a tortured soul. Would I meet a similar fate if the Baron thought I crossed that line, despite his love for me? The undead wanted me to trust them, but who could I really trust? Because of my knowledge of Bram's fate, I wondered how long it would be possible to safely walk between the worlds of mortals and immortals. The undead were just as fallible and prone to mistakes due to their emotions as Shorts. Except, of course, the Magus. He seemed to be unflappable, even when he was confronted by Simone and Harold's treachery. I wish that I had been able to spend more time with Bram. I had so many questions that only he could answer. I would now have to find the answers on my own. It was time to stop my mental meandering and face the task at hand.

"Goodbye, Professor Bishop. You taught me well. I forgive you." I placed the rose on his casket. I returned to the car and asked Jasper to take me to a bagel deli on Santa Monica Boulevard. When we arrived, I told them to wait for me outside. I was starting to feel a sense of what it meant to be a Baroness. I walked inside and saw my reason for coming.

"Hi Grigoryi." The surprised monk looked around to see who had accompanied me. "I just wanted to make sure you were okay."

"I'm good. One of your friends gave me enough money to get an apartment," he replied, "and the deli had an opening." He leaned over the counter and whispered, "Are you okay?"

"I am, thanks for asking." I saw his boss looking our way. "I'll take a dozen assorted bagels, a large container of jalapeño cream cheese and a small black coffee. Also, can you describe who gave you the money?"

As he put the bagels in a bag he said, "The guy in Arabian robes. He said it was because I tried to help you. I'll never judge anyone from the Middle East again. He gave me $5,000."

"You were brave," I replied. Somehow, I was not surprised by the identity of his benefactor.

"You were awesome, standing up to evil that way," he said and walked over to the register.

"We will keep that a secret," I smiled and handed him $50. "Keep the change."

"Thank you. I hope you come by again." He handed me the bag and coffee.

I was glad he was doing well. Funny how contact with a vampire could change the direction of your life. I sipped my precious cup of caffeine all the way back to Stone Canyon. Still, I felt ready for a nap when I got back. I gave the bagels to Tillie, greeted my birds and went upstairs to sleep. I had to rest up for a night with Tristan. I quickly fell into a deep sleep. It had been an emotionally exhausting morning.

In the evening Tillie woke me with a tray. "The Baron will be here soon," she informed me with a smile. I realized I had overslept and ran to the shower. Then I changed into a pair of black slacks and an ivory silk shirt with crystal buttons. I was starting to dress the part. Anticipation of being with my husband again filled my head and heart. I started to eat the veggie burger Tillie had made for me when a wave of nausea hit. I ran to the bathroom and started vomiting into the toilet.

"Miranda!" a familiar voice called to me. I turned my head to see my beloved in the doorway with a look of concern. "Morning sickness?"

"I don't..." the words were cut short with a new round of heaving. The Baron quickly came to my side and gently held my hair back. "I think I returned just in time."

When the nausea passed he helped me to my feet. "I'm so sorry, I should be looking after you," I uttered. Then I looked down at the stains on my shirt and tears began to flow. Tristan helped me out of my blouse and gave me a wet face cloth.

"I have missed you," he whispered and held me in his arms.

"Are you okay? I mean, really okay?" I reached up and touched the back of his neck. It felt smooth. When I looked, only the slightest trace of a scar could be seen. Tears began to fill my eyes.

"Better than you, it seems," he smiled.

"So much has happened. I found the hockey rink, I went to the Narcissus' Club and danced with the Magus and then I buried Bram..."

"And became pregnant," he added.

"Were you as surprised as me?"

"Yes. I knew it might be possible but did not expect that after just one night together. Dr. Kyoto said that you are particularly fertile."

"You think?" I had to laugh. "That was my first episode of nausea."

"You should drink something to help settle your stomach. Weak tea?"

I nodded. "And saltine crackers or a dry toasted bagel." I pulled a blue silk blouse from the armoire. "Let's go downstairs. I think your friends would like to see you."

"I told them to leave us alone tonight," he said. Tristan got on the intercom and asked Tillie to bring up a cure for morning sickness. "Let's go to my bedroom."

"That's what got me in this state in the first place," I retorted and grabbed a robe.

He took my hand and led the way to his suite. Delilah was laying at the foot of the bed. She raised her head to acknowledge me and yawned. I scratched the back of her ears like she was a house cat.

"Good Evening, Baron" Tillie said and placed a tray on the small table. "Will there be anything else?"

"No, thank you," Tristan dismissed her and she closed the doors as she left. I poured myself a cup of herbal tea and added a little sugar. It was soothing. There was dry toast, vegetable broth and Jell-O. "She must have been expecting this."

"Sit down." Tristan said and gestured to the bed. I positioned myself so that I was facing him.

"I'm better."

He took my hands tenderly. "I have good news but it might be upsetting."

"Just tell me." I could not imagine good news that could be more upsetting than what I had experienced that week.

"When I mentioned fertility, it was not just ease of becoming pregnant. The doctor and Lady Lily are fairly certain there will be twins." He felt my hands tense up. "You will have the best medical care."

"How could they know so early?" My mind was racing.

"It has to do with the medical tests Lady Lily did when you came back from Point Mugu. Your hormone levels, among other factors. They are fairly certain we should prepare for multiple births. There is something else," he paused. "Dr. Kyoto thinks you should start eating meat."

Tristan had only been back 15 minutes and I was already pissed off. "He probably suggested I eat it raw. Tell Dr. Kyoto to go to hell. I'll eat more beans, greens and tofu. I'll eat more dairy products and peanut butter sandwiches!"

"Calm down Miranda, it was just a suggestion," Tristan tried to hide a smile. "You are feeling better."

I walked over to the table and ate the dry toast. Then I finished the soup. I passed on the Jell-O. Growing up in the heartland I had eaten enough Jell-O to last a lifetime.

"I missed you but at this moment I don't know why!" I said and fell into his arms.

He laid me on my back and gently let his hand rest on my belly. His eyes had the look of desire and assurance that made me feel at peace. I realized that Tristan really loved me.

"I promise I'll do everything in my power to care for you and the children."

"They really think it will be twins?"

"Yes. Lady Lily told Tillie to have some food items on hand in case of nausea, she thinks you'll experience everything sooner than other pregnant women." he raised up on one arm. "It has been many years since the Magus has made an appearance at the club. You have no sense of what an honor, or what a message, that sent to the vampire world. I heard you danced well," he said with a bit of pride.

"Yeah, Gus and I are pals now," I responded, which caused Tristan's eyes to get big.

"Gus?" he said with disbelief.

"That's what I call him. In Illinois, everyone has a nickname. Like you might be called Stan," grinned. "He told me his name is Desmon Dontinae, so I did a Google search and that's just the scientific name for vampire bat, clever but not his real name."

"He's from Mesopotamia. Just stick with the Magus," Tristan warned. "He is fond of you but I wouldn't push it."

I snuggled into Tristan's embrace. It felt so good to be with him again. I loved his scent. His lips and hands began to unleash sensations of pleasure. We happily shed clothing and escaped into the realm of pleasure. As much as I was enjoying my husband, my mind at times recalled that the mouth providing exquisite kisses had also ripped into Simone's throat. I can't explain how I could hold all these thoughts and feelings at the same time and still have an orgasm, but I did. Temporarily, his overwhelming impact on my senses seemed to take over. My mind was finding a way to compartmentalize the loving Tristan from the violent avenger.

"I want a grilled cheese sandwich and some fresh mangoes," I uttered, suddenly sitting up in bed.

Tristan laughed. "I guess my work here is done. Now to feed you."

"And some steamed edamame," I added.

Tristan walked over to the intercom and placed my order. "Anything else?"

"We have to tell my parents." My husband appeared to cringe. "Are you actually afraid of my mother? How funny! C'mon, you have a panther for a pet."

"Delilah is reasonable," he replied. I threw a pillow at him. "Don't you fear Lena?"

"You have a point," I replied. "I think the Magus is more powerful but Lena looks on you as her only child."

"She never left my side while I was healing. It was a mixture of the blood of Lena, Kyoto and the Magus which caused me to recover so quickly. I am stronger now than before. I am only beginning to realize my new abilities."

"It is strange that your blood is the reason I survived as a child and that Al survived his attack when you consider that taking the blood of others is your main source of sustenance. They all gave their blood to you? Amazing!"

"They treat me differently than the others. Lena once said it is because I come from a mixture of noble and common blood, which has made me strong," he said. "Our children will be strong."

My hands touched my belly. "They will need to be."

"Can't contacting your parents wait until tomorrow night?"

"I suppose."

Just then Tillie knocked. I covered myself as she brought up another tray.

"Maybe we should have a little kitchen put in upstairs," I suggested.

"Baroness, I think that is a very good idea," she smiled and left with the other tray.

We spent the rest of the evening joking, talking about how to explain our marriage to my parents, discussing the Point Mugu crisis, giving him my perceptions of the vamps at the club and making love. I had a feeling this might be the most carefree we would ever be. It was also the night I decided Polly's fate. I fell asleep by his side at about four in the morning. He stayed up reading a book on pregnancy for a couple of hours. I found it lying next to him in bed when I got up in the early afternoon. For moment, I got a glimpse of how my life was effecting him. I might be struggling with the whole vampire lifestyle but he was equally anxious about my world. I tiptoed to my room and started making lists of names for the babies.

CHAPTER 24

JUST ABOUT SUNSET, I was sitting at the kitchen table eating a peanut butter and blueberry jam sandwich with a glass of milk when Sergio plopped down in a chair.

"I'll share," I joked.

"No thanks. I'm going to cut my vampire teeth tonight."

"To each his own," I replied. I could have asked for details, but honestly I did not want to know.

"Lena is mentoring me, it's quite an honor," he ignored my disinterest.

"I bet she has very sharp teeth," I responded.

Sergio laughed "It's good she didn't hear you say that. I want her to be in a good mood. Speaking of moody vamps, what is with the Baron? I have never seen him so nervous."

"He's up?"

"I just saw him in the library. He was pacing and barely acknowledged me."

"In-laws," I said. "We are going to call my parents tonight."

"That will be enough to send him out with me later," he replied. I kicked his ankle.

"Don't encourage the father of my children to go out on some bloodsucking field trip."

"Who is the target? Maybe I'll join you," Lady Lockporte asked. She sat down across the table from me. "Must be a worthwhile target if Lady Hauser has picked it." She looked at my sandwich. "That's disgusting."

"White supremacist who beat a migrant worker to death, got off on a technicality," Sergio said.

"He'll regret that," Lady Lockporte said. "I'll tag along."

"Would 'break a leg' be appropriate?" I inquired.

"Sure, thanks," Sergio responded.

"Excuse me, I'm going to soothe Tristan."

"Soothe?" Lady Lockporte questioned.

"He's going to talk to my parents tonight."

"This is a night of firsts," Lady Lockporte replied.

I found Tristan online in the library looking up Blackhawk scores and players from the last 20 years. I walked over, put my arm around his shoulders, and kissed his neck.

"Hey sweetie, it's Okay, you don't need to do this. You won't be quizzed about ice hockey."

"I want to seem as normal as possible," he replied.

I had to laugh. "Not a chance, Baron Mordecai."

"They will hate me!"

"All they will care about is that you love me, want the baby and that you're financially stable. Once they are assured of that, they will want you to like them," I explained. "I think we can hold off on telling them about twins."

"We won't have to visit Rossville. Will we?" He looked like a condemned prisoner expecting a harsh sentence.

"No. They will want to see where we live. We can invite them to come next month. It will take my mom weeks to prepare to fly out," I replied.

"How shall I address them?"

"Lord and Lady Ortega," I replied then started to laugh.

"You are not making this easier." He looked extremely anxious. His undead characteristics usually gave him an advantage with his opponents but not with my mother. "Shall we get this over with?" he asked.

"Just call them Connie and Pete," I grinned and dialed the number. "Hi mom."

"Randie, are you okay? Pete, Randie is on the phone. Wait a minute hon', I'll put you on speaker phone," she said loudly.

"Hi dad!"

"Hi Randie, how is your car holding up?" Asking about my car was one of the ways my dad expressed affection.

"It's fine. I've got some news for you." I decided not to beat around the bush. "I got married. My husband is here listening in," I added so my mom might filter herself a little.

My mom blurted out a series of rapid fire questions. "You're married? Who is it? Is it that Cuban? When did this happen?" Tristan's eyes got big. "How long has...."

"Connie, let Randie talk!" My dad demanded. "I guess we should say congratulations. Who is the lucky man?"

"Thanks, dad. He's my publisher, Baron Tristan Mordecai. I'm sorry you couldn't be at the wedding. It was all sort of sudden but we are very happy." I stopped to let my words sink in.

"Randie, I don't know what to say," my mother uttered. "Are you okay?"

"Yeah, I'm fine, except for a little morning sickness."

"That explains a lot," my mother responded.

Tristan looked like he wanted to crawl under the couch.

"What kind of name is that?" my mother blurted out.

"Lithuanian," I replied.

My dad took over, "I'm going to be a grandfather. That's great news! Is Baron a nickname?"

"No, dad, it's a title. He's really a Baron. His parents are deceased. He has lived here a long time. But don't worry, you can call him Stan," I added to my husband's horror.

"Hi Stan, welcome to the family," my mother said. "I wish we could have met in person." The last was clearly a barb directed at me.

"Good evening, Pete and Connie, I look forward to having you visit us soon," he said stiffly. "I will do everything possible to make your daughter happy." I gave him a thumb's up and waited for some response from my mother.

"I'm sorry we missed the wedding," my mother sniffled. I knew she would be a bit tearful. "I hope you'll send pictures," she said wistfully. "I guess you met at work?"

"Yes, Miranda is my favorite writer," he said.

"That's good," my mother responded. "You live in L.A.?"

"I moved into his mansion in Bel Air," I replied to give Tristan a break.

"Mom, remember how you used to say I needed a maid. Well, now I have one. Lolly and Al are really happy for us."

"A maid?" Her mood seemed to brighten.

"And a butler and a chauffeur. Tristan spoils me."

"You were already spoiled," my father joked. Tristan smiled slightly.

"When are you due?" my mother asked.

I had been expecting that question. "In about eight months. I'm feeling okay, except for a little morning nausea."

"The doctor urged her to eat meat," Tristan said. I jabbed him with my elbow.

"Thank God," my mother responded. "You sound sensible, Stan."

"I'm eating well. Stan got a present for you, season tickets for the Blackhawks." I was hoping to change the subject.

"Season tickets? That's too much," my father protested.

"Not at all," Tristan replied.

"We'll make your reservations to fly out, just let us know when you can come. Mom, we can go shopping with Lolly."

"That would be fun. Give her a hug for me," she replied. "I always thought she would marry first."

"Yeah, you never know how things will work out," I said.

"Try a little honey with peppermint tea to settle your tummy. I wish I could be there," she sighed.

"I know mom, me too! Just let us know when you can get away from the restaurant. Love you guys, talk soon," I nudged Tristan.

"Yes, it was very nice to talk with you. I am looking forward to meeting you both in person," Tristan said.

My parents said their goodbyes and I hung up, relieved it had gone so well. Applause erupted from the doorway to the library.

"Bravo, Stan!" Sir Diego joked.

"Thank goodness you didn't marry the Cuban!" Sir Franco added. Sergio, Sir Ruben and Lady Lockporte entered the room.

"I would not have missed that for the world. Tristan, for a second you actually looked scared," Lady Lockporte laughed.

"This does not leave this room! Do you understand?" the Baron stated loudly.

"No problem," Sergio looked at Sir Ruben. They both started cracking up.

"What a gathering," Lady Hauser said as she entered the room. No one spoke. They all politely nodded to acknowledge her arrival.

"Baron and Baroness, you are both well?"

"I'm fine," I said. "Thanks for taking such good care of Tristan." She sensed it was not easy for me to express my gratitude to her and smiled graciously. The Baron was pleased to see the two most important women in his life getting along.

"Come Sergio, you must prepare," Lady Hauser said.

"May I witness his coming of age?" Lady Lockporte asked.

"Of course," Lady Hauser responded.

Lady Hauser walked out of the library with Lady Lockporte and Sergio following behind.

"Any plans for tonight?" Sir Diego inquired.

"I'd love to kill a hockey puck," the Baron responded, "but we need a goalie."

"I could try..." I began.

"No!" my husband and Sir Diego said before I could finish.

"Don't look at me," Sir Franco pulled on the cuff of his shirt.

"How long will you be staying?" the Baron asked.

"Dear friends, we must head home tomorrow night. The Magus thanked us for our assistance and said we could leave at any time. We will return in a few months or sooner if requested."

"You are always most welcome," the Baron responded.

"*Mi casa es su casa*," I stated.

Sir Diego laughed, "Gracias."

"The Narcissus?" Sir Franco asked.

"Of course," Sir Diego responded.

"I think we shall wait here for news of Sergio," the Baron replied and looked at me. I nodded.

"You deferred to another besides the Magus and Lady Hauser. My stars! Miranda, you have bewitched my old friend," Sir Diego said as they left.

Sergio was taken to Lady Hauser's penthouse suite. Her butler, an old Russian gentleman, greeted him with new respect. He was shown to a bedroom where black clothing had been laid out for him. It was similar to the suit that Miranda had worn at Point Mugu.

"You think this is necessary?" Sergio asked.

"The first few times they may have a chance to utilize their weapons. Eventually the speed and skill of your strikes will be enough to prevent that," Lady Hauser replied.

"You are an assassin in training," Lady Lockporte added, and they left him to change.

The ladies stood on the balcony looking out on the lights along Santa Monica's coast. The butler brought them each a small silver cup of blood.

"Will Sergio be joining you, Lady Hauser?" he asked.

"Not tonight, Ivan, that will be all," she replied.

They knew Sergio would respond better to this test if he were thirsty. Lady Lockporte sensed the elder vampiress' concern regarding Sergio's ability. They spoke in hushed tones.

"Do you worry because he shares Simone's blood?"

"Yes. I have always had concerns about the Pentacles and Simone was a very poor specimen. Sir Sudovian must get his House in order," Lady Hauser replied.

"Sergio could be enriched by the blood of another House," Lady Lockporte responded. "I also think his strength of character will help him. He risked much to be with you."

"Yes, he did," she smiled. He walked up behind them. "Sergio, you are ready."

"I feel like Spider-Man," he said, looking at his new clothes.

"When you approach your target, you will find your body will begin to adjust to the task at hand." Lady Hauser put down her cup and walked back inside with him. The living room had two large sofas upholstered in gray silk. A painting of the Notre Dame cathedral in winter hung on the wall. Several small silver boxes encrusted with jewels were on a nearby coffee table. She indicated to Sergio to stop several feet away from her.

"You must keep eye contact. It will help you judge his next move and assess his emotional response. The second he looks away attack, because he is about to. I will demonstrate a classic technique." Without any warning, she moved on him in a mock attack. He tried to fend her off but in a second she deflected his arms and got her hand about his neck, then squeezed a pressure point that almost made him unconscious. Lena drew him close to her open mouth. Then let him go. He managed to stay on his feet.

"Okay. I can do that," Sergio said, feigning confidence.

With incredible speed Lady Lockporte picked up one of the boxes and threw it at Sergio's head. He caught it just before impact. "Watch it!"

"You also want to increase your peripheral awareness," Lady Lockporte smiled. "Your hockey playing will help you tonight."

"And my tennis arm," he added. "You are certain of his crime?"

Lady Hauser looked directly at Sergio. "Never question my judgment."

"He is a vicious wolf attacking lambs," Lady Lockporte stated.

"Forgive me," Sergio responded with downcast eyes. He could not help but think, "Are we the good wolves?"

Lady Hauser's chauffeur picked them up in a black Escalade in front of the building at midnight. They drove to Long Beach and turned onto a run-down street near the warehouse area. Only half of the streetlights were working and some of them just flickered.

"Park behind the blue SUV," Lady Hauser directed. The chauffeur parked, then put on gloves and walked over to the SUV. He produced a long, thin strip of metal, then slid it down the driver's window. With a quick motion, he unlocked the door and opened it just long enough to release the hood. He raised the car hood, disconnected some wires, then closed it. He returned to the Escalade and nodded to Lady Hauser.

"Now we wait," she instructed Sergio.

About one o'clock, a group wandered out of the bar wearing leather vests, some with shaved heads, and all with swastika tattoos and needing shaves. They were drunk and loud as they parted ways.

"He's wearing the red bandana; his name is Jed," Lady Hauser said. "Wait until he is alone. He is the only target."

Jed dropped his keys in drunken fashion as he got into the SUV. He was buzzed on alcohol and grandiose delusions. He had gotten away with murder. He waived as his friends drove by. They called out his name. He knew they feared and respected him now. He had noticed the Escalade as he got in his old car. Jed imagined getting a bigger piece of the meth trade and buying a car like that. He unsuccessfully tried to start his SUV, then tried again. "Piece of shit!" He banged his hand on the steering wheel, popped the hood and got out of the vehicle.

"Now!" Lady Hauser commanded.

Sergio got out of the Escalade, approached the SUV and stood several feet away from the man leaning over the engine. Jed was straining to see what was wrong in the dim light when he sensed he was not alone. He turned to see a man in some kind of wet suit staring at him.

"What's your problem?" he asked loudly.

"You," Sergio responded softly.

Jed stared at him and tried to think clearly. He looked away just as his hand slipped into a vest pocket for his .32 revolver. Sergio jumped him quickly and the gun went flying into the street. Sergio felt a strange sensation in his mouth. He picked up Jed by his neck and held the struggling, terrified man off the ground while he carried him into the shadows of the nearby alley. His hold on Jed's neck made it difficult to cry out.

"Never kill again and I will let you live," Sergio told him. "But first a taste." He threw the frightened man to the ground, then jumped on him, like a cat on a mouse. Sergio allowed Jed to see his fangs.

"Get the fuck…" Jed cried out but was silenced as Sergio's fangs pierced his neck. He blacked out for a few seconds. Sergio tasted the warm, salty fluid. It went down his throat like fine wine. He wanted more but pushed Jed away from him. He was not sure he could take a life. Sergio felt the rush as his body responded to Jed's blood. He forced himself to walk away. He realized his night vision was suddenly improving.

"Gutless wetback," Jed yelled as a knife went flying towards Sergio but was easily deflected by his protective clothing. Sergio turned and faced the man.

"You are a worthy target!" Sergio leaped on him and tore into Jed's neck. He died almost instantly. Sergio drank deeply then threw the body in a dumpster. As he turned towards the entrance to the alley he saw Lady Hauser staring at him with a satisfied smile.

"You passed the test, though your hesitation was noted. We must leave quickly."

"You were right about him," Sergio uttered as they got into the Escalade. He was instructed to sit on a piece of plastic sheeting while he removed his bloody garments. Lady Lockporte assisted with cleaning him up. Then the sheeting was deposited in a laundry bag while he put on clean clothes.

"How do you feel?" Lady Lockporte asked.

"Like a fully charged battery. All my senses, my capabilities seem stronger. It's an amazing rush. How long will it last?"

"Some of the enhancements will be permanent. The euphoria will fade over the next 24 hours but not your strength. With each fresh meal you will increase your powers," Lady Hauser replied. "We do not fully become vampires overnight."

"That is why you, the Haute Caste, are so extraordinary," Sergio exclaimed. "Now I'm beginning to understand. Your strength has come from thousands of …"

"Assassinations," Lady Lockporte interjected, "combined with HH blood."

"Our actions are precise, intentional and achieve multiple purposes. We protect the vulnerable members of society, eliminate some of the trash and increase our powers. An unsanctioned attack is not acceptable, unless it is to safeguard the Houses," Lady Hauser explained.

"Who chose my target?"

"The local Haute Caste," Lady Lockporte replied. "Which in your case is the very, very Haute Caste."

CHAPTER 25

WHILE WE WAITED to hear news of Sergio's big night out, Sir Ruben joined the Baron and me in the kitchen. I had managed to convince Tillie to get some sleep and allow me to fix my own dinner. I had groceries delivered to the house earlier. It was a strange sensation to know I could afford anything I wanted. My husband was amused by my vegetarian cooking.

"Even before my transformation I could not imagine a meal without meat," he said. "I hope you won't try to impose your unnatural diet on our children."

"My unnatural diet?"

Sir Ruben laughed. "Our diet precisely fulfills our nutritional needs and it's 100 percent natural. Unlike Shorts, our taste buds have evolved." He ran a hand through his curly hair and tugged on his black cotton T-shirt. "Any Angus in the fridge?" My husband nodded and Sir Ruben pulled out a bowl of dark red chunks.

"Can you eat that in the other room?" I asked, as seeing raw meat was starting to make me queasy.

"Sure, if you'll eat your tortured soy beans in here," he replied. "Poor things, never had a chance, torn from their bushes."

"Enough, I get the point, go enjoy your carcass elsewhere," I pointed to the dining room. Sir Ruben grabbed a fork and left.

"How long has Ruben been a vampire?"

"Two-hundred years. Lady Lockporte and her brother are among the youngest members of the Haute Caste. Despite his casual pretense, he honors his House with finely honed martial arts skills. Though I fear it will take at least another 100 years for his manners to improve. I blame the culture of North America."

"Yeah, Europeans were politely involved in genocide," I responded.

"The Nazis were warm-bloods," Tristan replied. "That period was one of the Parliament's biggest regrets. We took out many of the SS officers but it was not enough. It was difficult to stay in hiding, so we ended up going to England, Scandinavia and the U.S. during the war. We provided much intel, which helped the code breakers. We are proud of that but, we could not stop the millions who were murdered. In Rwanda, we were also sickened by the slaughter. Lady Kananga's House took out many of those who were slaughtering the innocent but there were not enough of us to stop it. The killing fields in Cambodia were another place where our efforts fell short." He paused, then added with a sigh, "We did what we could." I had turned off the stove and stood staring at my husband in disbelief.

"The Trail of Tears," Sir Ruben walked into the kitchen with an empty bowl. "We visited some of those responsible in Washington, D.C. but could not stop it."

"You are like Templar Knights," I uttered.

My husband had a slight smile "In a way, though I'm not sure Saint de Molay would agree."

"The sad thing, my dear vegetarian friend," Sir Ruben began, "is that we have too many worthy targets, or W.T.s as we like to call them. I never have to drink bagged blood, it's just that sometimes I like to take a little time off."

"I had no idea. I mean, I knew you picked people you did not approve of but I did not realize you see yourselves as global guardians of humanity."

"We hold ourselves to a very high standard and take the responsibility that comes with our gifts very seriously," the Baron responded. "That is what Sergio is learning about tonight."

"Don't you ever question if it is right to take a life?" I asked.

"We only take the lives of those who don't ask themselves that question, like the S.S. officers," the Baron responded. "We are the law for those who believe that they live above the law."

"I think Sarah is back. Time to critique Sergio's skills," Sir Ruben said. We went to the library. Sir Ruben and my husband began talking in low tones with Sergio who seemed quite animated. Lady Hauser sat in a velvet chair, watching the male vampires with a smile.

"Did everything go okay?" I asked, not sure how to appropriately ask about a vampire's first time.

"Yes. He is doing better than I expected. He was quick and decisive once he understood what was required. How are you feeling? Tristan mentioned you had some nausea."

"When I first get up but I've been eating fine."

"Dr. Kyoto will be by tomorrow night." Expressing concern seemed a bit of a stretch for her. Thankfully Lady Lockporte appeared in her hockey gear to get a game started.

"What are you doing? We only have about two hours left to play!"

Sir Ruben pulled out his phone. "Sir Diego and Sir Franco are on their way back."

"Splendid," the Baron was pleased. "I must get warmed up."

I went back to the kitchen and grabbed a carton of yogurt to eat during the game. When I got back to the hockey arena all the players were getting assembled. Lady Hauser had chosen to go home, which did not surprise me. It was Sir Diego and Sir Franco versus the Baron and Sergio. Sir Ruben was the referee. I did not envy his position. Lady Lockporte was protecting the goal. If no one was able to score, she would be the winner. My money was on her.

My husband hit the puck first and elbowed Sir Franco in the face. Chaos ensued as they began running into each other with great force. Sir Franco hit Sergio so hard he flew out of the rink and hit the wall of the building. Not even a Blackhawk player could have survived their blows. Sir Diego made the first goal attempt but Lady Lockporte caught the puck in her mouth! Then she threw it so hard it stuck in the wall. After some grumbling from the players another puck was produced. I wished I could have recorded the game. I decided that I wanted Lady Lockporte to teach our kids how to play. For an hour they pounded on each other, sometimes they seemed oblivious to the location of the puck. At one point Sir Ruben sat beside me.

"What is that?" he asked looking at my snack.

"Mango yogurt," I replied as I dug out the last spoonful. "Want a taste?"

He made a face. "Now I have morning sickness," he remarked and returned to the game.

It looked like they were about to pack it in when Sir Franco skated over to Lady Lockporte during a rare timeout. As he started to talk, he slipped a puck out of his pocket and threw it behind her.

"Score!" he exclaimed!

"Well done!" Sir Diego added.

Lady Lockporte decked Sir Franco. Sir Ruben decided the goal counted despite his sister's glare.

Everyone agreed to hang up their skates. Hockey has never been the same for me. I was relieved to see that in the seemingly grim world of my husband there could still be time for play, albeit super human play.

I caught up with Sergio as he was going to his room. "How are you doing?"

"Fine. I mean better than fine, great!" he replied.

"What happened tonight?" I had a new curiosity about his transformation.

"I learned that I made the right decision. Which is a huge relief because, you know, there's no going back."

"You killed someone?"

"It was an assassination, well planned." He looked at me with concern in his eyes. "You're wondering if you'll become like me. You have several years to decide. If it's right you'll know. I did."

When I got upstairs, Tristan was in the shower. I climbed into bed and waited for him. A bit of domestic normalcy if you did not count the black panther at the foot of the bed. I hoped Delilah would get along with small children and not see them as prey. Then I thought about Sergio. *Would he now see Shorts as prey?* He was right about my interest in, and discomfort concerning his transformation. It was too close to my situation. It was easier to dismiss the idea of becoming a vampire before Sergio did it. I rested my hands on my tummy. The precious new lives being brought into this world would need protection from the bizarre influence of their father's people. Hopefully, caring for the children would help ground me and keep me from dwelling on Sergio's choice. I tried to distract my brain by focusing on what would be needed to set up the nursery.

Tristan was warm from the shower when he climbed into bed and took me in his arms. "Great game," was all he said before helping my brain to escape further from the reality of my situation. It was so easy to be responsive to his touch, his kisses and his passion. My nipples hardened at the slightest touch. His tongue could coax the most delicious response from every part it touched. He easily lifted me on top of him. I loved to feel his hardness come inside me. The pressure from the friction of our bodies was overwhelming. Mini-orgasms erupted into earthquakes.

The Magus and Lena sat at a small table in his magnificent bedroom suite. Priceless works of art and pieces of furniture that had once been belonged to French kings decorated his room. Dove gray satin sheets with royal purple borders adorned the canopied bed. The Magus could be informal with his ancient friend and was simply attired in a long, white silk nightshirt. Lady Hauser was in stark contrast in black leather.

"So Lena, tell me, did he make you proud?"

"Yes. He hesitated as predicted but I could smell the change in his body chemistry as he started to walk away and when the W.T. attacked he was able to complete his first mission with enthusiasm."

"And afterward?"

"He was proud and elated. I imagine he made Lady Lockporte quite content tonight. She is easy to read." Lady Hauser smiled and shook her head. "Will they never learn that they can't fool us? You remember the intimate pleasures following our early escapades?"

"Vividly. You have always taken my breath away. I'm not sure there is time to reminisce tonight," he stated. Lady Hauser looked a little disappointed.

"I'm seriously considering letting Sergio become Sudovian's knight. I would like eyes and ears in the House of Pentacles who I can trust."

"I agree that the House of Pentacles should be investigated further. Perhaps it would be good for Sergio to spend some time away from me." She had a slight look of amusement on her face. "As long as my bed will not remain empty."

"Then I must oblige you, my lady," the Magus replied.

"The last time you said that was 100 years ago."

"You've always been fact driven," he smiled. "Perhaps you should rest here today so we can remedy my faux pas."

"As long as our pillow talk does not include your obsession with Miranda," she replied and unzipped her leather jacket.

"It is a small price to pay."

CHAPTER 26

TILLIE HEARD ME coming down the stairs and immediately started cooking. It was about 4 p.m. It was getting easier for me to be nocturnal. I checked on my birds. I named them after my two favorite vamps. Sir Franco seemed to be more obsessed with cleaning his feathers. Sir Ruben was noisier. They loved the attention and were riding on my shoulders when I heard someone clear his throat behind me.

"Yes Clive?"

"Will you be needing Jasper today, Baroness?" he inquired.

Despite all we had been through, he remained quite formal. "Yes, I'd like to run errands after breakfast and then I'm meeting Lolly for coffee at that deli we stopped at the other day. Thanks."

"Very well." He started to leave when suddenly Sir Ruben flew to his shoulder. I could tell it was a situation the Clive was not prepared for. Tillie walked in with a breakfast tray and laid it on the table.

"Oh my, Clive, what are you doing? That bird will ruin your jacket!"

Tillie took charge and the birds listened. She shooed them back into the cage and politely insisted I sit down and eat. She gave Clive a disapproving glance and, satisfied that she had achieved order, returned to the kitchen.

"How long have you been married?" I asked.

"A hundred and thirty years," he said with a look of satisfaction "I'm a lucky man, Baroness."

I dropped my fork. "How old are you?"

"One hundred and fifty-four," he replied and left the room quickly before I could ask any more questions.

I realized that the Baron was preserving them. Bram had been preserved at an elderly age but the servants must have been younger. They were aging very slowly. I wondered how much blood it took for this elixir of longevity and how often they would need to drink it. No wonder they were so loyal to him. I wondered how the blood I had received in the transfusion I got as a child was effecting me and possibly my babies. A million questions swirled in my brain as I ate my breakfast. Then I got ready to spend a few hours away from vampire central. I needed the break.

I went to the bank first and began what became a regular habit for me. I took out a $1,000 cash and spent very little of it. It was the start of my escape fund. I withdrew 10 $100 bills. You could fit a small fortune in a backpack. I did not like being deceitful but considering my situation it seemed like my only option. Unfortunately, there was no one I could confide in about my secret stash of cash that I could use to go off the grid. I grew up with a guy who, after serving in the military overseas, came back to the states for a few months. He was pretty unhappy as a civilian. I heard he robbed a bank then disappeared, some say he went to Costa Rica. I had time to figure out a way to disappear with my kids, if needed. For now I would go with what Tristan called "conflicted bliss."

I went back to my old apartment. It seemed oddly empty now and there was a for sale sign outside the building. Jasper helped me load some of my books, coffee mugs and photos of Rossville in an old suitcase. I also kept a few of my favorite T-shirts. I decided to donate the rest of my stuff. I looked around and thought about the first time Tristan had visited me here. I was so mad when he tore up my Bela Lugosi poster. I considered buying another one and started to laugh.

Jasper looked concerned, "Is everything okay, Baroness?"

"Yeah, I'm fine, just memories. This is all I want now," I responded. "It's about time to meet Lolly."

When we arrived at the deli, Lolly was already there, which was a first. We hugged, then found a booth. She looked great as always. She was wearing a turquoise scoop neck top and black jeans. I guessed the color must have been in style. I was in my usual drab comfy clothes but my wedding rings said I was more than a broke student.

"How are you, I mean really?" Lolly began.

"I'm okay. I have a bit of news. It looks like we'll have twins."

"Randie!" she shrieked, which turned a few heads. "Wow."

"I get a little nauseated at times but other than that I'm fine. Tristan is delighted."

"Tristan and his friends, they are treating you well?" she asked with a look of concern.

"Yeah, remember Jorge and Franco?"

"Isn't Jorge back in Cuba?" she looked surprised.

"He and Franco are part of the nocturnal mafia. They were never from Havana, more like Caracas. They were just looking after me."

She finished my sentence, "Until Tristan arrived on the scene. He is so protective. Unbelievable. I thought Jorge loved you."

"As it turns out, not so much. However, he is more than fond of Franco," I replied. Her eyes widened. "There are more night people in L.A. than anywhere else in the world." I decided not to tell her about the Narcissus Club. She might try and talk Al into going. I could tell that when she mentioned Tristan she was still attracted to him.

"Wow, I guess they like the warm climate. Al would like to thank Tristan."

"There's no need. It's just part of their code."

"They have a code?" she asked.

Just then Grigoryi came over to the table. "Good afternoon, Baroness. It's good to see you again."

"How are you Greg?"

"I'm well, thank you. What would you like?"

"I'll have the strawberry blintzes and dark roast decaf, black," I replied.

"And you, miss?"

"A whole wheat bagel, lightly toasted and veggie cream cheese. Coffee with cream," Lolly responded. After he walked away she said, "He sounded like an old friend..."

"New friend, actually. He was almost killed because of Simone. In his case, Jorge saved him. He's met Tristan, too." I was trying to simplify the situation.

"He knows? The waiter in this deli knows?" Her eyes got big.

"Greg is the only one here who does, besides us. I sort of feel sorry for him. Sometimes knowledge can be a burden, so I like to come by and check on him."

"I know. It's so weird to believe in a culture others consider fantasy that has remained undetected for so long."

"Except in Hollywood," I replied with a grin.

"So, what are they like, the others?"

"Like us. They get in and out of relationships, they get bored and party or play hockey or just assassinate someone," I replied.

"They play hockey?" she looked amazed, apparently missing the last comment. Just then Grigoryi arrived with our food.

"This looks great" I responded.

"I told the cook it was for my friends," he said with a big smile.

"Thanks Grigoryi, this is Lolly, she met some of the people you met." I was hoping to not sound like a complete idiot.

"Nice to meet you," Lolly said.

"We are very lucky, I think. Please excuse me. I must get back to work," he said. "Glad to meet you."

I assumed he meant lucky to have survived the meetings. We talked about my parents coming out, the puppies she and Al adopted and what I might want for the nursery. Al had heard from James. He was settling in nicely back in Montana. She said he asked about me. I told her she was free to tell James anything she wanted. It was good to be out with my best friend. We left a $50 tip. Grigoryi waived as we walked out the door. I would have liked to offer him a job helping Tillie but I thought he would be better off building a life in the world of ignorant Shorts like James was doing.

I asked Jasper to take the long way home. We drove along the coast for 20 minutes before heading back. I opened the window a little and breathed in the cool ocean air. The sunset was painted on the horizon in shades of orange and pink. It was a magnificent display of color and fading light. I closed my eyes as we headed back to Stone Canyon. It was going to be a long night of interrogating Dr. Kyoto and Lady Lily.

When I arrived, I noticed stylish light tan leather luggage was stacked by the front door, ready for Sir Diego and Sir Franco's flight home. I heard voices in the library. I stopped near the door.

"Be patient Tristan," Sir Diego said. "She has been through so much and now she will suffer through a pregnancy. In time, she will understand."

"I know you're right," and in a rare show of brotherly love placed his hand on Sir Diego's shoulder.

"You know, this is the first time I have ever seen you truly nervous," Sir Diego smiled.

"It's the first time in my life I have something to lose that I care this much about," the Baron responded.

"Ah yes," he replied. "I promise I will be here when the offspring are about to arrive."

"I can hardly wait," Sir Franco added.

"You will be most welcome. I'll keep you informed of the Magus' investigation into the House of Pentacles," the Baron replied.

I entered as they started to walk out. "Goodbye Jorge. Safe travels," I said and gave him a hug. "I will miss you and Franco."

"Take good care of my friend here. He is entirely under your spell," Sir Diego said and they walked to the front entrance.

Tristan gestured for me to sit on the couch with him. "Do you want anything?"

"No, I'm fine."

"Nausea?"

"Not so far. I even kept cheese blintzes down." I leaned into him and he placed his arm about my shoulders. "I'm not a China doll. I won't break."

He sighed. "I'm a bit lost when it comes to you and the pregnancy. Too many variables to feel entirely prepared. I usually know what to do."

"Shhh." I turned towards him and said softly, "Just love me and the babies. Make your plans, decisions and reactions out of love."

He had no words. Tristan looked away to regain his composure. Then he turned back to me. "Jorge says I'm experiencing love for the first time. All these centuries, all the women and I never felt such pain and delight."

"You were doing great till you compared me to all the other women you've fucked."

"There is no comparison," he replied with a smile.

"Good save."

"You won't talk like that around the children. Promise me that," he said in a serious tone.

"As long as you don't tear out anyone's throat around them," I responded a tad indignantly.

"Let's hope they have my manners, tact and patience," he smiled. I hit him with a decorative pillow just as Dr. Kyoto and Lady Lily arrived.

"Perhaps we should come back later," Dr. Kyoto suggested.

"Not at all. Good evening," Tristan responded. "Please, sit down."

"Perhaps we could go to the medical room, do a few tests and take the Baroness' vitals first," Lady Lily suggested.

"Of course," the Baron responded, then looked at me to see if I was on board. "Sure."

The medical room had more equipment than before, including a computer. Lady Lily took three tubes of blood. I could not help but feel a bit uncomfortable as the three of them had a laser focus on me while the blood was drawn. I imagined it caused a bit of an anticipatory high, like a junkie about to get a fix. She disappeared into a storage room that had been turned into a small lab. Dr. Kyoto suggested we go to the dining room to wait for the test results. Once we were seated, Tillie appeared with goblets for our guests and a bowl of veggie chili and cornbread for me. She also pulled out a bottle of Tabasco from her apron pocket.

"Can I have some blueberry yogurt too?" I asked as I started to dig in.

When she returned with the yogurt and assorted fresh berries. Dr. Kyoto watched me eat with a smile. "I'm glad you have such a good appetite."

"I've been wondering how my exposure to the Baron's blood and his genes will effect the babies," I said between bites.

"We can't say for sure," he replied and shifted a little in his chair.

"I'd appreciate an educated guess," I put down my spoon.

"Miranda, keep in mind that you are the first," the Baron said.

Dr. Kyoto folded his hands on the table. "We hypothesize that the children will be compatible with the Baron's genetic influence because you took his blood transfusion so well. We assume they will be warm-blooded but their cellular health will be remarkable."

"You expect them to be hybrids of some kind but you're not sure how much they will take after me," the Baron added.

Lady Lily entered and sat beside the doctor across from us. "May I respond?"

"Of course." Dr. Kyoto seemed as though he was relieved to have her help.

"We think the Short genes will dominate and that the vampire genes will tend to be recessive though perhaps recessive is not quite the right term. It might be more correct to say asleep. We believe that in time, as they mature, some of their father's traits might become apparent," she replied in a rather matter of fact fashion.

"Will they age normally?" I asked as my brain tried to deal with their response.

"Yes, at least until maturity when their cellular differences related to hormonal changes should become more apparent," Lady Lily responded.

"We assume," Dr. Kyoto began, "that their immune systems, ability to heal and intelligence will be greater than other infants, which of course will impact their development."

"Super babies?" I asked.

"This is, as you say, our educated guesses. Your blood tests from the hospital when you were a child showed an incredible compatibility," Dr. Kyoto continued. "It was as though you had received blood from a twin. More than just healing, you were transformed in a way. Over time, you seemed to show vampire qualities, your IQ increased, you never became ill and look young for your age."

"So, you wondered about how truly 'compatible' we might be," I uttered.

Dr. Kyoto responded "It became clear to us that you were quite different from others with your blood type. Call it evolution or even fate."

"Lucky me," I responded and could see the hurt in my husband's eyes. "I'm sorry," I added, but despite telling James my relationship with Tristan was fate, I was a big proponent of making my own destiny.

Lady Lily broke the tension. "Your blood work came back fine, except your iron is a little low."

"I can increase my leafy greens," I suggested,

"That might not be enough, especially when you consider the hybrid possibility," Dr. Kyoto responded. "Is there any beef that you might consider eating once or twice a week, just during the pregnancy?"

I had been expecting this. I figured that having twins might require such a sacrifice. "Despite my vegetarian vow, for my babies, I will eat barbacoa tacos with medium salsa and guacamole."

My husband smiled while Dr. Kyoto and Lady Lily looked surprised.

"Let Tillie know," the Baron said.

"I know she could look up a recipe." I was trying to be tactful. "But she has enough to do and it has to cook for hours to get it right and the spice combination is tricky, so let me just give her the name of a restaurant I like and have Jasper pick it up."

"Very good," Dr. Kyoto replied with a smile.

"I have another question, it's about my aging process. Since it's slowed down, could you tell me that when I reach 29, how old will I be physically? "

"I think," Dr. Kyoto responded, 'that you will be a little older than you are now."

"And when I turn 39?"

"You'll seem about 10 years younger," he responded.

"Thanks, I'll be the youngest looking mom ever," I said, hoping they would think my curiosity was about vanity.

The Baron cleared his throat. "Dr. Kyoto, do you think that due to the possibility of twins we should take any precautions when having sex, or do you think it is advisable to stop at a certain point in the pregnancy?"

"I must defer to Lady Lily on this matter."

"You are fine to have normal relations for now. When you begin to show, Miranda, you might want to try lying on your side. I think that during the last two months it would be wise to abstain," she dropped her gaze to the table.

"Thank you," Tristan responded. He seemed glad to get that over with.

"Is it okay if I just drink one regular cup of coffee a day? It would help my mood."

"If it is only one 8-ounce cup, that should be fine," Dr. Kyoto replied.

"Thank you," I said and looked at my husband with a self-satisfied smile.

They politely excused themselves. The Baron walked out with them as I finished my meal. If I would be 29 at 39, that could give me 17 years before my husband and the nocturnal clan would really pressure me to decide about transformation. The children would be grown. How could becoming a vampire ever seem like the right decision? That was what I was contemplating when the Baron returned.

"How are you doing?"

"I want to go to Starbucks." I replied.

"Tillie is making you a cup of Sumatran." he smiled. The Baron leaned over and gently kissed my neck with cool lips. He smelled great. "Maybe we should think about names." he suggested

"Magustine?"

"That's horrible." he laughed

"Let's go try out that new position."

"Perhaps we should consult the Kama Sutra?" he smiled.

"You probably wrote it," I joked.

"Well, Lady Hauser was involved."

"Shut up! I mean it" I responded and led him upstairs.

CHAPTER 27

THE NEXT EVENING Lady Lockporte and Sir Ruben joined the Baron in his suite. He was sitting at his desk looking at his monitor. The Tarot card, the Fool, was on the screen.

"She is gone?" Lady Lockporte asked.

"Yes, she is shopping for maternity garments with her friend Lolly," the Baron replied. "You may speak freely."

"Would you like us to continue surveillance on the dentist?" Sir Ruben inquired. The Baron opened a live camera feed of a rustic cabin in Montana. James' pick-up truck was parked nearby.

"Yes. I fear he will be important to watch for the next 20 years. Her parents, they remain protected?"

"If a mouse got in their home we would know it," Lady Lockporte responded. "What about the monk? I would enjoy expediting his entrance into heaven."

"Dear sister, I hardly think he is a worthy morsel for you, allow me the displeasure of tasting holy blood," Sir Ruben insisted.

"My wife thinks we allowed him to live because we are merciful. Let her hold onto that fantasy." He pulled up a file with an image of the Page of Pentacles. When the Baron opened it, the whereabouts of the monk were displayed. "He is at mass, hopefully praying for his worthless life. I'll never understand why anyone trusts the clergy. Allow Grigoryi to live as long as he amuses the Baroness. If Benedetto ever returns from Italy you may dispose of him." He stood and faced the Lockportes. "The Magus, Lady Hauser, and I are very pleased with the House of Plows. Your continuing loyalty, cleverness and diligence has not gone unnoticed. As a reward and a way to further Miranda's acceptance in our society, the Magus has approved a Grand Ball to honor your house. Only the House of Plows and their guests will be allowed."

"The other Houses will be so envious," Lady Lockporte responded.

"Hopefully it will encourage them to act in ways that will garner our pleasure. Please encourage the members of your House to invite a friend from the other Houses so that we might be able to gage their response to my wife's condition. Make sure Johann attends."

"I'll invite him myself," Lady Lockporte replied. "He loves to kiss the ass of the Haute Caste."

"That's a visual I didn't need," Sir Ruben replied.

"It will be on Sunday. Please tell Sir Steve to make formal preparations at the Narcissus Club. Sarah, this is a token of my gratitude for your service." The Baron handed her a small jewelry box.

"Oh my!" the Lady Lockporte exclaimed. She pulled out three diamond bracelets.

"They were Simone's. To the victor go the spoils," the Baron commented.

"I'll wear them to the ball."

"Ruben, you may have her Lexus," the Baron handed him a set of keys. "The title and registration are in your name. I was told there is a woman with HH blood who is ready and willing to become enlightened."

"Word gets around," Sir Ruben replied. "Her name is Pauline Barnes. She is longing to be transformed. The Magus and Lady Hauser find her worthy. Would you allow the House of Plows to conduct the ceremony at the Grand Ball?"

"She is a world-class surfer and a scholar with a degree in oceanography. This will add to the prestige of our House," Lady Lockporte said.

"I knew of her intelligence but not her athletic ability," the Baron said. He opened a file titled "House of Plow's Prospect." The picture of a young woman with straight blond hair cascading down her back and sitting at a beach café appeared. "Ruben, I heard that you discovered this new talent."

"Pauline was snooping around the Narcissus Club. Steven was considering her as a W.T. but I smelled her bloodline and could see potential. She has chased the perfect wave around the world and now seeks a new level of excitement," Sir Ruben said. "She already asked about using spray tanners to keep up her look."

"Vain, strong, thrill-seeking and intelligent," the Baron smiled. "A vampiress in the making. As long as she is not greedy."

"When her parents died five years ago she inherited a fortune, oil company money. She is not motivated by riches," Lady Lockporte responded.

"Good. Her transformation and education will be the responsibility of your House. Be sure she understands her loyalty must be to the Magus and the Haute Caste."

Lady Lockporte and Sir Ruben stood at attention and nodded as though receiving a command from a general. The inductee would be well schooled in respect for the social order of vampire society. The Baron dismissed them. As they walked down the stairs Sir Ruben asked, "Do you honestly think the Baroness will ever be respectful?"

"Quiet," Lady Lockporte whispered and looked back over her shoulder. "Never discuss your opinion of her in this house."

Lolly and I were shopping at the Beverly Center for stretchy yoga garments that would work until I needed maternity clothes. Jasper trailed along behind us carrying my bags. Lolly was in an upbeat mood, which countered my anxiety. We stopped at an organic food café for smoothies.

"You'll be a great mom. I think you'll be the grounded parent, aware of your kids' needs, while Tristan will be less involved in practical matters but a great provider," Lolly said as we sipped our smoothies.

I wanted to tell her she had no clue about what Tristan was like but held my tongue to protect our relationship. "Thanks. Motherhood is unknown territory. I think that you and Al were wise to start with springer spaniels. How are they?"

"The pups are fine, a little hyper but they are very sweet clowns. They make Al laugh, even when he's had a difficult case to deal with. Are you okay? You seem to be in a bit of a funk."

"I'm a little worried about my parents' visit. My mom has a good nose for something not being right. You've got to help me convince her that my husband just seems a little odd because he's Lithuanian. I can explain his nocturnal tendencies on international business concerns. I just don't know how to explain his diet."

Lolly's eyes brightened. "Al can help! He can say he advised Tristan to do a juice cleanse."

"That will be good for a few meals but I'm afraid he will have to eat then go barf if he is going to appear at all normal. But I didn't tell you the best part," I said with a mischievous grin. "I told my dad to call him Stan."

"Nice. You are such a twit. You know some of my girlfriends who were at the engagement party are still asking about him," she almost sighed.

"Yeah, he has that effect on women. It's getting late. I better get back to Vlad."

"Randie! Say hello for me and Al." She was oblivious to my irritation.

It's was about 9 p.m. when we pulled out of the parking structure. Jasper's voice came on the intercom, "The Baron would like us to meet him at a boutique. It's about 15 minutes from here. He mentioned a gown."

"Sure, thanks." I was surprised he did not just pick it out himself.

We parked in front of a small, chic clothing store down a side street in Beverly Hills. A woman was waiting at the door to gush over me.

"Wonderful to meet you, Baroness, please come this way," the gray-haired matron dressed in black said. She had large diamond solitaire earrings and a chunky gold watch. I followed her to an area in the back of the store where Tristan was seated on a velvet couch. I realized there were no other customers in the store.

"What's going on?" I asked as he took my hand and pulled me beside him.

"A private fashion show. You'll need a gown for the grand ball to honor Lady Lockporte and company."

"When and where?"

"The Narcissus on Sunday." He kissed my cheek then motioned to the store owner. A red-headed model came out in a low-cut, backless, silver dress with slits up the side. She was focused on the Baron.

"We have napkins bigger than that," I said.

Tristan shook his head. A dark-haired woman came out in a dark red dress that hugged her hips and showed her cleavage. She tried to stay focused on her task.

"I like it."

"Something a bit more formal." Tristan demanded. The older woman disappeared for a few minutes, then a blond model appeared in a black lace gown that flattered every curve of her body.

"Perfect!" Tristan exclaimed. The model smiled at him.

"Yeah but what am I going to wear?" I replied.

"Miranda!" he gave me a look that warned me not to make a scene "It will show off your jewels."

"You want me to dye my hair too? Why did you even want me here?" I stood up and headed for the door.

"Please have it sent over tomorrow night with a seamstress," the Baron instructed.

I got in the car and told Jasper to take me to a doughnut shop on the way home. I was not in a mood to witness women fawning over my husband. He enjoyed it way too much. I could sense he was considering a discrete sexual encounter with the last model. About 30 minutes later I was sitting in my bed with a box of a dozen assorted doughnuts and a large black coffee. The Baron walked in and closed the door. He looked amused by my antics. "That isn't decaf, is it?"

I took a big swig of coffee and said, "Go away!" while avoiding looking in his eyes, then I grabbed a chocolate frosted donut and took a big bite.

"Caffeine and sugar, that's great during pregnancy. Miranda, what did I do that was so terrible?" He looked baffled.

"Were you shopping for dresses or women?" I snapped.

"Why, is it a problem that I appreciate beautiful women?" His amusement was becoming irritation. He walked over and sat on the edge of the bed.

"A little too much," I said and took another bite avoiding looking at him.

"Monogamy is not a natural state for a vampire." I thought I was ready for anything he had to say at that point but his response completely threw me. He continued, "When you live as long as I have, it is only natural to have a series of affairs. What you as a Short might consider as immoral we think of as recreational activity. Relationships may span a few hundred years but there is never a demand for monogamy, we just keep it trivial."

"So now you think of our marriage as trivial? So I guess you wouldn't mind if I fucked around on you?" I had to put it out there.

"You're not capable of having an inconsequential affair."

"Oh, but Mr. Undead can? What makes you think that for me anyone but you would be inconsequential?"

He leaned closer, unbuttoned his shirt, took my hand and placed it on his chest. "I have a vampire's heart, my human years were a very short span of time." He stared into my eyes with the same look of longing I had seen in my apartment months ago. I snatched by hand away still fuming. "You cannot expect me to be some banal creature that lives under your command. That is not the person you fell in love with. I accept your jealous nature, though I find it petty, as I know it is a sign of your strong feelings for me. I cannot promise that I will be faithful but I can be honest with you. I have never felt so deeply for a woman as I do for you. The unique aspects of our relationship could never be duplicated. No one else you could have sex with will ever come close to what we have, so you won't."

I dropped the donut. He reached over and took my hand. Though his touch, his words, his scent and his gaze were getting me hot and bothered, I was still furious. I was not about to succumb. "Since I am so special, and as long as we are married, I expect you to be monogamous. If you don't agree, we can divorce and I can hook up with other vampires and see how they compare with the great Baron Mordecai!"

A flash of anger shown on his face. He withdrew his hand and stood suddenly. The Baron left without another ward, slamming the door behind him. He had been blindsided by my remarks. He obviously expected I would be romanced into accepting his values. I would not be the wife who waits at home wondering who he is with tonight. Now he was experiencing being petty. I bit into a jelly-filled donut. Maybe I would write about Polly telling off the Count and Sidney tonight.

About an hour later Sir Ruben saw his sister in the hall headed for the hockey rink."I wouldn't go in there; the Baron is really upset with the Baroness. I think he is running out of pucks, so I left," he warned.

"Perhaps he is in need of counsel," she responded and headed out the door towards the rink.

The Baron was hitting pucks so hard they had torn holes in the goal netting and were taking big chunks out of the walls. "Damn her!" he cried as he sent another puck flying into the lockers. Lady Lockporte said nothing. She sat on the side of the rink and waited while watching him carefully. The Baron rarely lost his temper but since he had become involved with Miranda it was becoming a regular occurrence. She was glad he was not upset with her. Several minutes passed before he spoke.

"She thinks I should live as a monk. She will not accept her place. Nothing I do is enough. She makes stupid demands, then pouts!" He hit the ice so hard his hockey stick broke into pieces.

"Would you like some advice?" she asked in a soothing tone.

"No! Well, yes, if it will help the situation," he responded, dropping the broken handle of his hockey stick. He walked over and sat beside her. She could see the distress in his face.

"She's not pouting. She is plotting," Lady Lockporte said in a calm voice. "That's what we do when we are upset with a lover. Vampire or Short. Say whatever you have to say to make her happy, even if you don't mean it, because if you don't appease her she will act out her plots."

"I told her I would be honest," he said.

"Then you have already lied to her, it will get easier," she said with a slight smile.

"If she is like this as a Short, can you imagine her as a vampiress? She will be impossible and incredible," the Baron returned the smile.

"All the more reason to keep her affection. Whatever it takes."

"But monogamy?" he said, getting a little wound-up again.

"Something to consider for the short term but at least the appearance of faithfulness, dear Baron," she replied.

CHAPTER 28

I FELL ASLEEP in my room in the early hours of the morning after spending the night writing. I did not try to reach out to Tristan and he apparently decided to let me cool off. I was, however, making progress with my novel, a welcome way to process my stress. I allowed Polly an escape route from the Count and from the pressure of her old boyfriend. My heroine sneaks away just before dawn. She travels to Denmark to consider her options before flying to Alaska to start a new life. Polly is no longer the innocent in many ways. She is aware that the unthinkable might actually be reality. Polly will also be aware that she does not have to live her life waiting on a man to complete her, no matter how amazing he might seem. I did not complicate her life with a pregnancy. The vampire baby daddy discussion was too close to home. To lighten the ending a little, I added a humorous scene between the Count and Sidney when they realize she has rejected them both. A truce is declared and they part ways but there is a hint that this story will be continued as the Count makes plans to visit the States. When I woke up in the late afternoon I read over my recent pages and felt satisfied with my work.

Tillie brought my breakfast tray. "Will you be needing anything else, Baroness?"

"This is fine but tomorrow could you include prunes?"

"Of course. That is your cup of regular coffee. Your gown fitting will be about 7 p.m."

"Please tell me when he wakes."

"Of course," she replied and left. Her professional demeanor would prohibit asking me how I could ever be mean to the Baron but I was sure everyone in the house knew we argued last night. I starting eating breakfast but could not keep it down. After spending 10 minutes in the bathroom I asked Tillie to bring me some saltines and tea. So much for my one real cup of coffee allotment. When Tillie returned Lady Lily was with her. I could tell she had just woken up.

"Are you all right, Baroness?" Lady Lily inquired.

"It's just nausea, sometimes it happens with the first meal."

She took my vital signs. "Your morning sickness began quite early in the pregnancy, which is probably due to twins and their parentage. We must be careful that you don't become dehydrated. This is ginger tea which might help with the nausea. I'll just take another blood sample," she quickly, took my blood. "Are you having any other problems?"

"Just the Baron," I responded.

Lady Lily turned to Tillie "We don't require anything else." Tillie left quietly.

"It's better not to allow the servants hear about your relationship issues but you can talk with me. I have a Ph.D. in clinical psychology."

"I thought you were a nurse or a lab tech," I said a bit surprised.

"I have several degrees. Now, what has upset you?"

"You should be talking to the Baron. He doesn't have a clue about women."

Lady Lily laughed. "I thought you were going to talk about trying to wrap your mind around knowing vampires really exist but you want joint therapy. Amazing!"

"I've already accepted that he's an egotistical ass vampire!" I stated.

Lady Lily tried to be more serious. "What has he done?"

"He thinks he should be able to have any woman he chooses and it shouldn't bother me 'cause I'm so special to him. He's no different than any other cheating husband."

Lady Lily chuckled, then she took a deep breath and said, "He is Baron Mordecai. He can have any woman he chooses. If you can accept his undead reality, why can't you accept his sexual appetite and prowess."

Tears welled up in my eyes, though I tried to hold them back. "Because I can't stand the thought of him being with other women, no matter how insignificant he might think it is."

Lady Lily put her arms around me while I sniffled. She was very kind. She handed me the cup of tea. "I have known the Baron for ages. He has never shown a woman the sort of attention he shows you. As they say, you've caught a tiger and now you want him to become a house cat. Can't you love him as he truly is, without conditions?"

"I don't know," I responded honestly. "I can accept the fact that he sucks people dry better than being unfaithful to me."

"Perhaps you could let this go for now, just enjoy the evening with your husband," she said. She fixed my pillow and pulled a throw over me. "Rest for now, it seems the nausea has passed."

"Thanks, I'll try." I fell asleep quickly. I think there was more than ginger in the tea.

An hour later Tillie woke me to say the seamstress had arrived. I asked for 20 minutes to take a shower before letting her come up. While I was lathering up Tristan slipped in, startling me, then he began washing my back. I tried to stay mad but that was all it took. Without a word, I turned and succumbed to his passion. He effortlessly lifted me and then entered me as the water rained down on us. He cradled me in his arms while he thrust inside me again and again to the beat of a primal rhythm. The look in his eyes was of a distant time and place where lovers could exist alone. I wanted to be there with him at that moment. I held onto him tightly hoping to never let go. My body trembled as I climaxed and cried out. He gently put me down and kissed me deeply.

"I accept your apology," I dried off.

He patted my fanny. "Don't start." Then he left.

Tillie insisted I eat while the 90-year-old seamstress with a heavy German accent pulled, tucked and pinned till the dress fit perfectly. I had probably gained about 5 pounds but the gown just made me look voluptuous. I almost got a glob of peanut butter on the gown. The seamstress glared at me.

"Tillie, what is next for this evening?"

"I made a pot of minestrone soup if you get hungry later, and Jasper will pick up those barbecue tacos you like so much," she replied, content that I was keeping food down.

"Thanks. It's barbacoa but close enough." I put on some comfy jeans and a striped cotton T-shirt with some logo that added $100 to the price.

"Where's my husband?"

"I believe he is in his suite," she replied and scurried off.

When I entered his room, Delilah walked over and rubbed her head against my thigh. A sound came from her throat that had to be purring. I scratched her ears. "Sweet kitty."

The Baron had a picture of a blond woman at a cafe pulled up on his monitor, which he closed.

"Is she a W.T.?" I asked.

"No, she is going to be transformed," he smiled.

"Lucky girl!" I quipped

"It seems you're feeling better."

I walked over to the desk and sat in his lap. "A little. Did you talk to Lady Lily?

"Yes. She had a splendid suggestion. She thinks it would be helpful if you met alone with the Magus to gain a greater understanding of our kind. You will have an unprecedented chance to ask him any question you would like. He has granted you this favor but desires that it happen tonight."

Jasper is waiting downstairs. I will be here when you return." He stood and placed me on the ground. Then he lowered his head and kissed me passionately. Then he lowered one of his hands to my belly. "You are the most beautiful woman I have ever known."

"Coming from you, that is really a compliment," I smiled.

"Go, before I regret saying it," he replied, "and please try to be polite, he is more powerful than you can imagine."

Jasper drove the Bentley to a gated entry off the Pacific Coast Highway near Paradise Cove. I had driven by it many times. A driveway with palm trees and flowering shrubs led to a mansion that looked like it belonged in a Caribbean plantation. As Jasper and I approached the door it opened and Clive's counterpart greeted us. He wore white pants and a blue linen shirt.

"Baroness, this is Rupert, he will show you to the Magus," Jasper said.

Rupert looked Indian or Pakistani, about 6 feet tall, thin, with short gray hair and a neat moustache. "Please follow me, Baroness," he said with a proper English accent.

I was guided through a large foyer with black and white tiles, potted ferns and black lacquer Chinese furniture. Exotic antiques, beautiful Japanese paintings of tsunamis and large vases of fresh lilies lined the hallway to the library. I was left alone to wait for his highness, which I had expected. The room was about the same size as Tristan's library but one of the walls of books had been replaced with dozens of computer screens. If this display of spyware was meant to increase my paranoia it certainly worked. There were live feeds from different corners of the world and one of the New York Stock Exchange. One screen showed the Stone Canyon residence. I noticed a familiar scene. It was Rossville! The head of the vampire world was keeping tabs on my parents.

"What the fuck," I uttered, staring at the screen.

"Good evening Miranda, I hope you haven't waited too long." The Magus entered the library wearing a beige polo shirt and matching khakis, looking more like a golfer than the leader of the undead. His thick dark hair was slicked back.

"You've got a surveillance camera on my parents? Really?"

"It's purely for their protection. I left the screens on so that you would know that it is not only your well-being that concerns us but also your loved ones. Please sit down." He gestured to a small table set for two near a picture window that looked over a cliff to the Pacific Ocean. Far below, the sea glistened in the moonlight. I wondered about the TV screens that were blank.

As I sat down an Indian woman in a tailored, pale blue dress, maybe in her 50s, entered with a tea cart. She placed a small plate with lemon cake and fresh berries with cream in front of me.

"Will there be anything else?" she asked with a soft British accent.

"Baroness?" the Magus inquired, his dark eyes examining me.

"Thanks for the tea but I'd rather have a cup of regular coffee."

"Sumatran," he told her. She left to fix my brew.

I started eating the delicious cake. "Thanks."

"The Baron and Lady Lily wanted me to speak with you to help you understand our culture." He added a bit condescendingly, "I would be glad to address any of your concerns."

"My husband thinks he can be unfaithful and that should not matter to me."

"That's why you have been considering going off the grid?"

My eyes flashed anger. "Why don't I just eat while you read my mind."

"I only get bits and pieces. I find your thoughts confusing and no, I won't burst into flames," he smiled.

"Welcome to my world."

The coffee arrived in the nick of time. "That will be all, Sari."

"You must have understood enough to know my decisions will be based on what is best for my children. At the moment, that means staying with their father." I glanced up at the screens. "You can relax, Tristan!" I called out loudly.

The Magus laughed "You're right, he is listening." His appraisal of me seemed to be changing.

"Not much in this world of yours is what it seems. He isn't just listening, he's here. I can feel him nearby, I noticed his scent. Your scent is similar to his but his has a touch of evergreen. Hey Tristan, come on down!"

"Vampire abilities! The Baron arrived shortly after you. What other abilities have you noted?"

"Hell if I know, you're the great and powerful wizard, you tell me," I finished the coffee. My sensitivity had occurred gradually and until that moment I had not felt it so strongly.

"Amazing, Miranda," the Baron said from the library doorway "You picked up my scent through the doors." He walked over to me, leaned down, kissed me, then sat on the plush burgundy velvet sofa.

The Magus moved across from Tristan in an ornate chair and signaled me to join my husband on the sofa. He started looking at his laptop on the table next to him. "Of course!" He exclaimed and turned the screen towards us. It looked like some sort of lab test results. "It must be a recessive gene."

Tristan stared at the test results, which meant nothing to me. "Her blood is like Lena's. That explains it."

"I don't think Lena will appreciate the comparison," I said, not sure I liked it either.

"Your blood work continues to show unexpected changes. The pregnancy has triggered cellular mutations related to the transfusion you received as a child. Lena's genes resided within Tristan's blood and has become apparent in you. The extreme sensitivity to other undead, that comes from Lena. We sense each other, pick up scents, but not at such a distance. You are a mortal with some Haute Caste vampire qualities. I believe your children will be even more gifted. Your very special blood type has given you the qualities of our kind. Yet, you have not been transformed. You walk in daylight and eat vegetables. Fascinating!" the Magus exclaimed.

"You know, I'm kind of over being special. I just want some normalcy in my fairly bizarre life. I can't help what is going on with my body but I can do something about my marriage." I was not ready to take in how much I had changed. I wanted to talk about what brought me there.

"We are discussing an evolutionary breakthrough we thought would not occur until our children were born. The blood you received was just to heal you," the Baron explained.

"So, I healed really well. Now I want to fix our marriage."

"Sexual fidelity is that that important to you?" The Magus said a bit surprised.

"I won't pretend it doesn't matter."

"Because you think your parents live some monogamous fantasy?" the Baron asked.

I took a breath to calm myself before responding and looked down at my feet. "My mom was having difficulty getting pregnant. The stress caused my dad to have an affair with a waitress. She kicked him out and cried for a week. Two weeks later she realized she was pregnant. My dad moved back home and eventually my mom forgave him. She hired all the waitresses after that." I finished my coffee and avoided the Magus' gaze. I did want him to see my weak side. It had been painful that my dad betrayed my mom like that. I did not want it to happen to me. "I would rather get a divorce, here and now, than live with you having sex with other women. I don't want to live a lie." I looked directly at my husband. "No vampiresses either."

"My devotion to you is not a lie. I've given you my heart."

"I want your word and other parts!"

"Miranda, our kind does not think sexual behavior has any more importance than reading a book or playing a sport," the Magus responded. "It is a recreational activity."

"Really? Then I think Tristan should leave so you and I can have sex." They stared at me speechless. I got up and walked to the door. "I'm going home, so you can discuss how to deal with a possessive, pregnant mutant. I have lots of questions, Magus, but I don't want to hear any more about how lucky I am tonight." Then I walked out on them without waiting to be dismissed.

The Baron turned to the Magus "How can someone so bright and gifted be so unreasonable? I feel like tearing someone's throat out!" He stood and started pacing.

"She has extraordinary potential," the Magus said with a Cheshire Cat grin.

"Miranda is an extraordinary pain in the ass. Perhaps I should take Sarah's advice and just lie to make her happy."

"Sarah does not realize your wife's abilities. If Miranda catches you in a lie, she will find a hundred ways to punish you." The Magus paused to let the Baron consider his words. "Perhaps you could be faithful until the babies are born. She will be so involved in caring for them she may not notice or even care about your indiscretions then," the Magus stated. Though it was worded as a suggestion, the Baron knew it was a command.

"Lets us hope the babies will arrive early," the Baron scowled.

The Magus spoke on the intercom to Rupert, "Please invite Dr. Kyoto to join us."

Dr. Kyoto entered with a pleased expression. "I have some interesting findings."

CHAPTER 29

I SAT IN the kitchen devouring barbacoa. To my surprise, Delilah joined me for a few minutes before Clive took her outside. The big cat had decided I belonged to her, just like the Baron. Though I was sure that if forced to choose, she would go with him just like everyone else in this house. I now knew that the Magus could read me and perhaps Lady Hauser could too. but obviously my husband could not. My thoughts about escaping only seemed to amuse the Magus. That was fine. It might be years from now but I would continue to hide money and plan. The children were my priority. I had the feeling they would be allowed to develop in their own way. I was trying to deny that we were a sort of science fair project for the undead. A line from an old song played in my head, "Surrender, surrender but don't give yourself away." The barbacoa was delicious. It had been several years since I ate meat. Once the children were weaned I would go back to being a vegetarian. I would find a way to protect the children and myself. My feelings for the Baron were all over the map. Would I ever be able to walk away from him? Sir Ruben interrupted my thoughts.

"I can't wait for the ball. I stopped by the club and sampled the beef, delicious."

"Want to sample this?"

"Charred carcass? I think not. How are you? How was the meeting with the big cheese?"

"I'll tell Gus you called him that," I grinned.

For a second Sir Ruben looked worried, then he saw my expression and laughed. "Gus?"

"I hate to harsh your buzz but I think every room in this place is wired for the Haute Caste's spy channel."

His expression became more serious. "Where is the Baron?"

"I left him with the Magus. They are trying to figure out what to do with me."

"Then he may be late getting home." Sir Ruben replied with a smile. "I heard you're a little jealous."

"More than a little and it's more like protective."

"I see. Our cultural norms are different. We have certain loyalties to those we favor but we don't expect exclusivity."

"I do, which is why it will happen," I responded and finished eating my taco.

"Rock on, Baroness!" he exclaimed "I've got to prepare for tomorrow night. Lady Kananga and her retinue are flying in."

"I like her," I replied.

"I'm fond of her House," he whispered and went to his room.

I fell asleep around four in the morning and about an hour later Tristan joined me. I barely woke when he came in and cradled me in his arms. When I woke at noon, he was sleeping soundly with one hand resting on my belly. I carefully got out of bed without disturbing him. When I got to my room I found a sheet of stationary on the desk with a message in burgundy ink, "Don't divorce me." He was worried. Good! I did not want him to take me for granted. I folded the note and placed it in my jewelry box.

I wandered downstairs and found Tillie in the kitchen pulling fresh cinnamon rolls out of the oven. "Would you like an omelet?" I nodded and sat down with a mug of caffeine. "Some shoes were delivered this morning."

Three boxes were on the kitchen table. I recognized the designers' names. They must have cost thousands of dollars. One by one I pulled them out and tried on pieces of shoe porn. Beautiful black stilettos with red soles, a pair of 5-inch platforms with a jeweled buckle and a delicately embroidered pair of open-toe shoes with 3-inch heels. I wanted the stilettos but knew I'd probably just hurt myself, so I settled on the open-toe shoes.

"Baroness, would you like me to fix your hair tonight, or have a stylist come in?"

"The Baron liked the way you fixed my hair. If you could make those cascading curls again, that would be fine."

"Of course, Baroness," Tillie smiled with pride.

"Will Lady Kananga be staying here?"

"No, the Baron purchased a property next door to accommodate all the visitors."

"I didn't notice any houses for sale," I commented.

"There weren't, but the Baron made a generous offer and the neighbors accepted and moved out a couple of weeks ago," Tillie replied in a hushed tone. "Now the grounds can be expanded. Better for your growing family. The Lady Lockporte and her brother will stay there when your parents visit. Vampires are not fond of hotels."

Across town, just after sunset, several vampires gathered at the Narcissus Club to oversee the set-up for the ball. Sir Steve stood near the back doors where beef, clean linens, blood and extra tables were being delivered. A dozen Shorts from a party rental company were setting up the extra tables and chairs.

Johann complained, "I have more important things to do than wait on a truck! I'm not some warehouse supervisor." He played with his diamond ring set in a five-pointed star.

Sir Steve rolled his eyes. "You could at least pretend to be useful," he replied. As Sir Steve started to walk away, Johann's phone rang.

Sir Steve overheard the self-important vampire say, "Of course, my lady." He could not help but wish that Lady Lockporte had not invited the House of Pentacles to their party. He did not want to spend such a special occasion with members of a disgraced House. Recognition from the Magus was rare. He was proud to belong to the House of Plows and looked forward to an evening which would add to their prestige. Sir Steve placed a chair in the center of the room which would be used for the transformation. Johann wandered into the ball room apparently doing nothing. Sir Steve gave him a disapproving glance.

"Make sure the reflecting pools are filled. Show one of the rental workers the bucket by the sinks in the back." Sir Steve enjoyed barking orders at Johann.

Johann mumbled, "I got up early for this? Just wait…" and wandered off.

To my surprise, someone from a salon came over to give me a manicure and a pedicure. Tillie had arranged it. It did feel good to have my feet massaged. She was a thin young woman from an Eastern European country with an accent I had a hard time understanding. She did a great job. I tried to tip her but she refused as apparently Tillie had already taken care of that. She apparently believed that handling money was beneath my status.

Tillie informed me that painters were here to paint the nursery and asked me to meet them upstairs to pick out colors with the decorator. Nice that my input was requested. When I got upstairs, a man and a woman in coveralls were standing beside a man in shorts and a vintage Hawaiian shirt. His hair was blond and spiked. My best guess was Eurasian but it was L.A., so who knows.

"Baroness Mordecai, it's a pleasure to meet you. I'm Frederick. Now let me show you some possible colors for the walls I've picked out. I also have some drapery swatches."

He walked into Bram's old room without waiting for a response. So, this was to be the nursery. I was glad it was by our rooms but it felt strange to use the room where Bram suffered and died. I took a breath to compose myself and entered. All the furnishings had been removed, even the pictures that had been on the wall.

"Let me see the colors please."

"Of course. It's my understanding there will be twins but the sex has not been determined?"

I was a little surprised he knew so much but realized he would have to know to plan the room. "Yes, twins."

"Splendid. What about some combination of yellow and green? Here's a nice pastel yellow and we could have antiqued dark green ivy painted about the windows. It would match the castle mural the Baron requested." Frederick held out a dozen cards with shades of yellow and green.

"Castle mural?"

"Yes. It will have the family crest on the castle wall. I'm sorry, I assumed the Baron had talked this over with you." He seemed a little surprised.

"I want the walls to be pale periwinkle," I asserted. He almost dropped his color cards. "No castle. I would like flowering vines with yellow, pink and lavender flowers around the windows and little blue songbirds. I want a big rainbow painted across that wall. No castle, no family crest. Do you understand?"

"Yes, of course, Baroness, if you're sure."

"I'm sure. Now show me the drapery swatches."

I chose curtains that would let in a lot of light and asked that the cribs be painted with the same flowering vine. "I'll buy the bedding and other decorations. Thanks Fred!"

He left a little downhearted. I guess he had been excited about the castle. Maybe I should have kept the castle and had little bats flying above the towers.

I did not like that decisions were being made for me disguised by minimal options. I could choose shades of yellow and green to go with the castle. Really! I knew I was being kept under surveillance and that my servants were also spies for my husband. I was allowed to fly around inside a large, very comfortable cage. In high school my motto was ,"Tell me the rules so I can get around them." My beloved husband did not grasp how heightened my abilities had become. Smell, taste, sight, strength and, I'm guessing, better reaction time, not to mention reading people's feelings. I could not help but wonder if I would be reading thoughts soon as well. In general, I was more sensitive to my environment. I was also feeling more confident, less overwhelmed by the vampires' strong personalities. When the Magus granted me an audience I did not become anxious and timid like most of the undead. I knew he wanted to have a good rapport with me. It was not just the pregnancy. I mattered to that nocturnal egomaniac but I was not sure why.

I spent a few hours going over my manuscript and getting it ready for my publisher. He came into my room to talk about the night's ball. I handed him the manuscript. "Remember this, it's the book that got me into so much trouble," I said.

"I'll send if off to an editor."

"You aren't going to read it first?"

"I read it last night before I came to bed. I approve of the Count," he added with a smile, "though I would have preferred a different ending. You can still change it."

"No!" I replied curtly.

"Very well, it's your fantasy. We leave for the ball in an hour," he said and left.

I could have fired back that I wished I was Polly, but I was not in the mood to fight with him. I wanted to enjoy myself that night. I soaked in the tub, then called Tillie to fix my hair. She also brought up a bowl of vegetarian chili and a grilled cheese sandwich made with Brie. I chowed down and felt fine. My appetite was getting extreme but I was eating for three even if the other two were tiny.

My mom and dad called. "Honey, how are you? How is the Baron, I mean Stan? Is the weather nice? It's been humid here."

"We are fine. I'm adjusting well to being married and no morning sickness today," I replied.

"Let Stan know we got the Blackhawk tickets. That was so nice of him. What size does he wear? We want to send him a Blackhawks T-shirt," my Dad piped up.

"Large, he's about 6 foot 3 inches but he's thin. I think he will love that. Great idea." I could not wait to see him in a T-shirt.

"We framed the wedding picture and put it over the couch. You look beautiful, and he is very handsome," my Mom sighed.

"Pictures of Tristan are rare, he is extremely camera shy but he made an exception for you guys."

"Are you eating enough? Taking prenatal vitamins?" My mom asked.

"Stan has a family doctor and a nurse who make house calls and check up on me weekly. I'm in good hands. They say I'm fine."

"Did you eat some beef?" My Dad inquired.

"Barbacoa tacos!"

"That's my girl! Were they any good?"

"Not as good as yours but close." I knew he was smiling on the other end. "Maybe you could make some for me when you visit."

We said our goodbyes after discussing their travel arrangements. Los Angeles would be enough of a culture shock without adding vampires pretending to be normal. I was more anxious about my parent's visiting than living with vampires. What would Freud have said about that? I told myself to stay focused on the task at hand. Tillie finished curling my hair. Then she helped me slip on the gown. It was a garment that transformed the wearer. The black lace neckline revealed enough of my shoulders and cleavage to be very flattering. There was a slit up the back which made it easy to move. I put on the ruby pendant, which unknown to me had become infamous in vampire circles since Simone's demise. I also put on the bracelet from Lady Kananga. I kept my makeup minimal as my clothing and jewelry added enough drama. The heels gave me just enough elegance and height. Tillie looked in one of the drawers in the armoire and pulled out a small silk clutch and handed it to me. When I opened it, I found tissue, my lip balm and a little dagger. "You really think it's necessary?"

"Just be careful, Baroness. You don't want chapped lips," she replied and left.

I went to my husband's suite. He was dressed in a black silk suit and white shirt with a black and white tie with tiny geometric shapes that glistened slightly. The suit was cut to flatter his muscular frame. He smelled great. The Baron nodded his approval of my appearance.

"Miranda, you look every inch a Baroness. Very regal." He walked over, took me in his arms and kissed me deeply. I will always remember that kiss. "Shall we go?"

I was feeling like pulling him down on the bed but I said, "Yes. Lead the way."

Jasper drove the Bentley to the front door of the club and let us out in grand style. Sir Steve was at the door and smiled warmly. We were shown to the table I had sat at before but the club was more crowded tonight. The well-dressed undead were staring at me as we walked across the floor. I looked around. Apparently, except for the Magus, we were the last to arrive at the ball.

"They can't all be from L.A.," I muttered.

"They are members of the House of Plows and their guests. They have come from many places to be honored tonight, though I believe seeing you matters almost as much as the Magus' praise. You are unique," Sir Steve replied as he escorted us to our seats.

"Yeah, well, so is everyone else," I commented.

I saw Sir Ruben dancing slowly with Kabedi. Her radiant smile was just for him. He had combed his red curls and shaved. It was strange to see him in a suit. Kabedi wore yards of silver glistening fabric wrapped about her like a sari. Lady Lockporte joined us with Johann. He held himself stiffly and did not sit at the table, but rather placed himself behind her chair and politely nodded. The Baron ignored him but I smiled in return. His stare was studious and cold. Lady Lockporte was in the best of spirits. She wore a low-cut burgundy gown with black roses made up of thousands of beads covering the bodice. Her long red curls had been pulled back to keep them out of her way during the transformation.

"I can't wait to show the House how to properly pass on the gift. It is rare to be able to display one's skills to such a large audience, not to mention before the Magus."

"Yeah, I can tell you're pretty stoked," I replied, trying not to let her know that the whole idea was repulsive to me.

Small plates of raw steak cubes were place on all the tables with small silver forks. The Baron ate a couple of pieces and appeared to enjoy it. Shot glasses of blood were placed on all the tables. Sir Steve placed one in front of me. I started to refuse and he whispered, "Cranberry juice." Did I mention that I really liked Sir Steve? "Don't tell the others," he said with a smile.

The Magus entered with Lady Hauser on his arm. The room fell silent. He wore a gray shirt, a black vest and a black tie with a diamond stick pin. He could have just walked off the set of a *Godfather* movie. Lady Hauser wore a pale lavender gown made of somewhat transparent material that suggested she was in great shape. A platinum crescent moon covered by diamonds hung about her neck. They stopped in the middle of the room behind a reflecting pond. Their reflection made them seem almost magical.

"We have come tonight to honor the House of Plows," the Magus paused and the undead throng politely clapped. "Lady Lockporte has for many years embodied loyalty, strength, valor and humility in her leadership of this noble House." Again, there was a pause for polite applause. The Magus nodded towards Lady Lockporte. "She will honor us tonight by transforming a most charming, intelligent and talented prospect who has requested to be able to join the House of Plows." The applause was louder for the chance to see blood spilled. I noticed how the faces of the vampires seemed to light up at the suggestion, even Tristan. Elegant chairs were brought to our table as the Magus and Lady Hauser joined us.

Lady Hauser commented that I looked well. I just smiled to avoid having a conversation with her. She fawned over my husband, complimenting his attire. The Magus watched me without speaking. Perhaps he did not need to ask. Lady Lockporte excused herself from the table to prepare for the ceremony, followed by Johann. To my delight, Lady Kananga joined us in a black satin tuxedo which emphasized her tiny waist. She had a warmth that could not be diminished by her undead nature.

"I meant to tell you last time," she said. "It's about the bracelet. I'm glad you appreciate its beauty. Like you there is much more to it. If you push down and slide the lion's head back, a blade will appear. It is very sharp, like a razor," she smiled.

"Thanks. Kabedi had mentioned something about that," I replied. I could not help but wonder why she and Tillie were so concerned about arming me. Even Sir Sadeghi had given me a lovely knife. That was not counting the one Tristan had stuck in my ninja boot. Maybe it was a way they expressed affection in this culture, or maybe I had more to worry about than I thought. At that moment, I glanced at the Magus. He nodded slightly, perhaps responding to my thoughts. I was about to ask Lady Kananga why I might need it now but the lights dimmed and a hush fell over the crowd. I noticed Sergio watching from a nearby table.

An overhead light fell on the chair in the center of the dance floor by the main reflecting pool. The blond woman I had seen a picture of on Tristan's computer was being led to the chair by Sir Steve and Sir Ruben. Lady Lockporte followed behind them. Pauline Barnes sat down with a faint smile on her lips. She wore a black satin nightgown and nervously slid the strap down on her left side. Sir Steve held towels and bandages. Sir Ruben had a bottle of O positive blood and an IV bag. Lady Lockporte held up a ceremonial blade to the crowd and then bowed to the Magus. Sir Ruben secured the IV needle in Pauline's arm. She made no sound, she did not even wince.

I whispered to my husband "What did the Magus do before IVs?"

"Goat skins and hallowed out bones. Lena was the first successful transformation." he whispered back.

"Let the transformation begin," the Magus called out.

Lady Lockporte leaned down and bit into Pauline's chest wall. The young woman cried out for an instant then seemed to pass out. Lady Lockporte quickly drank deeply, putting Pauline in shock. Then she raised her head, her lips dripping with blood and, with the ceremonial blade, lightly cut her own wrist and held it to the mouth of the prospective vampiress. Muffled cries of excitement could be heard from the undead crowd. Sir Steve withdrew three syringes of blood from Lady Lockporte and emptied them into the IV bag filled with O positive. The prospect, Pauline, began to suck on Lady Lockporte's wrist. The bittersweet scent of HH blood filled the room. As Lady Lockporte reached out to steady herself, Sir Ruben put his arm about her. He began to give her sips of blood from a silver cup while she was still bleeding into Pauline. The ceremony lasted about five minutes. Finally, Lady Lockporte withdrew her wrist from the prospect. Sir Steve bandaged Pauline's chest, then quickly put pressure on Lady Lockporte's wrist but it was already starting to heal. The new vampire was gently carried out by the Magus' servants to his limousine, with her IV bag held high. She would be watched over by Lady Lily at his mansion for a couple of days before being tutored by Lady Lockporte.

I was feeling a bit queasy. All around, I could hear comments about what a lovely ceremony it was. It was horrible. It is one thing to watch a horror movie and it is another thing to live in one. I just kept thinking about that poor young woman.

"Baron, don't you think it is delightful to have such a high quality, young vampiress enter the House of Plows after such a tragic incident with the House of Pentacles?" Lady Kananga asked.

"It will undoubtedly help the morale of some but not Sudovian's people," the Baron responded. "You may have heard that Sergio will become the knight to the House of Pentacles."

"Nice tactical move," she replied.

"Sorry to put a damper on the fun but I'm feeling a little queasy. Could we go home now?" I asked, looking a little pale.

"Of course, but I was hoping to speak with Lady Hauser and the Magus. Perhaps Lady Kananga could accompany you to Stone Canyon."

"I would be glad to. Come Baroness, we'll find Jasper." Lady Kananga gently took my arm. "I'm sure it was quite upsetting to see your first transformation. In time, the raw beauty becomes apparent."

As we got in the Bentley I saw Johann helping Lady Lockporte into her Jaguar. Sir Ruben was standing nearby with Kabedi. He called out, "Thanks Johann. Take good care of her."

On our way back to the mansion Lady Kananga explained that both the transformed and the one who gives the gift need to rest after the event. They are both in a weakened state for a couple of days. "Though she is HH, which means she will take the transformation more easily. A new member of the Haute Caste has been born."

"Sergio is not HH. Does that mean he can't join the royals?"

"Despite his relationship with Lady Hauser, he can never be one of us. It's what Simone was demanding, to be given Haute Caste status."

"Understanding a situation you involve yourself in does not mean acceptance," I replied. "Sergio knew he could not be on an equal basis with her now but still chose to be transformed. I think he still hopes that will change." Lady Kananga glanced at me. "The Baron refers to people who think beyond their status as 'The Fool.' He is not referring to you. You and the children will find a unique place in our society. Sergio is lucky, he is being appointed knight to Sir Sudovian. He can go no higher."

"Despite what I said, I honestly don't think he regrets it."

"I've never known of a vampire who wanted their life to go back to the way it was," Lady Kananga said confidently.

We dropped her off next door and Jasper took me back to our home. Just as we arrived, Johann and Tillie were helping Lady Lockporte to her room. I waited till they were down the hall to the guest wing to quietly slip into my husband's suite. I did not feel like being fussed over by Tillie. I laid the gown across a chair and crawled into the comfy bed. A sleepy Delilah barely acknowledged me. I hoped Tristan would be home soon.

CHAPTER 30

AS I WAS falling asleep I heard a knock. I called out, "What is it?"

"It's Clive, Baroness. I'm sorry to bother you, Delilah needs to go out."

"It's okay Clive, you can come in," I was sleeping in my slip but I covered up to avoid any impropriety.

"Delilah," he called out from the doorway. She slowly stretched and got to her feet. It was as though she enjoyed making Clive wait for her. Truly a royal cat.

"Don't bother to knock when you let her back in," I told him.

"Of course, Baroness," he replied.

I lay back down and was soon drifting off to sleep. I was not sure how much time had passed when I heard the door open. I tried to ignore it but something woke me up. It was an unfamiliar scent that stirred my senses. A vampire but not one that was familiar to me. I reached for the lion's head bracelet. The figure closed the door and slowly, silently, approached the bed. I pushed on the lion's head and heard a click. The gray figure stopped moving. I hit the light switch. Johann lunged at me, trying to get his hands around my neck. "No!" I screamed before he could silence me. It felt like he was crushing my wind pipe. His eyes were filled with hate. I blindly struck at his face with the blade. The scent of his blood filled the air. Suddenly he released me. Johann fell backwards covering his face, moaning, as blood flowed down his suit. Clive burst into the room with Delilah. With a screeching growl, she pounced on Johann, knocking him to the ground and began ripping at his body with her razor-sharp claws. I screamed and scrambled to my feet. Tristan ran in and helped Clive pull Delilah off the shrieking assassin. He lay shaking on the ground.

"Miranda!" he came to the bed and held me in his arms.

"He was trying to kill our babies, it wasn't just me!"

"You're trembling. I should have come home with you. Clive, call Dr. Kyoto and Lady Lily!"

"I'm okay but who else wants me dead?" I demanded.

"We will find out who is involved," the Baron said in a somber tone. "So sorry, Delilah, but the Magus will decide his fate after he is allowed to confess his sins." Jasper and Clive removed the snarling cat. The Baron kept one arm about me as he called the Magus. He explained the situation in coded language. I was able to gather that a "surprise visitor" would be delivered to his estate soon. The conversation was so short, I had the feeling it was not much of a surprise to the Magus.

Clive returned and regarded the bloody, shaking remnants of Johann. "Lady Lily and Dr. Kyoto will arrive shortly. Shall we remove this trash?" Jasper arrived, carrying a roll of plastic sheeting.

"Yes. You and Jasper may take what is left of him to the Magus now" Tristan replied.

"No...No.." cried Johann though his speech was faint and garbled. Jasper and Clive wrapped up the moaning vampire and quickly carried the weak assassin from the room.

"Thank Lady Kananga!" I held up the knife bracelet. "It saved me."

"The Magus will reward her and I will give her my gratitude." He stroked my head gently. I snuggled into his chest and stopped trembling. "Before you, no mortal ever fought off a vampire successfully." He put his hand under my chin and looked into my eyes as though trying to see my soul "You've done it twice. Your fame will grow."

"I think I'd rather be known for my writing. You almost got here just in time."

"I was talking with Lady Hauser about your book. The Magus interrupted and said that you were in danger. Are you sure you're okay?"

"I think so, but now I'm hungry," I said and looked up into his eyes.

"You never cease to amaze me." He put a silk robe about my shoulders. He was about to call Tillie when I suggested we go downstairs while Tillie cleaned the room.

"The Magus has amazing powers," I said leaning on my husband as we went downstairs.

My husband smiled. "Yes, and it is enhanced by technology. This house is wired for surveillance."

When we got to the kitchen, Sir Ruben arrived breathless, "Did he hurt you?"

"No. I'm upset but fine."

"That bastard! I'm going to check on my sister."

"Word gets around quickly" I remarked.

"The Magus said he would start an investigation immediately. I imagine Sir Steve will be in charge. We will find out who is behind these attacks. Luckily for him Delilah dislikes the taste of vampires. The audacity and stupidity of this attack makes me wonder if it was planned quickly because Simone and her henchmen failed."

I found a baguette, some chicken salad and cheese. Tristan watched me intently. "I'm okay," I said as I started to eat and then paused. "The adrenaline rush is gone. You think I'm just getting used to being attacked?" I took a bite of chicken salad. "Wow, I didn't even think about eating meat. It just sounded good."

Dr. Kyoto and Lady Lily walked into the kitchen "You must be craving protein," Lady Lily responded. They fussed over me for a few minutes and, after taking my vitals, pronounced me unhurt.

"Normally I would expect bruising to develop about your neck but there are no signs of injury," Dr. Kyoto said, "which would make sense if you were a vampiress, but not ..."

"A Short? Good thing I'm enhanced. You know, I think Johann could use your help more than me." I took another bite of bread, then went over to the fridge for some apple juice.

"We saw him briefly, you cut off his nose. Hopefully Tillie will find it, it wasn't with him," Lady Lily said. "Your blood pressure is back to normal. That's a very short recovery period."

"You don't have to be afraid of me," I said and smiled at Lady Lily.

"How did you..." she stared at me.

"I don't know. I sense things. I just felt Johann in the room." I emptied the glass of juice. The cool, sweet beverage was a welcome bite of normalcy. "Dr. Kyoto is amused and Tristan is thrilled."

"Absolutely, you're evolving so quickly. You're stronger than I had hoped for," Tristan responded with pride. "Your physical and emotional recovery time is impressive."

"Most people would not want a meal right after being attacked," Dr. Kyoto commented, "but you are pregnant."

"Exactly." Images of Wonder Woman flashed in my head, then I took another bite of bread. I felt like taking a bite out of Johann. "I was fighting for the babies," I replied.

Sir Ruben entered the kitchen "That should make you mother of the year. Lady Lockporte is fine. She seems to have slept through the excitement. Boy will she be pissed when she finds out. So, what is with the House of Pentacles?" No one wanted to speculate about that question. "I would hate to be Sudovian."

"How is Pauline?" the Baron asked to change the conversation.

"She appears to have accepted the transfusion well. What a night. Interesting times since the Baroness came to town. So many questions," Sir Ruben replied. "But I get the hint we should wait for the facts. If I can be of any service."

"Thank you, Ruben," my husband said in a serious tone "Your curiosity is understandable. Tomorrow night we will discuss an appropriate course of action."

"Yes, the dawn is approaching, we shall return tomorrow," Dr. Kyoto said.

Lady Lily handed me a small lacquer box with loose tea inside "If you have any difficulty sleeping." She turned to Sir Ruben "Make sure Lady Lockporte drinks a few more ounces of O positive before you retire."

"Dr. Kyoto, I have this feeling you are hiding something from me," I stated.

He stared at me with a slight smile. "Baroness, I was waiting for a more serene moment but I suppose it will not matter." He looked to the Baron, who nodded approval. "The tests indicate that you will have triplets."

"Tristan, you knew this?" I asked astonished he had kept the news from me.

"I just heard last night. It's still very early but it looks likely."

"Triplets? You should have a vasectomy!" I exclaimed

Before he could respond, Tillie entered with a baggie full of ice and a small bloody object. "Here you are, Dr. Kyoto."

"Thank you, Tillie. Please get it to the Magus." He bowed slightly to the Baron, who responded in kind and they left quickly.

"I guess more congratulations are in order," Sir Ruben responded. He looked at the Baron, "Good job citizen!" then he took a small cup of blood to his sister's room.

"I always thought I'd be like my mom and have a hard time getting pregnant. Wow! Triplets! How can there be enough room in me!" I looked down at my tummy.

"I don't have a suitable response to that" the Baron said with a slight smile.

"I want to sleep in my room tonight" I said. He looked a bit disappointed. "With you." His face brightened.

"Of course," he replied.

At LAX, Sergio and Lady Hauser boarded a private jet with heavy shades pulled over the cabin windows. The Magus ordered they leave immediately when he heard of the attack. It would be a long flight to London. They were to report on the state of the House of Pentacles to the Magus. Lady Hauser disliked being ordered about by anyone, even the Magus. To make matters worse for Sergio, she still had not quite forgiven him. It would be a very long flight for Sergio.

CHAPTER 31

MEMBERS OF THE Haute Caste all over the world were notified of the attack. An unprecedented mobilization took place. Sir Sadeghi and several members of his House went to London to meet with Lady Hauser and Sergio. Many of the Haute Caste and members of their Houses descended on Los Angeles. About 50 Haute Caste vampires arrived, longing to be at the disposal of the Magus. It seemed that for many years a bit of a rebellion had been fomenting within the younger ranks. Like Simone and Harold, the restless Common Caste wanted to be made members of the Haute Caste regardless of their lack of HH blood type or character. My appearance and acceptance into the Haute Caste circles brought their demands for fairness out into the open. Perhaps that is what the Magus wanted all along, to flush them out. I felt like a hunting decoy. The blood banks were going to be getting a lot of withdrawals. Several months ago homes had been bought in Malibu, Venice Beach and Topanga Canyon to house the visitors. The property next door had been the last home acquired for the undead hordes. It felt weird to be on the side of the royals as I had always imagined myself to be one of the struggling masses. I would have to throw out my Che Guevara T-shirt.

When I woke in the early evening, Tristan was till sound asleep. I left him in my room and wandered downstairs. I visited with my birds, who were very happy to have my attention.

"I'm glad you like them," a familiar voice commented. Jorge yawned in the doorway.

"Jorge!" I gave him a hug.

"That was a horrible flight," a slightly disheveled Sir Franco complained as he came into the room.

"I've never seen your hair messed up," I said.

"I know I look a fright, don't remind me," Sir Franco muttered and headed off to their suite.

"Don't mind him, dear Miranda, how are you?" Jorge inquired with concern in his voice.

"I'm ...." my words stopped as tears began to fall. Jorge just put his arm about my shoulders.

"Franco and I will stay close. We will stay through the pregnancy." He gave me his monogrammed handkerchief.

I composed myself. "Thank you. This is the first time I've cried since Johann attacked me. You should have seen his eyes. I don't understand why." I looked at him hoping for an explanation.

"Perhaps we will find out more from the Magus tonight. For now, why don't you have some breakfast while I see about our accommodations."

"Thank you for coming."

I sat in the kitchen slowly sipping my coffee and eating buttered scones, hoping not to be nauseated. A young, tall woman with long dyed blonde hair and blue eyes entered with Tillie in the rear carrying her luggage. She eyed me with a slight smile. She wore black everything and high-heeled boots. The scent of jasmine mixed with her blood type.

"Baroness, I'm so sorry I wasn't here to fix you something," Tillie apologized and dropped the bags. The vampiress gave her an irritated glance. "May I present Lady Anastasia."

"Hi. I'm Miranda," I replied. "There's O positive in the fridge."

"Charming," she responded with a Russian accent that sounded a bit like a purr.

"I have to ask, the Anastasia that got away?"

She merely nodded and walked off to the guest wing where Sir Jorge and Sir Franco were housed. Tillie followed behind. Wow! So now a tsarina was staying in the asylum. I thought about famous people who had died young and wondered if they had opted to be people of the night. I finished my cup of caffeine. Clive walked by followed by the nursery painters. The lids on the cans of paint they carried had a blob of periwinkle blue. My wishes were being carried out.

Tillie returned and started pulling out pots and dishes. "I'll make a cheese fondue for you. Is there anything else you would like?"

I did not have the heart to ask for jalapeño poppers. "That would be fine, thanks." I think the guests were a bit on the diva side. She would have her hands full catering to their whims. "I'll be in the library."

I lay on one of the leather couches and stared out the window at the night sky.

"Good evening Baroness" Sir Steve said and sat down on the opposite couch.

"Hi. What brings you to Stone Canyon?"

"Your popularity" he replied a bit sadly. "One of us will be near you at all times, by order of the Magus. I should have figured Johann would try something. Cowardly Pentacles! Thankfully, you seem unharmed."

"Yeah. I'm a little overwhelmed by all this but okay. Anastasia arrived."

"I've had a crush on her for a very long time," he stated.

"Just a crush?" I was surprised to hear the undead express innocent longing.

"Very few get close to her," he said softly.

"How long have you been undead?"

"I was born in Brooklyn in 1810. I got harassed a lot when I was young, so I joined the circus. That's where Ruben found me."

"So, you never left the circus!"

"I like this amusement park much better," he replied.

"I was just starting to enjoy the rides, then last night it went to hell. I thought the rogue vampires had been eliminated, that I could pretty much feel safe among you. Now I'm not sure who to trust, present company in the house excluded."

Sir Steve's expression became serious. "The Magus has called upon his most loyal nobles to keep you safe. He is meeting with a few of the Nobles from each house to insure their loyalty. We will root out the immature, foolish, greedy rebels who dare to call themselves vampires. They have no self-discipline and no respect for our social order."

"Anastasia is here protecting me?"

"Lady Anastasia is one of the foremost assassins in the world, like Sir Sadeghi. She hates anyone attacking royals, as you might imagine. Rest assured you will be safe," he replied confidently. "Franco and Ruben are also very skilled."

At the Magus' estate in a small garden house, Johann was handcuffed and shackled to a steel bed that was bolted to the floor. He had been cleaned up and a large bandage covered his nose. In a leather chair on the other side of the room sat the ruler of the undead, contemplating the traitor's fate. Johann stared at the ceiling afraid to look at the Magus. The wait, the uncertainty of how he would be tortured, the deep wounds from Delilah and the pain of having his nose stitched on were putting him over the edge. Johann saw no chance for a reprieve. He finally broke. "I will tell you whatever you want to know," he sobbed.

"What member of the Haute Caste's commands are you following?" the Magus demanded in a soft but chilling tone.

"You won't believe me," Johann replied.

The Magus walked over to the bed and placed his hand on Johann's sweaty forehead. Tell me," he commanded in a louder tone.

"It's the only true lady, it's Lady Hauser!"

The Magus cried out "That wretch!" so loudly the small building's windows rattled.

When he touched the trembling man he was able to read enough of his thoughts to know he spoke the truth. "She said it would keep us pure. That in time you would realize we were right," Johann sniffled. "She promised to make me a lord."

"And Sudovian?"

"I only know she was going to blame it all on him, then replace him with Harold or me."

"Who else?" The Magus placed his hand back on Johann's forehead.

"Besides Simone and Harold, I know of no one else, I swear!"

The Magus walked towards the door.

"We were so stupid to question your judgment, to believe her! I am so sorry. Just end my miserable existence, I beg you."

"I will not be that kind," the Magus responded and left the garden house.

CHAPTER 32

SIR DIEGO, THE Baron, Lady Anastasia, Dr. Kyoto, Lady Lockporte, Lady Lily, Sir Ruben and Lady Kananga arrived at the Paradise Cove estate in the early evening. They were shown to a large private office which overlooked an oriental garden and koi pond. No small talk or pleasantries were exchanged. They all knew the severity of the crime they were to deal with but not yet who was responsible. The Magus entered wearing a taupe linen suit. They all rose and slightly bowed their heads. He greeted them with a nod and thanked them for coming. They would do anything to stay in his favored circle.

"Please be seated." He settled into a dark green leather chair. The others made themselves comfortable on the plush couches and loveseats.

"Will Sir Sadeghi and Lady Hauser be joining us online?" Lady Kananga asked.

"No," the Magus replied, which caused some suspicious looks. "I have had this room debugged. The rest of the house is being checked tonight. Your residences are also being checked tonight. A scrambling device is keeping this meeting secure. What I am about to tell you deserves the utmost confidentiality." He paused and a heavy silence fell on the room. "I am extremely saddened and angered by what I have to report. Johann has confessed that the mastermind behind the attempts on the Baroness is none other than Lady Hauser."

"Impossible," the Baron uttered. "She would never..."

"You have proof?" Sir Diego asked, quite shaken as well.

"I'm not surprised," Lady Anastasia said coldly and Lady Kananga nodded.

"It is unthinkable," Dr. Kyoto responded.

"I was able to read his thoughts enough to know he told me the truth."

"Lady Hauser has always protected me," the Baron said. "How can this be true?"

"May I respond?" Lady Anastasia asked. The Magus nodded. She turned towards the Baron. "You did not see the jealous, possessive side of her nature. Lady Hauser often tried to keep other vampiresses away from you and the Magus."

"Except Simone," Lady Kananga added, "because she knew you would never become overly fond of her."

"She is jealous! That is what this is about?" the Baron wondered out loud.

"Not in the least. She wants to be the Magus," Lady Lockporte stated, which caused years of suspicions and dislike to come pouring out of the flood gates.

"It is about power. She is afraid of being eclipsed," Sir Diego said. "She covered it up so well, appearing to be bringing the Baroness into our world. Lady Hauser is very aware of the Baroness' potential. She did not foresee how quickly she would progress, or her ability to protect herself. She apparently manipulated the disgruntled, rebellious vampires so they would do her dirty work," Sir Diego said. "They thought they could count on her for favors. Amazing. How could we have been so blind?"

"Not all of us were," Lady Kananga replied. "She used the Baroness to upset the commoners, but when she started seeing the Baroness as a threat tried to eliminate her."

"Sudovian?" Lady Lily asked. The room became quiet. "Sir Sadeghi? Sergio? Were other Houses involved?"

"Johann did not know of others involvement, he was kept ignorant," the Magus responded. "Sir Sadeghi has never been suspect. He is aiding me."

"What will you do? Can you destroy her?" Sir Ruben questioned. This was the question they all were thinking about.

"I shall remove her from our world. Tomorrow, I will tell those of you in this room and Pauline how it will happen. It will take several of the Haute Caste to trap her."

The room fell silent as they considered what the Magus was planning. A way to dispose of the Haute Caste was mind boggling and a bit frightening.

"I have difficulty believing she would turn against us," the Baron stated.

"She didn't turn on you," Lady Anastasia responded, "but your wife and your offspring. In her mind, they threaten her hold on you and, I dare say, the Magus."

"We must at all cost protect the Baroness. Sir Franco and Steve are with her now. Even when you are with your wife, another will be close by," the Magus instructed.

"It will be my honor to protect her," Lady Anastasia said.

"We are all willing to do whatever we can to safeguard the royal family," Dr. Kyoto said. "But what is the plan to deal with the present threat?"

"For now," the Magus replied, "I will keep Lady Hauser in London. Let it be known that Johann was decapitated by Delilah and could not be saved though I will keep him alive as he might still be useful to us. Lady Hauser and her traitors think they have covered their tracks. I believe she will try to make Sudovian the focus of our attention. His involvement is still unknown. The Baroness must be told that she is not to have any communication with Sir Sudovian, Lady Hauser or Sergio until we are certain all guilty parties have been discovered."

"I must not have contact either. They would detect my anger," the Baron responded.

"Your in-laws are coming so you have an excuse for being occupied," Sir Ruben said with a grin.

"Don't remind me," the Baron muttered.

The Magus looked at Lady Anastasia who was wearing a black lace tank with tight, black and gray, leopard print jeans. "Though I have always appreciated your fashion sense, I'm afraid you'll have to wear a white lab coat, like Lady Lily, around the visitors."

"I shall be a consulting physician with a specialty in multiple births," she responded a bit like a royal decree. Lady Lily rolled her eyes without Lady Anastasia seeing it.

The Magus, with a fleeting smile, fought back a laugh. "We have two very difficult tasks. We must ferret out the traitors and apprehend them for justice. Secondly, we must try to appear normal to the Baroness' parents."

"Send me to London," Sir Ruben replied.

"I plan on sending you, Lady Lockporte, Lady Kananga and Pauline because you and your sister are formidable foes and the only ones her parents may recognize from your stays in Rossville. I believe Pauline may be useful with exposing Lady Hauser as she has little knowledge of our newest member. Lady Kananga, your strength, speed and wisdom will be needed to successfully capture Lady Hauser. In another day, Lady Lockporte, you and Pauline shall both have recovered from the transformation and be ready. It will give the young vampiress a chance to prove herself. Don't you agree she is quite promising?"

"She hated to have to wait so long to be transformed," Sir Ruben replied.

Dr. Kyoto added, "Her blood work is very healthy. She consumed a pint when she first woke like it was mother's milk. She will be ready."

"And loyal?" Lady Anastasia questioned.

"She is quite devoted to my dear sister," Sir Ruben said.

"Excellent," the Magus responded.

"Perhaps I could be more useful in London!" Lady Anastasia protested.

"My lady, we are not sure all the traitors are abroad." The Magus stated. "I know that, save for the Baron, none of you are particularly fond of Lady Hauser. That is why you and Sir Sadeghi are part of my loyal inner circle."

Lady Kananga commented, "Forgive me for being so blunt but I have always thought she coveted your position."

"I was aware of her tendencies but never believed she would act on them," he responded sadly. "It seems my judgment was clouded by our centuries to-gether. She has become toxic to the vampire world and must be stopped."

"Miranda has always strongly disliked her," the Baron said. "I should have trusted her instincts."

"Lena has always been a bitch to me," Lady Lily interjected in a polite tone which caught everyone off guard. Suddenly they all began laughing, even the Magus.

"Lily!" Dr. Kyoto responded, trying to find composure.

"Very well," the Magus said. "Please see to the well-being of the Baroness. Good evening."

Sir Steve and Sir Franco seemed to find amusement in watching me eat as we sat at the dining room table. They sipped silver cups of O positive while I downed the cheese fondue. I was just starting on lemon meringue pie when Sir Franco remarked, "I worry about the children."

"Really! Your diet sucks!" I smiled.

"Low blow," Sir Steve replied.

The Baron, Sir Jorge and Lady Anastasia arrived, which halted the banter.

"How are you feeling?" the Baron asked and leaned down to kiss my forehead.

I noticed Lady Anastasia smile. She seemed to approve of the Baron's relationship with a Short.

"I'm okay. What happened to Johann?"

"We'll talk about that later."

As I stared up at Tristan it suddenly became clear to me. "It's Lady Hauser! I knew it! She's behind all this, isn't she?" I shouted out.

"Everyone, please leave us," the Baron said.

"You should try to keep your thought reading to yourself," Lady Anastasia remarked as they left. "I'll take the first watch."

"It happens so fast, like an avalanche of thoughts and pictures," I told him.

He sat beside me and took my hand. His eyes were so beautiful, so sad and yet reassuring. I could also sense the love he held for me and the children.

"You are right. It is Lady Hauser," he got a little teary. I could feel him fighting back sadness and replacing it with anger. "We will deal with her. She does not know Johann confessed to the Magus. You must not have any contact with her, Sergio or Sir Sudovian. Any little thing you might say or feel could tip her off. She will remain in London while Lady Kananga, Lady Lockporte, Sir Ruben and Pauline are sent to bring her to justice and find out if anyone else is involved. If at any time you sense that something is wrong, you must tell me."

"I will," I picked up a napkin and dabbed my eyes. "I feel so sorry for Sergio. He really loves her."

"I feel like I'm turning my back on my dearest friend," the Baron said, "But it seems I have never really known her. She would have had you and the children killed to secure her position in the vampire hierarchy."

"You still don't understand. I never believed her devotion to the Magus. She is too egotistical to accept a number two position. I bet she has been trying to undermine him by encouraging the young vampires to rebel for 100 years. Her attacks on me are attempts at solidifying her power, weakening the Magus, and she wants you to be her second in command. If Johann had been successful, she would probably have comforted you and pretended to find out Johann was responsible and killed him before he could talk. The Magus must realize this, see her end game. Everything she does is for show, to achieve her goals. If you had once gotten in her way she would have plotted to eliminate you too. She does not feel love for anyone but herself."

The Baron looked at me like he had never truly seen me before. "All this time I thought I was teaching you."

"That's the problem with you and all the other undead, it's your Achilles' heel. You underestimate everyone. Lena is worried about me because I'm something she has not dealt with before, an uppity Short. She thought I could be killed and that would be the end of it. Lena now knows she miscalculated, which must bug the crap out of her. I'm not sure about my abilities but I just cut off a vampire's nose, so I think I can defend myself."

"I am worried about Lady Lockporte and Lady Kananga dealing with her in London. Her powers are legendary," he said.

"Yeah, but she never played ice hockey or hunted in Africa. They'll be fine. They understand how she thinks. They won't underestimate Lena, like you and the Magus did. He chose the right people to send to London."

"Lady Anastasia and Lady Lily expressed a strong dislike for her as well. I'm beginning to understand the ability of women to read other women."

I slowly shook my head. "Not getting women is a flaw shared by all men. Short or undead," I added. I put his hand on my belly. "And you'll probably have a daughter who will confound and amaze you as well."

"And a son? Tell me I'll have at least one child I can easily understand."

"Let's go pick out names for boys and girls. I want to have a list before my parents get her."

We went up to the Baron's suite but never got around to picking names.

CHAPTER 33

WHEN GRIGORYI GOT off work, the Baron's chauffeur was waiting for him in the parking lot. He requested that Grigoryi have a word with someone in a limousine, a Mr. Dontinae. His anxiety level increased as he approached the vehicle. He knew it had to be another vampire. The thought of running seemed to be pointless, they would find him eventually. The chauffeur opened the door and he climbed in. A man with dark hair, brown eyes, possibly Greek, spoke to him. He had seen him once before.

"Grigoryi, I believe you might have some information that could be useful to me."

"You're one of them, aren't you?" Grigoryi whispered. "The undead."

The Magus merely nodded. "I think you may have had contact with other of my kind recently, am I right?"

Grigoryi replied, "Yes. Did I do anything wrong? I've tried to cooperate. I just want to help Miranda, I mean the Baroness."

"Describe the person who contacted you."

Grigoryi felt himself squirm under the Magus' scrutiny. He was not sure if he was helping the Baroness, but fear for his life caused him to respond honestly. "White with short, straight dark brown hair, long red nails and lots of pearls," he went on. "I think I saw her once before that night at the beach with you."

The Magus stared at the little monk and considered how wise it had been to show him mercy. "What did she ask of you?"

"She said I was to let her know when the Baroness came by and who she was with. To help protect her. She gave me $1,000 and this phone to send her updates."

"Anything else?" the Magus seemed to stare into Grigoryi's soul.

"Yes, but I didn't do it. I'm sorry but it didn't feel right. She wanted me to put this powder into her coffee, said it was vitamins." He pulled a small baggie out of his pocket and handed it to the Magus. "I was going to get it tested first."

A cold anger filled the limo, making Grigoryi start to tremble. The Magus looked at the powder, then back at the monk. "Most assuredly not vitamins but I have no doubt poison, probably arsenic!"

"I didn't know. I swear. I was afraid of her, so I acted like I would cooperate," Grigoryi stammered.

"Have you had contact with any other vampires?"

"There was an Arab, not the one at the beach, this one had Western clothes. He paid me last week, said it was from that woman. He told me to keep sending updates. Here, take the phone, I don't want any part of this."

"Keep it but the only updates you will send is that the Baroness has not come by, even if you see her. Do you understand?"

"Yes, yes, I'm sorry, I will do anything to keep her safe." He paused for a moment looking at the Magus and asked, "Who are you?"

"I am the Magus."

"You really exist!" Grigoryi stared at him, wide-eyed. "I remember you at the beach, you came in the helicopter. I didn't know you were the king. The monks thought you were just a legend your highness, whatever I can do."

With a look the Magus cut him off. "You understand that contacting a monk is an extremely rare event and is meant to impress upon you the importance of this matter and following my directives. You will be contacted again to find out about any communications from the vampiress. As long as you truly help to protect the Baroness your life will be spared. You are not to tell anyone about meeting me. You're lucky I don't care for your blood type. Get out!"

"I will do whatever you say!" he exclaimed and quickly exited the limo. The chauffeur handed him a fat envelope with $5,000 in $100 bills, then he uttered a prayer, asking for forgiveness for almost poisoning the Baroness. He decided to light some candles before the evening mass. As much as he liked the California lifestyle, he was seriously considering moving back to Italy. It would be good to see Benedetto again. There were just too many vampires in L.A..

The Magus arrived back at his estate to meet with the group who would represent him in London. He would have liked to take on Lady Hauser himself but he feared leaving the Baroness, as she was still a target and he still had important matters to attend to. They assembled in the library where the Magus sat before an array of monitors which were displaying activities around the world. Pauline looked at the international sites with great curiosity. The Magus turned off all the monitors but one. It was a small private hotel near Sloane Square in London. Hardly the kind of residence the Haute Caste would entertain in.

The Magus turned to Pauline. "Pauline, you look well. How are you feeling?"

The tall, thin, blonde wore tight jeans and a white dress shirt. Her complexion was a bit paler than before. She respectfully stood when he addressed her. "I'm fine, sir."

"Splendid, please sit down. You will have an important part to play in unraveling the insidious plots of Lady Hauser."

"I am honored."

"Lady Lockporte, your House is crucial to our success," he said.

She was dressed in black pants with a paisley silk blouse that complimented her hair and complexion. "Dear Magus, we are eager to correct this outrageous situation."

He nodded to Sir Ruben. "They are set to meet momentarily. She recently acquired this property but does not stay here." The Magus turned back to the screen as a Rolls Royce pulled up to the Annandale House Hotel and Lady Hauser wearing a hat and veil went inside alone. Ruben's eyes went wide seeing the image of Lady Hauser on the screen and blurted out. "What the...?"

His sister, sitting next to him, cut him off poking him in the ribs with her elbow.

He whispered, a bit too loudly, "How is that possible? We can't be seen on camera."

The Magus, still facing the screen with a slight smile answered. "I have had a new technology developed that can detect each vampire's unique biometric and heat signature. It then superimposes the avatar so they can be watched on screen."

Silently everyone in the group looked from the screen to each other then back to the screen. They were more than a little shocked to find out that the Magus could now remotely watch them anywhere.

A few minutes later their individual silent contemplations on this new information were broken as a London taxi showed up and a man in black trench coat with collar turned up, sunglasses and a hat was seen entering the hotel. He turned and removed his sunglasses as he opened the door. Momand was easy to recognize.

Lady Kananga muttered, "Idiot." She stared down at her lap.

"And Sir Sudovian?" Sir Ruben asked.

"No other members of the Haute Caste are known to be involved."

"Sam called me this evening," Lady Kananga reported. "He was contacted by Momand, asking if he was satisfied with being my knight, feeling him out to see if he could be brought into this conspiracy. Sam told him he is grateful for his position. She is running out of young vampires to manipulate"

"Yes, I have heard of other aides to the Haute Caste who were contacted recently, and they were afraid to tell anyone until now," the Magus said.

"Franco, Lily and I were not contacted," Sir Ruben said a bit defensively.

"I am glad to be of the House of Plows," Pauline stated. "What may I do to prove it."

"Momand I shall leave to Sir Sadeghi and I hope he will be merciful."

"I would not be," Lady Kananga retorted.

"Lady Hauser is another matter. She has one very human fault, jealousy. That is where Pauline will be useful. Lady Hauser does not care about Sergio being with a distinguished member of the Haute Caste," the Magus glanced at Lady Lockporte, "but she would be mortified if he were with a young vampiress like Pauline."

"Magus, sir, I am attracted to women, I don't think..."

"Dear Pauline, I know that but they do not. Pretend to be seductive, flirtatious and when he responds that will be enough to upset her. You enjoy sports, talk about his last professional tennis match. Then when Lady Hauser is taken down, you must subdue him, so he can't interfere." Pauline's face lit up at the thought of restraining Sergio. "That is what we require of you, now please go prepare yourself for the trip."

She politely nodded and left the room. The Magus waited a few minutes before continuing. "When Lady Hauser is distracted, one of you will put this arsenic into her cup. She had intended to give it to the Baroness. When she tastes the tainted blood, it is crucial that she is injected immediately." The Magus handed a filled syringe to Lady Kananga and to Lady Lockporte. "Then you and your brother will handcuff and shackle her."

"It will be a pleasure," Lady Lockporte responded.

"Sir Sadeghi will handle Sir Sudovian and Sergio," the Magus said. "A truck with a locked freezer chest will be at your disposal. Place her in that freezer. Once in that suspended state, transport her back here."

"We can be frozen?" Lady Kananga uttered. "Of course."

"Not destroyed but powerless till..." Lady Lockporte said.

"At least 500 years," the Magus added grimly. "It will take a long time for me to begin to consider forgiving her. Now you know the way to stop the Haute Caste. Do not tell anyone else, ever. To the rest of the vampire world she will simply disappear."

At the hotel on Sloane Square, Momand entered the top room where Lady Hauser waited. She sat on a small Victorian loveseat. He bowed to her and she raised her hand so that he might kiss it in royal fashion. He did exactly what she wanted. She adjusted her pearls as he waited for her to speak.

"Momand, did you call that wretched monk?"

"Yes, he said he has not seen the Baroness for a week. Perhaps Johann's attempt will keep her from going out."

"I knew I should have sent you. The House of Pentacles are quite useless," she sighed. "The Magus sent a message that Lady Kananga, Lady Lockporte, her brother and the new vampiress will be joining us to assist in the inquiry. They should arrive tonight."

"Shall I start a rumor about Sudovian?" he asked.

"Mention to Sadeghi that Sudovian seemed very upset that Johann had been killed. That he was quite surprised that the Baroness was unhurt," she replied.

"Of course."

"And Momand, I hope you will keep Lady Kananga distracted during their visit."

"It will be my pleasure," he said with a slight smile, "though I would greatly prefer your favors."

"You shall have my favors after we see Sudovian humiliated and a new head of the House of Pentacles shall be named. Be gone. We both need rest. These secret late afternoon meetings are tiring."

When Momand arrived back at Sir Sedaghi's mansion in Knightsbridge, he quietly made his way to his suite, past the paintings of desert scenes and through the hallways with antique Persian rugs. He opened the door and took off the black trench coat, feeling exhausted by the long hours required for a rendezvous with the Lady Hauser. He settled into the ivory silk sheets and turned off the small crystal lamp by his bed, causing his room to fall into pitch blackness. Momand looked forward to being the master of a fine house. His relationship with Lady Kananga was enjoyable but not exactly bringing him up in the ranks. Lady Hauser knew she could rely on him. She understood how clever and talented he was. His fatigue and fantasies of power distracted him. He drifted off thinking his future was bright. A figure clad all in black hidden in the darkness stepped toward the bed. There was a lightening quick flash of steel. Before he could make a sound, Momand's dreams were ended. The lamp was clicked on. Momand's head rolled onto the floor as blood gushed all over the bed. Sir Sadeghi had struck quickly and stepped back before blood could splatter his garments. He looked down with disdain at what was left of Momand. He wiped his blade upon the covers. With a dark countenance, he called to his servants, "Dispose of this trash. I shall not allow it in my House." Then he walked down the hall to his bedroom and placed his sword in a scabbard set in the headboard of the bed. Sir Sadeghi sent a text message to the Magus, "It is done."

CHAPTER 34

I STOOD ALONE in the nursery looking at the freshly painted decor. A bright rainbow adorned the windowless wall. I tried to imagine three babies blissfully sound asleep in their new world, unaware of the storm that had heralded their creation. I rested my hands on my abdomen hoping to reassure them that all would be well. They were now the focus of my life. The servants were busy preparing the guest quarters for my parents. All the vampires had moved to the mansion next door except for my husband. This would be interesting.

"It will only be four nights, you are sure?" the Baron asked anxiously from the doorway.

"Yes. My parents had to close the café while they're gone. They won't stay any longer."

"Do I look presentable?" he asked. "Is this casual attire necessary?" I had to laugh. He was wearing a powder blue polo shirt, jeans and the running shoes I had bought for him. He hated the look.

"You look fine. My dad only has one suit. He only wears it to funerals and weddings. Dressing like a regular person will help the two of you bond."

"Surely we'll dress for dinner?"

"You are dressed for dinner," I grinned.

"I never spend time with Shorts, besides you. I'm afraid I will offend them," he said. "Or they will offend me," he added quietly.

"I heard you. I can guarantee my mom will, she offends me. C'mon Stan, we have to get to the airport," I remarked with a grin. "Their flight gets in about 8:30."

"Jasper will pick them up."

"Not happening. You have to greet my parents at the airport. If you don't, I guarantee you'll get off on the wrong foot with my mom."

"That's a terrifying thought."

"Exactly." I grabbed his arm and headed downstairs.

We got to the terminal exit about 15 minutes before my parent's plane arrived. Jasper appeared nervous and asked the Baron a couple of times if he needed anything. My husband was perturbed by the sea of humanity.

"All this contact just makes me hungry," he whispered. "Perhaps I could disappear for a moment with that pickpocket." He looked toward a young man in jeans and a T-shirt who seemed to grab something from the backpack of the person in front of him, then slip into the crowd.

"Does the thought of spending time with my parents make you want to kill someone?" I whispered back. He merely smiled.

"Randie! Stan!" My mom yelled as she ran to hug and kiss me and then, to the Baron's shock, she also grabbed him. She was a small, energetic woman with short brown hair and glasses who always wore pastel knits.

"Nice to finally meet you," the Baron said stiffly.

My dad arrived with their carry-on luggage my mom had dropped in her hurry to greet us. He was a thin man about 5 feet 10 inches who could never gain weight. He had an easy smile and soft brown eyes. His hair was kept so short that I never knew if it was straight or curly. He put down the bags and gave me a hug. Then to my husband's relief he held out his hand instead of hugs. The two men looked each over and seemed satisfied. It has always amazed me how men communicate on a primal level.

Jasper took the bags "Is there more luggage, sir?"

"No that's all," my dad responded, a bit surprised by the chauffeur and clearly feeling a bit awkward about having someone carry his luggage.

"How are you feeling, honey?" my mom asked.

"Fine, the morning sickness subsided the last few days. How was your flight?"

"Okay I guess, it's only my second flight ever. Your dad slept most of the time." She smiled and whispered to me, "He looks like a guy on a cover of a romance novel."

"He inspired my writing, didn't you, Stan?" I said loudly.

"At times. So you are optimistic about the Blackhawks?" he inquired of my dad trying to ignore my mom and me.

"Yeah, it's going to be a good season. I think we'll win the cup again but the Oilers are predicted to give us grief.

"Yes, I've learned a lot about the game from some Canadians I know." The Baron smiled. "Perhaps you'd like to hit a few pucks while you're here."

"I'm not much for the beach, a hockey rink sounds great," my dad replied, "I used to play on the town pond as a kid." The Baron glanced at me as we stopped by the Bentley. I flashed him a thumbs up. Jasper put down the bags and opened the door for my mom.

"Thank you," she said. She poked my dad and whispered to him, "Tip him."

"That's not necessary," I told her, "he works for Stan."

Jasper smiled. "It is my pleasure to be of service to the Baron, the Baroness and their family."

"Can you come to Rossville?" my mom quipped.

"Are you in need of help?" my husband inquired.

"Mom, be careful about what you say. Just about anything you might mention, even as a joke, he will try to make happen."

"I was only joking but thanks," she said.

"Thanks for picking us up at the airport, I'd hate to drive in this traffic. Nice car!" my dad remarked.

"It's kind of late for you, so I didn't plan anything for this evening." My dad looked relieved. "Lolly and Alan will have dinner with us tomorrow. I wanted to go shopping for some furniture for the babies' room tomorrow afternoon."

"It'll be good to see Lolly. She's sweet. When are they getting married? I thought she would never settle down." My mom was good at combining a compliment and a dig.

"Alan is supportive of her career, so they are pretty happy. Not sure when they'll get married."

"So, have you come up with any names yet?" I knew my mom was just getting started with the inquisition.

"Not yet," the Baron responded. "We were looking at names online last night, which made me wonder why you named your daughter Miranda. Is it a family name?"

"I was in the Navy," my dad replied, happy to get in on the conversation, "and Miranda means 'admiral.' It's a good name for someone who is strong willed."

"You mean stubborn!" my mom laughed.

"Well chosen," my husband replied.

"If you think I'm stubborn, just spend some time with your son-in-law and you'll know there's no hope for your grandchildren."

As we drove up Stone Canyon, my mom gasped, "Just look at these homes, Pete, they're huge, who could live here?" She hadn't quite wrapped her mind around the Baron's wealth, but then I wasn't sure I had either. I understood there was nothing remotely like this in our town, or the whole county for that matter. When the electric gates opened and we drove up to the mansion, she gasped, "Oh my!"

"Welcome to our home," the Baron said as we got out. Clive and Tillie greeted us. I quickly explained that they were staff.

"Let me show you to your suite. I'm sure you would like to freshen up after a long trip," Tillie said. "I've got a light meal planned for this evening, if you're interested. Of course, I can fix anything you might like."

"I'm sure whatever you fixed will be fine," my dad responded.

My mom was speechless and wide eyed while my dad took it all in stride as they were shown to the spacious bedroom with French doors which opened to a small, private rose garden. The garden had high walls to keep Delilah out. The bathroom had gold plated fixtures which looked like koi fish. There was a whirlpool bathtub for two. The bed linens and towels were shades of lavender with pale turquoise embroidery.

"Wow, this place is beautiful!" my mom exclaimed.

"This is the Baron's favorite residence," Tillie told her as she pulled back the bed covers.

"How many homes does he have?" my mom inquired.

"His business concerns sometimes require staying abroad," Tillie replied, not wanting to say too much about the Baron's affairs. "When you're ready, please come to the foyer and take the hallway straight back, past the library to the dining room." Tillie smiled and left.

My mom looked at my dad and said, "I think we need a map."

"I just hoped she'd marry someone with a job," my dad said and started unpacking.

At Heathrow, Sir Sudovian's chauffeur and butler met the tired West Coast visitors. They were driven to a beautiful townhome in Knightsbridge owned by Lady Kananga. Her staff had their rooms ready. Lady Lockporte sent a note to Sir Sudovian, thanking him and requesting to meet with him, Lady Hauser and

Sir Sadeghi to discuss the situation at 9 p.m. the next night. Lady Kananga had her house swept for bugs the previous day and allowed only her most trusted servants to be at the townhome. They gathered in the rather modern living room filled with African carvings and brown leather sofas with brightly colored pillows. Pauline was asked to simply flirt with Sergio to keep him distracted, then she was excused before they rehearsed how to take down Lady Hauser. She was kept from the details as they feared her thoughts might be more apparent to Lady Hauser. The others knew how to shield their minds from her prying.

After they finished going over the details of the take down, Lady Kananga confided in Lady Lockporte. "I fear for Pauline, she is being exposed to a level of knowledge about our kind that even more mature vampires would struggle with understanding. Lady Hauser's betrayal must be kept a secret."

"She is more sophisticated than most young vampiresses and has not lacked worldly status. I don't think she will be so easily impressed or overwhelmed as some might be," she responded.

"Keep her close, train her well so she keeps the proper respect due to the Magus."

"Of course," Lady Lockporte said and they both retired.

In Bel Air, the Ortega's found their way to the dining room where Miranda was feeding her birds.

"I don't know what to say Randie, I never expected all this."

"I was overwhelmed at first but then you start to get used to it," I replied. "I'm glad you're here. Tillie is a terrific cook. Come sit down."

Almost on cue Tillie appeared with bowls of French onion soup. Toasted bread with melted Gruyere cheese floated in the delicious broth. She returned with watercress salads and small bowls of tropical fruit sprinkled with candied ginger and coconut.

"What would you like to drink? Wine, iced tea, coffee, Perrier or juice?"

"Iced tea, sweet, for me," my mom replied.

"Perrier," my dad said with a smile.

"Enjoy!" I told him and began eating.

"Aren't you going to wait for your husband?" my mom asked a bit irritated with me.

"Nope, he's taking care of some business and will be a while. Besides, he is on a special high protein diet Alan has him on."

My dad started with the soup and made a few comments about how delicious it was. "I can see I'm going to have to get a few recipes from her." My mom seemed to enjoy her meal but ate quietly until Tristan joined us.

"Are your accommodations satisfactory?" he asked as Tillie brought him a silver goblet.

"Yes, very nice. Much more than we are used to. Thank you," my mom replied. "Aren't you going to eat anything?"

"I ate earlier. My work schedule keeps me up most of the night with international affairs, so I tend to eat at odd times," he replied. "This cranberry juice is all I want at the moment."

"So, you're sort of a money manager and a publisher?" my mom inquired.

"Yes, something like that," the Baron replied curtly. He was not used to having to explain his affairs.

"I'm looking forward to being a grandfather," my dad interjected, trying to smooth over an awkward moment. "You're sure it's triplets?"

Just then Dr. Kyoto and Lady Lily appeared in the doorway. "I'm sorry that we're late."

"Not at all, perfect timing," the Baron said, clearly relieved to have the subject changed. "Dr. Kyoto and..." he paused for a second and realized that it would require explaining if he called her a Lady, "and Dr. Lily are looking after Miranda. Please sit down. This is Pete and Connie Ortega."

"May I bring you something?" Tillie inquired.

"Just tea," Lady Lily answered for them both.

"How is my daughter doing?" my mom asked. "And the babies? My husband was wondering how you can be sure there are three?"

"Naturally, we checked our results but it seems they are a very fertile couple. All indications are that she is carrying triplets. Her blood work, blood pressure and sonograms indicate a healthy pregnancy," Dr. Kyoto responded.

"She was slightly anemic, so we added some supplements and changed her diet somewhat and now that all has been resolved," Lady Lily added.

"I get a little tired but other than that I'm fine," I said.

"It's nice that you make house visits," my mom remarked, "didn't know anyone did that anymore."

"The Baron is an old friend and we are glad to be of assistance," Dr. Kyoto replied.

"We have set up a small medical office with some lab equipment here so the Baroness can be monitored at her convenience," Lady Lily added

"So your both OB/GYN doctors?" my mom asked.

"That is my specialty. Dr. Lily is a psychologist, though she also has a degree in hematology."

"I always thought Miranda could benefit from a shrink," my Dad chuckled.

"I like your dad more and more," the Baron replied, looking over at me with a slight smile. The boys were bonding at my expense. It was worth it.

Tillie served the tea and everyone was quiet for a few moments while they drank and ate.

"We also have a colleague, Dr. Romanov, who will be looking in on the Baroness as well. We wanted to be sure that she would always have prompt access to medical care. The UCLA Medical Center is just minutes away," Dr. Kyoto added to further assure my parents.

"I'm relieved to know that, thank you," my mom sighed.

When my parents were ready to retire I explained that I would probably sleep in and not get up until about noon, but they were free to wander around downstairs, check out the mini hockey rink and the library. I promised to give them a tour of the upstairs the next day. The evening had gone better than I had expected.

Alone upstairs, the Baron asked, "Why is she so concerned about what I eat or what I do? Does she suspect something?"

"Are you kidding? She's a mom," I replied.

"I will try harder to seem normal," he said quite seriously.

"Good luck with that!" I replied, trying not to laugh. "You may as well tell Delilah to be a house cat while you're at it." I sat on the bed and scratched behind her ears. "Let's just help them accept some of the truth a tiny bit at a time."

"This is going to be a long four nights," he sighed.

I laughed and said, "Only three more."

CHAPTER 35

SUNSET OVER LONDON was obscured by the fog, which had not burned off that day. It was about 65 degrees. Sergio prepared for the dinner party by picking out a linen suit and white shirt he thought Lady Hauser would approve of. He had not been happy about the attention she had been showing Momand. He looked out his townhouse window a few blocks from Lady Kananga's home and felt alien in the gray city. He missed the L.A. nightlife at the Narcissus Club. The Pentacles he had met were wary of being judged by the West Coast vampire. They feared experiencing the same fate as Simone and Harold. He felt shunned by most of the them. Sir Sudovian's staff asked about how a Short could bewitch the Baron. Sergio had replied that they were just two exceptional people who had fallen in love when fate brought them together. He thought the less he tried to explain it the better. The thought of a vampire being in love was disturbing to them. Lust was understood and loyalty, but not romantic love. It was thought of as a juvenile state left behind in the world of the warm-blooded. Everyone knew she was a descendant of de Molay, which set her apart from the rest of humanity but still did not make her undead. He sighed, "I wish I had joined the House of Plows."

Later that evening the vampires from Los Angeles descended on the home of Sir Sudovian on the outskirts of London. It was a stone mansion set on 25 acres with a lovely swan pond. The security fence which surrounded the mansion was disguised with lush shrubbery. The long driveway was gravel until they got close to the mansion, then it became cobblestone. It had at some point been a royal hunting lodge. When Lady Lockporte, Lady Kananga, Sir Ruben and Pauline arrived, the rest of the guests were already assembled.

"This is like my family estate in upstate New York," Pauline quipped, "but a little older."

Sir Ruben laughed, "I don't think New York was a state when this place was built."

Pauline would keep her distance from Lady Hauser and the others were wearing their best game faces. They were shown to a large banquet hall with a stone fireplace where Sir Sudovian, Lady Hauser, Sir Sadeghi and Sergio were waiting. Sergio was the first to greet them. He was glad to see his friends. He shook hands with Sir Ruben and bowed slightly to the ladies. Sir Ruben was relieved that Sergio remained so clueless. He was happy to start a conversation with Pauline. The young vampiress was attentive to Sergio and stayed by his side as they walked to the large, oblong table.

"We are grateful for your help with this grave matter. The sooner the bad apples are discovered, the sooner the House of Pentacles can restore its honor," Sir Sudovian said. "Please be seated." As was the habit of the Haute Caste, Lady Lockporte and Lady Kananga sat on either side of Lady Hauser. Like ladies in waiting to a queen, they appeared to show deference to the senior vampiress. Sir Ruben, Sergio and Pauline sat at one end of the table and Sir Sadeghi sat beside Sir Sudovian at the other end.

"Momand should be coming later, Sir Sadeghi sent him on an errand," Lady Hauser whispered to Lady Kananga, who merely smiled in response. The fire burning in the large fireplace cast shadows on the faces in the dimly lit room. Pauline began asking Sergio about his tennis career and he was happy to fill her in on all the details. She appeared to be interested and amused by his accounts, when in reality Pauline was quite bored. Her performance was catching the attention of Lady Hauser, who appeared a bit annoyed. Sir Sadeghi sat watching the situation stone-faced as always. He would have made a great poker player.

"Do you have any news to report" Lady Lockporte inquired of Sir Sudovian. A servant placed silver goblets filled with O positive in front of each of them. A second servant placed small plates of cubed raw steak beside the goblets. Pauline laughed at something Sergio said.

"Sergio," Lady Hauser glared and said. "May I speak with you?"

"Of course," he stood and followed her to a corner of the room where she reprimanded him for being a little too welcoming to the young vampiress. At that moment Lady Kananga poured the poison into Lady Hauser's goblet. It was seen by Sir Sadeghi.

"Sir Sudovian," said Sir Sadeghi, wanting to get his attention, "does it not seem like these rogue vampires are a very small group and that Johann may have been the last member?"

"Yes," he said, then cleared his throat nervously. "To answer both questions, we have not been able to find any evidence of others' involvement in this plot, though we hope that with your assistance we can be assured our findings are correct."

At that moment, Lady Hauser and a subdued Sergio returned to the table. Pauline smiled at him but he just looked toward the center of the table. Lady Lockporte asked if Sir Sadeghi would be kind enough to make a toast for the success of their mission.

"Members of the Haute Caste and honored younger members of this most distinct community, our survival and ability to protect our kind lies in our loyalty to our code of conduct. We are gathered here to see that it is preserved." He lifted his goblet and all followed. Then everyone took a drink of the precious fluid.

"Poison!" Lady Hauser dropped her goblet as Lady Kananga jabbed her with a needle in the neck. "No!" Lady Hauser screamed. She struck Lady Kananga so hard her body flew through the air and smashed against a stone wall. Everyone was on their feet. Lady Lockporte jabbed a second syringe into Lady Hauser's back. "Cowards!" Lady Hauser cried out.

"That's for Miranda!" Lady Lockporte exclaimed.

Lady Hauser turned quickly and put her hands on Lady Lockporte's throat. Lady Kananga leaped on Lady Hauser and they all fell to the ground. Lady Hauser smashed Lady Kananga's head on the ground. Lady Lockporte stabbed the elder vampiress' shoulder with a dagger. The scent of HH blood filled the room. Lady Hauser slashed at Lady Lockporte's face with her nails. Lady Kananga hit Lady Hauser in the back of the head with a heavy silver serving tray with such force it cracked her skull. Then the drugs finally kicked in. Sedated, the vampiress staggered to stand and then hit the floor.

"Stop!" Sergio began to yell but a swift blow to the stomach by Pauline and an equally strong blow to his head sent him reeling. Sir Ruben looked at Pauline with new respect, then ran to his sister's side with handcuffs and shackles he had hidden earlier. Lady Hauser was moaning on the floor.

Sir Sudovian had jumped up initially but was held back by Sir Sadeghi, who said simply, "She was the mastermind, she was going to put the blame on you."

Then Sir Sadeghi released him. Sergio got to his feet and tried to go to Lady Hauser. Pauline stood before him but she only slowed his progress. This time he sent her sprawling across the table.

Sergio grabbed the heavily sedated vampiress and cried, "What have you done to her?"

"Elephant tranquilizers," Lady Kananga replied, "and a little poison she had intended for the Baroness."

Pauline started to jump on Sergio but was stopped by Lady Lockporte. Sir Sadeghi grabbed Sergio's arm and pulled him away. "You will understand in time. You were blinded by your feelings for her but she was just playing all of us to try and gain more power. She has been plotting to become the Magus for centuries. It is why he kept her so close."

Sergio had such high regard for Sir Sadeghi and his sword that he did not fight him. In his gut he knew it was true. He had been nothing more than an errand boy to her. Still, he hated to see her so helpless. He stood slowly, his eyes downcast, and walked to the other side of the room with Sir Sadeghi. "What will happen to her?"

The Haute Caste vampire looked at him with sad resignation. "She will disappear."

"You can't kill a member of the Haute Caste!" Sir Sudovian insisted.

"I didn't say she would be killed," Sir Sadeghi responded, "I said she would disappear." He led Sergio and Sir Sudovian out of the room.

"The truck has arrived," Sir Ruben announced. He helped Lady Kananga to her feet.

"I will give her one more injection before she is locked up," Lady Lockporte added, holding a linen napkin to her bloody cheek. She slammed another needle into Lady Hauser's arm. There was a garbled response then she fell limp.

"I'd like to rip her heart out," Lady Kananga exclaimed.

"Good luck finding it," Sir Ruben replied.

"Ruben, will you do the honors?" Lady Lockporte asked.

Pauline assisted Sir Ruben with lifting Lady Hauser and whispered to Sir Ruben, "Remind me never to piss these ladies off."

He put the unconscious vampiress over his shoulder and carried her to the waiting truck, which had a free-standing freezer in the back. After wrapping more chains around her body, he unceremoniously deposited her into the freezer, which was belted and locked.

The West Coast visitors gazed in the back of the truck, quietly considering what they had just participated in. No member of the Haute Caste had ever been disposed of. Despite the rumors that would be whispered, they knew this truth could not be shared. There would be no need to swear anyone to secrecy. There would be no honor or bragging rights. It was a tragic situation. They also did not want anyone else to know how to incapacitate and imprison the Haute Caste.

Finally Pauline spoke, "I want another chance at him. Sergio sucker punched me."

Tense laughter broke out. Sir Ruben replied, "Don't worry about it, you did fine."

The Magus lay in his bed contemplating the roots of treachery. He waxed philosophical about the nature of betrayal and the unmet desires of those who would act in such a way. Power was the aphrodisiac that those with flawed characters craved. He was aware that Miranda was not at all interested in worldly power. She was only now becoming aware of some of her gifts. He knew she would use them appropriately in time. A text message from Sir Sadeghi interrupted his thoughts: "All is well. They are on their way home." The Magus smiled and was soon in a deep sleep.

At the Stone Canyon mansion, Tristan sat in a chair in the dark, gazing at his sleeping wife. When he read the same message, he had mixed feelings. Lady Hauser had groomed him and protected him. Now he understood that her supposed affection was meant to insure his loyalty when the time came to challenge the Magus. She had greatly misjudged his devotion to the greatest vampire. He crawled into bed beside Miranda, who barely stirred. He had to believe that she and their children would be safe now.

CHAPTER 36

WHEN I GOT up, my husband was sound asleep. I patted a sleepy Delilah and headed back to my room to change. I knew my parents had been up for hours and Jasper had given them a tour of the downstairs and the grounds. I showered and dressed quickly. I picked out a silk flowered blouse and white capri pants which my mom would approve of. No matter how old you are, your mother's opinions seem to carry weight. Mom is always mom.

When I got downstairs, Tillie had breakfast waiting for me. I was halfway through an omelet when my parents walked in.

"There she is! You've become a night person," my mom exclaimed.

"I try to keep Stan's hours," I replied. "Have you eaten?"

"Yeah, she took good care of us," my dad replied. "That's quite a car collection, and that mini hockey rink is unbelievable."

"Which car would you like to go shopping in?" I finished breakfast quickly.

"I like the car we were in yesterday," my mom replied, "very smooth ride."

"It's a Bentley," I smiled. She would never be happy in a Chevy again. I finished off my breakfast. "Lolly's going to meet us at a children's boutique at the Beverly Center. Let's get going."

"You husband isn't coming?" my mom asked in a tone that sounded more like an accusation.

"He was up all night taking care of the international business that pays for all this. He'll join us later," I explained in an assertive fashion that surprised my mom and amused my dad.

The sights of L.A. and the Beverly Center stores kept my parent's attention. I was hoping to keep them distracted so I could avoid more lifestyle questions. Lolly warmly embraced them. I was happy to let her reassure my mom about my spouse.

"Isn't the Baron a great guy! He has been very good for Randie. She didn't want to have much to do with him at first and tried to send back the fabulous presents he sent her. It was too funny," Lolly said.

I did not remember it being quite so amusing at the time but this version was perfect for my parents. Just enough truth.

"In essence, he was my boss so I wasn't sure getting involved was a smart idea but he won me over." *Or maybe just wore me down.* I thought with a smile.

"We're pretty impressed, too," my dad said.

"They have some beautiful baby furniture here. I just wanted a little input from you all." I realized my central Illinois accent was coming back. We walked around the store looking at truly beautiful cribs, bedding and other nursery items. My mom loved a crib that looked like something out of a fairy tale. It was antique white, it could be rocked and had a small crown design in gold on the front. We all agreed it would be perfect. The sales lady almost fainted when I asked for three.

My dad looked at the price and said he could buy a car for that. "Maybe they should come with engines," he quipped. I reassured him that Stan could well afford it. He didn't seem totally convinced but he let it go.

"Would you mind if we go to a casual place for lunch? It's a deli where a friend of mine works. You'll like him mom, he used to be a Catholic priest."

"Used to be..." she started.

"It's a long story, he is considering becoming a regular Joe."

"Well, some regular food sounds good to me," my dad said.

The deli was crowded but Grigoryi managed to get us a table. I introduced my parents and said, "They are new to L.A. and don't know much about the lifestyle here."

"It's a very interesting place but a little too exciting for me. I'm thinking of going back to Italy," Grigoryi said. My mom nodded approvingly. He handed out the menus nervously. "Baroness, would you like to check out our newest bagel flavors? They were just baked."

"Sure, I can get a bag to take home." I followed him to the deli counter.

"I'm not supposed to say anything but I owe you, a lot," he spoke quickly. "There was a vampiress, short dark hair, who wanted me to report on you. She wanted me to put something in your drink. She said it was vitamins but I didn't believe her. I didn't tell her but I wouldn't do it. Then later, this other vampire said he was the Magus. He asked if she had contacted me and got angry about her trying to harm you. I think he stopped her, because she hasn't contacted me again."

I steadied myself by putting my hands on the deli counter. "You're sure he was the Magus?"

"Yes. I saw him go off in the helicopter that night. He had dark straight hair, tall, thin, and scary, dark eyes. The Magus seemed very pissed at her. He didn't want me to tell you. I felt like he would do anything to protect you."

"Thank you, Grigoryi. Thank you for protecting me. You are very brave. I won't tell anyone you told me this." I didn't have the time to make sense of all this now. "Did my husband talk to you?"

"No, never," Grigoryi blurted out. "He has never contacted me, which is fine by me." '

"Please bring a bag of assorted bagels to the table." I started to walk away but turned and told him, "You talked about going back to Italy. I think it would be safer for you there. Please, go to Italy soon."

When I returned to the table my dad asked if I was okay. "You look a little pale."

"I'm fine, just a bit of nausea, it comes and goes quickly."

"Why doesn't Jasper join us?" my mom asked.

"It's his job to look out for us, he wouldn't consider joining us. Trust me," I replied. I smiled and hoped it looked sincere.

Lolly was able to keep the conversation light during lunch. I tried to add a few details about our crazy days at UCLA. To my relief, I was able to keep some blintzes down. As we left, I gave Grigoryi a large tip that I hoped he would use to help him return to Italy.

We parted ways with Lolly. "See you tonight," she said and was off to get a manicure/pedicure before our dinner party.

I asked Jasper to take us for a drive up the coast highway by Malibu. I knew my husband wouldn't be awake yet. I was sure that he had been very busy with affairs of the Haute Caste last night. For now, I had to act like everything was great for my parents. Jasper parked by a public access area. We walked down by the beach. The sunset was painting the horizon deep shades of pink and orange. A few diehard surfers were trying to catch one more wave. Seagulls were crying out as they attacked remnants of a picnic. Southern California in all its glory.

"So, do you like living here?" my dad asked with a note of concern in his voice.

"I really do. Sometimes I miss seeing snow fall in winter, but this is hard to beat."

"You miss snow?" my mom chuckled "You really do need that shrink."

"I can't seem to wrap my mind around what your husband does for a living but I'm sure he must be good at it. He seems to be a very responsible young man," my dad said. It was funny to hear someone refer to the Baron as young.

I smiled at him. "He is. He is excited about the pregnancy." *So is the rest of the vampire world,* but I kept that to myself.

"I just wish you lived closer," my mom sniffled. I put my arm around her shoulders. "You can visit any time. Just let us know and we'll arrange it."

My dad took a step closer to the beach. He was very uncomfortable with any display of emotion except yelling at a sports teams. I think it had been hard at times for my expressive mother to be in love with such a stoic man.

Jasper cleared his throat, "Shall we be going, Baroness?"

"Yes. Thank you."

As we walked to the car my mom said, "I just can't get used to you being called a Baroness."

"Me either," I laughed.

Lady Lockporte, Lady Kananga, Sir Ruben and Pauline were wakened as their private jet arrived at LAX. To their surprise and honor, the Magus personally greeted them, along with the Baron.

"You have done well. Such a distasteful affair," the Magus stated as they descended from the jet.

The Baron was there to assure them he understood and accepted what they had done. "I am grateful," he told them solemnly.

The Magus looked at his trusted Haute Caste, "Thank you for your valor." To the surprise of everyone, the Magus began to board the jet. "I must take care of the traitor. None but me will know her whereabouts. There will be no chance of revitalization unless I feel forgiving. I don't imagine that will happen any time in the next 500 years, or even in 1,000."

They all bowed to the Magus. "Terrible business," Sir Ruben whispered to Pauline. "Remind me never to piss him off."

The Baron left in the Spyder without another word. He was not ready to hear any more of the details. The others seemed to understand. They got into the Magus' Escalade and were driven back to the Paradise Cove estate to recover.

CHAPTER 37

I WAS UPSTAIRS changing into a denim cotton sleeveless dress that would disguise my expanding belly when I heard my husband return. I was surprised he did not seek me out. I found him in his suite sitting in an overstuffed chair petting Delilah. He stared down at the floor like someone who was emotionally exhausted.

"Are you okay?" I asked, not sure if the undead ever were.

He looked up at me with sadness in his eyes. "You are safe now," he said.

"What has happened?"

"All you need to know is that Lady Hauser has been taken care of," he replied softly.

"I felt sympathy for Bram but I don't for her."

"We will never speak of her again. Do you understand?" Pain and anger flashed in his eyes. It was not a question. It was a command.

I did not respond but it was not over for me. I would not be left ignorant. Information was crucial to survival in the world of the undead. I wanted to know who had looked out for me. Who I could trust. Though, this was not the time to continue the discussion. "I'm going to finish getting ready. See you downstairs."

I closed myself in my room for a few minutes. I took a deep breath and wondered if the babies and I were truly safe now. My thoughts turned to Sergio and Grigoryi. Lady Hauser had hurt so many people. My husband felt betrayed, Grigoryi was fearful and Sergio was undoubtedly heart broken. The Haute Caste would be in disarray and struggling to establish unquestioned order, equilibrium. At the center of this bizarre state of affairs was the Magus, my alleged protector. That was disturbing and comforting at the same time. My husband did not mention the role the Magus had played. I wanted to talk to the supreme vampire alone again but not tonight. Now it was time to reassure my parents that all was well in Bel Air, or should I call it Hell Air.

I found my parents out on the patio sipping iced tea with Lolly and Alan. Lolly looked amazing in tight black ankle pants and an orange silk tank. A dozen gold bracelets adorned her wrist. Her hair was pulled back with several braids cascading to her shoulders. Alan wore the same old boring, pale blue tailored shirt and khaki Dockers with expensive Italian loafers and no socks. It was sort of his uniform.

"Hi Randie," Alan stood and gave me a hug. "I was just telling your parents about what an outstanding man your husband is."

"Yeah, he's a keeper," I replied.

"A zookeeper," my mom muttered, looking past me wide-eyed.

The Baron stood on the other side of the sliding glass door with Delilah. He yelled through the glass, "It's okay, she likes all of you."

"It's fine. This is Delilah, our cat."

The Baron slowly opened the door and walked the panther over to the table.

"We waited until you were rested to introduce her. We were afraid it might be a bit much the first night."

My father held out his hand a bit tentatively and the big cat brushed against it with her head. Everyone breathed a sigh of relief. "That is some kitty!"

"Do you think she'll be okay with the babies?" my mom asked.

"They could not have a better guardian," the Baron assured them.

I got on my knees and put my arms about her neck to let my parents see how sweet she was if you were on her good side. "She attacked an intruder once. I feel very safe having her around." As both looked from me to Delilah, I realized that that might not have come out as reassuring as I had intended.

Mustering all her courage, my mom walked over and very stiffly patted the panther on the head. "If you say so."

"Clive, will you take her to the play yard?" Tristan called out.

The butler appeared and led Delilah to the exercise yard.

"I think dinner is ready," I said. As we walked in the dining room I whispered to my husband, "That went better than expected."

Tillie started us off with tomato bisque soup. It was delicious. My husband was able to handle a few spoonfuls of the soup. The main course consisted of rare prime rib, au gratin potatoes and asparagus. My mom watched the Baron consume some, shall we say, extra very rare meat and ignore the rest of the meal.

In her typical, subtle fashion she inquired, "Stan, are you all right? You barely touched your food."

"I'm accustomed to eating later in the evening," he replied curtly.

"Besides, he is on a high-protein, low-carb diet that Alan set up for him," I added.

"This is great Tillie. The prime rib is perfect and the asparagus is cooked just right." My dad was trying to ease over an awkward moment.

"You have a beautiful home," Lolly said. "I love the artwork."

"When we're done with dinner I'll show you the upstairs, then maybe we can have coffee and desert in the library." I added.

"Do you have any other pets?" my mom inquired a bit nervously.

"Just the birds." I replied. She seemed relieved.

Lolly made a point of walking beside my husband as we went upstairs. I showed them the children's room. My mom loved the rainbow. Then I showed them what I called my "writing room."

Unfortunately, the Baron heard my mom say. "You write about those horrible creatures in this beautiful bedroom? It doesn't make sense to me. I would think this would inspire you to write romance novels."

I saw him wince and knew it took a lot of self-control to remain polite. I quickly interjected. "The stories are in my head, I could be anywhere and be thinking about my next chapter. I like this room because the colors, the furnishings. are all about comfort. I write better when I'm at ease."

"You know I'm your biggest fan but don't let the kids read your books until they're teenagers!" my mom stated in a rather authoritarian voice.

"Perhaps we could get illustrated editions for the nursery," the Baron said.

"Good one," my dad responded and patted the Baron on the back, not realizing that he probably wasn't kidding.

There's was a bit of nervous laughter and we moved on to the master suite.

"This is really Delilah's room but she lets us share it with her." I noticed Lolly looking intently at the large bed covered in black and white satin bedding. I did not want to know what she, or anyone else, for that matter was imagining.

"The black and white touches are dramatic but balanced. It works," she exclaimed. "Who was your decorator?"

"I told the decorator what I wanted. It was my design," Tristan answered, showing a bit of pride.

"It's sort of dark," my mom commented, continuing to get under my husband's skin. "But it is roomy."

"He sleeps during the day. Makes sense to me. Remember when I worked nights at the cannery and we put heavy blinds on the bedroom windows?" my dad said.

The Baron smiled at my dad.

"This Escher is fascinating." Alan pointed to the drawing of angels and demons.

"I'm the angel," I smiled.

"Not always," the Baron countered. "Let's go to the library, a couple of business associates from Central America will be joining us."

To my delight, Sir Diego and Sir Franco were waiting for us.

"Senor and Senora Ortega, how nice to meet you. I'm Jorge Diego and this is my assistant, Franco Verde."

They shook hands and I could tell my dad was won over. My mom was a bit uncomfortable. She was having to deal with a lot of strangers. In Rossville, she knew most of the people who came by the coffee shop. Lolly did a good job of acting like she had never met them before.

"Your daughter is very bright and beautiful. They are a charming couple, no?"

"Yes, they are. Thank you," my mom replied. Complimenting me was a good move on Sir Diego's part. My mom seemed to look a little more at ease. "What business are you in?"

"Drugs," Sir Franco responded. Both my parents' jaws dropped until he continued. "For pharmaceutical companies. We supply rare vegetation used to develop some of the newer heart medications."

I could have kicked Sir Franco. I saw the look of relief on their faces when he elaborated. In the back of my parents' minds, they had probably wondered if the Baron's empire was based on cocaine trafficking. Later I later learned he was not lying. The importation of exotic vegetation for drug research was one of Sir Diego's ventures.

"We are partners in several investments. The pharmaceutical industry is highly profitable," the Baron explained.

"I know," my dad replied. "The Lily Corporation pretty much owns Indiana. I can see how you have done well for yourselves."

"Some drugs are quite helpful for treating mood and thought disorders," Alan added, "but others become prescribed addictions. I think it is the physicians' responsibility to not prescribe or over prescribe those medications as the pharmaceutical companies won't stop if it makes a profit."

"Quite true," Sir Diego said. "Our drugs target cardiac and hematology concerns, nothing habit forming. We hope to find ways to preserve blood longer, aid in transfusions and reduce bleeding."

"We hope to help, not hurt humanity," Sir Franco added and looked at me with a satisfied grin.

"Enough business talk," Lolly sighed. "What are you going to name your offspring?"

Tillie arrived with chocolate mousse and petit fours just in time. I was ready for my one cup of regular coffee. The vampires and Alan said they were on diets or had already eaten and just politely sipped coffee. The chocolate mousse was divine.

"She's a great cook," my dad said.

"Names?" Lolly asked again.

"We haven't decided. I kind of like Desmon." I saw Sir Franco almost drop his cup.

"I like it," Lolly stated.

"And maybe Tomas, for grandpa," I said to my parent's surprise.

"That would be nice," my mom commented.

"I like Marie Antoinette Ortega Mordecai," my husband responded.

"Perfect for a baroness," Sir Diego replied.

"That name may not bode well...." I started to say.

"They will make their own destinies, like us all," the Baron replied.

"I've always loved the name Marie Antoinette," my mom said, "and Dorca."

"We can talk about this more, closer to the due date," I said and finished my coffee, trying to end the discussion.

My mom and my husband had agreed on a terrible name. I feared that was a done deal. To my relief they started talking about the weather differences between the coast and the cornfields before they could suggest another name. A few times I noticed my mom watching Sir Franco. Finally, my husband said they had business to attend to and would return in a few hours. He said goodnight to my parents and kissed me on the cheek.

Lolly and Alan also said their goodbyes and I noticed how she looked after the Baron as he left with Sir Diego and Sir Franco. His vampire charisma still seemed to be working on her. I would have to limit her contact with him. My mom did not seem smitten and wanted to talk with me when my dad turned in.

We sat alone in the library. She had a worried expression. I could see the wheels had been turning for some time. "What is it, mom?"

"I don't mean to pry but your husband seems like he is trying to hide something."

"What do you mean?" I asked a bit anxiously.

"He stays up all night, he's got this strange diet to stay fit and tries very hard to let us know what a big hockey fan he is, like that would make him normal."

"He has business concerns all over the world," I replied, wondering if she even had a clue he was undead.

"Your bedroom is so creepy, like some gothic porno movie set. You can't tell me it's normal."

"Gothic porn? C'mon, mom, Lolly liked it. He likes decorating."

"Exactly, and he wants to name your daughter Marie Antoinette. What kind of man would even think of that?" She was staring at me.

"A man who loves French culture?" I replied, struggling for a response she would buy.

"Does he spend a lot of time with that Franco?" she demanded.

"Mom! You think he's gay?" Relieved, I exploded in laughter. She did not realize how glad I was that she came up with that explanation. "He is very attracted to women. Did you think my pregnancy was due to artificial insemination?"

"I thought that might be why the medical specialists were here," she said with a foolish expression on her face. "Then when I saw the big cat, I thought about those gay guys in Las Vegas. I'm sorry. I was just worried about you. I feel so stupid now. Promise me you won't tell him."

"Believe me, he would forgive you, he would be amused at the thought," I smiled and patted her hands. "It's true he's a little different but you know, he's a Baron."

"Are you happy? Really happy?" she asked with tears in her eyes.

I placed her hands on my tummy. "I'm feeling much more than that. I love my husband and he returns that love in amazing ways like putting a doctor's office in the house."

She dried her eyes with a napkin. "If you say so," she smiled. "Am I wrong about Franco?"

"No, you just didn't realize that he is with Jorge. They've been together for years."

"That's nice. As long as he isn't with your husband," she chuckled. I could not wait to call Sir Franco a home-wrecker.

CHAPTER 38

AFTER 10 HOURS including a stop to refuel, the Magus' jet landed at a private air strip near Barrow, Alaska. It was ten o'clock in the morning and the sun would not set till ten o'clock that night. No vampire would ever choose to visit Barrow. Only his pilot and his butler were on board. The pilot charged the battery of a Humvee that was kept in a garage by the desolate airstrip and moved it into the shadow of the plane. The Magus wore heavy clothing, a mask, sunglasses and a hat to protect him from the sunlight. He covered the short distance to the vehicle very quickly. It was 40 degrees. A pleasant day for the citizens of Barrow but his California staff did not care for the cold. The freezer was quickly transferred to the vehicle and they headed for the cabin several miles from the town overlooking the sea.

The Magus had several places around the world where he could stay without anyone knowing his location. This hideout had been chosen years ago when he decided it would be a good place for a troublesome Haute Caste vampire to be retired. He never thought it would be his oldest companion. Though the large cabin they parked next to appeared rustic, it was very luxurious inside. Silver goblets, the finest linens, leather couches and a few Persian rugs made the cabin more hospitable. The Magus retired to his windowless bedroom suite and climbed into his four-poster bed, exhausted.

The pilot and his butler plugged the freezer in. They would take turns watching over it while one of them slept. The butler placed a liter of blood in the refrigerator for the Magus and fixed sandwiches while the pilot lit a fire the stone fireplace. They ate quietly as they had no desire to discuss the long night that lay ahead of them. The pilot, Bernard, was retired from the Royal Air Force. He was a well-mannered British gentleman of 50 who made a point of showing he was not a bit racist towards Rupert. The butler never let on that he knew the pilot used hand sanitizer after their hands touched while handling the freezer.

Bernard took the first watch. Rupert cleaned the dishes after they ate, then after making tea for the pilot he laid down on a couch in front of the stone fireplace. The cabin was quite cozy now.

Rupert lay on the couch for an hour but he did not sleep. He peered over the couch and saw Bernard slumped against the freezer. He quietly walked over, shook him to check if the sedative had taken effect. He gently placed the pilot on the rug "Sweet dreams old man," he whispered. He then took a pair of cutters out of his cooking gear and began to cut the ropes that were wrapped around the freezer. The clippers made a sharp clicking sound with each cut. He nervously looked towards the Magus' bedroom. The house was quiet except for Bernard's snoring. Finally, he was able to pick the lock and unlatch the freezer. He opened the lid and almost started to cry. The beautiful vampiress who haunted his dreams was gray and lifeless. Her once proud face was scratched and her hair was disheveled. She had promised him immortality but now looked powerless and lifeless. Rupert pulled her body from the freezer and took her over by the fireplace.

"My queen, what has he done to you?" he whimpered. Rupert held her close to the heat. Her skin began to look a little less gray but still she seemed lifeless. Tears welled up in his eyes.

"I trusted you," the Magus said in a low voice like the hiss of a snake. Panic seized Rupert. He dropped the vampiress and ran to a window to pull back the drapes. The Magus leaped upon him and pinned the butler against the wall beside the window as the sunlight came streaming in, falling on the inert form of Lady Hauser on the floor. The vampire's powerful jaws pierced the butler's neck and blood sprayed on the wall. Rupert died quickly. The Magus became oblivious of everything as he felt a rush from the adrenalized blood. The sunlight began to take a toll on Lady Hauser's frozen body. Her skin began to smolder and there was a putrid smell in the air. Her hair sizzled. For a second her eyes opened then turned opaque as she became blinded by the sunlight. The Magus heard her utter, "No!" then fell silent. He dropped Rupert's body and pulled the heavy drapes back across the window. He wiped his mouth with the butler's sleeve. The Magus laid a heavy blanket over Lady Hauser to stop further burning. He did not wish this fate on any vampire.

Bernard was alive but heavily sedated. The Magus would have to take care of the mess. As he lifted Lady Hauser's charred body, one of her hands fell off. Her sapphire ring came loose from the burned flesh. He put the ring in his pocket and placed her hand and body back in the freezer. The smell made him nauseated. The Magus was surprised by how badly the sunlight had damaged her in a frozen state. "Frozen vampires are much more vulnerable to the sun, good to know," he thought. The Magus closed the latch and found rope in the kitchen to rewrap the freezer. He knew that under the best conditions she would recover to some degree from these horrible injuries, but under the present conditions she would never heal right, especially if she was not freed for 500 years or more. One of her admirers had sealed her fate. "Karma, my dear," he said with a grim smile. "You now appear as you truly are."

Rupert's disloyalty was disturbing. He would have to be suspicious of everyone now. He put the butler's body in a large trash bag and cleaned the blood stains off the wall. He did not want to upset Bernard before a flight, though he believed the old R.A.F. pilot would be so embarrassed about allowing himself to be drugged and outwitted he would say little about Rupert's demise. After putting on a clean wool sweater and slacks, he laid down on the couch to rest until nightfall. The fresh blood would help him recover from the long flight and the brief fight with Rupert. He fell asleep wondering if his cabin was the kind of place that Miranda imagined her Polly would escape to in Alaska. Perhaps she had picked Alaska because it was inhospitable to the undead. He would not tell her about this cabin. He never wanted her near Lena's resting place, though the Magus did want to give Miranda a refuge, someplace even the Baron did not know about, if she should ever need it. He considered all his properties and suddenly Washington came to mind. He had a lovely home overlooking an inland waterway. She could handle the winter climate. There were no vampires there, as it was too small of a population to sustain a community. He would give it to her as a secret present upon the birth of the babies. Despite her disrespect at times, he felt he could win her over. Miranda was safe for now. If there were others, they would be waiting for Lady Hauser to reappear. They would have a very, very long wait.

In Los Angeles, I took my parents to lunch at the Paradise Cove restaurant where James and I had brunch. That date with James now seemed ages ago. They really enjoyed the scenery. My dad was a little uncomfortable with not being allowed to pay for anything. I just explained that my husband would be offended and he seemed to accept that. My mother seemed to be more at ease now that she thought my marriage was not just so the Baron could have offspring.

"I never imagined that you would have this kind of life," my mom said.

"I'm still trying to get used to it," I replied.

"Desmon is an interesting name," she stated.

"It's the name of a good friend of Tristan's. Sort of a mentor. He's out of town or I would have introduced you."

The seafood was delicious. I had salmon and my parents had Chilean sea bass. I loved seeing them so delighted by a meal they were not involved in preparing or serving.

"We are getting very spoiled," my mom said.

"Maybe we should expand our menu, add French onion soup, and maybe chocolate mousse. I got some recipes from Tillie," my dad suggested.

"Oh Lord, now you're going to change the coffee shop to a French café," my mom chuckled. "He will never be the same, Miranda."

"Well, I was going to wait until tonight but now that you mention improving the restaurant," I dug into my purse and pulled out a check from my husband. "The Baron wants you to have this so you can make a few improvements." I handed it to my dad.

His eyes got big. "You've got to be kidding. Look, Connie!" He handed her the check.

"Two hundred thousand dollars?" she asked in a whisper.

"It's okay. I had him get a certified check to make it easier to deposit."

"I have never seen a check for so much money," my dad uttered.

"Maybe you can hire more help," I suggested.

He started to hand the check back. "Your husband doesn't have to do this."

"It was his idea, he just wants to be a considerate son-in-law," I responded.

My mom took the check from my dad. "We could really fix up the place."

"A new oven!" my dad replied.

"You can even go on a cruise if you want," I added.

"A cruise!" my mom exclaimed. "Oh Pete! A cruise! You know how much the Johnson's loved the Bahamas." She quickly put the check in her purse as though someone might try to snatch it.

"With three babies on the way, are you sure?" my dad asked, concerned.

"We are, it's fine. Sometimes it's even hard for me to grasp how wealthy he is, so don't try, just enjoy."

"We will make a donation to the ambulance fund." My mom was feeling a little guilty about her good fortune. "They've wanted a new one for years."

"You're such a good Catholic," I smiled.

"A nice donation, don't start giving it all away," my dad added. "I'm a practical Catholic."

"Oh I won't," my mom chuckled.

It was good to see them so happy together. It had not always been the case. They worked hard to make their marriage successful. Perhaps I could learn something from them, though I was not sure it would apply in my situation. I still had not decided how much I would allow my husband to influence our children.

As the sun set, the Baron rose and went to the mansion next door. He wanted to meet with the vampires who had taken Lady Hauser prisoner. He was also hopeful they could shed light on the Magus' whereabouts. He was now the second most powerful vampire in the world. Lady Hauser's crimes were an important reminder to him of the corrupting influence of status. He would be very careful to never cause the Magus to doubt him.

The mansion next door was a modern work of art, very high tech, which helped the Baron make it quite secure from trespassers and from cyber hackers. Computers had been set up in the library, creating a center of operations for the North American undead linked to the Magus' computer. He did not want Miranda to be aware of the kind of surveillance that was done on her behalf. It was much more than pictures of her childhood. He had a wealth of information about anyone she had contact with, including banks. He was aware she was taking more cash out of the bank than she was spending. He also had access to the private details of the world's prominent vampires. He imagined they had some suspicions but none knew the degree to which they were spied upon. His next door office was off-limits to even his trusted allies.

To accommodate his guests the walls of glass at the back of the house that looked out on the garden had been covered with heavy electric blinds. The sun roofs in the bathrooms had been removed. The sleek wood and marble used in the construction was quite attractive. It had a sophisticated ambiance that Lady Kananga appreciated. She was sitting on a olive green leather couch, sipping from a goblet in the living room when the Baron arrived.

"Good evening."

"Good evening, Baron," she responded. "The others are still primping but should be here soon. I like this guest residence."

"It is the least I can do after the service you provided."

"I took great satisfaction in my work," she replied with a smile.

"As did we all," Lady Lockporte said as she entered with Sir Ruben and Pauline.

"You have my gratitude," the Baron stated and bowed to them. The honored vampires said nothing but felt very lucky to be in his good graces.

Lady Anastasia entered. "May I join the party?"

"Please," the Baron responded.

"Would one of you fill me in on the details of your visit to London?"

Lady Kananga nodded to Lady Lockporte. "I would not be reporting our success if not for Lady Kananga's strength and speed," she said. Then she recounted the entire affair, stopping at the moment when the Magus left in his jet with the freezer. They sat quietly for a moment as they each processed what they had experienced. Lady Anastasia wished she could have been involved.

The Baron broke the silence. "Your courageous protection of our community will not be forgotten. Pauline, I hope you appreciate how fortunate you were to be allowed to participate."

"Yes, I do," she said, making little eye contact.

Sir Ruben laughed. "She wants another chance to beat on Sergio."

The Baron smiled. "That won't be necessary. I spoke with him last night. He was saddened but understands why it had to happen. He is loyal to the Magus." Pauline looked a little disappointed.

"Any clue as to where the Magus went?" the Baron inquired.

"No." Lady Kananga replied. "Personally I'm glad I don't know. I just hope it wasn't Africa. I would not want my land contaminated by her presence. Samuel called, he is concerned about the many rumors about Lady Hauser. What would you like me to tell him?"

"Tell him that Lady Hauser has retired to pursue enlightenment. I shall take over her responsibilities until another high priestess shall be named," he said. "Now for a more pressing issue, dinner with my in-laws. The Lockportes are excused as they might be recognized."

"I would rather watch a sunrise," Lady Kananga said.

"Sir Ruben is going to tutor me on the history of vampires tonight," Pauline said. She looked at Sir Ruben, who nodded.

"Well, since the real doctors are not around tonight, I shall make a house call," Lady Anastasia announced.

"Thank you Dr. Romanov," the Baron stated. "Sir Diego and Sir Franco?"

"They were up late at the Narcissus and seem to be sleeping in," Sir Ruben replied.

"Pete and Connie are leaving tomorrow, right?" Lady Lockporte asked.

"Yes," he said sounding relieved. "I'm not sure which has been more upsetting, Lady Hauser's alarming betrayal and subsequent abduction in London, or spending three nights with my in-laws."

We gathered for dinner about 8 p.m. My parents were fascinated by Dr. Romanov. They had never met a Russian before. They would have been blown away if they knew her pedigree.

"When the Soviet Union fell apart, that was something," my dad commented.

"They were better off with the czar," she responded.

My husband decided to change the subject. "What do you like the most about Southern California?"

"The food," my dad replied just as Tillie brought in a platter of barbacoa tacos. She returned with bowls of seasoned rice, refried beans, salsa and guacamole.

"I think you will like this," I began filling my plate.

Then Tillie brought in plates of leftover very rare prime rib which she served to the Baron and Lady Romanov. Her highness picked at her food.

"You should try the tacos," my mom said.

"No thank you," Lady Romanov replied curtly.

There was an uncomfortable pause, then the Baron replied, "Dr. Romanov also follows the high-protein, low-carb diet. I haven't felt this well in years."

"I can't very well tell my patients to do something, then ignore my own advice," Lady Romanov said, taking a bite of barely seared raw meat.

"You both look pretty fit, so it must be working," my dad observed. Lady Romanov gave him a condescending smile, which lowered my anxiety level a bit.

"Pete, would you like to hit a few pucks with me after dinner? You must try the rink at least once. I've got some skates in your size," my husband told him.

"That would be great!"

"What about you, Mom, you want to play?" I asked.

"No thanks but it would be fun to watch. I'll take some pictures."

Lady Romanov dropped her fork. Everyone looked up at once. *Oh crap*, I thought.

"I hate to have my picture taken, so if you don't mind no pictures," the Baron requested.

"Though, of course, you may take pictures of your lovely daughter and our home if you wish." He continued.

"Okay, I'll take some tomorrow morning before we leave," my mom said a little hurt and confused.

"He's a Baron. He just doesn't want his life getting in the tabloids." I was hoping to get away with a lie. "He is very private. Sort of a phobia he has."

"Okay I guess," my mom responded.

In Barrow, Bernard was waking up. He had a throbbing headache from the sedatives. When the Magus explained what had happened he became upset with himself and a little sad. The pilot had felt a certain fondness for Rupert. He told himself the butler must have fallen under the spell of a bad woman. He helped the Magus burn Rupert's remains and then throw them off a cliff into the ocean.

"Appropriate, isn't it, sir? Though I'm sure he would have preferred the Ganges."

"Undoubtedly," the Magus responded. "Now we must bid au revoir to the lady."

They put the freezer in the back of the Humvee and drove about half a mile to the edge of a very deep crevice. They pulled out the freezer and, without ceremony, tipped it into the crevice. Bernard held up a powerful lamp but the freezer had fallen beyond their vision. The Magus had studied the temperature of the crevice and it stayed below freezing all year long.

"Wait for me in the vehicle," the Magus said. He waited until the pilot was in the Humvee then he turned back to the dark, craggy, hole. "You have not made it easy to forgive your deceitful, malevolent, greedy heart. You were right to fear Miranda, though you never really understood why. In any case you should have properly feared me." He climbed into the vehicle and they headed for the airstrip.

CHAPTER 39

I RODE TO the airport with my parents. Thankfully they had accepted saying goodbye to my husband the night before. His eccentricities were easier to ignore when they began to understand how wealthy he was. It was a beautiful, late summer day. I was glad they had visited and relieved they were leaving before something happened that might have revealed my husband's true nature.

"Tell Stan I think he missed his calling, he would have made a great hockey player. That last goal almost tore the net," my dad said.

"He prides himself on being in shape," I responded. I knew my husband had held himself back during the game last night in an attempt to seem more normal.

"I wish you could come out for a visit but with your pregnancy, it's probably better you don't travel now," my mom sounded a little sad.

"I promise that we'll visit with your grandbabies so you can brag to all your friends."

Her face lit up. She patted my hands. "You know we'll come out the week you're due. I want to see the triplets come into this world."

"You better!"

They insisted that we said goodbye at the departures curb. I could not help getting a little tearful. Normalcy was taking a flight back to Illinois, leaving me surrounded by nocturnal crazy fuckers. I was glad Jasper was driving. I sat back and closed my eyes on the way home. The visit had gone better than expected but now I wanted to meet with the Magus alone. He knew a lot of secrets and it was time he shared a few with me. My husband would not discuss Lady Hauser but I bet the Magus would. I had Jasper stop by the bank. I withdrew a thousand dollars, just to be on the safe side. Then we went home. I was ready for an afternoon nap.

The Magus' plane arrived about the time Connie and Pete were taking off. He descended from the jet inside a hangar that allowed no outside light. A silver Rolls Royce with darkened windows was waiting. He turned to Bernard before getting in the back of the limousine, "You'll get a substantial bonus and I know that I can rely on you for the utmost discretion. I value your loyalty."

"Of course. Thank you, sir," he replied and closed the door gently. He loved the Rolls and did not mind riding in the front with the chauffeur in the least. Several more lucrative flights for the Magus and he might own his own Rolls Royce. He could be very discrete for the kind of money he received from the Magus.

At his mansion, a few personnel changes had been made. The Magus had transferred his former staff to another of his residences and had the staff from his Chicago home flown in. They barely had time to unpack before he arrived. They were older Polish immigrants and felt lucky to have such a generous employer. Months might pass before he would visit Chicago but they had kept his residence in Highland Park spotless and ready. They also appreciated the tonic from their employer that kept them feeling youthful. They had known about vampires in the old country and felt it was better to be under the protection of one than to be on the menu.

The chauffeur had given them a quick tour of the house before going to pick up the Magus. The Rolls pulled into a small building which was a four-car garage. The Magus stayed in the limo until the garage doors were tightly closed. Then he took a passageway that led directly to the master suite. Rupert's replacement was waiting there. A pair of black silk pajamas were laid out on the bed. He was a robust man with gray tinged blond hair and bright blue eyes.

"Thank you Paul, that will be all. I do not wish to be disturbed till I rise at 10 o'clock."

The butler nodded and left the room quickly. He had no idea what his predecessor had done to garner the Magus' displeasure and Paul did not want to experience it. He would make sure that no one disturbed his employer.

I arrived back home and went straight to my husband's suite where he was still asleep. Delilah raised her head slightly, yawned, then did a slow, languid stretch with her eyes barely open, then appeared to go back to sleep. I crawled into bed, sliding close to his comforting presence. His eyes momentarily opened. His hand slid over to gently touch my belly, then he fell back into the deep sleep of the undead. "I love you, Tristan," I whispered. It was true. There was no explanation for my attraction. It was not because he was undead. I had not felt attracted to any of the other vampires, except maybe Jorge, though in the past I didn't know his undead nature. Our souls were somehow inexorably intertwined. Deep inside there was a fateful attraction that could not be denied, though I had tried. I drifted off to sleep thinking of names for our offspring.

Several hours later I was slowly wakened by my husband's tender touch and soft kisses. Like many men he woke up ready for sex, a trait apparently shared by men undead or not. My parent's visit had temporarily diminished his sex drive. I was glad he was back to his old self. His hardness entered me. My brain felt a rush of intense pleasure. I was lost in the urgency of his thrusts. My back arched. I held onto him so tightly that my finger nails cut into his shoulder. I yelled, "Tristan!" Then we collapsed like marathon runners at the end of a race. Delilah made a sound that sounded like a sigh of annoyance. "Sorry if we disturbed you, your highness," I uttered, reaching down and patting her head.

A few minutes later my husband rose in all his naked glory and turned towards me. "I'm glad you used my proper name. I never want to be called Stan again, by anyone." Then added, "except your parents."

"Understood," I chuckled, "though I'm not responsible for what other's might call you."

"Everyone else already knows," he replied curtly.

"Thanks for being so good to my parents."

"You have devoted parents, they deserve my respect," he smiled, "even Connie."

"That was hard, sorry about that. I didn't get a chance to tell you, she thought you and Sir Franco were having an affair."

"What?" he responded, genuinely surprised.

"She thought that you were staying up all night going to dance clubs with him and Jorge. It was the only way she could explain your nocturnal lifestyle and keen sense of fashion."

"Amazing woman," he smiled. "I shouldn't be surprised considering your imagination."

"I need it to be a writer. She just hasn't found an outlet for it."

"Tonight I will meet with the Magus, we have much to discuss. I am now second to the most powerful vampire in the world." He began to get dressed.

"Yeah, but you still put your pants on one leg at a time," I commented. He gave me a questioning glance, clearly puzzled. "My dad always says it means that we aren't all that much different."

"I'll be sure to share that with the Magus," he smiled.

"Okay, he is a little different. I do want to talk to him again. It's important."

"I will pass on your request but I don't think he will talk to you about Lady Hauser."

"You can be such an asshole!" I threw a pillow at him.

"Imagine what I might be like if I did not love you," he responded.

"I have, Godzilla."

"No one ever called me that!" He threw the pillow back at me.

I ducked. "They lacked imagination. Besides, that's Baron Godzilla! Dr. Kyoto and Lady Lily will come by to check on you and do some lab work. I should be back after midnight." He kissed me gently on the forehead and left.

I realized it must be odd for him to tell anyone his schedule. The fact that he was attentive to me and made an effort to explain himself to me mattered. His new position would cause strain on some of his old relationships. He was now owed more respect. I would have to ground him whenever I could. The last thing I wanted was for him to become arrogant like Lady Hauser. The babies would only know him as daddy. He was wrong about the Magus. Sooner or later I would find out about what happened to Lady Hauser. There was no one he could confide in who was not part of the vampire world except me. The most powerful vampire in the universe would want someone to let his hair down with. I was the most logical person for that, as I would not do anything to upset him because of my offspring. Any threat to him would only come from his nocturnal kingdom, not me.

I dressed and went down to the kitchen. Tillie brought over a tray with croissants, Camembert cheese, thinly sliced roast beef and a mixed-greens salad with fresh raspberries. I was becoming used to being a carnivore again. By the time Dr. Kyoto and Lady Lily showed up I had cleaned my plate and emptied the salad bowl.

"You look well, Baroness," Dr. Kyoto commented as he and Lady Lily entered the kitchen.

"Would you mind coming to the office for some tests?" Lady Lily inquired.

"Sure," I replied and followed them to the little medical office where he took my vital signs and listened to my lungs. Lady Lily drew a few tubes of blood.

He asked me several questions and all my answers seemed to satisfy them that I was doing well. Then they had me lay back and they took turns listening for baby heartbeats. Then a strange, very human thing happened, they both smiled.

"You both look happy," I remarked, sounding a bit surprised.

Dr. Kyoto regained his stoic composure. Lady Lily responded, "We are pleased to find you doing so well."

"I feel okay. Just sort of pudgy," I remarked. They weighed me and I had gained 12 pounds.

"You are progressing as expected. Your weight is fine," Dr. Kyoto said.

"I encourage you to rest more, get off your feet more and keep your exercise light," Lady Lily commented.

"My understanding is that sex is still okay."

"Probably, we will have to see how you are doing over the next month," Lady Lily said. Remember, frequent small meals. Lots of protein."

"I think this pregnancy might be harder on the Baron than on me."

Dr. Kyoto chuckled as I left the office.

To my delight, Tillie was waiting in the kitchen with my cup of caffeinated wonderfulness and a bowl of crème brulee. I sat down and began to savor my first spoonful when Lady Lockporte and Sir Ruben entered.

"Hey Baroness, how are you?" Sir Ruben asked and plopped down beside me.

"Good evening, Baroness, "Lady Lockporte greeted me and stood on the other side of the counter. "We are your bodyguards for tonight."

"Will you please just call me Randie?"

"Can't do that," Sir Ruben responded. "Now that you are really Haute Caste."

I sighed, "My husband got the promotion, not me. So, tell me what happened to the wicked witch?" Sir Ruben looked at his sister. She seemed to be trying to come up with a safe response.

Lady Lockporte looked me straight in the eye and finally said, "We don't really know. The Magus went off with her, we don't know where and we don't expect to see her again for a very long time, if ever. She has lost her power, her status and her disposition will remain a mystery."

"Then why do I still need protection?"

"Good question," Sir Diego said as he entered with Sir Franco.

"We aren't quite sure if anyone else was involved," Sir Franco explained, "though since the chief instigator and her henchmen have been dealt with, we are fairly certain you are safe. But, until we are sure,"

Sir Diego gently put his arm around my shoulders, "You, my dear Baroness, are to be protected by order of the Magus."

"It's amazing," Sir Ruben added, "that a Short could be so feared and so respected by vampires. We are supposed to look after you but we don't know what to do with you. It's like a kitten scaring Delilah."

"Even kittens can bite and scratch," I replied.

"Good evening, Baroness," Lady Kananga said from the doorway. "May I speak to you all in the library?"

I grabbed my coffee and followed everyone through the house. I was glad to have so much company. I was afraid I would have to spend the evening alone, waiting for my husband. It was an amazing gathering of talented vampires. As I stood there I realized that they waited for me to be seated on the couch before they sat down. Even Dr. Kyoto and Lady Lily joined us.

"The Magus has given me the honor of letting you know first about his latest decision. Sergio will be a knight for Sir Sadeghi. The House of Pentacles will not have a knight for the time being."

"This is huge," Sir Ruben said. "He has allowed a Pentacle to join the House of Swords."

"Yes, this is historic," Lady Lockporte looked over at me. "This is because of you. I can't explain it, but your existence has been a catalyst for change in our world, a welcome change," she added

"Also, Kabedi is requesting to be assigned to the House of Plows," Lady Kananga said. "I haven't told the Magus that I'm agreeable yet."

"I'll do anything, really anything," Sir Ruben pleaded with Lady Kananga.

"What do you think, Lady Lockporte?"

"I think he could be more polite and respectful," she said in a serious tone.

"I will, I promise I will," Sir Ruben said and actually got down on his knees. "Please approve her request!"

Lady Kananga smiled. "I gave my permission yesterday. Kabedi is waiting for you to call and help her make arrangements."

"Thank you!" He pulled out his phone out and ran from the room.

"I'm glad he's happy," I said. "Shouldn't Lady Anastasia be here to hear the announcements?"

Lady Kananga responded, "She is on her way to London at this moment. The Magus is sending our roaming vampiress on a special mission to help clean up the House of Pentacles. Her breeding allows Sir Sudovian to feel flattered by her attention instead of threatened or insulted. If any of us had been given the task, our pretentious brother would have been offended."

"It's the dawn of a new age for our kind, dear Lady Lockporte," Sir Diego said. "Perhaps we will become more unified."

They chatted about how the social structure of the vampire world might be changed by the Magus' decisions. Now and then I was mentioned as a catalyst.

"I did not choose to be part of this cultural revolution, I suppose I was born into this role." Not that I had any idea.

"That doesn't seem to matter. Intentional or accidental you are the spark," Lady Kananga said. "Your children will be the explosion that will cause us to rebuild our civilization. I look forward to this challenge. The undead existence had become so mundane the last 300 years."

"I've only been alive 23 years. It is still hard to realize how long you all have been...well, around." I replied.

"We all remember when you were born," Sir Diego said with a smile.

"Everyone waiting to find out about your blood type," Dr. Kyoto added.

"The Baron was elated that you were a girl," Lady Lockporte said.

"I don't think I want to hear anymore," I responded and they laughed, which was kind of an odd experience, seeing a group of vampires laugh and not in a menacing way.

"It's the same with your pregnancy," Lady Lily said. "It is exciting. A mystery."

"It just feels like heartburn," I replied.

"I hope they will sleep through the night. You were not very fun as a baby," Sir Diego added.

"You looked in on me while I slept as a baby?"

"It was easy. Your parents left their house unlocked. They probably still do," he replied.

"Do you think the babies will be sort of nocturnal?" I asked.

"We can only hope. Do you think they'll call me Uncle Franco?"

"Do you realize they will spit-up on your silk shirt?" Lady Kananga said with a smile.

Sir Franco made a face.

"You should be so lucky to get their royal puke on you," I replied.

Sir Ruben returned smiling and asked, "Hockey, anyone?"

"Not me. I'm waiting up for Baron Godzilla."

"You didn't just say that," Sir Ruben uttered. He turned to his sister, "And you think I'm bad." The others acted as if they hadn't heard my comment. Most of the Haute Caste decided to go to the Narcissus club to break the news about the Magus' decisions and to celebrate, except, of course, my bodyguards, who excused themselves to play hockey until the others left for the club.

I sat alone in the library for a few minutes. I should have been horrified by the thought of the undead looking after my children but they felt like family. I imagined that it must be similar to having mafia hit men for uncles, except they lived forever and drank blood. I could not explain why but I had this strong feeling that my kids would be able to handle the weird world they were being born into. In any case, I would do everything possible to keep their little half-royal butts safe.

CHAPTER 40

THE MAGUS WAS standing in his office with the attorney, Mr. Beaudine, when the Baron arrived. The leader of the vampire world was dressed in a lavender polo shirt and tan slacks. The computer screens were dark and no refreshments had been served. Mr. Beaudine was wearing one of his best Italian suits but clearly he was an employee and appeared slightly uncomfortable.

"Congratulations on your marriage," Mr. Beaudine said but did not attempt to shake the Baron's hand. The Baron merely nodded. The Magus sat in a leather chair at his desk and indicated they should be seated. The Baron chose a stuffed chair and the attorney seated himself last in a hardback, antique oak chair. The vampires were his only clients. For a very large monthly retainer he gladly catered to their demands and eccentricities.

"All of the late Lady Hauser's real estate, bank accounts, stocks, etc. will be yours, my dear Baron, though the townhouse in Santa Monica will go to Sergio," the Magus explained. "I will keep the jewels, as I gave her most of them." He fingered Lena's sapphire ring which he now wore on the little finger of his right hand.

"I'm sorry for your loss," Mr. Beaudine said. He was not quite sure what had happened and as with many interactions with the Magus, he was just as happy to remain ignorant.

"Don't be," the Magus responded, "though I will miss her."

A little taken aback, the lawyer presented the Baron with the documents, which included a will and deeds to her properties around the world. He had bribed a few officials to be able to have the papers drawn up and notarized in two days. In the 20 years he had served the Magus, this had been the first will. The dates on the will showed that it had been drawn up last year. That was expensive. The death certificate was more difficult and expensive. All in all, he had done a splendid job.

"I have put all the documents on a disc as well." He placed it on the desk. "Will there be anything else?"

"That will be all," and with that the Magus dismissed him. Mr. Beaudine left quickly. "He is afraid of our displeasure but the money keeps him coming back. Greed helps people overcome their fear."

"Like Johann. What is to become of your reluctant guest?" the Baron asked. "I would gladly dispose of him for you."

"I've decided to allow him to return to our society as a symbol of my mercy to our kind. If there are other traitors I want them to let down their guard while I figure out who they are."

"You can't allow him near my wife!"

"He doesn't want to be anywhere near her," the Magus replied "He will be sent to London where Lady Anastasia will observe how the Pentacles respond to him as well as keep an eye on him. Johann has repented and pledged his loyalty. He will be very helpful. You may tell your wife his nose is healing but he will sport an interesting scar. It will add to her legacy."

"I've heard that the Houses fear her. I find that amazing. How can someone so vulnerable be so frightening? She is hardly the warm-blooded monster they make her out to be. Spoiled brat is more like it," the Baron smiled.

"I'm not sure Johann would agree," the Magus responded.

"May I ask about the circumstances surrounding the disappearance of Lena?"

The Magus looked at the Baron intently. He placed a hand upon his arm. "She is secure in a very remote location, immobilized and badly injured. If I ever choose to bring her back she will be close to unrecognizable with very little power. In that state, I might pity her rather than hate her."

"I accept your judgment in all things, my dear Magus. I shall not speak of this again. I refused to answer any of Miranda's questions, then she demanded an audience with you, alone."

The Magus smiled. "She is bold and undaunted. Imagine what your children will be like."

"More disciplined than she is, I will make sure of that, I assure you."

"Tell your beloved wife that I shall not see her again until the children are born. Then I shall give her my undivided attention," the Magus said.

"As you wish. Thank you for my new status and for the wealth you have bestowed upon me." The Baron got on one knee before the Magus' chair. "I swear my eternal loyalty," then he bowed his head.

"I never doubted your loyalty. You have always understood me and what is required," he said, looking fondly on the Baron. "I've only been concerned with your ability to be patient with Miranda." The Magus gestured for him to stand.

The Baron smiled, "I have never become so angry with someone without tearing their throat out."

"Keep playing hockey," the Magus laughed softly.

The next several months became a monotonous but tranquil time for my husband and me. From time to time, members of the Haute Caste from all over the world would visit to pay their respects. During this time I never saw the Magus and had no idea where he was. We would go to the Narcissus now and then but the last two months I spent a lot of time in bed. The House of Plows and the House of Arrows were primarily in charge of my security. Sir Steve even helped me hone my knife throwing skills. My husband would go out from time to time to hunt down some poor wretch who he had decided had escaped justice. It helped his mood. Sometimes in the evening a group of my vigilante vampires would discuss recent court cases and who might deserve their appetite for wrath. Then it was , rock, paper, scissors to decide who would do the honors. Yes, rock, paper and scissors decided who would take a life. Sir Ruben, to my surprise, seemed to come out on top the most. I think he had some ESP ability that he hid from the others. Sir Ruben and Sir Franco's bickering could always make me laugh. It helped me avoid dwelling on the dark side of their natures.

All the vampires were doting and comforting to me at night. As the due date got closer the Baron rarely left the mansion. Even when we could not be intimate he would rub my shoulders and gently hold me. My room had been set up as a birthing center. Delilah never left my side for long. Lolly and Alan would come by every few days in the late afternoon and bring fresh bagels or some healthy treat. They told me that Grigoryi had taken my advice and left for Rome. I was glad, he would be better off there. My parents had made plans so they could fly out in a couple of weeks.

Lady Anastasia visited with news of Sir Sudovian's efforts to clean up his House. She reported, "He is quite anxious to please me and the Magus. All his staff and his close vampires have been under scrutiny. Johann has been given a butler's position, which he seems grateful to have. His nose scar is the talk of the House. Some say he was brave, though extremely foolhardy, to take on the Baroness. I was constantly besieged with questions about you. Johann has been telling them how you seduced the Baron with your great beauty."

I looked down at my body, which now housed three babies and started to laugh. "In a sort of Sir Rubenesque, voluptuous way, I suppose that is true." I was lying in bed with several pillows which Tillie had recently fluffed, supporting my back. Even so I could never get totally comfortable.

Lady Anastasia appeared quite happy to be the Magus' special emissary to London. Though not very maternal, she presented three antique lace Christening gowns for the babies, which like everything at eight months made me tearful.

"You don't care for them?" she inquired as I sobbed.

"No, I'm very touched, they're lovely," I began sobbing again and suddenly a great pain ripped into my gut "Tristan!!! Get Tristan!!!" Water suddenly gushed out of me, soaking the bed.

Lady Anastasia went to the door and called out, "Dr. Kyoto! It's time!" Suddenly the room was full of people. Tristan ran to my side and put his arm about my shoulders. Dr. Kyoto and Lady Lily pulled back the sheets and positioned my legs to see how imminent the births might be. The Lockportes, Sir Diego and Sir Franco were standing by. Tillie ran in with sterilized sheets.

"The Baron, Lady Anastasia and Tillie stay, the rest of you out," Lady Lilly commanded and pointed to the door. They all cleared out. Tillie removed the wet bedding and gently slipped the sterile sheets under me.

"Fuck!" I yelled as another wave of pain grabbed me.

Dr. Kyoto hooked up a fetal monitor and monitors for my vitals as well. "Try to take slow even breaths, like we practiced. You're doing fine."

"Ow, I'm not doing fine! I think they want out!"

"Put this on her forehead." Lady Lilly handed the Baron a cool, wet face cloth, then she started an IV.

"I love you," Tristan said. He was holding my hand and looking nervous and clueless.

"Damn that hurts," I cried out. The pains continued for another hour at about the same intensity and timing, then suddenly they started coming more frequently and the pain doubled. "It's worse, the pain!" I screamed something unintelligible. I squeezed my husband's hand hard and he tried to smile.

"I'm going to give you an epidermal then make a small incision to help you," Dr. Kyoto told me calmly.

I felt a sting, then it passed. It was nothing compared to the labor pains. I saw the helpless expression on my husband's face and for a second felt sorry for him. For several more minutes I felt like I was expelling my insides.

"I can see a head," Lady Lily cried out. Tillie grabbed a warming blanket.

"Push when you feel like it," Dr. Kyoto said.

I closed my eyes so tightly when I pushed that afterwards I had slightly blackened eyes. I let my body do what had been written into my genes. I cried out each time the wave of pain would start. I thought I was dying. Then suddenly the pressure let up a little. I opened my eyes to see Dr. Kyoto help my oldest child into the world, wet and pink.

"A boy! Baron! A healthy boy!" he exclaimed and then handed the crying baby to Lady Lily. She suctioned and wiped him off, did a quick evaluation and then started to bring him to me but the terrible pain returned.

"Again, it's happening again!"

A few minutes later Dr. Kyoto exclaimed, "Another healthy boy!" and handed the crying infant to Lady Lily. She performed the same procedures and evaluations for a second time.

My husband was beaming as he kissed my cheek and put the cool cloth back on my forehead.

"You're doing fine. Your vital signs are fine. I can see a shoulder. Try not to push for a moment. I'm going to try and help position the baby," Dr. Kyoto said.

"I can't stop this!" I cried.

"Okay, I see the head, push!"

I screamed bloody murder again and the last baby arrived in a wave of blood. I was crying, "Is my baby okay?" I apparently passed out for a few seconds.

When I become aware again, I heard Dr. Kyoto saying, "She needs a transfusion! Now!"

Dr. Kyoto wiped his arm with an alcohol swab and motioned to Lady Lily. She looked surprised when he handed her a syringe. He nodded toward his arm. She filled the large syringe with his blood. She inserted it into the IV port and slowly depressed the plunger. I felt as if a wave of energy had flowed through me and though slightly light headed. Then Lily hung up a rare bag of HH blood from a mortal source and connected it to my IV.

"My baby!" I cried out.

Lady Anastasia came up to me holding my youngest "She has arrived and is perfectly healthy!"

"A girl?

"A Baroness!" Lady Anastasia exclaimed.

"I want to hold all of them," I cried.

The Baron handed me our first born, "May I introduce Tomas." Then he took the second born from Tillie and placed him gently in my other arm. "And Desmon." They seemed so tiny and precious, I was almost afraid to touch them. Lady Anastasia handed our daughter to my husband. He gently placed her on my chest, "and finally, Marie."

"Their Apgar scores are perfect," Dr. Kyoto announced. "Though they are couple of weeks early they are fine. They each weigh just under 7 pounds. Amazing."

"Of course their Apgar scores are perfect," my husband said. He was smiling like I had never seen him.

I looked over at Dr. Kyoto and Lady Lily. All I could get out was, "Thank you." Lady Lily seemed quite concerned about me. "My dear Baroness, Tillie and I shall attend to you while Dr. Kyoto, the Baron and Lady Anastasia care for the babies in the nursery."

It was the first time I heard Lady Lily give Dr. Kyoto an order and he did not question it. As they opened the door, jubilant cries could be heard from the vampires in the hallway.

"Call my parents!" I yelled at my husband over the celebration in the hallway. "Oh, and Lolly too!"

"We will take care of everything. Now, you need to be quiet and rest. You lost a lot of blood but you will be fine. All is well!" Lady Lily said.

"They are beautiful" I said to her. "Somehow the pain doesn't matter now."

Tillie changed my night gown and put clean sheets on the bed while Lady Lily helped clean me up. Tillie opened a window to air out the room. It was three o'clock in the morning.

"It's February 13," I said.

"Friday," Lady Lily added.

"How weird,'" I muttered.

"Not really, it's what I expected. You helped me win a bet with Dr. Kyoto."

"You'll be a good mum," Tillie stated. "Drink a little tea, then get some rest." She gave me a few sips of weak herbal tea. "I'll sit right here by your bed."

The Baron returned to check on me. I smiled weakly. I had never been so exhausted. Every muscle in my body ached.

"Our babies are all okay?" I asked a bit anxiously.

"Yes, they are perfect! You won't believe it, Sir Franco and Sir Ruben got teary. You may want to blackmail them with this knowledge." He kissed me and held my hand.

"How is she?" He asked Lady Lily.

"Better than expected after having triplets. The blood transfusion has stabilized her nicely."

"I can give her some," he insisted.

"That won't be necessary," she responded. "Did Dr. Kyoto check the babies' blood type?"

The Baron looked at me as he answered her question, "They are all HH."

"That is great news," Lady Lily said.

"Vampires will respect them?" I asked.

"Absolutely," my husband replied.

"Who is caring for them besides Dr. Kyoto, maybe Lady Lily should...." I began but my husband interrupted.

"They are in good hands. The Magus arranged for a pediatric team from the UCLA Medical Center to be on standby. They just arrived. They'll care for Tomas, Desmon and Marie while we sleep."

"The Magus?" I asked.

"You will have an audience with him tomorrow night. I talked to your parents and they're making arrangements to fly in tomorrow. Lolly and Alan are still in New York, she wants you to call her tomorrow."

"Did my mom cry when you called her?"

"Yes, as soon as I told her the news, then she gave the phone to your dad."

"I should be with my babies." I tried to get up but fell back on the bed.

"You'll have plenty of sleepless nights with them but now you must heal and recover a bit," Tillie said and fixed the sheets.

"Baron, I must ask you to sleep in your suite tonight. She will not rest well with you in the room," Lady Lily said, taking charge to everyone's surprise.

"I hate to say it but I think she's right," I responded.

Tillie nodded in agreement. "I'll stay with her all day."

"Very well, my love. I shall respect Lady Lily and Tillie's knowledge of these matters." He turned towards Tillie, "Do not hesitate to wake me if anything happens."

"Of course, Baron."

He kissed my forehead and then left to see our offspring again before retiring.

"Thank you. I think I need to get my strength back so I can hold my beautiful babies again." I started to tear up. "Tristan's genes helped them. They're early but they'll be okay, won't they?"

"They are magnificent. I am honored to have been chosen to assist with the birth of your children. Thank you for being so brave." Lady Lily assured me she would check on my little ones before she went to sleep. "That was amazing to see Dr. Kyoto give his blood to you." She gave me a low bow and then left the room.

Tillie closed the window and pulled the blinds so the light of dawn would not wake me later. She settled into a rocking chair and began to knit. I was soon asleep.

CHAPTER 41

THE MAGUS TOOK particular care in dressing for his meeting with Miranda. He did not want to wear too formal attire, nor did he want to dress casual. A special, intimate conversation deserved the appropriate look. His walk-in closet resembled a small clothing boutique. He looked over the vast array of the shirts and picked out a dove gray silk shirt then chose matching linen slacks and finished with a pair of dark gray Italian loafers. The Magus looked through the collection of jewels that had once belonged to Lady Hauser. He picked out a very rare 10-carat tanzanite pendant set in white gold. He placed it in his pocket carefully. *It will look much better on the Baroness*, he thought and decided not to tell her who it used to belong to.

He arrived at the Stone Canyon mansion as the last hues of the red washed sunset faded. It was unheard of for the Magus to be seen so early in the evening. There was a knock on the door of the nursery and Clive announced that the Magus had arrived. Somehow at that moment the audience with him did not seem so important. I was sitting in one of the plush chairs in the babies' room quite astonished by Tomas, who was sucking on my breast. "I'm really doing this, I'm really feeding him," I said to the RN who had shown me how to position my nipple so his tiny mouth could grasp it.

The nurse from UCLA smiled. "More milk will come in soon as your body responds to the demand." She gently took Tomas and handed him to Tillie. He began to squabble. Tillie quieted him with a bottle. Clive entered, staring at the floor the whole time. "The Magus will speak with you on the patio, Baroness."

"Tell him I'll be down in 10 minutes," I replied. I could see the look of astonishment on Clive's face even though he was looking down.

"Ten Minutes?"

"Tell him I'm attending to my children and will gladly see him in 10 minutes," I replied.

Clive left without another word looking as if he dreaded having to deliver my message. Tillie just smiled. The nurse handed me Desmon. I swear he grinned. Maybe it was just gas. In any case I nursed him a little as well, then gave him to another nurse who had a bottle. Then it was time for Marie. She fussed a little until she could grasp the nipple, then she was fine. She was an ounce bigger than her brothers. I was sure she would be able to hold her own with them. I regretted having to leave them for even a short time but I had a lot of questions concerning their safety. I handed my little girl to the RN and went downstairs. My baby blue night gown and white lace robe would have to do as I did not feel up to getting dressed, and decided that it wouldn't be wise to keep the Magus waiting any longer.

I saw Clive standing by the sliding glass doors to the garden. He seemed more than a little surprised at my attire but tried to hide it. "I'd like a cup of decaf and some cookies. Thanks."

"The Magus already requested it for you," he told me.

I looked outside and saw his highness sitting at a wrought iron table for two with a silver coffee set and pastries. "Please tell the Baron where we are when he wakes." He nodded and opened the door for me. I was beginning to feel more comfortable with giving orders to our servants.

The Magus actually stood as I approached. "Good evening, dear Baroness. How are you?"

"I'm sore and a bit tired but feeling much better. I apologize for my attire but after feeding the babies I didn't want to keep you waiting any longer." He brushed off my apology with a wave of his hand. I quickly overcame my embarrassment. After all, it was my house and he had arrived earlier than I expected. "Aren't our children amazing? They are so healthy." I sat down. Negotiating stairs was a little hard on the stitches. "Could I have a pillow?" I called out to Clive. He produced one in record time, then I was more comfortable.

"Though I'm told many people claim that their children are special, they could not compare to the unique qualities, stamina and intelligence of your triplets."

"Thank you. Please relieve my anxiety. I must know that Lena can't harm them. What did you do with her?"

"A select group of the Haute Caste went to London, subdued and secured Lady Hauser. She is now, shall we say, imprisoned in a very remote location. You need not be concerned about her again. You should be thanking Sir Sadeghi,

Lady Kananga, Lady Lockporte, Sir Ruben and Pauline. In the process of removing the despicable creature to the secret location, she was inadvertently burned by sunlight. Her body is now scarred beyond recovery and, except to a very minimal degree, she will never be powerful again. She has been secured deep in the earth. If I ever decide to bring her back, she will survive on the outskirts of our society."

"Where is she now?"

"That I will not tell you or anyone for that matter. The Baron does not know either. It is better if you both do not know, though I will say it is very far from you and the babies."

"Don't ever free her. She will never forgive any of us," I stated flatly.

"I've considered that. I hope to not revisit this subject for a at least 500 years," he said. "Now to more pressing matters. But first I would like you to eat something."

"I'm fine. Tillie gave me a veggie burger when I woke up and a protein shake."

"Yes, I'm sure that was delicious," he grimaced slightly, "but I had these pastries flown in from Paris." I think you will enjoy them."

I took a bite of a light, crisp pastry layered with dark chocolate, hazelnuts and custard. "I see what you mean, these are amazing. Thank you! Now please tell me about the pressing matters." I continued to eat the wonderful pastries. I was very curious about what could matter more than Lena's disposition.

"I like to think in logical if not scientific terms, but sometimes fate has a way of aiding science. When a descendant of the finest Templar Knight married someone with HH blood, some called it a sign but I saw an opportunity," he said, gazing at me intently.

"I already know about my heritage...." I began but he held up a hand to quiet me.

"No, you don't, there is something important you need to know. There is no polite way to relay this information," the Magus began in a low voice. "You know that when your parents were having difficulty conceiving, your father got distracted by a pretty face and your mother kicked him out for a few weeks. Then your mother decided to go to a women's civic club convention in Chicago to spend some time alone to think."

"I know all this. My mom told me she forgave him when she realized she was pregnant and my dad has been true blue ever since," I replied, a bit annoyed to be discussing such personal matters with him.

He paused before saying, "What you may not know is that your mother met someone in the hotel bar in Chicago."

"I don't like what you're insinuating. My mom wouldn't pick up a guy in a bar. She doesn't even drink!"

"He was a charming vampire and she had had two glasses of wine. Understandable under the circumstances," he said in a serious tone. "After becoming acquainted with him she felt positively adventurous, slightly intoxicated and let the stranger walk her to her room. Then, well she may not want to remember but you were conceived that night."

"Liar! That's not possible, my mom would never...." I stopped as it dawned on me I was raising my voice to the Magus.

"She is human and fallible," he said with a tiny smile. "And I don't lie."

Even though I was upset and confused, I realized the Magus had just let me get away with insulting him. I knew better than to press my luck. "You're saying my biological father was a vampire? That can't be! I'm an Ortega. I'm a Short," I responded anxiously.

"Your father believes you are his daughter, and in all ways you are, except biologically. I'm sure your mother has decided he's your father as well. It's just that he is sterile."

"Sometimes even the doctors aren't right." I protested. "Wait, wait! How would you know all that. It isn't possible." My head was spinning, I felt like my world was imploding.

"In his case the doctor was correct. When I realized that your mother would be the last de Molay, I came up with a plan. A vampiress worked nights at the café long enough to seduce your father, causing the separation. Your father's blood is HH, so the vampire's blood type never raised suspicion. Your mother believes you are a miracle that saved their marriage." The Magus paused to give me a chance to process this revelation.

"This doesn't make sense, my mom never had a transfusion of vampire blood. How can you explain her becoming pregnant by a vampire?" I asked, hoping to disprove his words but my gut told me to hear him out.

"Some of your female ancestors had, shall we say, exposure to male vampires, especially your grandmother, but they never got pregnant. Yet our presence over the years had a molecular impact, like someone having a positive TB test because of exposure but no symptoms. For a year small amounts of blood were secretly added to your mother's diet at their café in hopes that it might improve the chances of her becoming pregnant with a vampire. Those who helped us thought the blood was meant to help her become pregnant by your father. Only I and another member of the Haute Caste knew the real plan. We patiently waited for an opportunity. The trip to Chicago worked out perfectly."

"Oh my God you're serious! My father was a vampire? Don't tell me it was Tristan! Just when I think my life couldn't get more fucked up!"

"No. That would have compromised the genetic health of your offspring, and unthinkable even for us."

"Are you telling me you are my father?" I felt like I was having a Luke Skywalker moment. I was starting to feel nauseated.

The Magus smiled. "Unfortunately that was not in the cards for me. The honor went to another. It was important that if your mother became pregnant, the baby be aligned with a Haute Caste House. Belonging to a House assures greater acceptance for you and your children. When the time is right, your lineage will be announced."

"Who is my father?"

"Guess," he said with a Cheshire Cat grin.

Instantly, I knew. Somehow I knew. "Sir Sadeghi! I remember how he looked at me that night on the beach. His kindness to Grigoryi for trying to help me. The knife he gave me."

"Very good. Yes. You are of the House of Swords."

"So that means that I'm the first mixed-blood child!"

"Yes. I will let you tell the Baron now if you wish but no one else. It seems Lena suspected you might have had a connection to me and saw it as a threat to her, so she tried to have you killed in Rossville. She never knew the truth. Sir Sadeghi and I were able to shield our thoughts from her."

"Deep down I always knew she hated me."

"Yes. According to Johann she hired some men in Chicago and they set up the accident that almost killed you as a child. Luckily those mortals were inept assassins. I only recently discovered that she was responsible."

"That bitch!" I could not consider the attempt on my life right at that moment but I would talk about it with my husband later. I had to know more about my biological father. "Why didn't Sir Sadeghi tell me when he was here?"

"He wanted to give you more time to become accustomed to our kind."

"Why did you choose Sir Sadeghi?" I knew the Magus had planned my conception.

"There are three vampires that I may depend on without reservation: your husband, Lady Anastasia and Sir Sadeghi. Luckily, he has a similar complexion, hair color and dark brown eyes like your father. "

"Do I look like him?"

"When you smile," the Magus replied.

"When I was growing up, my mom said I didn't look like either of them, that I looked like my grandmother."

"Yes, well, unconsciously she recognizes us, even in you, Though I don't know if she will ever consciously admit it. That is why she will accept any excuse you give her to explain your husband's nocturnal schedule."

"She actually thought he was gay!"

"She is an interesting woman," the Magus replied tactfully. He pulled a small satin drawstring bag out of his pocket. "Sir Sadeghi wanted to be here for the birth of his grandchildren but worried about being recognized by your mother." He handed me the bag. "He will visit after your parents leave, but in the meantime he wanted you to have this."

I opened the satin bag. Inside was a gold frame that held a miniature portrait of Sir Sadeghi. "My other dad." I started getting a bit tearful.

"And this is a small token of my regard. I hope you will consider me a very protective guardian." He reached over, took my hand and placed something in my palm and closed my fingers over it. I opened my hand to a gorgeous tanzanite pendant. "You and the children will always have access to me."

"Thank you. I am still trying to understand what all this means," I replied awkwardly and looked at the jewel. "The color is amazing, I've never seen a lavender-blue gemstone like this," I said, holding it up to the light. I guess in a way if not for you I wouldn't even exist. I should be yelling at you and running away from all the lies about my conception but it's like I'm finally starting to understand who I am." It suddenly struck me. "I'm half undead."

A rare fondness shown in his eyes. "Half-vampire. Your response to the transfusion from your husband was incredible. Other mortals will show a decline in time if they don't get more blood but not you. You recreate your own blood cells with vampire and mortal traits. The warm-blooded traits seemed to dominate during childhood but as you age your vampire qualities are slowly beginning to show. We assume it will be the same with your offspring."

"My sense of smell, my ESP and my strength. That explains subduing Johann," I mused. "I'm even becoming more nocturnal, though luckily my appetite hasn't changed."

"Thank you for naming one of your sons after me, I am truly honored," he smiled.

"Tristan has to know but I don't want the kids to know. Not until they are grown."

"Pete will be their only grandfather," the Magus stated, "until you are ready to tell them. Sir Sadeghi wants it this way as well." He took a piece of paper out of his pocket with information about one of his properties.. "If you ever need to get away, this is a place no one but you and I will know about."

There was a softness in his expression I had never seen before. I took the incredible pendant and fastened it about my neck. I placed the piece of paper in the bag with the portrait. Tears filled my eyes. "You know I used to hate you."

"I know," the Magus smiled. "You were quite amusing." Tristan appeared through the patio doors. The Magus gave him an almost imperceptible nod.

The Baron slid open the glass doors. "Good evening, Magus. Miranda, Clive just brought your parents from the airport."

I slipped the small bag into my robe pocket. We exchanged an almost conspiratorial look. Tristan looked puzzled but fortunately before he could ask any questions my mom, with my dad trailing behind as usual, ran past my husband and hugged me tightly. "Honey, how are you? Where are my grandbabies?"

"I'm fine. It was rough but the babies and I are okay. Mom, dad, let me introduce you to a dear friend of Stan's, Desmon."

"So you're the guy one of my grandsons is named after," my dad observed. He held out his hand to the Magus. I thought Clive was going to faint. The Magus stood and shook his hand quickly, in an awkward fashion, like someone not familiar with the act. It was hard not to laugh.

"It is nice to meet you. Tristan was very lucky to marry your daughter," he smiled. "Now if you'll excuse me." Without another word he was gone.

"Let's go see the children," the Baron said.

"Did I say something wrong?" my dad asked me as we walked up the staircase.

"No, he was just about to leave when you arrived, some important business meeting," I replied. Lying seemed to be getting easier for me. Perhaps that was another vampire characteristic.

"That's a beautiful necklace," my mom said.

"Thanks." I did not want to explain who gave it to me. If it wasn't from my husband she would not understand.

As we walked up the grand staircase my husband walked a few feet behind my mom and me chatting with my dad. When we got to the nursery, Tristan took over.

"You have a mini neonatal unit here! Oh, my grandbabies!" my mom exclaimed, then tears began flowing. "I was afraid they would be weak!"

"They are Ortegas, you should know better," my dad said and beamed with pride as he touched Tomas' cheek.

"May I present in order of birth," the Baron announced, "Tomas!" He gently picked up our sleeping son. Then the RN lifted Desmon. "And this," continued Tristan, "is Desmon!" The RN placed the second born in my mom's arms. She sat down in the rocking chair and began to gently rock him. Tillie handed Marie to my dad. "And finally, this is Marie, she can be a bit fussy like her mom." My dad smiled. Then I got tearful.

The Baron smiled with pride. The nurses excused themselves. My children were content and sleepy after their feeding. It was one of those sweet moments in time that you want to forever remember in tiny detail.

"You look good,. Miranda, but you should be sitting down," my mom said. I sat in one of the plush chairs.

"I'm really okay though it is better if I am sitting on pillows. Dr. Kyoto and Dr. Lily have taken very good care of the babies and me."

"I'm glad we didn't have to visit them in the hospital. Thanks for all of this, Stan," my mom smiled at my husband.

"Anything for my family," he replied.

"Are you going to play hockey with your brothers?" My dad asked Marie.

"But of course," my husband answered. "She can be the goalie." He looked at me. "One of our friends has already asked to coach them."

"Oh my Lord," Tillie uttered and we all started laughing.

Near Barrow, Alaska, an old elk wandered away from the herd. It stumbled and fell down a deep, craggy crevasse to its death. The elk's broken body trickled blood. Before it became frozen, some of the crimson elixir formed a small pool on a dented, broken freezer. Several wolves who had hunted the old elk paced back and forth at the edge of the crevasse looking for a way to get to the fresh carcass. The scent of death and blood filled the cavern from the still warm body. Despite their hunger, a sound, a terrible wail, startled the wolves and caused them to retreat into the darkness.

CHAPTER 42

MY PARENTS STAYED for a week. The UCLA nurses were only needed part-time as my parents spent most of their waking hours in the nursery, then the Baron, Sir Jorge and Sir Franco would join us in the evening. I was always tired but very content. My parents were delighted. When I saw my father holding Tomas, I became tearful but hid it from him. He could never know they were not his biological grandchildren. My mom made a special effort to befriend Sir Franco. I knew she felt guilty for thinking he was having an affair with my husband. She even invited Sir Jorge and Sir Franco to visit Rossville.

"We have a few antique stores, you can get some good bargains," she told him.

"So I've heard," Sir Jorge responded with a droll expression. "Unfortunately, we will be going back to Caracas soon."

"Mi casa es su casa," my dad stated.

The Baron laughed. "I think that is the only Spanish your daughter knows."

"I told her not to take French," my dad responded. "Please be sure the kids learn Spanish."

"I will personally give them lessons, Senor Ortega," Sir Jorge responded. "Their heritage is important."

"Well, I only speak English and I've done fine," Connie asserted.

"Yeah, but wouldn't you like to know what my mother said about your turkey stuffing?" my dad asked.

"She didn't like it? All those years she seemed to enjoy my cooking!" My mom seemed truly hurt.

"Mom, calm down, he's just joking. We all love your stuffing. Dad, knock it off. In fact, we hope to be in Rossville for Thanksgiving," I replied.

"We do? When is Thanksgiving?" my husband responded.

"You don't know when Thanksgiving is?" my mom asked, rather shocked by his ignorance.

"It's not big in Lithuania, mom," I responded and wondered if vampires drank turkey blood. "It's in November. The babies will be old enough to travel by then."

My mom and dad excused themselves to pack. Sir Jorge and Sir Franco said good night to the babies and headed for the Narcissus Club. I excused Tillie, which left my husband and me alone for the evening. He was very attentive to our children. They brought out a soft side that few have ever seen. After finishing feeding our offspring and tucking them in, we sat down in the plush chairs. It was the first chance I had to speak with my husband since my meeting with the Magus, when I wasn't exhausted."

"It is good to have a moment alone with you, Miranda. You are amazing, my love, and so are the children."

"I can't believe you changed a diaper. If only Sir Ruben or Sir Franco had seen it!"

"I'm the second most powerful vampire in the world and that's what impresses you?" He looked dumbfounded.

"Absolutely. The babies bring out your human side. Wait till you read them *Green Eggs and Ham*!"

He looked baffled, "Green Eggs and Ham?"

"You know, Dr. Seuss, children's books."

"No, really, I don't know. Besides, isn't that something you should do?"

"I can't imagine you telling Marie you won't read to her."

"Well then, I suppose," he smiled, "I can't either."

"I've been waiting for the right moment to talk with you about my conversation with the Magus." I got up and closed the door. Then I turned off the baby monitor. I pulled my chair close to his.

"This must be serious. I hope I won't be asked to take sides," he said.

"No, you don't have to worry about that. Did you ever wonder about how compatible I was when you gave me the transfusion as a child?"

"I was just so relieved that I did not question it."

In a soft voice, just above a whisper, I said, "Pete is not my biological father."

"I don't understand." My husband responded with a look of surprise. "He has HH blood. No one else...What did the Magus tell you?" he demanded.

"Our children are not the first born of a vampire and a mortal."

"That's impossible, I would have known!"

"Shh!" I pointed to our sleeping offspring. "Only two members of the Haute Caste knew, though Lena had her suspicions."

"The Magus told you this?" he asked in a hushed tone.

"Yes, and he said I could only tell you. It's hard to believe but my biological father is really Sir Sadeghi. He spent one night with my mom when she was separated from my dad. They had been secretly slipping vampire blood into her juice at the café to boost compatibility and fertility. The Magus and Sir Sadeghi were the only vampires who knew that my father is sterile. The Magus believed that it was important that our bloodline not come to an end, so he planned it all."

The Baron just stared at me. "The Magus said the blood given to your mother was to help her conceive but he never mentioned...." It was an uncomfortable and rare feeling for him to be so surprised. "You are Sir Sadeghi's daughter?"

"I'm of the House of Swords." I took the miniature out of my pocket. "He sent this to me."

"That explains the extraordinary health of the babies and your ability to take on vampires. The children will have even more of our qualities," he nodded with a bit of enthusiasm. Then his expression became concerned. "Lena suspected something. It explains her hatred of you."

"Lena thought it might be the Magus. She was worried about me taking her place. The Magus found out she was behind the accident I had as a child."

"Lena! In the end, her treachery only made you stronger. You have the genes as well as the blood of the elite Haute Caste. My feelings for you blinded me. I should have seen your connection to Sir Sadeghi. How could I have not detected your heritage?" He truly looked confused.

"You had no reason to question where my HH blood came from. The Magus and Sir Sadeghi were very careful. Lena never let on about her suspicions because she was a manipulative criminal, always trying to keep you in her loyal circle. Lena only wanted you to think of me as an ungrateful Short. When you were injured and she stayed by your side, she was grooming you. making sure you would feel obligated to her, keeping you away from me. She would have pressured you to choose her over the Magus and me." I touched his hand. "The Magus saw Lena for who she was but kept her close to keep an eye on her. He seems to have some regrets or reservations about disposing of her but she would not have a lost a minute to regret, if her plan had worked. I would be dead, the Magus disposed of and she would have used you to keep the rest of the Haute Caste in line."

"You were able to see her true nature," he said "She transformed me. You were exposed to her blood through me but it effected you differently."

"I'm of the House of Swords and so are the children."

"Yes," he smiled. "You have a right to be proud. It is an honorable House that has served our kind well, though Sir Sadeghi recently executed his aide, Momand, as he was linked to Lena."

"The Magus didn't tell me that. She got her claws into so many young vampires. How sad," I sighed.

"Lena merely helped us weed the garden. Lady Anastasia reports that the House of Pentacles is behaving themselves. The threat appears to be over but we must still be vigilant."

"I'm sorry that Lena deceived you," I said. "I know that can't feel good."

He smiled grimly. "My dear, she is dead to me. If her withered corpse ever surfaces, she will wish she stayed in the ground. The Houses know only that the Magus made her disappear and no details will ever be released. Fear can be helpful when dealing with egotistical vampires."

"I'll remember that. The weird thing, I mean if it is possible for my life to get any weirder, is that I'm starting to like the Magus. He has my back."

He smiled. "As long as I have the rest of you." The Baron walked over to me and held out his hand. "You are not a vampiress yet you are truly of the Haute Caste. The undead world has nothing but the highest regard for your Haute Caste father. That will bode well for you and the children. Lady Anastasia told me that you had unique strengths. I'm starting to understand why. All this time I thought it was exposure to my blood but I was only enhancing your hybrid DNA. Would the Lady of the House of Swords care for a massage?"

"As long as you're not expecting much more. This mighty mortal still has stitches," I replied as he pulled me into his embrace.

Near Barrow, a private jet plane landed at the Magus' airstrip as the sun was setting. A figure clothed in black with dark glasses over a ski mask descended onto the landing strip. He made his way to the Hummer. He pulled a set of keys and a map out of his pocket. Then he quickly got in the vehicle. He headed towards the craggy crevice on the Magus' property.

In L.A., a screen in the Magus' library displayed the activity. "Now I have proof," he thought. "It was a two-headed snake." He sent a text message to an old friend. It seemed another trip to Alaska was in order. He called the police department in Barrow and reported that his car had been stolen and that an unauthorized jet had landed on his property. He warned them that it was probably a well-armed drug dealer. Then Magus pulled up Bernard's bank accounts. He saw a recent deposit from London of $100,000. The pilot had divulged the location. He recognized the accounting firm that had made the payment, though the Magus had already recognized the member of the Haute Caste even with his face and head covered. The Magus would not regret disposing of the treacherous vampire but thought, *What a pity, good pilots are hard to come by.*

A few hours later the Magus slipped into Bernard's apartment. His hair was covered by a net and he wore surgical gloves. The Magus noticed a book about the history of Rolls Royce on a coffee table and picked it up. He proceeded into the bedroom and stood over his sleeping servant. "Greedy fool," he whispered and clutched the sleeping pilot's throat so that he could not yell. In the dark room, a faint light showed Bernard's bulging eyes. His legs thrashed the bed covers.

"You were disloyal. That was an act I cannot forgive," the Magus stated coldly. He hit the struggling man's head so hard with the Rolls Royce book he fell back unconscious. The Magus lowered his mouth to the pilot's throat and bit deeply. In a few minutes, his hunger was satiated. He took a razor out of Bernard's bathroom, slashing his throat, disguising the bite marks. Then he took his wallet, a watch, a phone and the laptop computer. He opened the dresser drawers of Bernard's desk and scattered items to look like a robbery.

Back in his limo, he received a reply to his message. "I'll meet you in Barrow tomorrow night. I appreciate the invitation. C.B." The Magus smiled. C.B. was not the most powerful vampire but he was one of the most dependable assassins.

"Excellent!" the Magus said aloud.

CHAPTER 43

JASPER TOOK MY parents to the airport at about 10 in the morning, which seemed like three in the morning to me. They had a great visit and took lots of pictures of the babies and me to show their friends. They saw what they wanted to see and ignored the signs that my household was bizarre, to say the least. Any explanation I gave for my husband's hours or liquid diet was accepted. Human denial can be very convenient. It helps people sleep at night.

After they left I checked on the triplets. I was aware that my children smelled of HH blood, though a little sweeter. They had adorable pink cheeks and peach fuzz on their heads. Differences in their dispositions were starting to become apparent. Desmon slept the best, Tomas was the loudest and Marie fussed the most when her diaper was wet. They still looked so tiny but Lady Lily and Dr. Kyoto were quite happy with their weight gain. I left Tillie to look after them and went back to bed. I could not read people's minds but I could feel their intentions. Tillie had nothing but love for my children. The vampires surrounding my children now were protective. Though I tried to be very quiet, Delilah grumbled and then resettled herself as I climbed into bed beside my husband. I was accustomed to his cool body temperature now. His scent was comforting to me. I fell asleep listening to his slow, even breathing.

The Magus was sleeping in his private jet as it flew back to Barrow. Normally he would not have involved the police but it would take a day for the Magus and C.B. to arrive and settle matters. Fortunately, he had made a nice contribution to the local sheriff's campaign last year to insure good relations since there was no vampire community to rely on for security. He hoped his uninvited guests would be properly entertained till they arrived.

A private jet arrived at the Barrow airport as the sun was setting. It had flown to the northern outpost from New York. The pilot, a tall, dark haired, woman in her late 20s, rented a car then drove back to the airstrip where a lone passenger debarked from their plane. From the airstrip he was taken to a hotel. The pilot made all the arrangements for the hotel suite, then carried the baggage for her employer, a short man with brown wavy hair to his shoulders, a pale complexion and dark piercing eyes.

"I'm sorry the accommodations are so rustic," she said with a soft Italian accent, closing the door to their room. It had a king bed and a couch near the door. She walked over to the window and closed the heavy drapes.

"This will do until the Magus arrives. Antoinella, my breakfast." He chose not to stay at the cabin as he did want the local police to confuse them with the trespassers.

"Of course, Sir Borgia," she said and pulled a bag of blood from a small cooler. Then she took a silver goblet and emptied the bag into it. Antoinella handed the goblet to him with both hands, taking care to not spill a drop.

"You must rest," he stated. She started to protest. "I insist. You may take the bed. I will study a map of this area." The exhausted pilot merely nodded and laid down. Sir Borgia had saved her from being beaten and raped in Rome many years ago. She would do anything to please him. She had been homeless for a few years when Sir Borgia found her. Antoinella had no fondness for the world of mortals. Sir Borgia recognized her intelligence and enjoyment of risks so he had her trained as a pilot. Sir Borgia knew Antoinella longed for the night when he would pass on the gift of immortality. After a few minutes she was fast asleep.

Luckily for Antoinella she had AB blood, not his favorite, quite easy to turn down. He was hungering for the blood of the Haute Caste traitor. He drank the last drops of O positive from the goblet. The land seemed inhospitable but the people of this place knew it could provide for them, as did the vampires. If needed, elk, moose and wolves could provide sufficient blood for his kind without having to feast on the locals and draw unwanted attention. Sir Borgia ran his jeweled hand slowly over the topographical map. He noted a few possible hiding places. *A cave would be an appropriate dwelling place for the traitors*, he thought.

A few hours later Sir Borgia received a text message from the Magus. He woke his aide and they headed for the cabin. The Magus had hired a former air force pilot who was quite jaded from combat and seemed to enjoy the mysterious high life of his new employer. He was a tall, lean man from Oklahoma named Cody. Paul, his butler, was also present when they arrived. The sandy haired pilot smiled at his female counterpart but she ignored him. Cody was sent into town to buy dinner for himself, Antoinella and Paul. He was not aware of the true nature of his employer. Sir Borgia and the Magus sat down in front of the fireplace. Their servants stood nearby.

"Sudovian was found near the crevasse by the Police. He paid no heed to their authority. They fought with him and he was shot. He is in the hospital now, under arrest and heavily guarded. I should be hearing from the sheriff soon. His pilot is in custody and appears to know nothing about the reason for the flight. They found amphetamines on the pilot, so he'll be in jail awhile," the Magus smiled.

"And the vampiress?" Sir Borgia inquired.

"That is the interesting piece of the puzzle. It seems I underestimated her. When I examined the area, the freezer was empty. An elk carcass was down in the cavern but no trace of what is left of her."

"Could she have been carried off by wolves?" Sir Borgia asked.

"She may have carried one of them off. I think she was gone before Sudovian showed up. I believe she has kept away from civilization because her grotesque remains. I left her charred and blind but she could have survived, she was not beheaded."

"A mercy and a curse, most impressive," Sir Borgia responded.

"Meanwhile, Sudovian will suffer the penalty that comes with such grievous deception, treachery and lies."

"What do you wish me to do to him? He is a member of the Haute Caste."

"No longer. He is barely a vampire in my eyes," the Magus responded.

"Excellent!" Sir Borgia exclaimed.

The Magus' phone rang. It was from the Barrow Police. The wounded prisoner had somehow knocked his guards unconscious and escaped. He politely thanked the chief for all he was doing and hung up. "The waiting is over."

"The map I studied indicated he would not have time to make it to any city before sunrise. In a town this size his presence would be noticed, so I assume he is either in a cave by the sea, an abandoned shack or he went back to the plane looking for his pilot.," Sir Borgia stated.

"He is not on his plane but I'm sure he is nearby where he can watch the airstrip," the Magus said. He opened a laptop that had been on the coffee table. "We can check the surveillance video."They watched the footage from a half hour before. There was a police car parked by the plane. The officer appeared to be taking a nap. A figure dressed in dark clothing, a knit cap and sunglasses was seen running by the far corner of the airstrip, then he disappeared.

"It should be easy to follow his scent," Sir Borgia said. Cody arrived with hamburgers and fries.

"Please stay here, have dinner and rest while we take care of some business," the Magus stated. "We will fly out as soon as we return." The staff knew better than to argue, though Antoinella did not want to be left out. The Magus and Sir Borgia left in the rented car. She grabbed her bag of food and sat alone by the fire.

"You're welcome," Cody said. He turned to Paul, who joined him at the table. "What's her problem?"

"She is very fond of her boss," he whispered.

"That short guy?" Cody asked surprised.

"That short guy could kick your ass," Antoinella yelled. After that they ate in silence.

The rental car stopped a quarter mile from the airstrip behind some scraggly bushes to avoid being seen by the police. Sir Borgia grabbed a large backpack. They walked in the direction where Sudovian had last been seen. Soon they picked up his scent. His wounds had not fully healed which made the smell of his blood easy for them to track. They came to the opening of a cave in a small, rocky hill. For a second the Magus thought he picked up a bitter scent as well but then it was gone. Sudovian's blood permeated the air. It was pitch black inside the cave. Sir Borgia pulled a flashlight out of his backpack. When he illuminated the cave, a hideous scene made them both wince.

"Lena!" the Magus exclaimed.

A charred, bent-over figure with eyes that glowed white was feeding on the slashed neck of Sudovian.

Sir Borgia hit her with enough force to send her snarling form crashing against a far wall. He leaned over Sudovian, who could barely speak. The Magus came over and in a whisper the wounded vampire uttered, "She said my blood would bring her back."

"That was probably the only unselfish thing you have ever done," the Magus responded. "You really should have chosen someone more worthy. Finish him."

Sir Borgia pulled a very sharp, long, curved blade from his backpack. "Goodbye, Sudovian. I could never stand Prussians." He slashed Sudovian's neck three times before the vampire's head was completely severed and rolled on the ground. He picked up the dripping head, holding it upside down and offered it to the Magus. The ancient vampire drank from an artery, then dropped the head like an empty soda can. The blood was potent but added little to his powers. Sir Borgia drank from what remained of Sudovian's neck. The heady sensation of Haute Caste blood was amazing. He felt stronger, more aware and a rare sensation of satisfaction filled him. He put the head in a plastic bag and dropped it in his backpack.

They turned towards the vampiress. She was struggling to get to her feet. Her hair had white streaks. Where her skin had started to heal she looked wrinkled and old. It was shocking to see a vampiress who had aged. "Magus," she asked, "Who is with you?"

"Sir Borgia, my dear. He came to pay his respects to Sudovian," the Magus replied.

"Ah, your favorite henchman," her scarred face managed a slight smile. "Forgive me for failing to destroy you."

"On the contrary," the Magus replied, "I appreciate how your subversive activities have helped me be rid of some of the disloyal members of the House of Pentacles."

"Shall I?" Sir Borgia asked, holding up his bloody knife.

"Perhaps someday"

"Why do you allow me to survive?" she asked in an astonished tone.

"You were once my oldest friend. Unlike you I have not forgotten how we helped each other so long ago when the world wanted to exterminate our kind. So I will give you a chance. This last chance. You'll find a way to exist here. I forbid contact with any of the undead. You will never cause harm to the Baroness or her children. Do you understand?"

She bowed slightly. "Yes." She wanted to insult him but she would wait until one night when she imagined she would be stronger.

"You are lucky it is not my decision," Sir Borgia said.

"Papal bastard!" she snarled. Then her tone changed. "It's true that Tristan is a father?" Lena inquired.

"He is the proud father of healthy triplets," the Magus responded.

"They are dangerous," she whispered.

"They are the future," the Magus responded, "which you will never know if you don't abide by my conditions."

"We will let you dispose of the body of the late Mr. Sudovian," Sir Borgia instructed.

"Au revoir, Lena," the Magus said and they left the cave.

"I never expected you to be so forgiving."

"I haven't yet. Years of wandering, blind, in desolate Alaska will be punishment enough. For now, I will leave her to become a creature of legends, like Bigfoot. If she ever leaves this place without my permission or contacts anyone, then she will be executed. The power she has had over men amazes me. Much can be learned from her downfall and her survival skills."

"Much can be learned from women. I have never considered women the weaker sex," Sir Borgia added. "Underestimating my sister, Lucretia, caused the undoing of many men, which is why I believe that we should finish Lena now."

"Yes, your sister was an incredible foe. I was always glad that she was fond of me. Thank you for your offer, Sir Borgia, but enough vampire blood has been spilled this night. Please jettison the Prussian's head when you are flying over the ocean. This has been a terrible night. I hope never to have to terminate a member of the Haute Caste again. Sudovian gave me no choice. Old friend, I believe I must make myself more available to the vampire world, allow them to question me about the royal triplets. Calm their fears about change. How is Antoinella doing? She seems very devoted to you."

"I find her a very promising candidate for a transformation. She is probably sulking at the moment because she was kept from witnessing the beheading."

"She seems like a lovely young woman. We have a new vampiress, Pauline. She is brilliant and enthusiastic as well. I did not bring a vampiress of the Haute Caste with me because they are all so angry at Lena for shaming their kind. Lady Kananga and Lady Lockporte would have torn her head off with their bare hands." They got in the car and drove back to the cabin. Before they entered the building the Magus put his hand on Sir Borgia's sleeve. "I will need someone to take the reins of the House of Pentacles. I would like to bestow the honor on you."

"To the Victor, go the spoils. I would be honored." He patted the backpack.

CHAPTER 44

I BEGAN MAKING plans for the baptism. My parents would not be able to come as my father had injured his shoulder and needed surgery. At first I was disappointed but I realized that their absence meant Sir Sadeghi could be present. I think my husband and the rest of our nocturnal community breathed a sigh of relief. The ceremony would be stressful enough without keeping up a façade of normalcy for my parents. Sir Jorge kindly said it was "quaint." Sir Franco protested that he did not know what to wear. My husband humored me. Mr. Beauvais, his attorney, had pull with the church and managed to arrange it for 10 p.m. on a Friday night. The warm-blooded would be represented. Lolly and Alan had convinced James to attend with them as I still wanted him to be one of the godparents. Lolly was also asked and accepted the honor. Of all the people I was close to who knew about the Baron, James was the most normal. Since dealing with the undead did not trigger a relapse, I wanted him to become one of their warm-blooded guardians. James sent me an email stating he accepted the invitation for the sake of our friendship. I read the response to my husband, who was lukewarm about the idea.

"He won't be staying long?" he asked rising from the bed.

"Just coming in for the weekend. He is rightfully scared of vampires, including you," I replied.

"Good," he said with a smile.

"I will never do anything to make you think I am not totally faithful to you, and I would not put my friends in jeopardy again. I just want the kids to have a regular Joe in their lives."

"He will be perfectly safe and I will be gracious to the loser."

"What an asshole!"

He pulled me into his arms "Yes, but I'm your asshole. He is not."

"Congratulations," I grinned. Then he pulled me down on the bed and the stitches did not seem to matter anymore.

An hour later we were getting dressed when the Magus called my husband. He hung up the phone after a very short conversation. "There will be a meeting at the Magus' home. You are included."

"When?"

"Now! Meet me downstairs quickly. I'll instruct Tillie to have Clive and Jasper help with the children. I'll drive the Spyder." He quickly left the room, still buttoning his shirt.

The baptism was a few nights away. I hoped that whatever was going on would not interfere with it. I checked on the babies quickly. To my delight, each was in the arms of a devoted caretaker. Jasper looked quite comfortable rocking Desmon. I got to the front steps just as my husband pulled up in his favorite red sports car. It was the first time I had been in it since my escape to the reservoir.

"Can I drive?" I asked innocently.

"Get in!"

He drove through the streets of L.A. like he was on a race track. He had a radar detector that helped him avoid the police. I suspected that it was not a model available in stores to the general public. I was holding on to the edge of my seat even though I was wearing a seatbelt. The Baron noticed and laughed.

"The Magus just returned from a trip which involved exposing the Haute Caste vampire who plotted with Lena. He has an important decision to announce. I promise I will get you there safely."

"It was Sudovian," I said. I touched the ruby pendant he had searched for at the beach. "He was never content."

"You're probably right but the Magus did not identify him or her."

"Sometimes I just get what is going on, I can't explain it. Can I have the ruby put in a different setting?"

"Of course, but why?"

"You know he probably had it put in this setting thinking it would one day go to Lena." A shiver went down my spine.

The cars parked at the Paradise Cove mansion were impressive. Porsches, Bentleys, Corvettes, Lamborghinis, Rolls Royce, a Lotus, a McLaren and a Tesla. So at least one member of the Haute Caste cared about the environment. We were ushered into what could only be called a small ballroom where chairs had been set up in a semi-circle to accommodate a few dozen influential vampires. I later learned the meeting had been called for two nights ago, but the Baron and I had just found out as the Magus did not want me brooding about it.

I recognized about half of the undead. Sergio and Sir Franco, the Lockportes, Lady Anastasia, Sir Steve, Pauline, Lady Kananga, Dr. Kyoto and Lady Lily were whispering about the possible reasons for the gathering. There were others I had seen at the Narcissus Club and some I did not recognize at all. They all seemed to know me. Though we were seated in the center I suddenly felt a presence behind me, I turned quickly. It was my father. He looked my age except for his dark brown unfathomable eyes.

"Good evening, Baroness," he said with a warm smile, which somehow did not fit his normally somber appearance. He wore the long robes of the desert. "May I visit the royal infants after the meeting?"

"Of course!" I responded, then a hush fell on the room as the Magus entered. He was dressed in a black silk shirt and black pants. He wore a gold symbol for eternity on a chain about his neck. Everyone stood. My husband did not take a chance and grabbed my arm and pulled me to my feet before I had a chance to think. The Magus sat and gestured for us all to be seated.

"This is an historic night for our kind. The social order based on loyalty and respect which protects our civilization was threatened from within. Sadly, some of our kind had to be disposed of. The House of Pentacles is in need of a new lord." He paused and no one said a word. "Fortunately, a distinguished member of the Haute Caste has graciously accepted this difficult undertaking to restore this house's former glory. Sir Borgia, please come forward."

It was like some bizarre awards ceremony. The Magus handed Sir Borgia a framed picture of the King of Pentacles card. There was a polite round of applause.

"Borgia, as in the Pope's family?" I whispered. The Baron merely nodded. Sir Borgia smiled at me, then took his seat.

"When does Jack the Ripper show up?"

My husband turned and glared at me, clearly quite irritated.

"I also have the honor of presenting the card of the Empress tonight. She is the only warm-blooded person to ever be allowed into our inner circle. Her unique qualities are only beginning to be revealed. I shall present the card which denotes her station as the Empress to the mother of the royal triplets, Baroness Miranda Ortega Mordecai."

He held out the framed picture card to me. The artist had captured my likeness well. I stood and accepted the present, then sat down quickly. I was a little confused and taken aback, not exactly sure what this meant. My husband was beaming with pride. There was the same polite applause. I wondered about how happy they could be with a Short in their midst.

"We are in need of a High Priestess as the Lady Lena has been removed from our community forever," the Magus paused and you could have heard a pin drop. "Lady Anastasia Romanov has agreed to take this most important position."

Lady Anastasia rose, dressed in her black finery and took the framed card of the High Priestess. "I am honored." She bowed to the Magus. Now there was much whispering along with the applause. She was the second vampiress in their history to be honored with this position.

"Now, I show you the future," he turned on a large screen and there were our babies being held up to the camera in the nursery. "May I present Tomas, Desmon and Marie."

"Thank you," my father whispered from behind. It was lucky he had said that because I was just about to yell at the Magus for not asking my permission.

Suddenly Tillie screamed, "No!"

I saw her grab Tomas from Jasper and turn her back to the camera. Jasper jumped in the direction of the nursery door. "Stop!" he screamed.

Clive had put Desmon down and now raced to help his brother. "Baron!" I heard Clive yell. Then blood spattered the camera lens. Tillie screamed again as a man with his back to the camera hit her so hard she fell to the floor unconscious.

"No! No!" I yelled. Lady Kananga held me back as my husband, the Magus, Sir Jorge, and several other vampires ran to their cars. Sir Steve and Sir Ruben stared at the screen frozen in disbelief. I pushed them aside, I had to see what was happening.

"Don't hurt my babies!" I cried. Then the man picked up Marie and as he turned to leave. I recognized Sergio.

"No! Stop him!" I screamed. I turned to Sir Ruben. "Take me home. Now!"

Sir Ruben drove us in Sir Sadeghi's Rolls Royce. Lady Kananga was there for me but knew better than to talk.

"She is just a baby. How could he take her?" I cried.

The scene at the mansion was grim. I ran up the stairs. The hall was splattered with blood leading to the nursery. "Your sons are fine," Sir Sadeghi assured me and motioned to me to go to my room. My husband had the boys nestled safely in my bed, asleep. Dr. Kyoto and Lady Lily had found Desmon and Tomas unharmed but the servants were severely wounded. Tillie had a concussion. Clive's neck had been slashed but fortunately missed his artery. Blood loss had made him pass out. Lady Anastasia was giving a syringe of her blood, with the help of Sir Borgia, to save him. Tillie was laying down in the Baron's suite. Jasper was conscious, though he had a stab wound in his arm and one in his side. Lady Lily dressed his wounds while Sir Jorge prepared a syringe of his blood to help Jasper heal.

I could not stop the tears as I gazed at my sons. "Whatever he needs, please give it to him," I urged them. "Just get my baby back!"

"I assure you," Sir Borgia said, "Baroness Marie will be returned to her home safely."

"Miranda, our daughter will not be harmed," my husband promised and put his arm about my shoulder. I turned and buried my face into his chest.

"The House of Swords will do whatever is needed," Sir Sadeghi stated. He walked over to his grandsons and touched their heads so gently it did not wake them.

"He wants Lena. I think we should take him to her," Sir Borgia said.

Lady Kananga entered with the Magus. He looked positively menacing. "No Mercy! We shall take care of this tonight." Then he turned to me. "Baroness, use your gifts, be with your daughter, help us find her," he commanded.

I pulled away from the Baron and stood with my eyes closed and my arms down at my sides. I took a deep breath and held Marie's sweet image in my thoughts. The room went silent. Nothing happened. I opened my eyes and looked at the Magus. He simply nodded his encouragement. I closed my eyes again and took another deep breath and suddenly I smelled the ocean. I glimpsed moonlight. I saw a dark figure and the glint of a knife blade, then I saw my daughter being carried to a small house. She was alive! I started trembling and felt my husband's arms keep me from hitting the floor.

"She is alive," I said trembling "He has taken her to a small beach house. I'm sorry that's all I saw. I don't know where she is."

"Simone's house, Venice Beach. Sergio requested that property," the Baron said. The Magus left, followed by his deadly crew. I could not believe Sergio could do such a terrible thing. He had become a monster for the love of Lena.

I sat on the edge of the bed and stared at my sons. Somehow, I had to protect them from the intrigue of the vampire world.

Lady Lockporte and Sir Ruben came upstairs. They had been asked to secure the property. There were no signs of any other intruder than Sergio. Though normal cameras were useless, they had equipment that could show the unique heat signature of the undead.

"Franco and Pauline went with the others. Lady Anastasia is helping Dr. Kyoto and Lady Lily," Sir Ruben reported.

"What would you like us to do?" Lady Lockporte asked with sadness in her eyes. If I did not know better I might think she had been crying.

"Please supervise the Magus' staff, be sure the nursery is cleaned up and ready for Marie's return," the Baron directed.

"Of course." She turned and left to take care of her task.

Sir Ruben came over to me and took one of my hands. "What can I do? Do you need anything? I think Tillie would be getting you a cup of something if she could."

"No. I just want my baby," I cried.

"I want to tear him apart," my husband stated flatly.

"You and me both. Most of all I want to destroy Lena." I could feel her influence in this horrible event.

"I believe the Magus will now change his mind about her life sentence," he said grimly.

In Venice Beach, a few very expensive cars parked a block from Simone's house. Several vampires quietly surrounded the small building. Barely visible in the darkness they silently entered through the windows, hardly disturbing even the air. Marie was crying, Sergio had her in a back bedroom, he was trying to give her a bottle. "Shut up! Shut up!" he shouted as she refused it. He laid her on the bed and picked up a cell phone. "I can't get her to drink. She won't quiet down. I can't stand the noise!"

Lena responded, "It doesn't matter, they will find you soon, just make the Magus promise to let me come back before you return her! He will agree to anything to get her back unharmed. He will keep his word. You have the knife?"

"Yes!" he said.

"Then you know what to do!" Before he could respond she hung up the phone.

"Shut up!" he yelled at Marie and reached for the long blade he had wounded the servants with but it was gone. He stared at the spot on the bed where he had placed it, looking confused. He never realized the rescuers were behind him. They moved so quickly that the distraught Sergio did not have a chance to respond. Lady Kananga gently scooped up the baby and handed her to the Magus. Marie stopped crying immediately.

Sir Borgia pinned Sergio to the ground on his back while holding the long knife to his neck. Then he spit in Sergio's face. "You are a disgrace to all vampires and an embarrassment to all Italians." Sergio suddenly freed one arm and pulled a small knife from his boot and stabbed Sir Borgia in the arm, he barely winced. Pauline reached down, pulled the knife from Sergio's hand, then drove the blade deep into his side. The Magus motioned to Sir Borgia to let him go. Sergio lay on the floor writhing. Pauline picked up the phone and handed it to him.

The Magus ordered, "Tell her I agreed and that you will see her soon."

"No, I can't betray her! She will never believe me." The lower caste vampire stared back at him. The Magus raised his free hand and held it above Sergio's chest. The scar from his transformation began to bleed. He writhed in pain. Sergio cried out, "Stop, please stop! No more, I'll do it, I'll do it. The Magus lowered his hand and the pain appeared to subside. After a few seconds Sergio took a deep breath, raised the phone, then pushed the call back button. He delivered the message as the Magus had commanded. Lena cackled so loudly with delight that everyone in the room could hear. Pauline grabbed the phone, hung up and handed the phone back to the Magus, who put it in his pocket. It would be easy to track her. He looked down at Marie who was resting in the crook of his arm and seemed quite content now.

Sir Sadeghi politely asked, "May I have the honor?" The Magus nodded. Sir Jorge pulled Sergio to his feet by his hair. The vampire moaned and held his hands over his bloody chest. Sir Sadeghi removed his sword from beneath his cloak.

"I'm sorry your pain will be over so quickly!"

Sergio looked shocked as he suddenly realized his immortality would be short-lived. "You can't! I did not hurt her! I did as you asked. I'm one of you!"

"You were always a mistake," the Magus stated in a disgusted tone and nodded to Sir Sadeghi.

With a silent swing of Sir Sadeghi's sword Sergio's head lay on the floor. "Don't let his blood go to waste," the Magus said in a matter of fact tone.

"Sweet!" Pauline responded with a smile and began to drink from his neck. Sir Borgia said, "I like her enthusiasm."

One by one, they all drank of his blood except the Magus, who held Marie. He looked into her innocent soul and felt somewhat shaken. He reluctantly gave the baby to her grandfather. "I almost hate to have her out of my sight. Please take the little Baroness home."

Sir Sadeghi gently took Marie from the Magus. "It's interesting that the babies cause us such great concern. It has been centuries since my heart raced like this, since I felt strong emotions."

The Magus touched Marie's tiny hand. "Quite true. I shall not return directly to Stone Canyon. I must make arrangements for the disposition of Lena before I meet with all of you."

The vampires quietly took care of Sergio's remains. The Magus called the Baron as he left the beach house. "All is well. Sir Sadeghi will return Marie to you immediately. She is unharmed and perfectly fine."

All the Baron could say was, "We are most thankful."

CHAPTER 45

AS I BREASTFED Marie tears were rolling down my cheeks. I was sitting on my bed, her brothers sound asleep beside us. Lady Lily had examined her completely and assured me that she was unharmed and in perfect health. When she was abducted, I kept thinking it was because I had done something wrong, that because I loved a vampire our children would be cursed. Now sanity had returned. I knew it was really because Lena was a sociopathic bitch. My husband was downstairs in the library with the most trusted of the Haute Caste, waiting to hear the Magus' plan. I wanted him to banish her to the lowest abyss of hell. I still held a tiny amount of pity for Sergio. Love had driven him to do a horrible thing and he paid dearly for his blind, stupid, devotion. Love for my children was driving me to make a difficult decision. I dried my tears and looked at Marie's sweet, innocent, content face. I would do everything in my power to protect my children.

The Magus' maid, Ania, and her younger, plumper sister, Zofia, were looking after Tillie, Clive and Jasper in their rooms downstairs. Clive was much improved though his neck wound have a residual scar. Jasper was already up and about though he walked slowly due to the pain in his side. Tillie wanted to be taking care of the babies, but Lady Lily was adamant that she had to rest to allow her brain a chance to heal from the concussion. I knew they would have given their lives for my children. They all were recovering quickly due to the Haute Caste blood they had been given.

In the library, all who were present at the rescue and those who had helped with the wounded sat quietly discussing the death of Sergio. From his Paradise Cove mansion, the Magus called the Barrow Police and notified them he would be in town for a couple of days and provide for his own security, so there was no need for them to check on him. He also made certain his jet was ready. Then he sat quietly deciding who would help with the task of destroying the second oldest vampire in existence. He thought it was important for some of the Haute Caste to witness his ability to cause the bleeding from the transformation scar when he questioned Sergio. With the assassination of Lena his invincibility might be imagined. When the details of Sergio's death became known it would help to maintain his position of authority. He would utilize his powers as needed to protect his vampire domain. None knew the extent of all his powers, not even Lena. He knew more about his kind than anyone, which assured his undisputed position of power. He had made a rare mistake by underestimating Lena. That would not happen again.

When he arrived at Stone Canyon an hour later he was dressed entirely in a black suit as though attending a funeral. His cold anger could be felt as he entered the library. All present rose but he gestured for them to sit.

"I am most pleased and grateful to have witnessed your response to this crisis. One day Baroness Marie will be grateful as well," he smiled grimly. "The task at hand is to destroy Lena. Let it be known she spit on the mercy that was shown her. There can be no chance for her to corrupt any more of our kind. Sir Borgia, I would like to use your pilot, Antoinella. I shall require several of my trusted and accomplished assassins. Lady Anastasia, Sir Borgia, Sir Sadeghi and Sir Steve. Her powers have diminished but she is apparently still quite clever. We will talk about the plan on the flight. Dear Baron, I request that you and the other members of the vampire nobility look after the safety of your household until we are assured the threat has been finally and totally removed."

The vampires who would stay behind were disappointed. They had greatly resented Lady Hauser and all wanted to be part of her unprecedented and historic demise.

"Baron," the Magus added, "please assure your wife that we will be back in time for the baptism."

"Of course," the Baron said. "Please tell Lena that I despise her and wish that her end would have been by my hand."

"With pleasure," Sir Borgia responded.

Pauline was irritated that she would not be able to participate in the execution. "What is so special about the assassins the Magus chose?" she asked Sir Ruben.

He grinned. "Have you ever heard Lady Anastasia enter a room?"

Pauline thought for a moment and replied, "Good point".

"We can do things quietly. They do them silently. Sir Sadeghi kills so perfectly the only sound is his blade cutting through air, then the thump when the head hits the floor."

"Maybe he could teach me his technique."

"Get in line," Sir Ruben responded with a nod. "It's good Steve will be there to represent our House; his knife work is superb."

Sir Sadeghi visited the children before he left. It was beautiful to see his stern face melt into delight around his grandchildren. I excused Ania so we could talk openly.

"Hi Dad," I said for the first time, smiling.

"That's Sir Dad," he laughed. "I've wanted to have this conversation for many years. The Magus advised me to wait, he knew it would not be safe. I have watched you from afar for so long." He picked up Desmon. One of his grandson's tiny hands hit his chin, making him smile. "He will be strong."

"It's just hard to believe you were with my mom."

He gently put Desmon down, then picked up Tomas. "She was under the influence and upset with your father. As you have found we have...an effect on the warm-blooded. That's all you need to know. I have immense respect for her. She is a good woman and obviously a good mother and will be a wonderful grandmother."

"Okay, Dad," I smiled. "You are right about her and I don't want to know any more."

He kissed Tomas' head, then laid him down beside his brother. "Look at his wise expression, those dark eyes." Then he turned to his granddaughter. "So little Baroness," he held Marie tenderly. "That old vampiress seems to fear you the most. What does she know, or guess, about you?"

"You don't think Sergio just took her because she was the closest to him?" I asked.

"It wasn't chance. He did as Lena commanded. She had a reason. She has Sudovian's cell phone, that's what she used to contact Sergio. Their phone messages showed that she had planned the attack to occur during the Magus' meeting. He was told to take my little Marie." Sir Sadeghi handed her to me.

"Some women have no clue about sisterhood, having female friends, they just see them as competition, it's pretty sad."

"Lady Anastasia said something similar to me, in London," he smiled. "I'm very proud to be your father even if it must remain a secret for now." He gently placed his hand on my cheek. "I will take personal delight in eliminating this threat to my family. I look forward to the day when I can proudly reveal your bloodline. Then the vampire world will know that there was already someone conceived by a vampire years earlier, and it only enriched our world." Sir Sadeghi bowed slightly and turned to leave.

"Thank you. Sometimes I feel that the kids and I don't fit in anywhere. In some ways, I feel alienated from everyone."

"You are Haute Caste from the House of Swords, even if your appetite is a bit odd," he smiled. Then he kissed my forehead and left. I had the feeling that his outpouring of affection for the children and me was a rare event in his long existence, which he enjoyed very much. Normal is strange and strange is normal down this rabbit hole. I thought of hanging a sword on the wall in the kids' room but my parents would not understand.

"Only a baby and already at the center of a storm," I muttered. She looked at me with questioning eyes and I could see a resemblance to her grandmother. Marie fell asleep nursing. I laid her down next to her siblings. They were all so beautiful but the responsibility of raising them was terrifying. They were three-quarters vampire, yet my normal genes seemed to be enough to keep them warm-blooded. The pediatrician from UCLA said that besides their rare blood type, they were fine, thriving in fact. He had even asked about my diet during the pregnancy. I just told him I ate a lot of barbacoa tacos. Lady Lily and Dr. Kyoto took over their medical care to avoid any more questions.

The Baron entered with Ania, she would watch over our babies while I had some dinner and time with my husband. There was only an hour before sunrise. The nursery had been cleaned and the cradles had been moved back to their room. Paul was still getting some stains out of the hallway carpet. He smiled politely. I wondered if after seeing what happened to our servants he did not question if the job was worth it. In the kitchen, Zofia was pulling vegetable lasagna out of the oven. It smelled great. She had made a tossed salad and cut up a baguette, which she served with seasoned butter. I was starving. I drank a tall glass of iced tea. I could never seem to get enough food and fluid in me these days. My husband watched me with a pensive smile. He had barely touched his goblet of O positive.

"Are you okay?" I asked.

"I will be when I hear that Lena is no more," he replied. "This was hard for the Magus. He gave her a chance though she did not deserve it and she betrayed him again. He regrets showing her any mercy. We have monitored Johann and there has been no contact. If there had been he would have been disposed of immediately. Sir Jorge and Sir Ruben are flying to London to make sure the House of Pentacles is loyal. Even a hint of disrespect for the Magus and they will pay dearly, though I think that the greedy and overly ambitious undead have been found out." He took a drink. A slight red stain appeared on his lips.

"I know you wanted to go after Sergio tonight. Thank you for staying with me and the boys."

"It is a new and at times painful sensation to care for others more than for yourself," he said. "Being with you is more important than personal revenge but yes, I wanted to cut his head off slowly." He finished his drink.

"Did you love Lena?"

He looked into his goblet. "She saved me from growing up as an orphan, an outcast. I was dependent on her and grateful for what she had done for me. Now, like the Magus, I must face the reality of her character and actions. I've gone from sadness to rage and back," he replied.

"It's called grief," I said. He gave me a puzzled look.

The Lockportes arrived with Delilah. "We let her have the run of the grounds, she did not find anything but a sorry squirrel. We can cut back on her steak tonight," Sir Ruben announced. The big cat rubbed against my chair. I patted her large, perfectly shaped, sleek head. She had been out in her pen when Sergio came earlier. I felt safer with her loose in the house.

"I have to know, why Barrow? Why on earth would the Magus have a house there?" Lady Lockporte asked.

The Baron smiled. "If you needed to get away from other vampires, just for a little while, would it not be the last place they might look for you?"

"Second only to the South Pole," Sir Ruben quipped.

"Where would you like us to stay?"

"Next door will be fine. Sleep well today. We will have the Magus' staff and I dare say that Jasper and Tillie will watch over the household as well. Thank you for your efforts on behalf of our children," the Baron said.

"Thank you," Sir Ruben replied. "It's never this exciting in Toronto."

Lady Lockporte just shook her head, "We'll see you tonight. Rest well."

Lady Hauser had found some strange allies in the desolate, rocky caves near Barrow. After being revitalized by the elk that had fallen into her craggy cell, she decided to hunt them. Relying on her senses of smell and hearing, she had managed to kill another old elk that she found staggering behind a herd and shared it with a pack of wolves. She bled a little on the carcass before she shared it with them. She wanted their acceptance and she hoped to enhance their strength. She noticed their scent changed a little. Lena bled a little more on the carcass. She heard them growl as they fought over it. Lena sat very still as she was in no condition to fend off wolves. Somehow, they seemed to accept her. She kept her breathing steady. It became very quiet. Suddenly a wolf lay down beside her. She breathed a sigh of relief.

CHAPTER 46

AFTER THE MAGUS had discussed his plan to trap and eliminate Lena, the assassins settled in for a long flight. The window blinds were pulled down and pillows and blankets had been provided to help them sleep. Sergio's head was on ice in a large insulated container. Antoinella felt privileged to be the pilot. She was in charge of flying the Magus. He had not spoken to her directly but she knew he had asked for her. Hopefully this would help her chance of becoming one of them.

Sir Borgia had difficulty falling asleep. He was trying to get inside Lena's mind, a dark place indeed. He knew her treachery had no limits, which he grudgingly admired. Any other being in her condition would be an easy kill, but not this ancient vampiress. He imagined that she planned to kill Sergio and use his blood to fuel her recovery. He wished that he had been able to finish her during the last visit. With every night, he knew she was becoming stronger. Despite his abilities, he was relieved to not be taking her on alone. Eventually he was able to slip into the arms of Morpheus.

The jet landed a few hours before sunset. The assassins stayed on board and slept until it was dark. Then they took the Humvee to the cabin. They all changed into their dark, puncture proof clothing, similar to what Miranda had worn that night at the beach. They sprayed their suits with a special compound to mask the scent of their blood type. They wore soft, pull-on booties with tiny spikes. They were quiet but still had traction. They put on collars with very large, sharp spikes for additional protection, which gave them a goth touch. Sir Sadeghi had a special matte black sheath to house his sword. The hilts of a dozen very sharp knives could be seen sticking out of Sir Steve's vest. Lady Anastasia was fond of guns; she carried two pistols and an assault rifle was slung across her back. The Magus never used weapons, he preferred hand-to-hand combat and was proficient in several forms of the martial arts. All this against an injured, blind opponent, but then again it was Lady Hauser and no chances were to be taken.

"Rest for the flight home," Sir Borgia said to Antoinella. He knew she wanted to accompany them. The pilot grudgingly laid down on the couch in front of the fireplace.

It was a clear night. The moonlight was helpful as they walked over the rough terrain. Sir Sadeghi carried the airtight container with Sergio's head in it. The Magus, imitating Sergio's voice quite well, left a voice message to meet at the crevasse, then turned off the phone. They removed the head from the container and placed it on a rock next to the deep abyss so the scent would be obvious, they then moved back 100 feet behind some large boulders. A short time later there was the sound of shuffling feet as Lena made her way towards the head.

Lady Anastasia, Sir Sadeghi and Sir Steve were shocked by the wretched condition of the once great vampiress.

"Sergio," she called out. She stopped short. Immediately she knew he was dead, then she sensed the presence of the Magus. "You killed him? Bastard!" she turned as though trying to pick up the smell of his blood.

"He's not alone," Lady Anastasia called out to her.

"You brought Anastasia to destroy me? She is nothing!" Lena yelled. "Cowards, you can't hide your stench from me. Borgia, Sadeghi and that doorman! That's the best you could do? I have assassins as well!" Suddenly a pack of at least a dozen large wolves crept up behind the vampires. They snarled, showing sharp, yellowed fangs. Sir Steve sent knives flying, taking out two of them. Lady Anastasia opened fire with the assault rifle, killing three more and injuring a few others. The largest wolf leaped on Sir Borgia, pinning him to the ground. It lunged for his neck but got a mouth full of spikes. The vampire pushed a dagger deep into its throat.

Four wolves leapt to attack the Magus. He moved so quickly that they landed on the bare ground a foot away from him. Then he jumped on the largest and with a single move broke his neck. The others started snarling and backing up. He threw the dead wolf's body out into the dark tundra. The wolves ran away. Apparently, the Magus was a weapon with which they didn't want to contend.

Sir Sadeghi saw Lena trying to flee. He grabbed her and knocked her to the ground. "Why did you go after Marie?" She pulled herself up into a sitting position. She held herself up straight and for a moment it was easy to imagine her in pearls looking regal again. She did not have the strength to pull off that illusion for long.

"I despise those children!" Her voice was harsh and cruel. "You have no idea what has been unleashed! You think you are powerful now, just wait until they mature!" The rest of the assassins gathered around her now. "But that Marie, she will be cunning. The female must be more cunning to survive, you will see. I almost had the power! Magus, you chose mortal trash over me. You fathered Miranda! You created that ungrateful, ignorant monster." She sniffed the air as if trying to find the Magus. "You should all be attacking him!"

The others looked at the Magus in surprise, even Sir Sadeghi managed to look puzzled. "No. I am not Miranda's father. You have been so wrong about so many things." He slowly shook his head. "It is difficult to understand now why I ever transformed you. A mistake I will now rectify."

"My wolves will find you, no matter where you try to hide," she spat at the Magus, putting her hands up to cover her neck. She looked afraid, truly afraid, which was shocking for the vampires to witness. The Magus nodded to Sir Sadeghi. Sir Borgia pulled her up by her white hair. She was a pathetic, scarred, aged vampiress with white eyes that glowed in the moonlight.

"I'm Haute Caste!" she shrieked. "The High Priestess!"

"You are nothing! You will shame our kind no more," Lady Anastasia replied with a sneer.

There was a whoosh and her body fell to the ground. Her head fell a short distance away. Sir Steve placed a plastic container under the head to catch the dripping blood.

The Magus sent a text message to the Baron. "It's over."

Silently they followed the plan that had been explained on the jet. The only difference was that the Magus had them keep watch for the wolves that had escaped. He could sense them somewhere out in the darkness, watching their every move. Sir Steve helped Sir Borgia cut up the withered body of Lena and place it in a body bag. Lady Anastasia poured lighter fluid on Sergio and Lena's heads. Sir Sadeghi built a small funeral pyre. Sir Steve rolled their heads into the flames. As the fire crackled a wolf howled in the distance. The Magus leaned over the remains of one of the wolves. He recognized Lena's scent in the blood of the wolf. He had never considered that Lena would expose wolves to blood from the Haute Caste. They seemed to have bonded with her. It would be wise for them to fly out tonight. Frankly, the Magus had no desire to ever return to Barrow. Tomorrow, he would tell his realtor to put the cabin up for sale. He walked over to the fire and stomped the skulls so hard they shattered and sparks flew. "Bury them."

"Gladly!" Sir Borgia nodded to the Magus and with Sir Steve dug a deep hole. The bone fragments were thrown in, then covered with soil and rocks. They put out the fire and headed back to the cabin. Sir Sadeghi and Lady Anastasia carried the bag full of pieces of Lena and headed to a small cliff over the ocean. Piece by piece, the last of the vampiress was thrown far out into the water. They wiped their hands on the moss covering the damp earth. Lady Anastasia took a deep breath of the ocean air. Sir Sadeghi took her arm and walked back with her. They had admired each other for many years but this was their first physical contact.

When everyone had returned to the cabin, they gathered around the table. Antoinella was included in the bizarre honor. The Magus dipped a small glass into the container of blood and put a few tablespoons into six silver goblets. "May we never taste Haute Caste blood again," the Magus said with a sad expression, then emptied his goblet. Her blood left a bitter taste in his mouth but he immediately felt an adrenaline rush. Lady Hauser's blood had 10 times the impact of Sudovian's. The others followed his example. Yet with the surge of vitality that rushed through their veins, they were aware they had witnessed their own mortality. They had known the Common Caste could be slain by them but had not wanted to think the guillotine method of execution could also apply to the Haute Caste. Loyalty to the Magus had kept them safe. Now they would be even more devoted to him.

Antoinella steadied herself with the table. "Wow," she uttered. Her heart was racing, and she felt nausea building. She made her way to the kitchen and started to vomit. She saw Sir Borgia holding her hair out of the corner of her eye. Then everything came up into the sink. "Sorry," the embarrassed young woman uttered, wiping her mouth with a towel.

"O positive will go down easier, just wait till you are transformed," Sir Borgia responded.

"You mean it?" she asked, tears falling down her cheeks.

"You have earned it." He walked away to avoid the embarrassment of witnessing anymore tears.

The assassins reported tasting the same bitterness and feeling especially invigorated by Lena's blood. Despite the rumors that would be generated, Lady

Anastasia and Sir Sadeghi went off to one of the cabin's bedrooms for 20 minutes while the others prepared to leave. The Magus carefully saved the remaining blood in a glass jar, which he placed in the cooler which had transported Sergio's head. No one dared ask what he was going to do with the blood.

When the Baron got the Magus' message, he was helping me with the babies. They had been moved back to their room. He held up the phone so I could see the message as I was feeding Tomas. I felt an incredible sense of relief. She would never be near my children again. "Ding dong, the vampiress is dead," I sang to my son as tears of relief started to flow.

My husband smiled. "Lovely! But please don't teach that to them." He wiped my tears then his expression became somber. "Two of the Haute Caste have been executed. The details will not get out but rumors will be rampant. Now our immortality will be questioned by the vampire world though our powers will still be respected. I fear our position has been jeopardized."

"Associating with me should have already done that," I smiled.

"Your social stock has actually increased. You are the envy of many a vampiress, and they think you must be an artful seductress to have captivated my affection."

A familiar odor was in the air. I laid Tomas on the changing table. As I wiped his darling little butt, I said, "If they only knew."

CHAPTER 47

BY THE NIGHT of the baptism, everyone had returned to L.A.. Sir Sadeghi and Lady Anastasia were staying with the Magus, quite an honor for any member of the Haute Caste. I was considering the possibility that I might have a Russian czarina for a stepmother. The Lockportes, Pauline, Sir Borgia and Antoinella were staying at the neighboring villa and keeping an eye on our security. Sir Jorge and Sir Franco were our guests.

Last night they had spent most of the evening holding the babies. Sir Franco had brought back several outfits for each of them from London. He seemed disappointed that they would wear the gowns Anastasia had bought for their baptism. Sir Diego rolled his eyes. "Franco spent more on the triplets than he did on himself. It was amazing." It was more amazing to see vampires rocking my children to sleep. Did I mention that Sir Diego bought his own antique rocking chair? It seems they found the triplets more amusing than the Narcissus Club. When Desmon spit up on Sir Franco's shoulder, I almost died laughing. He practically threw my son to Tillie as he ran to change his shirt.

My husband had arranged for a portrait artist to be at the church. He would make drawings that would be used to capture the historic event in paintings. I just wanted family pictures. Lolly assured me that she would take photos of the babies and me. She had helped me pick out a light blue dress with an ivory lace bodice and ivory heels. The Baron wore a dark gray suit with a white silk shirt, open at the neck. He looked very handsome. He fastened the ruby pendant about my neck. The new white gold setting had the large glistening gem framed by Ceylon blue sapphires. They reminded me of the color of his eyes.

We arrived at the church a little before 10 o'clock. The priest was trying to be pleasant but was noticeably flustered. He had a slight Italian accent. Father Rinaldi was 50, plump and had a shiny, bald head. The warm-blooded guests arrived first. James appeared well and a bit nervous. His warm smile lit up the room. He looked less stressed than our last meeting. His healthy tan made him stand out from the vampires. I was surprised to see him in a suit. "Thanks for coming. Let me guess, Lolly bought the suit."

He nodded. "She can be very adamant when it comes to fashion."

"Tell me about it, she picked out my whole outfit." I gave him a quick hug. He looked around nervously. I whispered, "It's fine, you're protected."

"Alan assured me of that. All the same, tell the Baron I'm dating." He smiled at the babies. "They look very healthy." I could tell he wondered how normal they could be. He even shook the Baron's hand to congratulate him.

My husband was a bit uncomfortable with the physical contact but tried to be polite. "Welcome, my wife insisted you be the triplets' godfather."

"I'm honored," James responded, which seemed to put my husband more at ease. Lolly and Alan went on and on about how beautiful and obviously bright the triplets were.

"Of course, they are quite exceptional," the Baron remarked.

The Magus arrived in an ivory linen suit and matching Italian loafers. Soon the church was full of vampires in their finest black goth fashions, except for my father. He was in white robes with golden trim and a traditional head covering. Lady Anastasia wore black lace and gray Tahitian pearls. She looked content on his arm. They made a striking couple. The guests stood in a circle around the babies, who were side by side in their carriers on the table, calmly looking at all the people.

"Someday they might play futbol, I mean soccer, for Argentina," Sir Diego said.

"Hockey for Toronto," Lady Lockporte responded.

"They will be Olympic equestrians," Sir Sadeghi insisted.

"It will be their decisions and I think they will surprise as all by what they accomplish," the Magus said.

The priest came over and per the Magus' wishes proceeded to do the ceremony in Latin. One by one, the babies were anointed and blessed. Despite the strangers and the strange place, they quietly looked around. I think it helped that I fed them prior to the event. When it was all over, I spoke to the priest.

"I know this has been a little unusual, thanks for being flexible."

"Mrs. Mordecai, an old friend of mine, Grigoryi, talked to me before returning to Italy. He told me you helped him a great deal and that he thought someday you might seek the church for comfort. When I heard about the ceremony I requested to officiate. We are all God's children. You and your husband's generous donation will help us with our youth program," Father Rinaldi added.

The surprised look on my face caught my husband's attention. He came over to my side. "Is everything okay?"

"Yes. Father Rinaldi was just telling me about his work with youth groups and how our donation will help his efforts."

"Excellent, but now we must be going." Apparently my husband did not like hanging out in the church. As we walked away he said, "His kind has hunted us for centuries, not to mention torturing and killing your ancestor. I only agreed to this because it mattered to you and your parents."

"Father Rinaldi does not strike me as a burn-people-at-the-stake kind of priest," I replied. "Don't you think the babies handled their first big social event well? I'd like some pictures before we go and one with the priest," I said, not wanting to get in a big discussion of the church's dark side. I was glad that at least Father Rinaldi seemed enlightened. I was starting to keep a list of warm-blooded allies who might be helpful in the future.

Lolly took some sweet photos of the babies and me. I took pictures of Alan, Lolly and James each holding a baby. James picked Marie, which surprised me because I thought Lolly would hold her. Lolly picked Tomas. Alan seemed to be fascinated with the middle child. In some strange way, each of these people seemed to connect with their chosen child, or maybe vice versa. It was interesting to see their brief but important interaction. It was as though the babies were already finding allies as well. Before we left, I asked that Alan be included as a godfather.

The artist's sketches beautifully captured my husband with the children. None of the others desired to be in the paintings. I could not blame them for wanting anonymity. As we walked out, I thanked Lady Lockporte and Sir Ruben for coming and added, "I hoped it was not too uncomfortable for you."

"Not at all. It's just an old building," Lady Lockporte said.

"I'm glad we came, even if we are Jews," Sir Ruben added with a smile. "Though Lady Anastasia was saying she would have preferred a Russian Orthodox church."

"I'll keep that in mind, though I don't think there will be a next time," I said. "By the way, did Jews ever hunt vampires?"

"Are you kidding?" Sir Ruben said. "We were too busy trying to avoid people who were hunting us."

"Good point. I never thought about it that way."

When it came time to put the babies into their car seats, Jasper had more help than he needed. There was a procession back to Stone Canyon. The royal triplets were in the Bentley with me. Sir Ruben rode up front with Jasper. The Magus and my husband rode in the Spyder. Sir Sadeghi, Lady Anastasia, Sir Borgia and Lady Lockporte were in the House of Sword's white Rolls Royce. In the rear, Sir Diego, Sir Franco, Pauline and Antoinella followed behind in a Tesla. Sir Diego was quite concerned about the decline of the rain forest and insisted on an electric car. It was ironic that he could take human life without a second thought but the loss of a toucan, well, that was another matter. Still, I admired his desire to protect the environment. I thought that he and Sir Franco would be good influences on our children.

On the ride home I watched our babies fall asleep and considered how important those present today might be to their futures. It dawned on me that since they had no children of their own, the triplets were probably their only chance to experience parenting, something quite novel in their long existences. The discussion of which sports they thought the triplets might pursue was telling. They felt a connection to our children. I was glad they held affection for them but I was wary of how strong the vampire influence might be. Their father's influence alone would be difficult to try to balance out. I had a lot to think about as I stared at my babies on the long drive back to Stone Canyon.

CHAPTER 48

BACK AT THE ranch, plans for a hockey game to celebrate the baptism were underway. The Lockportes were in charge. Pauline now had her own uniform and locker. Antoinella wanted to play but was told it would have to wait until after her transformation, which was planned for tomorrow night. There appeared to be a little rivalry between the two young women. I was fascinated by the number of women who chose to be vampires. It some ways it gave them freedom, but the taking of life seemed so foreign to me, especially after giving birth. Also, they were still part of a culture dominated by males. The Magus was unquestionably in charge and my husband was second in the hierarchy, president and vice president of the nocturnal asylum that had become my world.

The Magus asked to meet with my husband and me in the nursery. The fact that he asked seemed odd but I chalked it up to politeness. When we got upstairs, Tillie and Ania were putting the triplets in their beds. Dr. Kyoto and Lady Lily were waiting for us.

"There you are, I was wondering why you did not come to the Baptism. Was it the church?" I asked them. The Magus excused Tillie and Ania and told them to close the door.

Dr. Kyoto replied, "We were very busy preparing something to keep you and the children safe."

"What do you mean? Safe from what? Lena has been destroyed, right?"

I looked at my husband who also seemed to be at a loss.

"I did not tell either of you until now because I had to confer with Dr. Kyoto and Lady Lily. Also, dear Baron, I was concerned that if I said anything to you the Baroness would sense a problem. So, I waited until we had a solution."

"What are you talking about? Is something wrong with my babies?" I began to tear up and walked over to their cribs.

"No, no, they are fine. Very healthy," Dr. Kyoto assured us. "This is purely preventive."

"Please explain," my husband said to the Magus.

"When we executed Lena, I realized that she had shared her blood with a pack of wolves. In a very short time, they had started to change, to accept and show loyalty to her, and they become stronger and very aggressive towards us. Before she died, she said they would be a threat in the future."

"A threat to who?" I asked. My breathing was becoming more rapid.

"You, the triplets and Haute Caste vampires," Lady Lily said looking down.

"We killed most of the wolves that attacked us but not all. We don't know how many but some escaped," the Magus continued. "I considered what the chances were that the wolves in Barrow could ever cause problems for us here. Then I thought about the coyotes in Los Angeles. The enhanced wolves could travel long distances to track their prey. They could survive anywhere a coyote could live. So I brought back a small amount of Lena's blood to have Dr. Kyoto and Lady Lily make a serum of sorts, if you will, an anti-wolf serum."

"We believe that with the scent of her blood from the serum, they will not attack you or the children," Lady Lilly added. "The Baron already has had enough of her blood to be protected but not you and the children."

"You want to inoculate the babies and me with the blood of that bitch from hell?"

"Just as a precaution," Dr. Kyoto explained. "We have very carefully calculated the dose each of you need."

"Dr. Kyoto and I have been inoculated and we are fine," Lady Lily tried to assure me.

"Yeah, but we aren't undead. We don't have a choice, do we?"

"You and the children are already touched by our blood," the Magus answered.

"You mean contaminated," I said and regretted it immediately. "I'm sorry, I didn't mean it like it sounded." The Magus waved it off apparently not offended.

My husband came over to my side. "I do not like this anymore than you do but Lena would not have made an idle threat. You and the children must be protected."

"Think of it like a measles vaccination," Dr. Kyoto said. He opened a small black bag and took out four small syringes.

"The measles don't have fangs. Are you certain this will be safe? I want to be vaccinated first and if I'm okay, then you can do it to the triplets."

The Magus nodded. Lady Lily cleaned the injection site on my upper arm. I clinched my teeth and Dr. Kyoto very quickly injected me. It only stung a little. Tears began to stream down my face. "I hate Lena, I still hate Lena. I will always hate her."

"You are not alone," the Magus said. He did something I did not expect. He held my hand to help steady me as the babies were injected. They each started crying. I picked up Tomas, my husband comforted Marie and the Magus cuddled his namesake. It was the first time I had seen the Magus hold one of the children. As soon as the babies stopped crying so did I. I felt a little warm, sort of feverish, but that was all. It passed quickly.

"What about the other vampires?" I asked.

"The Haute Caste have all been taken care of. Vials of the serum are being flown to every major city in North America to assure the protection of our kind, with the first going to the Canadian provinces," Lady Lily said.

"But if you need to protect me, then you must protect Alan, James and Lolly," I demanded.

"Alan is taking care of that tonight, he will attend to James before he boards his plane," Dr. Kyoto said. "We are taking every precaution possible to safeguard our kind and our enlightened companions. The servants have also been vaccinated," the Magus responded. "Also Delilah. We have made arrangements to vaccinate your parents as well but without their knowing what it is, of course. They will think it is for the flu."

"Let me take your vital signs while Dr. Kyoto checks the triplets." Lady Lily then asked, "How do you feel?"

"Fine I guess. I felt a little feverish for a few minutes and now oddly sort of energized."

"Your blood pressure, pulse and temperature are all within normal limits. You adjusted quite quickly."

"And the children?" the Baron asked.

"Fine, just a slightly elevated temperature. We will monitor them the rest of the night and Tillie will be mindful during the day," Dr. Kyoto said.

"If they seem to be having a reaction, you'll come get me right away?"

"Of course, we'll notify you and the Baron," Lady Lily responded.

"Splendid, let's watch a hockey match." The Magus patted the Baron on the back. I think he was relieved I had not created more of a scene.

I kissed each of the triplets on their sweet little heads and went to my room to change. It seems I adjusted quickly because I was a half-breed. I decided that being only a quarter warm-blooded must have made it even easier on the babies. I knew that the potential to be Haute Caste vampires was in them but without the transformation they would just be gifted Shorts, very gifted to be sure. That was fine by me.

Lena was still fucking up my life. Vampire-wolves! It was fortuitous that James had come to the Baptism. I would hate to have sent vampires out to visit him in Montana and try to give him an injection. He trusted Alan and Lolly perhaps more than he trusted me. I hated what my friends and family were still having to endure because of contact with me. I was lucky they were so understanding. I could not blame James for wanting to fly home right away. I stopped myself from imagining James driving up to a cabin in a Jeep with fishing poles in the back. That was not going to be my life.

Ania and Tillie were in the nursery as I walked by. Tillie gestured to me. "Marie is a bit fussy tonight. Would you like to feed her? That seems to calm her down. The boys took a bottle and went right to sleep."

"Of course," I replied and sat down in the plush chair where I was most comfortable. I held her closely. She began feeding as though very hungry. My sweet little daughter gave me a chance to focus on my primary goal, keeping my children safe. She stopped nursing for a second to look up at my face. She was so sweet and trusting. "Marie, you will be fine," I whispered to her and she returned to her dinner. She seemed to accept my assurances.

I had gone from angry to anxious to resigned and, finally, to determined. I had been seriously considering leaving since Johann attacked me. A possible plan had taken shape with the help of my parents. The thought of vampire-wolves hiding in Stone Canyon waiting to pounce was all I needed to make my decision to leave soon. The trick would be to get the cooperation of my husband by convincing him it would be in the best interest of the children, not to mention enlisting the Magus. I felt Marie grow relaxed and finally fall asleep. I held her for a few minutes and wondered about how she and her brothers would handle their crazy family. I had to give them every opportunity to develop normally away from discussions of Worthy Targets and royal titles.

I gently put Marie in the crib. Her tiny hand was clutching my UCLA T-shirt. She was strong. Tillie helped me carefully open her fist a little. "One day you won't need me," I whispered, "but until that day comes I will be close by." I checked on my boys, then went downstairs.

CHAPTER 49

THE HOCKEY GAME was memorable. The Lockportes played against the
Baron and Pauline. Sir Borgia was the goalie and came up with some extra rules.
It was decided that the goalie would get a point every time he stopped a goal.
The teams would get two points for each goal scored. The Magus sat beside me
keeping score because no one would dare question his numbers. Sir Diego and
Sir Franco cheered for the Lockportes. I, of course, rooted for my husband.
Antoinella stood near the goalie net, a dangerous location. She would do any-
thing for Sir Borgia. She sort of reminded me of Sergio.

Sir Sadeghi and Lady Anastasia asked to speak with me out in the hallway.
They were still in their formal attire. I was wearing jeans and an old T-shirt,
hard to believe we were related.

"You may speak freely," my father assured her.

"I smelled your bloodline the moment we met," Lady Anastasia said. "Luckily
for you it is a rare ability among the undead."

"Thank you for keeping it a secret," I said, a bit surprised.

"We will miss the hockey match," Sir Sadeghi said. "I wish to spend more
time with my grandchildren even if I just watch them sleep. They are amazing,
just like my daughter."

My eyes began to tear up.

"Would you mind if I hugged you? It's what Shorts do." He seemed surprised, then delighted and gently folded me in his robes. I felt secure. He exuded strength and maturity, a certain solidness. His embrace was comforting.
His scent had a touch of spice that I could not identify. I was lucky to have two
very devoted fathers in my life. He kissed the top of my head then released me.
Though we appeared close in age, the look he gave me could not have been more
paternal. I wanted to ask him more about his decision to father me, but that
could wait.

Lady Anastasia seemed to enjoy seeing the soft side of Sir Sadeghi. "It is interesting the effect you have on vampires. I can't help but wonder how the triplets will change our culture."

"I think Darwin would see us as a step in unnatural evolution but in the end, we're just family," I responded.

"You should be getting back to the match. Your husband will be wondering where you are," Sir Sadeghi said. As they started to walk away he turned and added, "I will always protect my family."

"I know," I responded and returned to the hockey rink. As I sat down, my husband glanced at me. I smiled to reassure him everything was fine.

"Sir Borgia is winning," the Magus told me. I looked at the board. The teams had each scored six points but the goalie had 27.

"This will be the last time they play by Sir Borgia's rules," I smiled. "They should have known."

"It's better this way. He has been known to be most unforgiving when he loses," the Magus replied.

Sir Ruben missed a goal. Lady Lockporte broke a hockey stick over his head.

"I think she is a bit unforgiving too," I added.

The Magus whispered, "They were a couple once, Lockporte and Borgia. They got in an argument which involved what you would call a knife-throwing contest, it wasn't pretty. They did not speak for 50 years until you brought them together to protect your babies. They are fairly civil now."

"Good to know," I replied. Then I whispered, "My father and Anastasia are a sweet couple."

"I don't understand why it took so long for them to acknowledge their attraction to each other," the Magus replied.

"You and Lena kept it private."

His stern look silenced me, then a weak smile came to his lips. He gently placed a hand on my arm. "Our relationship never resembled romantic folly, it was always about survival. However, for her it came to be competitive. Sex for her was purposeful but not loving, though I enjoyed it all the same."

"Sex without love would be empty and sad. It's not for me," I replied. I was surprised by the Magus' willingness to chat with me.

"How would you know?" he challenged me. "You're very quick to judge. Though perhaps if I ever felt affection and passion for someone like you do, I might agree."

"You have lived for centuries and still don't understand love?" *This is sad and unfortunate*, I thought.

"I have yet to experience it," he said with a serious expression, "though it may still be in the cards."

Upstairs, Lady Anastasia suggested that Tillie and Ania take a break while she and Sir Sadeghi looked after the triplets. Once they were gone, she took a diaper pin and made a prick in one of her fingers. Sir Sadeghi nodded. She walked over to Tomas and touched his lips. He began to suck as though nursing. Then after a few minutes she did the same for Desmon. Tomas began fussing, so Sir Sadeghi picked him up gently. Then she moved over to Marie. She stayed with her a little longer. "You will need a little more strength I think," she whispered. Then she pulled her finger away. Now Desmon began to cry. Lady Anastasia picked him up and he became quiet instantly. "You just wanted my undivided attention," she smiled.

Tomas yawned and closed his eyes while Sir Sadeghi walked him. "You'll be strong and in time very wise," he said to his grandson. He placed him back in his crib. Almost on cue Marie started to cry. Sir Sadeghi lifted her up like a fragile china doll. "Your highness, I did not mean to ignore you." She quieted down and stared at his face. "I think she likes my beard."

"I think they sense your paternal connection. Your scent and your eyes are like hers." Desmon had fallen asleep in Lady Anastasia's arms. "He is so precious." She returned him to his crib.

"You've had an exciting night little Baroness, now it's time to sleep," he whispered to Marie.

"How is it possible that they can melt our hearts?" Lady Anastasia whispered. "They awaken a feeling inside of me that has been dormant for so long. It is almost painful."

"It is their innocence. We were once like them," he smiled.

"No one has ever been like them, or their mother." Lady Anastasia gently touched Sir Sadeghi's cheek then stood beside him gazing at the babies. "You must try to guide your daughter to use her growing abilities appropriately, maintain her loyalty and teach our values to them."

He turned to her and whispered, "My dear, I will not leave her bereft of my influence. Besides their father, I have a trusted companion who will be looking after her and the children."

CHAPTER 50

BY THE TIME the marathon hockey game ended, it was near sunrise. Try as they might, the teams were not able to defeat the goalie. The final score was the Baron and Pauline with 26, the Lockportes with 32 and Sir Borgia with 58. Lady Lockporte asserted that when the Baron slammed her against the lockers outside of the rink, it should have been a penalty. Pauline thought that when Sir Ruben stole her hockey stick that should have stopped the game, but instead Lady Lockporte used that moment to score. The Magus said he would not intervene to avoid showing any partiality. Sir Borgia was obviously quite pleased with himself. There were a dozen new holes in the wall behind the goalie net. Antoinella wiped the brow of her benefactor, though I doubted he worked up much of a sweat.

We checked on the babies before retiring. They were fine. Tillie assured me their temps were normal though their lips seemed a little red. I pumped some milk so they could have some breast milk during the day. It made me feel a little sorry for cows. Then we fell into bed. Though we were both very tired, we made love. I was not sure if after tomorrow he would be in the mood so I wanted at least one more sweet, passionate, make-the-world-dissolve, half hour of sex to remember. Okay, 45 minutes. Then I fell into a deep sleep and did not wake until late in the afternoon.

After I showered and dressed, I tried calling my mom but she did not pick up. That was strange, so I sent a text message, thinking they were probably busy with the dinner crowd. I asked if everything was okay and a few minutes later I got the response.

"Your home is ready. We can't wait to see you. Love, mom."

A week ago, I had told my parents to expect a long visit. Since the children were born I had been setting aside the clothes, books, jewelry, etc. that I would want to take with me. Once I set a date then I wanted to move quickly. I could not imagine living with a brooding, resentful vampire. I worried about how it might impact the triplets. If the undead world was resistant, I had $20,000 in cash hidden in my room. I would find a way. After all, vampires had to sleep during the day, I did not.

I spent a couple of hours with my babies. Desmon was making bubbles and it almost seemed like he laughed with me. He already showed signs of being good at amusing himself. Tomas was very predictable and very serious about eating. As long as his tummy was full all was right with the world. He would take the bottle or breast without a problem. Marie was not so easy to please. She obviously preferred the breast but if push came to shove, she seemed to grudgingly take the bottle. I loved the way they smelled, well most of the time. Like Lady Anastasia, I could identify the different scents of vampires. It was more than blood types, it was bloodlines. I had this weird sense that the babies scent had changed a little but assumed it was from the Lena inoculation, though it was a bit different from the deceased vampiress. I helped Ania change their diapers and played with them until it was about time for my husband to rise. I would miss having Tillie and Ania's help.

I went down to the kitchen where Tillie had left breakfast for me in the fridge. The housekeeper was taking a well-deserved nap. She and Ania had been taking turns looking after the triplets. There was a plate with Camembert, fresh strawberries and croissants. She had even left a note reminding me to take my vitamins. I ground some Ethiopian beans the Magus had given me and made a fresh cup of the glorious brew. I was up to two cups of caffeine a night now. I put my meal on a silver tray and headed for the patio. I saw Clive going up to my husband's room and asked him to have the Baron meet me outside. I sat at a wrought iron table for two and slowly sipped my coffee while I went over in my head for the hundredth time what I would say. I was not about to ask permission; still, I had to break the news gently, which was not typically my style. I chose a beautiful garden setting for my declaration to give us some privacy. I ate some of the croissant with cheese as I was aware my brain did not function at its best on an empty stomach.

My husband stepped onto the patio. He wore a white silk shirt, barely buttoned, and black jeans. His hair was still damp from the shower. He looked as handsome and virile as the first evening we met, Like a lover who had died, he would not age but I would. In fact, knowing him was aging me considerably. He bent down to kiss me. I held the Queen Victoria mug up to my lips. He kissed my forehead instead. I was afraid of how his passionate kiss would impact my resolve.

"Is that cup an amulet for protection from me?" he smiled.

I already felt guilty. This was not good. I thought of the triplets. "It is time for the talk."

"Isn't it a little early to discuss having more children? Although I'm in favor."

"I'm not crazy. Not that talk. It's about protecting the children, giving them the best environment for more normal, healthy development."

"Are you reading this off cue cards?" he laughed.

This was not the response I expected. "Tristan, damn it, I'm serious. I'm going to take the children and move back to Rossville."

"You are taking everyone I love most in this world to one of the places I dislike the most?" He looked hurt but he did not sound all that sincere. Something was not right.

"It's not about you. I hate to leave you. I just can't bring the kids up surrounded by well-meaning vampires. I want them to have a better grasp of reality." That was as tactful as I could muster. "You can visit every month for a week," I added in a small voice and waited for the backlash.

"Really? You will allow me to see my children once a month? What about the Magus? Not to mention the others who disposed of Lena to protect you and the children," he asked sounding more upset, "and your father?"

I felt like crawling under my chair. "I thought about them. I can take the triplets up to Chicago for a visit now and then. I think the Magus has a house there. The others could visit with us there too so I won't have to hear Uncle Franco whine."

"Twenty-thousand dollars will not be enough to buy a home," he said with a make-you-squirm stare.

"We can stay with my parents until I find a place. Anyway, how do you know I have $20,000?" I put my coffee cup down.

"It's in your suitcase," he smiled.

"Tillie!"

"She loves you and the kids but she is still quite loyal to me," he said.

"I'll move with or without your help."

"So you've made up your mind?" he stared at me.

"Yes!" I replied staring back with my arms crossed.

"Very well," he said and handed me his cell phone. "Pictures of your new home. Your parents sent them."

I sat speechless looking at a photo of a mansion in the middle of the cornfields. "I don't understand."

"After our first conversation with your parents, I contacted them again and asked them to secretly find some land near town to surprise you. I bought 100 acres. They helped arrange the construction according to my wishes. Look through the photos. It was just to be for visits but the Magus thought you might decide to reside there. We had to make sure you had a secure and proper place to live."

"I don't believe this. They helped you? You aren't going to fight me on this?" I looked at my husband. He was not joking. "The Magus knew?"

"It was the Magus that convinced me you would be unhappy raising a family here. I realized he was right. I do not look forward to the time away from you and the children but I understand. I want what is best for them as well."

"I really hate having to like the Magus." I started looking through the photos. It resembled a Southern mansion. It had seven bedrooms. The master suite appeared to have only one small window. Every room was completely furnished. There was a huge stone fireplace with a royal crest on the wall. The kitchen had a chef's stove and an espresso maker on the counter. "You thought of everything! I can't believe my mom kept this a secret."

"There's an office off the kitchen where you can write. Your vampire book will be published next week."

"Tristan!" I dropped the phone and ran around the table to sit in his lap. "You really do love me and the kids enough to let us go!" I began to tear up. "Thank you for making this so easy." I kissed him. "I want to leave soon before some other weird crisis like vampire-wolves occurs." I looked in his eyes, I could see he was struggling with the separation. "They will always look forward to your visits and when they are older they can visit you here."

"And you?"

"I will be quite happy to see you too!" I kissed him again.

"I will hate the nights away from you."

"It will be hard for me too. I'll start working on a sequel. Vampires in the cornfields."

"I'm sure you will," he smiled and shook his head. "There are more photos." He picked up the phone. "The stables were completed last week." He showed me a large, long white building that could house thoroughbreds.

"I've never had horses besides, it will be years before the kids can ride."

"It's a gift from your other father, three Arabian stallions. They are magnificent."

"Sir Sadeghi?"

My husband nodded. "He sent his favorite groom to look after them. They are for more than sport. They will also offer protection." I wasn't sure what he meant but I figured I would find out in time. "There will be llamas and peacocks from Sir Diego. The llamas can also be very protective and the peacocks will warn of any intruders."

"My dream of a more normal life is becoming vampirized." My Little House on the Prairie had quickly morphed into a grand estate.

"Vampirized?" He smiled. "I like that. I'll have to tell the Magus. There is also a state-of-the-art security system. The house has solar panels. I also insisted on a water purification system because of agricultural run-off. Your father picked out two generators in case of power outages during storms. Your mother persuaded me to buy you a Jeep Grand Cherokee, she said it would be less conspicuous than a Range Rover and be great in the snow. She was afraid of offending people with a show of your wealth."

"I think the mansion and stables might accomplish that. They never said a word to me. That's why they didn't get upset about missing the baptism. They knew we were coming home."

"Ania has two cousins who will be your staff. They are already at the house. Stone Canyon will always be your home," he stated as Delilah came up to the table.

"I will miss her." I patted her sleek head. She rubbed her muzzle against my leg. I started to tear up. "Why are you being so understanding?"

"You haven't heard my condition," he said in a serious tone. His deep, blue eyes studied my face intently.

"What is it?" I asked rather curious about his demands.

"Miranda, you must remain faithful to me. Though you may not find this fair since you will not be available to me and I may have occasional, discrete sexual encounters. Be assured they will not effect my feelings for you."

I stood suddenly and stared down at him. "So that's how you're going to punish me for making the children a priority? Really? You don't know how hard it was for me to make this decision. You can't keep it in your pants while we are apart?" My voice was starting to get loud.

"Stay here then," he replied. "I prefer to make love to you than have sex with an exercise companion."

"Sorry, but the children matter more to me than who you're fucking. You don't have to remind me to be faithful, I married you, remember? If I ever choose to be with someone else, I will divorce your ass first."

"That will never happen," he said with confidence. "Why can't you be forgiving like your mother?"

"I can't believe you said that! Remember, she only forgave him after she got drunk and had sex with a vampire." I stood up and walked a few feet away, then turned to face him with my arms crossed.

"Do you want to get drunk?" my husband replied with a smile.

"You're such an arrogant prick! If it wasn't for the others I would pack up and leave right now so you can get on with your exercise program. Tonight I'll say goodbye to my vampire family. I'll get tickets for tomorrow morning." I started to walk in the house.

"The Magus' jet will be ready to fly all of you to the Danville airport. Just let your parents know to pick you up about noon. A plane is on standby for you," Tristan said with resignation. "Live wherever you like."

With tears starting to roll down my cheeks I ran back to him and kissed him passionately. "I will!," I said and went into the house to pack.

Sir Borgia came out on the patio and sat down across from the Baron. "I think everyone heard that she is leaving with the triplets."

"Cesar, tell me I'm not crazy for loving that woman."

"My friend, do you ever find her boring?"

"Never!" the Baron responded.

"Then you've chosen the right woman." He smiled. "Which reminds me, Antoinella surprised me by requesting to have her transformation take place in the hockey rink tonight."

"Yes, she has earned her immortality.. Please honor her request," the Baron responded. "Let us plan for midnight, I'm sure the Magus will agree. I could use a distraction. Will she be going to London with you?"

"Not if you might have need for her here," Sir Borgia responded. "She could always join me later."

"Perhaps," the Baron responded wistfully.

When I got to my room, Tillie was standing by with a complete set of designer leather luggage. She looked like she was fighting back tears. "I'll help you pack, Baroness. Ania is getting the triplets' necessities ready for the flight."

"Thank you, Tillie, you've been very good to me and the babies." I pulled the clothes out of the closet I had put aside to take with me and stacked them on the bed. "I'll leave the gowns and high heels here for when we visit."

Her face brightened a little. "Of course, Baroness."

An hour later I checked on the triplets. They had been quiet longer than usual. I found my father in his white robes sitting with a grandson in each arm rocking them. Lady Anastasia was giving a bottle to Marie, who immediately started fussing when I entered. She reluctantly handed her to me. "They are so full of potential," she said. "It is good to take them away from here. They will have enough time when they are grown to come to terms with their dual natures."

"No doubt" I replied.

"We helped plan your new home. Lady Anastasia picked out the linens and color scheme. You will like the horses," my father said to the boys. "They are a special breed, just like you."

"Antoinella's ceremony will begin soon," Lady Anastasia said.

We placed the babies back in their cribs and Ania took over. I followed Lady Anastasia and my father out into the hall.

"Is formal attire mandatory at a transformation?" I asked.

"Of course not." Lady Anastasia shook her head and replied barely above a whisper, "You don't understand the caste system. She is quite common. Any large room would be appropriate for her transformation. In our world, your blood is your destiny."

"They must have rented a bowling alley for Simone's coming out."

Lady Anastasia turned and walked away without another word. I returned to my room to make sure everything I would need had been packed. The hallway conversation strengthened my resolve to get the hell out of undead central.

The gathering in the hockey rink resembled the baptism. I started going from person to person getting my goodbyes out of the way. "Jorge, I will always hold a tiny resentment that you lied to me but I treasure your friendship. Please keep an eye on my husband."

"Remember he adores you. It's best to accept him as he is," he smiled. Sir Diego kissed me on the cheek. "I will be your vampire's keeper."

"I can't believe your taking those darling babies to that hell hole in the cornfields," Sir Franco said. "I should call a child abuse hotline."

"I appreciate your honesty but it will be better for their development. I turned out alright, didn't I?"

"Promise me you'll bring them to Chicago from time to time so we won't have to go back there!"

"I promise to bring them to civilization to see their Uncle Franco," I replied. He looked genuinely relieved.

The Lockportes gave me hugs. "Thank you both for stopping Lena. Please tell Steve that I hope one day he can teach the triplets some self-defense techniques. Toronto is not that far, you are always welcome in Rossville."

Lady Lockporte smiled. "If you ever need us, we will come to your aid."

Sir Ruben stood a little behind her shaking his head, which made me laugh. When she turned to look at him he said, "Go Bobcats!"

The Magus approached me in a black silk suit and a gray shirt. He was dressed appropriately for the transformation. I had not changed from my blue jeans and T-shirt. It was my common attire. Everyone was waiting for the Magus to nod his head so they could begin but he stopped to speak to me. I could not help but be relieved that this powerful control freak was not my father.

"Dear Miranda, you're starting to understand your new reality. I have no doubt that you are worthy of your station. Your children will be difficult to guide at times. They will be brilliant and manipulative but your love for them will keep their hearts open to you. Forgive me for not wanting to visit you at your new home. I will see you in Chicago next year."

I did something which caused a few whispers. I bowed slightly to the Magus. He smiled and patted my hand then walked away. I saw my husband smile at me as we gathered near the ice. I would never bow to him, Baron Asshole.

Everyone assembled in a semi-circle as Antoinella, dressed in a red satin dress exposing lots of cleavage, walked onto the rink. She looked like a glamorous actress from an old movie. Italian vampires had their own style. She was careful not to slip on the ice. It was a little cold. Sir Borgia stood beside her in a black suit with a red vest. His dark wavy hair hung down to his shoulders. His light brown eyes were focused on Antoinella's chest like everyone else. Jasper brought out a chair for the young woman to sit in. The Magus signaled to begin. Lady Lily stood by to assist.

When Sir Borgia bit into her chest, I looked away for a moment. Antoinella bit her lip to suppress a scream then passed out. Sir Borgia drank deeply. I sensed the other vampires' hunger. Lady Lily started a transfusion infused with Sir Borgia's blood. Then he stood, slit his wrist with a tiny dagger and held it up to the barely conscious woman's mouth. She began to drink. I noticed droplets of blood dripped down her chin onto the ice and started to feel light headed, then everything went black. The next thing I remembered was coming to as my husband carried me upstairs. I was in the safety of his arms again.

"What happened?" I asked as he laid me on his bed.

"You fainted but I caught you in time."

Lady Lily appeared quite concerned. She had a blood pressure cuff and took my vitals, which I thought was a bit over the top. "Her vitals are fine," she reported. "Still, I suggest resting for a little while. I'll leave you alone." She quickly left, closing the door behind her.

My husband lay next to me with his hand resting on my tummy. He looked at me with the same passionate concern he had displayed at the airport hotel. I was feeling aroused by his scent and touch. I recovered quickly. "Thanks."

"You seem to have an aversion to the sight of blood. That's unfortunate. You'll have to work on that."

"Maybe I should just stay away from undead social events," I responded.

He put his fingers gently on my mouth and said, "Quiet." The he kissed me as his hand slipped under my T-shirt. It did not take long and all our clothes seemed to disappear. He gently rubbed my clitoris till I moaned softly then he entered me with hard thrusts that made me cry out. It is a fine line between love and hate and sometimes while having sex you experience both and do not care which it is. Finally, we collapsed together and fell asleep.

After an hour I untangled myself from his arms and got dressed. He sat up with his glorious mane of white-blonde hair somewhat disheveled and said, "Stay here."

"We can't. It always feels right in your arms but outside the bedroom, this life isn't right for raising children," I replied and went to the nursery. Everything was set to go. Tillie would fly with us to help with the babies during the trip. I had wanted to take a shower before leaving but I was afraid my husband might join me and convince me to stay.

A few hours before dawn we headed to the airport. Jasper drove Tillie and Clive with the triplets in the Bentley. The Baron insisted on driving me in the Spyder. Neither of us spoke and I stared out my window to avoid his unhappy glances. We passed by my favorite taco stand, the monk's deli and the hotel where Tristan had revealed his true nature. Giant old palm trees lined the road near the airport. The trees had welcomed me to the city of crazy angels and now they seemed to honor my departure. We drove right up to the Magus' jet. Cody, the Magus' new pilot, greeted us and helped the servants get the triplets and all the luggage on the plane. I turned to my husband. "Maybe it will be easier for the children to assimilate our two cultures than it is for me, like second generation immigrants."

With a resigned expression he said, "They are Haute Caste, they will never fit in the ordinary world even though they may try. On the other hand, they will become very self-reliant. You can't hide from your true nature either. I shall be patient."

"Go to hell!" I muttered as I slammed the car door.

"I will see you in three weeks," he called out. "Say hello to your parents." He tossed something to me. I caught it and looked in my hand — it was the hair clip I wore at our first meeting. I looked at him with surprise. "You can wear your hair up when I'm not visiting."

Nine months later, Jacques Omar Ortega Mordecai was born and I had my tubes tied. He was baptized in a Russian Orthodox Church in Chicago. When my mom questioned why I named him Omar, I said it was after a character in an old TV mini-series *The Wire*. Fortunately, she had never watched it.

The next 19 years did not turn out at all like anything I had ever imagined or could have, for that matter. My children even surprised their father, not to mention the vampire world. Their coming of age is recorded in my second journal. No names have been changed to protect anyone, because who would believe me anyway.

ACKNOWLEDGMENTS

AS WITH MANY BOOKS this one has been in the works for a long time, in fact, thirty years. I started writing this book to cope with the stress of working as an addiction therapist. I had all but finished the book when a lightning strike fried my computer and destroyed all I had written. Unfortunately, not being very computer savvy, I had not created a backup copy. I was determined to resurrect the story, after all it is a story about the undead. Undeterred, with many pages of hand-written notes and a slew of new ideas, I dived in and started again.

I have always had what some may call an odd sense of humor and a little different view of the world than most people. One year, for Mother's day, one of my kids' elementary school teachers had given the class an assignment to draw a picture for their mothers. The teacher became quite alarmed when she saw the picture my child had drawn. It was a vampire bat with bloody fangs. I adored it!

Thanks to my late husband Ted who always told me to keep writing. Special thanks to Pam, who made it all seem possible. Thanks for the love and humorous support of all our kids and grandson who make it all worthwhile. Thanks to my husband Joel for his many hours of editing (he read the book at least five times), and my daughter Jenn for obtaining the cover artwork. Also special thanks to David Wogahn for essential publishing guidance and seemingly endless patience.

Miranda, the Baron, and all the other vampires and mortals that make up their world will continue with their intriguing adventures in upcoming sequels.

ABOUT THE AUTHOR

SUSAN GREW UP in So Cal with hippies and surfers, wrote for her high school underground newspaper and played in a garage band. Her adventuresome spirit took her to Central Africa while serving in the Peace Corps.

Back in the states she worked in Mental Health/Addictions for 30 years. Exposure to many cultures/subcultures and unique thought processes made writing about vampires a supernatural next step.

When not writing about Miranda's struggles with the vampire world, she volunteers at an animal shelter, and a Veteran's museum.

CPSIA information can be obtained
at www.ICGtesting.com
Printed in the USA
FSHW02n1651240718
50622FS